Limerick County Library
30012 00694520 7

D0262356

HALF-SICK OF SHADOWS

www.transworldbooks.co.uk

HALF-SICK OF SHADOWS

David Logan

Doubleday

LONDON • TORONTO • SYDNEY • AUCKLAND • JOHANNESBURG

TRANSWORLD PUBLISHERS
61–63 Uxbridge Road, London W5 5SA
A Random House Group Company
www.transworldbooks.co.uk

First published in Great Britain
in 2012 by Doubleday
an imprint of Transworld Publishers

A CIP catalogue record for this book
is available from the British Library.

ISBNs 9780857521163 (cased)
9780857520760 (tpb)

Addresses for Random House Group Ltd companies outside the UK
can be found at: www.randomhouse.co.uk
The Random House Group Ltd Reg. No. 954009

Typeset in 11.5/15pt Bembo by Falcon Oast Graphic Art Ltd.
Printed and bound in Great Britain by Clays Ltd, Bungay, Suffolk

2 4 6 8 10 9 7 5 3 1

For Christopher

Contents

Foreword

This novel is not just the joint winner of the inaugural Terry Pratchett Prize, but the joint winner of the inaugural Terry Pratchett *Anywhere But Here, Anywhen But Now* Prize.

Which meant we were after stories set on Earth, but perhaps an Earth that might have been, or might yet be, one that had gone down a different leg of the famous trousers of time (see the illustration in almost every book about quantum theory).

It could, we mused, be one day in the life of an ordinary person. It could be a love story, an old story, a war story, a story set in a world where Leonardo da Vinci turned out to be a lot better at aeronautics (or, indeed, where a Victorian poet laureate developed a deep affection for Morris Minors). But by and large you don't hear stories about being on an alternate Earth because the people on an alternate Earth don't know that they are; after all, you don't.

Imagine the shock, then, of finding out that someone considers your personal patch of reality to be an alternate one – an interesting but ultimately baffling anomaly amongst the strings of sensibly organized universes around it. David Logan's anomalous world, the world of the Manse, is an unsettling place to be, precisely because he springs that shock on his unsuspecting characters – an uncommon trick, which requires the audacity not just to make a new world from scratch, but to unmake it too.

After all, getting a second opinion on the rules of reality can be a dangerous thing – as you'll know if you are familiar with the poem from which *Half-Sick of Shadows* takes its name. Once you start to question the laws and promises that hold your world together, the whole thing can start to come apart. So step inside the world of the Manse, and watch it unravel around you.

Terry Pratchett
March, 2012

Before
Alf

1

The Stranger and his Time Machine

Before the beginning: nothing. Then, faster than a flash . . . everything: my universe and my planet in it. All things existed at once with their back-stories ready made – even some humans on my planet to get the species started. Alf said so. Sophia and I came later. We came a fraction short of five years before this particular story began. It began in August, on a morning shivery and brilliant. Or it might have been January? It could have been any morning; mornings were all the same when Sophia and I were a fraction short of five – except this one.

I dressed in clothes stiff with frost and went downstairs to find the fireplace black and speckled with ash. Granny Hazel snored in bed in the middle of the living room. I didn't stay there long. Mother, elbow deep in soapy water, washed dishes in the kitchen.

'Where's breakfast?' I asked.

'Not now, Edward,' she replied in her headachy voice.

She told me to go out and play with Sophia. So I did.

Sophia, by a frightening coincidence the same age as me to within mere seconds, wore her red winter and only coat. Mother said she would grow into it. She also wore white mittens and a white pom-pom hat. We were twins – whatever twins were. I assumed twins were children the same height and width, with the same blond hair, the same brown eyes, the same brain, the same everything. Twins were brother and sister and best friends. Twins were what we two were: two bodies but a single person – something like that.

Rain threatened. Rain always threatened, except for when it rained. Mother said we lived in a hole in the middle of the world that all the water drained into. Sometimes it snowed.

Sophia had gone around every pothole in the courtyard – and potholes were legion – smashing the ice. She crouched near the toilet. We had a wooden toilet at one end of the courtyard, like a coffin standing on the sole of its foot.

Near the toilet, and the septic tank, was the Hole.

The Hole was full of muddy water, often frozen over, like a lake for midgets. We called it the Hole because it was a hole and the biggest one we knew of. A giant tree once stood on the spot, but Father had taken against it and dug it out roots and all.

Sophia inspected the damage. Seeing me, she stood up, hammer in hand, wearing her worried face – essentially the same as her it-wasn't-me face but not quite so wide-eyed and innocent. She could pull an it-wasn't-me face even when as guilty as Eve with apples.

As I got closer, she felt the weight of the hammer in her mitten. I thought she didn't recognize me. That frightened me. If Sophia didn't recognize me, that meant . . . It meant something frightening.

She had translucent skin.

'What's wrong?' I asked.

Then she recognized me, her other half, and smiled.

When Sophia smiled all the ice in the potholes melted.

'Mother has one of her headaches,' I said.

'Which one?'

I shrugged. They all looked the same but had different names: today's headache, yesterday's headache, Tuesday's headache.

'Look!' said Sophia, pointing at the cemetery. The big black dog was wandering through the headstones. It had been wandering around the Manse for days. Mother told us not to go near it in case it was rabbit. I thought Rabbit was its name, though it was a mad kind of rabbit because it looked like a dog.

Rabbit disappeared behind an outhouse.

Sophia and I looked in the opposite direction – we must have done, otherwise we wouldn't have seen it coming down the Lane. The Lane was flat, not a hill. Strictly speaking, it had neither up nor down. But, to us, down the Lane meant from the Road along the Lane to the courtyard at the back of the Manse. And up the Lane meant from the courtyard at the back of the Manse and along the Lane to the Road.

The Lane connected us to the Road, and the Road connected us to the rest of the world. The Road weaved and wound this way and that as if the people who made it were drunk. It began somewhere and ended somewhere else. All roads do, and the Road must have too. Between its points of beginning and ending, the Road went past Farmer Barry's farm, past the Manse where we lived, and through the nearest village: Bruagh. I knew no more than that. That, and that the Road had potholes: new ones every winter, like rabbits, said Father. Potholes would turn out to be more important than I knew.

Not yet five years old, I had little idea of roads, beginnings and endings. They were not the sorts of things I thought about. The Road had always been the Road, as the Lane had always been the Lane, as if only one of each existed.

Only one of each did indeed exist, although I became aware, later, that there were many of their class, just as there is only one Edward Pike although there are many boys. Such matters can be confusing when you're not five yet. I would doubtless have despaired at my confusions if I'd thought about them, but I'd plenty of other confusions to be getting on with.

I didn't know it was a car, then. The light blue metal thing with windows and wheels sort of . . . frizzled . . . out of existence. It reminded me of Farmer Barry's lorry, but looked nothing like it. Sophia and I looked at each other. When we looked back towards the Lane, the thing sort of frizzled back into existence, but further up the Lane than it had been. Again, it advanced. A dust cloud would have risen behind it had not the ground been wet.

Sophia and I yelped, ran to the back door, darted inside, and clung to Mother's apron. Except we didn't because, first, we were immobilized and silenced with fear, and, second, we were immobilized with fascination. Especially when . . .

Frizzle. Vanish. Frizzle. The thing on wheels returned closer than ever to us and still on the Lane but only just. Two wheels bumped and splashed in Laneside mud. The thing slowed down.

. . . stopped. It stopped. Unintentionally, I thought.

The door opened and a man with a walking stick got out. He reached inside, withdrew a hat, and put it on his head. Obviously, the thing getting stuck in the mud upset him, for he slammed the door shut and hit it a kick with his boot. He did have two boots, having two feet, but he only kicked the door with one. The violence of his action imbued Sophia with the strength to run indoors. And she did. Open-mouthed and shivering, I remained. Powerless but intrigued.

The man approached me, but not in a frightening way. I knew nothing about clothing in those days, but his looked very nice, like Sunday best but better. The cane was ornamental rather than an aid for walking. He had a bushy beard like Father's, and it had dignified streaks of grey. He said something in a foreign language, which, I realized, after he said something else, was 'young man'.

'Young man,' he said in a funny accent. 'Are you deaf, child?'

'No.'

'No what?' he asked.

I had no idea what.

'No, sir,' said the stranger.

No sir what? It might have been some kind of puzzle.

I liked puzzles. 'What's that?' I asked, pointing at the stuck-in-the-mud thing on wheels.

'That,' he swung at the hips to where I pointed and swung back, 'that, my boy, is what would be on most planets that support organic life a major advance in transportation technology.'

I looked up at him. He looked down at me, and saw a small boy with eyes like marbles and the space between his ears unfurnished.

Said he, 'It's a time machine.'

It didn't look like a clock to me. It had no hands.

'Yes, my boy, a time machine. The intricacies of its workings are far beyond me, I'm afraid. I'm still learning, by trial and error, how to make the blasted thing do what I want it to.'

'What do you want it to do?'

'Work properly would be a start.'

'What does a time machine do?'

'It travels in time, naturally. See those . . . headstones?' He satisfied himself that they were indeed headstones. 'See those headstones?' I said I did. 'At top speed, my time machine could zoom to over there before it left here.'

As I looked towards the cemetery – because the man was looking towards it – I noticed Mother at the back door with her hands on Sophia's shoulders. Sophia stood in front of her like a fireguard, or a bearded stranger guard. Gregory's head peered over Mother's shoulder. Edgar's head peered over her other shoulder. Mother looked like she had three heads.

I hadn't eaten breakfast yet. My tummy rumbled.

'That's a graveyard,' said the stranger.

'Cemetery,' said I.

'Yes. Quite so. Cemetery.'

The cemetery was as old as the Manse, which had existed since the sixteenth century. Mother didn't explain centuries, but we knew there must have been at least twenty of them.

Though closer to my birth than my death – a reasonable

assumption – death, nevertheless, never strayed far from my mind . . . nor Mother's, Father's or Sophia's. I'm sure Death nurtured a relationship with Gregory too. How else would we be? What other states of mind could we possess? What else would occupy our thoughts with a cemetery for a back garden?

Sections of the Manse, the original building, still stood; they were built into newer sections with thicker walls designed to hide and support them. Sections of wall from the nineteenth century were visible, but all the rest came from the early twentieth. Even when we were tiny children Sophia and I were used to feeling the chills that suddenly were where no chills were before – like the dead passing through. Mother would tell us to close the door and keep the cold out. I thought the Cold was an entity, like the Bogeyman. The Cold, the Dark, and the Bogeyman were a supernatural trinity, like God but less spiteful. Of all the entities in the Manse and the land around it, the Cold filled it least balefully. We had learned to live with the Cold. Only the kitchen remained warm day and night and through the seasons.

'A large black dog,' said the stranger. 'Have you seen one?'

'Is it yours?'

'Yes. In a manner of speaking. You've seen it, then?'

'It was in the cemetery a minute ago.'

'Good! Then I'm in the correct place. And you are, unless I've made an error, Edward.' I neither denied nor confirmed it. He hadn't asked me to. 'I won't take up much of your time, Edward. No doubt you're busy doing whatever small boys do. I need to ask a permission of you. It won't work, at least not with complete success, unless I have your permission. May I ask?'

'Yes.'

'Will you be my friend?'

Gosh! I didn't know what to say. Nor did I see why he shouldn't be my friend if he wanted to. Some years of life and experience were necessary before I would think of such things as what we might have in common. The notion of ulterior motives was unknown to me. I'd never been told not to talk to strangers. I didn't know any strangers. I didn't know many not strangers either.

'Sophia's my friend,' I said. 'She's my sister.'

'Is that her?'

'Yes?'

'My word . . . Yes . . . Yes indeed . . . I wouldn't want to be your very best friend, Edward,' he said. 'I'd never want to replace Sophia as your very best and special friend. If I could be just an ordinary friend, that would do nicely. May we be friends?'

'All right,' I said with a smile.

We shook on it.

'Now, listen to me, Edward, my friend. What I'm about to say may be important, and you need to remember it.' I listened hard with both ears, my eyebrows lowered and my neck stuck out. 'You may, one day, want something from your friend . . . from me.'

'What like?'

'I don't know. But something important. When you want it, all you have to do is ask. Is that clear?' Clear as porridge. I didn't know whether to shake my head or nod it. 'Ask and it shall be given unto you, as the good book says. Seek and ye shall find.'

'That's from the bible.'

'Correct! What a clever chap you are, Edward. I'm pleased about that, because our friendship will change this social and cerebral milieu. You shall witness change. Indeed, my intervention necessitates change. Time itself, which you think fixed, may on occasions warp back on itself. But let's hope it doesn't happen too often. Ours is very much a friendship that requires a clever chap . . . Is that your mother?' he asked, looking past me again.

'Yes.'

'And are those boys your siblings?'

'No. That's my brother Gregory and my brother Edgar.'

'Gregory looks like a strapping fellow. Do you think he could help me push my time machine? It's rather stuck at the moment.'

I yelled at the back door. 'He wants Gregory to help him push his time machine out of the mud.' Nobody moved. Mother's hands might have tightened fractionally on Sophia's shoulders.

Turning square on to the back door, having taken a step closer to it, I yelled harder. 'He wants Gregory to help him push his time machine out of the mud.'

A vacuum followed my second yell, as though I were in a bubble, like a reindeer in a glass orb that snows when you shake it. Except I existed in my bubble, sensate, alive, a physical entity, and everything outside was plastic, stiff, inanimate. I began to feel very claustrophobic in there, until, just when I couldn't hold my breath any longer, Mother moved. Her head turned towards Gregory and she said something. Gregory hesitated before coming forward, pausing, then approaching me and the stranger.

'Sir, you have my warmest gratitude,' said the stranger. 'Our combined weight should get it over the rut.' He led the way to the rear of his machine. Gregory followed. I followed too, but only halfway. Silver letters on the front of the machine spelled MORRIS MINOR.

At first, the rut looked too deep for them to succeed. I couldn't see the stranger at the far side. Gregory's face turned red. But they got the machine rocking, and eventually it rocked over the rut.

'We did it!' exclaimed the stranger, and shook Gregory by the hand. 'Thank you, sir. Thank you.' As he wiped his hands with a handkerchief, Gregory ran back to Mother.

The stranger got into the machine and it came alive with a roar. I watched as it circled the courtyard and slowed to walking speed before stopping where I stood too much in awe to do other than stand and watch. A window in the machine sank, allowing the stranger inside to speak to me.

'Thank you for being my friend.'

I wanted to ask him something, many things, but didn't know what any of them were. The window went up again, separating him from me, and the machine took off. 'What's transportation technology?' I thought, too late.

The machine diminished in size as it went up the Lane.

Frizzle. Vanish.

2

The Night of Our Final Flight

It was darker than night but warm and giggly where we were. 'Who's the man that came here today?' asked Sophia. Before I had a chance to ask 'What man?' our bedroom door opened and we shushed.

'Oh my goodness! Where could they be? The Bogeyman must have stolen Edward and Sophia. There's nothing here, in their bedroom, but a hump in the bed, underneath the blankets.'

The hump was us and Mother didn't know. We put our hands over our mouths and giggled while trying not to.

'They'll miss dinner if the Bogeyman doesn't bring them back and they're not downstairs in five minutes.' (Tee-hee-hee!) 'It's strawberry jam on toast and hot, sweet tea . . . when you're done.'

Our bedroom door closed.

'Five minutes,' said Sophia.

'Strawberry jam on toast.'

'Who is he?' asked Sophia, one half of the blanket-hump.

'Who?'

'The man that Gregory pushed his machine out of the mud.'

I'd forgotten about him. 'I don't know.'

'What did he want?'

'I don't know . . . To be my friend.'

'Why did he want to be your friend?'

'I don't know.'

'I'm your friend.'

'You're allowed more than one.' I hadn't known you're allowed to have more than one friend until the stranger told me. 'You're my best friend.'

'I'm your best friend,' she repeated, with a giggle in her voice.

The mystery of the stranger and his time machine puzzled me for as long as the memory of it lasted, which, when you're stupidly young, isn't long. I'd more or less forgotten about it again by strawberry jam on toast and sweet tea time.

After strawberry jam on toast and sweet tea, after our trips outside with our bowels – which seldom moved as regularly as they should have, according to Mother – and after warming ourselves by the fire only to leave the living room and get cold again ten minutes later, Sophia and me had nothing left to do but look out of the window of our bedroom.

Getting sleepy as the sky darkened between day and night, Sophia and I looked through rain bubbles at nothing in particular: the Lane to our right, outbuildings in the middle, and the cemetery to the left. Sophia pointed at the Lane. 'Look!' I looked, and saw Farmer Barry's lorry, squiggly in a rain bubble.

Farmer Barry's lorry turned round in the courtyard so its back faced us. Farmer Barry had brought Father home from work. Father normally came home from work as he set out: on his bicycle. The bicycle was on the back of the lorry.

Also on the back of the lorry: a shining black coffin.

'Is that for us?' asked Sophia.

I told her I didn't think so.

'How do you know?' she enquired.

'We need two. They'd be small and white.'

Four eyes – ours – shifted from the lorry past the outhouses to the cemetery, or, as we sometimes called it, the back garden.

'Who's it for, then?'

'I don't know. Somebody dead.'

'But nobody's dead.'

'Granny Hazel nearly is.'

'Who's it for, then?'

'Granny Hazel, probably.'

We couldn't sleep. Tough luck. Mother – who was cross with herself for having forgotten our hot water bottles – made us get our nightshirts on, tucked us in and kissed us. When she left, we got up and looked out of the window again.

I wanted to go to the hot sun, but Sophia wanted to go to the cool moon. We went to the cool moon, and built sandcastles with moondust and played the same games we played in the courtyard.

Coming home from the moon, we saw a dot of murky light: the Manse. We flew over black trees and black hills of green. The Manse grew as we flew closer; the dot of murky light became our bedroom window.

'There's us,' said Sophia.

Our heads were two pale orbs behind rain-bubbled glass. Then our heads were two pale orbs with eyes. Sophia and I were two sad faces looking out at ourselves as we flew home from the moon.

Then we were up close through the window and back inside us.

'The moon's cold,' I said.

Sophia said we could go to the sun tomorrow.

As far as our eyes could see through the window, they saw nothing but night. Out there, past the clouds where night met the sky, there were stars. There were hundreds and hundreds of stars. Thousands. Millions – and whatever's bigger than millions – of stars.

Beautiful Mother, soot on her cheeks – her smiles would have been no less treasures had there been more of them – Mother must have floated upstairs, as she sometimes did, because we didn't hear the stairs creaking. Normally, the stairs creaked louder than the walls and roof. We heard the door, though. On each of our bedside tables, beside each of our lumpy beds, a dim candle burned in a glass bowl.

Between the candles, in the space between our beds, our bottoms in nightshirts were side by side, and the backs of our fine blond heads.

We turned round to see Mother's candle entering the bedroom, then Mother with our forgotten hot water bottles. 'Get into bed,' she whispered, cross because we were freezing to death in our nightshirts without enough sense to get back under the blankets. 'What are you looking at out there? There's nothing to see. You've nothing on your feet. Honestly!'

She pulled back the blankets on Sophia's bed and inserted a hot water bottle. Sophia got in. Mother folded the blankets over her like sealing an envelope. I got into my bed, and my hot water bottle joined me seconds later. 'Go straight to sleep, and no talking.' She blew out our candles and closed our bedroom door tight, leaving us alone with the Dark, the Cold and the Night Noises.

'Why did she whisper?' whispered Sophia.

My shrug was lost on my twin without candlelight, unless, with bigger earholes than me, she heard a shrug in the rusty bedsprings or frozen sheets.

'Are you awake?' I pretended to be asleep. 'Edward! Edward, wake up. Are you asleep?'

'Not yet.'

'Why did Mother whisper?'

'It's been a whispery day.'

'Why's it been a whispery day?'

'Some days just are.'

My answer satisfied her. It satisfied me too.

Some days were whispery the way some days were sad. Some days were noisy the way some days were happy. Whispery sad days and noisy happy days went together in a satisfying way, the way toast and jam go together although toast is hard and jam is runny.

I had a hot water bottle, which satisfied me too, because it meant my feet would soon defrost. In the absence of knitted bed hats, we pulled our blankets up to our eyes. We were snug although our exposed foreheads were chilly. Cold that ruled the day gone by, at night turned our faces straight like icicles.

Sophia and I had agreed, long before candles-out, and without need for words, that we should be quiet and sad too, although we felt happy – which was probably a sin. We were quiet and happy, but happy in a sad way because of Father's sadness at Granny Hazel's illness, which we thought we should share. We needed no one to tell us. We did not need to tell each other. Sophia and I just knew, the way we knew how to fly: tomorrow would be different.

Tomorrow, we would begin to forget how to fly.

'Edward,' said Sophia.

'I'm asleep.'

'I saw the White Lady with the fuzzy face. Did you see her too?'

'Yes.'

The White Lady with the fuzzy face was our ghost. When someone saw her, it meant somebody was going to die. I hadn't really seen her; I told Sophia a lie because I didn't want my twin to be all alone and afraid when she saw the White Lady with the fuzzy face.

Later . . . we should have been asleep, and maybe we were until the stairs creaked and the stairs creaked and the stairs creaked again. The landing floorboards at the top of the stairs creaked. The handle of our door grated and the door groaned open. We were four wide eyes, watching. A candle. A hand. An arm. Mother. Mother returned to our bedroom with the candle making her face look like the sun in night-time.

Sophia rose on her elbows in her bed and I rose on mine in mine.

'Granny Hazel has passed on,' said Mother, with neither sorrow nor a smile. I felt odd in a tingly way down my spine. 'I just thought I'd let you know. There's nothing you need to do. There's nothing anyone can do. Go to sleep now, it's late. Be brave.'

She and her candle left the room, closed the door tight again, and left us inside on our elbows with the Dark and the Cold. We had each other, and Mother had been brave. Sophia and I borrowed some of her bravery, although we didn't know for sure what to do with it.

Granny Hazel took ill a week before Farmer Barry brought Father, his bicycle and the coffin home in his lorry. We saw her taking ill as it happened, Sophia and me, and Mother and Gregory and Edgar too. All of us children were born in the Manse and had lived there all our short lives. Granny Hazel was born in the Manse too, and had lived there all her very long life.

On the day she took ill, Father worked late on the farm. The Manse's kitchen was hot and thick with the aroma of beef, potatoes, carrots and onions. Sophia, me, Edgar, Gregory, Granny Hazel and Mother had enjoyed stew and crusty bread for dinner when the first sign happened. Our empty bowls were stacked and ready for washing. Tea steamed from six mugs.

'I feel sick,' said Granny Hazel.

'I'm not surprised,' said Mother. 'The way you down it.'

Granny Hazel moaned. 'It wasn't the stew.'

She moaned again and toppled sideways off her chair.

Surprised but unfazed, Edgar and Sophia stared at the place where she had been. Gregory stared too, before turning to Mother, who pretended not to have noticed. I looked under the table to see where Granny Hazel had gone. Her eyes gazed at me unseeing.

'She's collapsed,' said Gregory.

Mother said it looked like it.

I emerged from under the table to see what would happen next.

'I hope she didn't bang her head,' said Mother, pouring herself another cup of tea. After blowing on it, she sent Gregory on the spare bicycle to tell Father at Farmer Barry's farm.

By the time Gregory returned – with Father pedalling twenty-four to the dozen behind him – Granny Hazel had come back to life. She had drunk a cup of tea and retired to bed, colliding with more walls than usual on the way. When she came downstairs the following day, she couldn't get back up. Father took her bed apart, carted the whole thing down to the living room and rebuilt it. He and Mother talked about getting a doctor for Granny Hazel, but nothing came of it.

Father didn't trust doctors. He said if the Lord makes you sick it's because you're supposed to be sick, and if the Lord wants to heal you He'll heal you. He said doctors suffered from having had an education. Education blinded people with false knowledge and fancy words from the facts of sin, the Saviour, and salvation.

Sophia and I remained quiet in bed after Mother left because Sophia had nothing to say and I was preoccupied with puzzling out passing on.

Whenever I tried to puzzle something out, Mother called me precocious. So I took to puzzling out in private. I wanted to puzzle out what Granny Hazel had passed on, and thought about asking Mother in the morning. Knowing it would be a silly question, I decided against it, and satisfied myself with the knowledge that when people die they pass something on.

But what?

I knew people passed on information. Sometimes Father told Mother Farmer Barry had asked him to pass something on – usually something about his wife's health. I used to think Mrs Farmer Barry suffered from halitosis. It kept her indoors. I knew about halitosis because Mother said Edgar had it. Mother corrected me when I made a fool of myself one day by saying the wrong word. Mrs Farmer Barry might have had halitosis too, but she definitely had tuberous sclerosis. When I asked Mother about tuberous sclerosis she told me to go to bed.

Noises like moving furniture came upstairs from downstairs. Father must have been shifting Granny Hazel's coffin into the house from the outhouse. How would he get her in? She was bigger than him and fat. He would have to roll her on to the floor first. I listened for a bump that never came. My brain fogged over trying to fathom the mechanics of it. The kitchen table was about the right size; the coffin would best go on it. Maybe Granny Hazel had enough life in her to walk to the kitchen. Father could give her a leg up.

I gazed at where the ceiling would be if I could see it in the Dark, and wondered if it was there even though I couldn't.

Lying there, I wondered if I could invent something better to do with a dead body than bury it. Use it as a scarecrow or something. We ate meat. A dead body had meat. Just today Mother said we were out of sausages. But we couldn't eat Granny Hazel if Father put her in a coffin and buried her – not that I'd want to eat Granny Hazel; she would probably make me ill.

In the Quiet, Dark and Cold, Sophia pulled me back from the rim of sleep. 'Who'll sleep in Granny Hazel's room now?'

'I don't know,' I replied, because I didn't know. Until then, I hadn't thought about it. I thought about it. I thought about it for longer than I thought. 'Gregory, probably.'

Sophia didn't answer. She'd gone to sleep.

Next thing I knew, the bedroom door creaked and candlelight came in with Mother – and Father too this time. I must have been asleep because no creaks came from the stairs.

Father had shaken Gregory and Edgar awake, and brought them in dressing gowns and bare feet to speak to all of us together. We were all there: Sophia and me in bed, Mother, Gregory and Edgar shivering, and Father, the white of his face glowing between his head hair and his beard. How could anyone say, as Mother did, that Gregory had inherited Father's square chin and strong looks? How did anyone know what Father's chin looked like? In Gregory, I could see only Father's ugly disposition, which, up to that point, Mother had never mentioned.

None of Father's strong looks or ugly disposition remained when my and Sophia's turn came to be born. Our birth called upon Mother's substantial resources. Even as a child, I saw shards of her in us: the splinters of solemn mood, the sharp edges of delicate features, and the jigsaw piece of sallow pallor. I was less a handsome boy than a pretty one. Sophia reflected Mother in every way. Mother depleted herself when she produced us. I came out of our birth best. Neither Mother nor Sophia came out of it whole. As Sophia gained strength through infancy and grew into childhood, Mother's remaining strength shrank in equal measure. They were ghosts of each other.

Father's voice crackled with emotion as he gave us our instructions for tomorrow: no dawdling, no talking, no laughing and no horseplay. We were to get up promptly, wash, and get dressed in our Sunday best. We were to be respectful at all times. Were we to step out of line there would be consequences. 'Justified consequences,' he said. I wondered how justified consequences differed from ordinary ones.

Our Sunday best should have been for church. We only attended at Christmas. The nearest church was two hours away and two hours back if the horse hurried and the cart kept all its wheels.

While Father talked, Gregory's and Edgar's feet turned blue.

Blue feet were common; we all had them.

But we didn't mind blue feet. We didn't mind groaning, crooked rafters. We were deaf to creaking walls and joints. We made peace with the wind that penetrated brickwork gaps like the breath of ghosts. We were accustomed to straining noises at night like the noise our gums made when Farmer Barry pulled a rotten tooth. Commonly, a whine somehow different from the usual whines awakened one or other of us – me, Sophia, Edgar, Gregory, Mother or Father – and sometimes a whine woke all of us together, and we would be twelve eyeballs in the dark. One of us might frighten another downstairs, or in the corridor, with or without our candles, as, unable to return to sleep, we prowled in search of dawn.

When Father had done talking, he left our bedroom without saying goodnight. He never said goodnight. Gregory and Edgar never said goodnight either. They limped out behind him and went to their room. Mother kissed me and Sophia, and muttered as she tucked the sheets in that we would catch our deaths, which made me aware, for the first time, of death's existence as my future possession, waiting for me to claim it, drumming its fingers, bored, because I had two left feet – according to Mother – and took ages at everything.

Sophia went to sleep before our parents went down the creaky stairs. I decided to stay awake and listen in case she woke. On that night, as on most others, I was useless at staying awake.

Granny Hazel, dead on the kitchen table, and only a floor or ceiling between us! She looked up at me with her eyes closed. I feared looking over the side of my bed in case she opened them.

3

Sophia's Promise

Poor Mother.

Mother rose before dawn even in summer when dawn came early, and we ate breakfast with sunlight streaming through the kitchen window and making the marmalade glow like orange jellyfish.

Every pre-dawn, Mother hurried downstairs in her high-neck blouse, V-neck pullover, cardigan, woollen socks, long skirt, and invisible green Wellington boots. She had ballet feet and a ballerina body. Either I saw her hurrying downstairs in my dreams or I've muddied her haste with images from books and movies: Jane Eyre, Blanche DuBois, Tank Girl, and the blind daughter in *Little House on the Prairie* whose name never made as much impact as her hair – which was like Mother's after she washed and dried it.

Sophia had similar hair. They were great, troubled women – not Mother and Sophia; they were just troubled – Jane Eyre, Blanche DuBois, Tank Girl and the blind daughter in *Little House on the Prairie* whose name never made as much impact as her hair. I became familiar with television years later. The Manse had no aerial in those days, nor television to connect it to.

Every day, Mother built up scrunched newspaper, firelighters, sticks and coals, and put a match to protruding paper ends. She watched the firelighters catch and flames embrace the sticks, then put the fireguard on the hearth. She smiled her first and often only smile of the day. Daily, she hurried to the kitchen. If the gas for the stove was too low – she could tell by the hiss – she pulled on her coat and hurried to the outhouse where the bottles were stored.

This morning, the gas had a strong hiss. Mother put the kettle on the ring to boil. Boiling took ages. Heat had first to change water from solid to liquid. Mother washed soot off her face and hands at the sink and dried them with a towel. She did this while spooning tea into the pot, a juggling act, like patting her head while rubbing her stomach. By the time she had stale bread – all the better for toast – on the board to slice, and the pan on the heat ready for oil, bacon, sausages, eggs, soda and potato bread, Father had resurrected himself upstairs.

Father, as usual, knelt at the side of his bed and thanked God for His gift of another day and plentiful bounty from the land. I heard him giving thanks and asking forgiveness through the thick walls and across the corridor. He prayed at listeners on the far side of the planet, and to a god I had a notion wore a hearing aid.

Mother cooked continuously, baking bread for future meals when she finished preparing imminent ones. The fire in the living room gave off a sweltering heat when lit, but most of the time the hearth sat black, like a hole in the wall. The bedrooms had fireplaces, but Father kept them empty to spare expense. He said sinners should never get so warm and comfortable they forget their need to repent.

When we repented, our teeth chattered.

The worst thing about the Manse was the toilet – a hole in a plank in a coffin-like box across the courtyard beyond the outbuildings, and a large bucket under the hole. Mother had the pleasure of emptying it daily, and twice daily when we were all blessed with freely moving bowels.

Father suffered from the need to perform excretory functions like the rest of us, which meant he suffered like the rest of us. Therefore, he prayed long and hard about what to do about our old-fashioned outdoor toilet. It served six needs and often had a queue. The Lord had given him permission to have a modern toilet built indoors, but the Lord had yet to give him a date and enough money. Father had spoken to builders and sought planning consent from whichever authorities had the power to grant or withhold it. I prayed for a positive verdict. We all did. An indoor toilet: we would truly praise the Lord for that! It would mean an end to bare cheeks frozen to the seat and fingers liable to snap off as we wiped our bums.

Six people go through a small fortune in toilet paper, which is why Father brought other people's newspapers home from wherever he could find them. Mother held a ruler against each newssheet and tore it into six smaller sheets. Daylight shone through a crack and we hurt our eyes reading stories with the endings missing, and pulled our pants up over inky posteriors.

The Manse contained other reading material: an encyclopedia and a dictionary – wholesome reading material, Father called it, but I had never seen him reading anything except his bible.

Candles hurt our eyes at night when we read the encyclopedia. Father made us use candles because lamp oil cost the earth. I liked the encyclopedia better than the dictionary. It had stories, and sometimes they made sense. It had more than a thousand pages, and three columns of writing on each page, which felt like reading for ever. While I enjoyed reading from the encyclopedia, I wished it had only one column per page and fewer pages.

The encyclopedia contained hundreds and hundreds of every letter in the alphabet, and had many pages devoted to words beginning with each one. So had the dictionary. An encyclopedia is a dictionary with true stories. On my fourth birthday, I started reading the dictionary at the beginning, intending to learn all the words through to Z. Alas, I gave up when the A entry introduced the word 'diphthong', which I made the mistake of looking up . . . something to do with two vowels. I looked up vowel . . . something to do with the speech tract. I looked up tract . . . a short pamphlet, often on a religious subject. Learning words involves more than meets the eye.

Newspapers and magazines were the Devil's work, especially newspapers – although useful for the toilet. They let the world's filth into the home, according to Father, which is why I never saw an intact one . . . except once, when Father must have forgotten to hide it. I saw my first bare-chested woman in that newspaper. She deserved pity more than anything else, having to walk around all day, every day, deformed. I thanked God, in my prayers, that neither Sophia nor Mother had breasts.

If Father had allowed newspapers, I would have been better prepared to encounter the world. Encountering the world, and possibly conquering it, was my destiny. Despite the absence of information – except in the encyclopedia – about life elsewhere on our flat planet – the one God made in six days – I knew we were safer in here, in the Manse, with the dead all around, than out there, in the world, with so much Devil's work going on.

There were other evolutions on the way. Running water! Electricity! I understood electricity to mean we would never run out of candles. Mother said everybody had electricity up north.

Me, Sophia, Gregory, Mother and Father had death on our lips, and in our eyes and ears. Edgar, however, came from a different planet. Nobody knew where Edgar's mind wandered when free to wander where it would. Mother and Father never scolded Edgar the way they scolded the rest of us when we needed scolding. I had an idea that he had a special status and, therefore, had been set apart. I assumed they liked him more than the rest of us.

I liked him too.

Father and Mother often quarrelled over education. Long before we were born, however, Father let Mother teach him how to read and write. Father never took to reading – apart from his bible. Writing came in handy for notes in the margins.

Mother thought so highly of education she sowed the importance of letters in the form of words on paper into our brains almost before we had teeth. I could sing the Alphabet Song – albeit twenty-six letters in a single note – before I could locate my mouth with a spoon. She taught us well. She gave us the gift of word boats. She made us one each by folding sheets of paper into tub shapes. When we came across a new word worth remembering, we wrote it down, cut it out, and dropped it in our word boats.

Gregory was by far the best at words. I came second best. Sophia used to be as good as me, but then she stopped, as if her head held enough of everything and had no space for anything new. By the time Granny Hazel fainted under the table, I had an ocean liner for a word boat and Sophia had a tug. Nevertheless, there were words I thought I knew but discovered, when called upon to use them, that I didn't. Words like posy. Edgar displayed as much talent as anyone when the words could go with pictures, but he was hopeless at non-picture words, like precocious.

He's a precocious child, Mother occasionally said. I, for my sins, held the dubious honour of being the precocious child in question. This invisible stamp, this identity, became all the heavier to bear because Gregory and Sophia were never referred to as precocious, and Edgar was its opposite.

When Father said precocious it sounded wrong, like a walrus performing a capriole. He said precocious as if he had a taste in his mouth like sour milk. He always directed his words to Mother, or the air; he seldom spoke to my face. He never punished me for being precocious, although his scowl was disapproval enough. I didn't like being precocious. I never knew if my precociousness leaked out like dribble.

When Mother called me a precocious child, however, precocious sounded special rather than warped. When I learned to read, and discovered how to use the dictionary, I trawled through the pris, the pros and eventually the pres. The word I sought remained elusive. It even managed to evade the encyclopedia. The meaning came to me some time later, as most words do to all people, by magic.

*

Suddenly, my eyes opened in pitch darkness. I had a space behind them where sleep had been. Morning had arrived, but not dawn.

'Are you awake?' I called across the gap between our beds.

'Where have you been? I've been awake for ages and ages and ages and ages,' replied my other half.

'You should have woke me.'

'I did, but you didn't wake. I dreamed. Did you dream it too?'

'I don't think so. What was it about?'

'I can't remember,' said Sophia. We often dreamed the same dream. Dreaming the same dream was like having four arms, four legs, and one head. 'Sometimes I can't remember my dreams, but I know I've had them. There's a big space where they were in my head . . . Mother's been up for hours and hours. Why hasn't she come?'

Not a clue on earth did I have appertaining to Mother's absence. Nevertheless, 'She's gathering eggs for breakfast,' I said.

I couldn't wait any longer. I needed to wee, which meant sitting on the edge of the bed, exposing myself to the Cold. While I went, Sophia went too. I went in my bottle; she went in her pan. It's a wonder our pee didn't freeze solid on the way down.

When we had done what needed doing, we jumped back into bed with shivery noises and wrapped our blankets tight against our necks. Just as our shivery noises stopped, Mother stormed our rooms and opened the curtains, first in the bedroom shared by Gregory and Edgar, then in the bedroom I shared with Sophia. If Mother stopped starting our days in this way none of us would have got up ever except to wee.

Mother had a sunny word for each of us as she shook us to life one by one. Gregory first – he took most shaking. 'Morning, dreamer.' Then, Edgar, 'Rise and shine, sleepyhead.' Sophia next, 'Come along, my angel.' And, finally, me, 'Hurry up, precocious one.'

Precocious was a Mother word, like reduce (over saucepans) and obligatory (over Gregory doing his homework). Sin and punish were Father words. Mother's words were prettier, in my opinion.

. . . and, last, Gregory again, 'Come on, you; shift your arse.'

On this particular morning, she echoed something she said last night: 'Don't forget what day it is.' As if we could!

None of us spoke much first thing in the morning. Mother said it was because we Pikes slept like the dead. I don't know why she said that; it wasn't true. We didn't speak more than a word or two at a time in the morning for an opposite reason: because the Manse's groans and whines often broke our sleep. There's another reason why we didn't speak: our jawbones took an hour or two to thaw.

Our harsh weather had chapped Sophia's red, red lips. They looked fatter than they were. She had a delightful pout. When Sophia pouted for a kiss, and when she thought hard about how to solve a problem – like how to turn the door knob with jam on her fingers – her lips formed a red bud.

When problem-solving, Sophia's eyebrows narrowed. She folded her arms across her chest – except if she had jam on her fingers. Problem-solving involved making herself as compact as possible. With eyes closed, eyebrows raised, and arms at her side, she presented her kissing pout while leaning forward as if lips were allowed to touch but toes had to stay apart.

Sophia threw back the blankets and sat on the edge of her bed, slumped and shivering. Her feet were white, tiny and sharp. A girl of her age should have had plump feet and piglet toes. I saw my first plump girls' feet when I went to school. It was a boys' school, but girls came to partake in a sports day. Until then, I thought all girls were skinny by nature. Sophia's feet were hard, like the stones ancient people used as knives to skin bears and lions. They wore the skins as coats and shoes because those were the days before shops.

I knew farms, churches, and houses because I'd seen them. I knew about shops too, although I'd never seen one. Shops were where you got things because you were out of them, like washing powder, matches and bleach; those were the kinds of things Mother most often found herself out of. Father only ever found himself almost out of gas for the cooker, which he cycled home with from Farmer Barry's farm in two green bottles, in a bag on his back. You needed money before you could go to shops. Everything costs money, Mother said and it didn't grow on trees. Shops were far away and maybe you had to travel across the sea in a boat to get to one. There were pictures of boats in the encyclopedia. One, called the *Titanic*, crashed into an ice cube and sank, drowning everybody except Robinson Crusoe, who washed up on a desert island and ate coconuts.

Edgar rose next. He collected water in a jug from the pail and poured enough into the basin to threaten his hands and face with damp. Sophia rallied at the noise from next door and did the same in our room. Sometimes the water froze overnight and first to the pail had to crack ice with the jug. Sometimes it froze outside, in the well, and Mother had to break it by dropping the bucket hard, or with a pole. One year she broke the bucket. The next year she broke the pole.

While Sophia tried to wash without allowing icy water to touch her skin, I edged my feet from under the blankets and rose bit by bit, even though I knew I would warm faster by rising all at once and getting dressed quickly. I dressed while Sophia washed. Then she dressed while I washed.

I dressed in hand-me-down-from-Gregory patch-arsed trousers, washed-to-see-through-thin white cotton shirt buttoned to my neck, and my heaviest pullover – which had holes at the elbows.

Mother came upstairs briefly to put a Windsor knot in my black tie. The hand-me-down-from-Edgar black jacket hardly fitted over the pullover; I looked stuffed. My shoes had such a high shine they reflected my face when I looked at my feet. I took off my jacket – wrestled with it for two whole minutes – so as to feel the benefit of it when I went outside.

Gregory, last as always, needed yet another shake from Mother.

*

Father appeared downstairs smelling of soap. Normally, he smelled of farm animals. The top half of his weatherworn face was as red as raw meat and the bottom half, shaved for the first time in years, looked like bone. He did it last night while we were asleep. His greying hair stuck upward and out. He must have washed it. No comb could tame its rebellion at the shock of shampoo, when it had known nothing stronger than water all its young life – and in its later life, water and a blob of grease. Father had dressed in a black suit shining with age.

Since his eyes in the hall inadvertently collided with hers through the open door to the kitchen, he mumbled Mother an aye-aye. He said aye-aye often, in preference to talking. I used to think he said eye-eye because everybody has two of them. He was confirming to whoever he said eye-eye to that they still had both.

'Sleep well?' she asked, with plainly feigned interest. Mother's enthusiasm always sagged when Father appeared. Sometimes she spat on to his eggs – I'd seen her doing it when she thought herself unwatched.

Nothing smelled better than the sound of frying bacon. I later went off bacon when I learned those crackle-fizzing strips of goodness were bits of cut up pig. But these were innocent times. Crispy aroma crackled out of the pan and snaked through the air. The bacon was for Father; we only received a crispy breakfast at Christmas. The rest of the time we got porridge and buttered toast – more than they got in China, Father often said, with cut up pig fat glistening in his beard.

Mother danced with kitchen utensils for partners; she and they were as one. She brought the kettle to the boil, milked the cups, turned the bacon and scooped it on to a tray to keep warm under the grill with the soda and potato bread. She fried sausages in the pan and buttered toast. Eggs were last. Father loved his eggs and bacon. Thick farm bacon with plenty of fat. He waited by the fire, reading his bible, for Mother to place the tray and saucer of toast and mug of tea and stacked plate of breakfast upon his lap.

Mother's enthusiasm returned by the time she reached the top of the stairs. She existed for us, her alpha and omega, she said often, having learned the phrase from Reverend Burrows. We loved to hear that we were her alpha and omega. It sounded grand even if we had no idea what it meant. At least, I had no idea what it meant, and I'm sure Sophia had no idea either. Edgar, to the best of my knowledge, never had an idea about anything. Gregory might have known. It was hard to tell what Gregory knew because he lied so often.

Father never missed a day at work, not even when snow reached the window sills, not even when thunder and lightning frightened our chickens to death, not even when he woke up in the morning dying from flu, or when one of us woke up dying from Plague, Famine or Ennui. He said he couldn't afford to miss a day at work. Father pedalled through summers and winters, through darkness and light, through thunder and snow blizzards to get to Farmer Barry's farm.

However, he had taken a day off work today to bury his mother. Her coffin occupied the kitchen table. We were to have breakfast on our laps in the living room. Father had shoved Granny Hazel's empty bed into a corner to make space.

Having already eaten one breakfast, Father waited for us to arrive for ours in his armchair by the fire. We arrived one by one. When everyone had presented themselves, Mother left the living room and returned a minute later with a large tray containing six small bowls of porridge so thick it was nearly biscuit.

Father gave thanks for the Lord's rich bounty, bearing in mind – lest we forget – that because of the Devil's work people were starving in China. Father always remembered the starving in China. If he kept on eating two breakfasts, Father would be unlikely to starve in China or anywhere else. I was truly thankful we had a fire on that morning; most mornings were too warm for a fire – Father said.

After porridge, Mother brought mugs of tea so hot they lifted skin from the roofs of our mouths, and a stacked plate of toast, the black scraped off and heavily buttered to hide the scars. We were big toast people in the Manse. Bread's cheaper than meat, Mother said. It fills you up and you don't have to kill it.

The toast-stack rapidly diminished. Edgar was butter and crumbs from ear to ear. Mother returned our empty mugs and plates to the kitchen when we had done.

The lamp flickered. Threadbare curtains kept out the bit of Cold that wasn't already inside. Cooked breakfast smells hung in the air. Father cleared his throat and said to Gregory, in a stern voice, 'Do you know what you've to do?' God help him if he'd forgotten.

Gregory said he did, and they left the room.

We waited quietly for them to return. I waited fidgety, wishing today was over. Sophia whispered to me, 'What's he to do?'

'What?' said Mother, before I got a chance to reply.

'Gregory. What's he to do?'

'Carry one end of the coffin. The end her feet are at, I dare say.'

'Oh . . . Why?'

'Your Father can hardly carry it on his own, can he?'

'I mean, why's he to carry her feet end?'

'I don't know, child. Just because!'

We were quiet again.

Occasionally, one or other of us coughed.

Father and Gregory didn't come back – at least, not as soon as I thought they would. Maybe Granny Hazel was too fat and they couldn't lift her. In case that was the reason, I made a suggestion.

'Mother?'

'What is it?'

'If Granny Hazel's too fat . . .'

'If she's too fat, what?'

'They could bury her a bit at a time.'

Mother made a noise, and covered her face as if she was going to cry, or laugh, I didn't know which.

We were quiet . . . again.

I whispered to Mother, 'What are they doing?'

'What needs to be done,' she whispered back, and, 'Shhh.'

Having done what needed doing, Father and Gregory washed and dried their hands at the kitchen sink; I heard the pipes gurgling and water running. I heard their Sunday-best boots on the floor tiles. Then they came to the living room with mud and blades of grass still on their boots even though they wiped them on the doormat.

Gregory looked flushed and his hair stuck out all over the place. He looked half mad. Father always looked flushed and half mad.

Father, standing at the door, instructed us to take our places.

I joined the line behind him, behind Edgar, who stood behind Gregory, who stood behind Mother, who stood behind Father. Sophia, a black bow in her blond hair, joined on the end and gripped my coat-tail. Our line would have been from tallest to smallest if Mother had been taller than Gregory, but Gregory and Edgar were both taller than her. Single file, we followed Father out of the living room, down the hall and through the kitchen.

Father and Gregory had removed Granny Hazel in her coffin from the table and put her outside, beside her grave.

Like a train with its six carriages standing on end, we followed the biggest carriage, Father, out the back and across the courtyard to the cemetery. I grew up thinking garden was another word for cemetery, like toilet and privy, potato and spud.

Poor Mother, a gossamer spectre of willowy grace, might have taken to the clouds if a windy gust had caught her off-guard. If a windy gust caught Sophia, I'd hold her down – unless the windy gust caught me too.

Father had conscripted Gregory to assist with the ropes.

Edgar picked his nose.

Cloud cracked above our heads as though God had a parcel to post through. Sun shone in the gap like a fanfare. We trod over mud and assumed our positions. I looked over my shoulder at the Manse – dark, bleak, with eyes and a mouth. The cloud-crack closed and the sky became the colour of concrete after rain. The Manse's shadow expanded, embracing the outhouses and green fields beyond.

I went somewhere else in my mind. I can't say what dream I took comfort in, or which nightmare I focused upon – perhaps one relating to the words 'Thy rod and thy staff, they comfort me', because the usage of anything resembling a rod or a staff brought tears and misery, never comfort. Father used a bamboo cane for the correction of his sinful children. When the cane was in another room, off came his belt, which he called the strap. How he relished clenching those yellow teeth and wielding the strap. We were to thank the Lord – and we did, because we knew no other way, even as we whimpered with lash burns on the backs of our legs and buttocks – that He had given us a father well able to keep us pious.

Sophia and I, holding hands, grew goose bumps. They were the same goose bumps we regrew daily. The ghost hand locked in mine had fleshless bone for fingers. Her wrist might snap at a sudden twist. She had arms like twigs, and bath-time shoulders like those on a victim from a ghastly prisoner of war camp like the ones I'd seen in the encyclopedia.

She had a lovely face.

. . . bloodless though it was, big-eyed, somewhat nervous, a little frightened perhaps, like a vulnerable forest creature wary of sudden noises. And there were plenty of those in the Manse.

Father looked like Isaiah, or Ezekiel, without a beard. He waved his palms Heavenward and shouted at the sky.

'Oh, loving heavenly Father who hast created us from dust and made us whole, who hast died for our sins and saved us, comfort us this day in thy manifest mercy. Be thou our strength.'

. . . and on, and on, until his voice was the same as the wind.

The chill should have kept me awake. Instead, I slipped into a doze on my feet as Father read Psalms from the big black King James bible with its thys, thees and thous, green pastures, paths of righteousness, valley of the shadow of death where I need fear no evil for the Lord my God is with me, and so on and so forth and on and on some more. The bible's pages were thumbed off-white at the edges. Its cover was floppy with excessive bending. Father had written an extra testament or two in the margins with his fountain pen.

Father called it the Family Bible. But it was his. He smacked my legs with the strap once for setting it on a shelf face down.

'Never put the bible face down! That's Satanism. Never ever put it face down. I won't say it again.' His bible occupied the kitchen table, the hearth, his chair in the living room when he got up to stretch his legs and potter a while as fathers do. The bible seemed to follow Father around, always one step behind him – or one step ahead. He would approach his chair, lift the bible off the cushion and sit down to read with it open at the correct page, all in such a fluid motion, without pauses of any length, you would think the bible an extra and perfectly functioning body part.

The cessation of Father's voice, and the scrape of casket on planks, roused me and gripped my attention. I returned from the place in my head where I had been, and noticed that Sophia had slipped her hand out of mine. She had left my side. Where had she gone?

A moment of panic! Me, looking around!

Mother gave me a reproachful look. I stiffened and stopped looking around. Her disapproval shamed me. When mother scolded us, we deserved it. 'Don't speak ill of the dead,' she said – often – if a snigger slipped out, or an unkind utterance concerning a deceased grandparent (never within Father's earshot, of course).

I watched Father and Gregory about the business of burial out of respect for Mother's wishes rather than respect for my dead grandmother. How could I respect her? I knew nothing about the old woman other than that she once produced Father. Granny Hazel used to sit by the fire with a face like curdled milk. Awake or asleep, the only difference was whether her eyeballs were on show. Worst of all, she always smelled of hours-old pee that saturated the bed sheets, soaked into the mattress, and penetrated the cushion on her fireside chair.

Gregory took his position on one side of the casket. Father took his on the other and said a silent prayer. Gregory had the longer side of the ropes that ran under what remained of Granny Hazel, now snug and sealed in her box. Father signalled with a nod. Gregory took his end of the ropes across the grave – Oops! Watch your step; it's slippery – and pulled them as though in a tug-of-war. The coffin moved towards the hole. Father steered from the other side. Together, they wrestled Granny Hazel into the grave.

His task complete, brushing his hands, Gregory returned to Mother's side breathing heavily. Breathless too, from effort and emotion, and glistening with sweat, Father took his place at the head of the grave, wiped his nose with a sleeve, and gestured with both hands for us to bow our heads for yet more prayer. I did. Then I looked up, to my right where the crumbling outhouses were.

Sophia appeared to be poking something with a stick.

Father's prayer would go on and on and turn into a sermon.

No one would miss me.

I found I had slipped away from the graveside before I had time to realize that doing so counted as more than an error of judgement – a sin. Like a thief stealing someone else's time, I tiptoed to my sister's side, my other half, my second skin. We shared a heart. Sophia was indeed poking something with a stick: the big, black dog. Dead.

Out of Father's earshot, wind blowing her voice across Hollow Heath, she sang, 'I fell in to a burning ring of fi-re. I went down, down, down . . .' She stopped singing and glanced at me, then turned her attention back to the animal. 'And it burned, burned, burned . . .'

'Stop singing. Father will hear you!' I whispered loudly.

She stopped. If one thing in the universe made us stop whatever we were doing, it was Father knowing we were doing it.

'You're supposed to be watching Granny Hazel getting buried.'

'So are you,' she argued.

'I came to see what you're doing.' Since she ignored me, I asked, 'What are you doing?'

'I found the dog, and it's dead.'

'It isn't ours,' I said, needlessly. 'We have chickens.'

Father must have shut them in the coop until after the burial.

'Can we keep it?'

'What for? If you throw the stick, it won't fetch.'

More a baton than a stick . . . 'What did it come off?' I asked, keeping my voice quieter than the prayer in the background.

Sophia shrugged.

The stick looked new. Was it a table leg? All the table and chair legs in the Manse were age-worn. It must have arrived here from outside. Small enough for Sophia's little fist, big enough to beat something with, a greater mystery than the dog. One leg of a table can't walk. Neither can two, three or four, but it must have got there – wherever Sophia picked it up – somehow. The dog had legs, so its presence posed no mystery. Then I felt highly pleased with myself because I realized the dog could have carried the stick in its mouth from wherever it came from to here, walked around for a couple of days looking for its master, the bearded stranger, then died – probably from exhaustion after carrying the stick so far.

'Why are you smiling?' Sophia asked.

'Nothing,' I replied, stopping smiling.

If you smile at nothing, people think you're daft, Father liked to say when he felt like a joke. This was as humorous as he got: a hint of sarcasm and a touch of insult. He had a smile like Lot's as he watched his wife turning into a pillar of salt.

Sophia bared the dog's fangs with the stick. 'Shall I ask Father if we can bury it with Granny Hazel? She likes dogs.'

'Animals and humans have separate graves, silly.' Immediately, I wanted to bite my tongue. Knowing I had hurt her feelings, I apologized. 'Sorry. You aren't silly; it slipped out.'

'That's all right,' she said, although I could tell it wasn't. For a while, we stood in silence.

The dog, a formidable beast if alive, had started going grey. Hair continues to grow after death; I knew that much from an overheard snip on the radio, but I had no idea whether it continued turning grey. Sophia lifted one of the dog's rear legs with the stick until her strength could lift it no more and the leg fell off the stick's end. It was a boy dog.

'Why?' she asked.

'Why what?'

'Why do animals and humans have separate graves?'

'Everybody knows that.' The hardest thing for a brother to do, in response to his sister's question, is admit ignorance.

'Why then?'

Unable to provide the correct answer, I could at least offer what seemed to me – given the little I knew – a rational possibility. I had no idea of how any sentence I began might conclude.

'It's because when you die you go to Hell, and . . .'

'Or you go to Heaven if you love Jesus hard enough.'

'And if a Hell animal gets buried with a Heaven human, it'll end up in the wrong place. Or it might be the other way round: if a Heaven human gets buried with a Hell dog. And if the Hell . . .' dog goes to Heaven? The argument became woolly in my head, and I petered out.

The dog wore a collar with a metal disc attached. I knew dogs' names were on metal discs because Farmer Barry's dog had one and its name was Fart. I couldn't pronounce the black dog's name at first. Neither could Sophia. We said Tenny, Tenny, Tennyson.

'Funny name for a dog,' I said, as Sophia and I stood up in case it came alive and bit us.

'I thought its name was Rabbit,' I said, while Sophia mightily tenderized the dog's flank with a rhythm and shoulder action like the ones with which she flattened braising steak for Father's

Sunday dinner (the rest of us usually got a pork sausage each).

Rain spat from Heaven like God firing darts to remind everyone of his omni-everything. God was like that: always drawing attention to Himself by parting Red Seas, and getting Himself crucified. I resented God's always having to be the centre of attention. I resented His big, preachy voice.

The rain pleased me. It meant Father would cut the service short and we could go inside and warm our backsides at the fire.

Granny Hazel's burial service ended sooner than I expected.

When I glanced back at the cemetery, I saw Father striding towards us with a face more thunderous than the weather. He must have taken off in pursuit of us immediately after saying amen. My heart either missed a beat or hiccuped and beat an extra one. Mother, Gregory and Edgar were following him. He looked over a shoulder and pointed them at the Manse. They veered towards it, as one, physically redirected by the force of his will.

Father descended like an axe to chop off our heads. My entire life – what there had been of it – passed before me. The encyclopedia flashed across my mind's eye, open at B for Boris the Hermit.

And then Father had stopped striding. He stood before us twelve feet tall, like Goliath. If I'd had a sling I'd have dropped it.

I'd expected Father to order me and Sophia indoors. I thought he would have barked a command that we were to wait in his study. I thought he would have changed out of his damp clothes, returned, then bent us over his desk and tanned our bare backsides with the strap. But something happened there, outside, beside the dead dog. Wet-faced with the rain, Father glared down at me as though I were a poo Tennyson had done on the living-room rug. At times like that – and there were many – I stiffened in expectation of an open-handed blow to my face. To my relief, he deemed me unworthy of his anger.

Instead of hitting me – or giving me a good shake at least – Father got down on one knee in front of Sophia. If she had possessed a sword she could have knighted him – the stick might have done. His nearness sent her half a step closer to me, as close as she could get without standing on my feet. With his hands on her shoulders, Father drew her a whole step back, closer to him. Then a bit closer still. So close to his face, I would have started blubbering, but Sophia was stone.

Sophia never cried.

Father's voice wavered near to tears in a way I had never heard before.

Far from being sad, I was happy she'd gone. We all were, except Father. I wondered what dead people did all day when they were closer to Jesus than ever. Sing hymns, I supposed; it must be like attending church for ever. Poor Granny Hazel. But old people like that kind of thing, although I couldn't imagine Granny Hazel getting off her chair for long enough to stand up for a whole hymn.

Father said to Sophia, in a way that made me swallow hard, 'I want you to make me a solemn promise.' When she didn't reply, he raised his voice: 'Promise me?'

Her head nodded like the stiff tail of a small dog, but her expression far from reflected a similar kind of happiness. She might pee herself. She had done it before this close to Father's face. We both had.

'You're a good girl.' He stroked fine strands of hair from her eyes with porcine, farm labourer's fingers. I noticed that his fingernails were clean. I'd never seen them clean before.

'You're my only daughter,' said Father. 'A daughter's place is to help her mother, and your mother's past the age now where . . . The thing is, what I want to say is, this is your home, and it always will be.'

She seemed to have no energy left to nod her head.

'Do you hear?'

Her eyes were huge and round, her lips pressed tight.

'Do you hear?'

At last Sophia's head nodded the way it would have done no matter what he asked.

'You must make me a promise. You must promise you'll never leave. Never leave your home.' He shook her, gripping her shoulders too hard. 'You promise?' Sophia nodded her head harder. 'Never ever desert your mother, daughter. Never ever leave your home.'

Father's grip relaxed.

He had never displayed great skill with words, unless they were part of a sermon of one kind or another. He seemed to speak to himself next, looking at the ground. 'Your mother needs you as all our mothers need us. She'll need you when her husband's long gone . . . Unless, Him knowing best, He takes her first.'

Father looked at Tennyson as though trying to remember what kind of beast it was. Sophia had dropped the stick. We stayed like that for a long moment, alive but inanimate like the dog, as though we were dead too, yet still standing with our eyes open. The Manse and everything around and inside – including us as a family – had death running throughout as surely as fat runs through meat. Maybe that's why the dog came to the Manse: to die – because it smelt death where we were.

Lightning snapped us in the wrong places. I saw Father and Sophia, and the outhouses and the toilet coffin and the dog's corpse and, somehow, they were behind me, as were the headstones and angels, in black and white like a photograph's negative. I saw them close up, then distanced. Sophia was a skeleton. Father, staring at the sky, prayed: 'The Lord giveth and the Lord taketh away. Thy will be done.' Lightning bolted. Thunder thundered like the Lord cross.

Father rose to his feet and staggered indoors like a shot cowboy, wounded, head low, leaving us there, his rejections, as rain grew heavier and we got wetter. We cared nothing about wet. We would rather swim across the cemetery, out to the fields and beyond, than sit dry indoors with Father for company. Rain pounded upon large pot-hole puddles that formed in seconds on the broken cement and gravel ground. Rain sounded like glass shattering on the kitchen floor.

The shape of Sophia's mouth asked: Never?

'What?' I shouted, and put my ear in her mouth.

'What does he mean by never? He said never leave.'

'I don't know. He means what he says.'

Mother waved at us from the kitchen doorway. I think she wanted us in out of the rain with some urgency.

'Does he mean never ever?'

'He did say never. Never is never ever.'

Her eyes grew wide and her lips parted in awe and terror.

'But what will happen if I do leave one day?'

'Awful things,' I said, thinking of Father more than anything else. Father represented all kinds of awful things.

'What awful things?'

Canes and straps and dead dogs flashed in my mind.

We jumped when the dead dog gave a spasm. We gaped into each other's faces, and sprinted, screaming, for indoors.

4

Sophia's Curse

Sophia's nerves and mine spent the rest of Granny Hazel's burial day settling. Our nerves had never been so nervous. Mother noticed it. As we sat at the hearth, building we knew not what with coloured wooden blocks, she looked down on us as if we had each sprouted an extra ear on our foreheads. Mother turned to Father who was reading his bible on an armchair bleeding discoloured stuffing like snot from a nose. 'It was too much for those two. Look at them; their nerves are on end.' Sophia and I looked at each other, but we still had flat hair and looked the same as always. Father grunted.

Granny Hazel had been changeless, present all my life, stinky on her chair but suddenly gone. The living room doubled in size. The kitchen became a pleasant place to linger. The air smelled fresher.

Granny Hazel's burial day became the day after Granny Hazel's burial day and the next day became the day after that. Sophia and I looked at each other's faces, pressed each other's noses and tugged each other's cheeks. We realized we were what Granny Hazel had ceased to be. We were alive.

We went round in circles, too inexperienced to know how to conclude our ruminations. But when we did we would conclude them together, because our heads were one and our tight circles were the same. We had yet to split and become ourselves.

The wind blew two slates off the roof. One of them killed a chicken, which was rubbery, but the chips fried up nice and crunchy.

A special game came into existence called The Promise – our new, favourite game. We couldn't begin to guess what the outcome would be, but no ending we could imagine looked like a happy one.

In dry weather we talked about the promise while bouncing rubber balls off the side wall. In wet weather we talked about the promise while flicking through the encyclopedia in search of information about nothing in particular. We whispered about the promise in our beds at night when we were supposed to be asleep. We talked about the promise to each other, exclusively, because we never thought of talking about it to anyone else.

When we lost interest in bouncing rubber balls off the wall, and in reading books that didn't tell stories, we played hide-and-seek in the cemetery – when the rain stayed away – and built very small snowmen in the cemetery when too little snow fell to build tall ones.

'I think Granny Hazel has it in for us,' whispered Sophia as we lay in our beds, the cemetery through the window in the Dark and the curtains drawn open. 'I dreamed she burned us down.'

'You didn't tell me,' I said.

'I only just remembered.'

As I thought of what to say, the bedsprings protested. Sophia punched her pillow and turned her back to me. 'Night-night.'

What would happen if the Manse caught fire? Sophia would have to leave it then! Maybe she could leave the Manse as long as Mother went with her. Mother going with her would be all right. But, then, they might both get lost. Lost in a dark wood, like Hollow Wood, but with wild animals, sinking sand and pirates, highwaymen, fire-breathing dragons and monsters and no way out . . . And so on, in the Dark, until yawns came and my eyelids drooped in the black middle between midnight and dawn.

Father moved Gregory and Edgar into Granny Hazel's bedroom at the front of the Manse, and moved me into their old room. Gregory got Granny Hazel's double bed, Edgar took his single with him, and I got Gregory's single. In making me change rooms, Father shut me off from Sophia at night-time. Sophia had a room of her own now with two beds, one of them empty. Separation from Sophia seemed like a punishment for something I never did.

When I asked if I could stay with Sophia, Father said I would do as he said, and Mother added, by way of unfathomable explanation, that Sophia would be a young woman one day. Although I didn't see what Sophia's becoming a young woman had to do with anything, I held my tongue.

My new room gave me a phobia I had no name for. Perhaps there's no better name for it than small-person-in-big-brothers'-former-bedroom phobia. Which isn't as bad as big-brothers-in-dead-granny's-bedroom phobia. My new room contained an odour of older brothers who broke wind too freely and washed too seldom. Sophia slept on the other side of the wall to my right. The junk room was to my left as I lay in bed. It had been reserved, since the beginning of time, for our future toilet – or bathroom, as Mother had taken to calling it because we were going to have a bath too.

I had difficulty getting to sleep in my lonely room. I awoke in the wee hours almost every night. Getting back to sleep took ages. Sometimes I got out of bed, wrapped in my sheets, and looked out of the window. When the moon hid, I saw almost nothing. When the moon came out, I saw the cemetery and miles and miles of fields stretching to the horizon.

Sophia and I lay side by side with only a solid wall between us, which we knocked secret codes on and hurt our knuckles.

Before Granny Hazel died, we were regular churchgoers. We went once each year, on Christmas Day. I hated church. It's no place for children or people with brains. Aged eleven months, I watched Mother staring down at me, cooing 'Ma-ma, Ma-ma', and my first words back to her were I hate church.

After Granny Hazel died, Father stopped going, which meant that the rest of us stopped going too. I never knew why Father stopped going; there were no signs that he had fallen out with God, but, obviously, he must have done. I don't blame him. I'd have fallen out with God too, if He'd killed Mother – and if God and I had been on friendly terms in the first place.

It was a Sunday. The day had been overcast and night came early. Evening approached candle-lighting time. Drizzle dotted the window, in morbid contrast to the scene within.

Gregory: jumping in the air, clapping his hands, jigging around the living room in a most non-adult and unsophisticated way. Sophia and I looking on, astonished that he should greet bad news with such delight. Edgar: cross-legged on the rug in front of the fire, ha-ha-hawing and clapping his hands in imitation of his older brother . . .

The promise had never been a secret. Neither Sophia nor I knew of a reason why the promise should have been kept from Gregory. Father never said that we had to keep it a secret. When Gregory started leaping around we wished we had kept it to ourselves.

'I'm glad you think it's so funny,' I muttered loud enough for only Sophia to hear. I felt like punching Gregory in the head. Had I done so, he would have been imprisoned for my murder.

Sophia knew no such fear. 'I'm glad you think it's so funny!'

He stopped abruptly and acted deadly serious. 'Oh, don't get me wrong: it isn't funny, little Soapy Soapsuds; far from it. It's a curse!' he announced. 'You're cursed! You're cursed!'

'What's a curse?' asked Sophia.

The living-room door opened. Father came in. We held our tongues and our breath. Father looked behind a cushion, scratched his beard – some of it had grown back. Having scratched his beard for half a minute, and inspected his fingernails, he left the room and closed the door behind him.

I had hoped that in Father's depression, because of his mother's death, he would do himself in by swallowing a tin of rat poison, or sawing off both hands and squirting blood all around the outhouses . . . Although he could only saw off one hand, unless he could saw with a foot, and I doubted he could. He might have sawn off both feet; or both feet and a hand. Alas, he hadn't sawn off anything and our lives hadn't improved.

'Go on, then, Eddy Bear: tell her what a curse is.'

'I don't know any curses,' I said.

Gregory went behind the sofa and placed his hands on the top as if it were a lectern. Pleased that I had thrown the question back to him, but unwilling to show his pleasure, he used the sofa as a stage prop. He stood behind it legless, like Punch or Judy. 'A curse, dear sister, is like a spell cast in ye olde days of witches and wizards and boiling pots of bats' blood, pee, bulls' bones and human hair all mixed together.'

'But what does it do?'

'It . . .' His search for a word ruined the performance; it also gave me an injection of joy, and I hoped all the words he wanted to find to define a curse were lost. 'A curse made by, say, Father, on, say, you, means that if you do something in the future . . . Never mind. Look; your particular curse is this: if you leave the Manse something bad will happen to you.'

'I already know that.'

'Then what more do you want from me, child?' He raised his arms in a shrug and dropped his head to one side. While holding that pose, he looked like a boy Jesus on a cross, apart from the polo-neck pullover, which I doubt they wore in Jesus's day, especially when they went to get crucified. 'The bad thing shall be something very, very, veryvery unpleasant.'

'What like?'

'All the people in the cemetery breaking into the house to eat you?' He did scary monster shapes with his arms and face.

'Stop it! Stop it!'

He monster-lurched towards her. 'We're coming all smelly and horrible from our graves to get you, strangle you, tie you up, boil you in a pot and pick your bones clean.'

'Stop it.' She ran away from him behind the chair Mother normally sat on. 'Dead people are in Heaven and Hell.'

'You're frightening her,' I said.

'Shut up, you wimp, or I'll frighten you in a minute.'

'Why don't you tell her the truth? What kind of thing?'

'How should I know? She'll turn into a frog or something.'

Sophia screwed up her face like when she had to take a spoon of castor oil. 'I think I'd rather sleep for a thousand years.'

'Right! I'm bored with this,' said Gregory. 'You won't have to worry about either frogs or princes, if you ask me. Just forget about the whole thing. I'm sure Father will too.'

Instead of simply heeding his advice, we told Gregory that we needed some kind of boundary and the old, fallen tree on Hollow Heath seemed like a good distance.

'Sounds good to me. That's your radius,' he said.

'What's a radius?' Sophia said, while I searched my brain.

'A radius is a line going from . . . It's half a diameter. It's the distance, in a straight line, from the centre of a circle to its rim, and the rim is called its circumference.' Gregory accompanied his definition with finger-drawing in the air. 'If you draw a straight line from circumference to circumference through the centre of a circle, that straight line's the diameter.'

In one voice, Sophia and I – neither of us had been introduced to mathematics beyond adding and subtracting – said, 'You what?'

'Imagine Edgar standing at the gate with a ball of string.'

There was a ball of string in the kitchen drawer which seemed just the thing for Edgar. 'Got it,' I said.

'Right. Sophia, imagine yourself walking away from Edgar with the string's tail end in your hand. You keep walking in more or less of a straight line. When you get to the tree, you stop.'

'Does Edgar follow me?'

'Don't be stupid. Edgar holds the string tight so no more unravels, just the amount that stretches from him to the tree. What you want is a length of string from Edgar to the tree.

'The length of string that stretches from the Manse to the tree is called the radius. Right? That's because the Manse marks the centre of a circle. You walk in a circle around the Manse, holding on to your tail end of string, and end up back at the tree. The circle you've walked in is the circumference. See? All the time, Edgar will be holding the ball of the string tight, so if you kept your end tight too, you would walk in a perfect circle.'

Sophia asked, 'What's the diameter, then?'

'I already told you. It's twice the length of a radius . . . Never mind . . . Look, if you really want to know, the diameter stretches from the tree, to Edgar at the gate, through the centre of the Manse and across the cemetery, into the field. You don't need to think about the diameter, or the radius or circumference for that matter. All you need to do is walk in the circle that the tight length of string lets you make.'

'Just walk round holding the string?'

'Just walk round holding the string.'

'What if I come up against weeds or a shrub too big to climb through, or stinging nettles or sinking sand? There's an awful lot of holes and things there. I wouldn't like to fall in. I might get trapped. Mother says to be careful.'

'It's all right to walk around things, but you can't let go of the string. You must keep it as tight as you can. Well, fairly tight anyway.'

Sophia looked to me for confirmation that Gregory was making sense. I knew her thoughts: what if her walk round the Manse turned out to be zigzags or a square rather than a circle? Or a rectangle or a triangle, although Sophia might have no knowledge of rectangles and triangles – I'd go over it with her later.

Meanwhile, as I imagined Sophia circling the Manse with her string, something occurred to me which Gregory had overlooked.

'But if Edgar's standing at the garden gate holding the ball of string,' I piped, commanding Gregory's attention, 'and if Sophia walks round the house the string will wrap round it and she'll end up against a wall unless it's a very big ball of string that never runs out. If there's not enough string she'll run out of radius.'

I looked at Sophia to see if she understood what I meant. If she did understand, I hoped she might explain it to me. With my attention elsewhere, Gregory took his opportunity and punched me in the head, which hurt him more than it hurt me because he had never broken the habit of punching with his thumb inside his fist instead of out. When he returned to the living room, after running his hand under the cold water tap, he said that we were stupid and he refused to have anything further to do with us.

Sophia and I, with Edgar's help, attempted to create the circumference outside which Sophia had been forbidden to venture. It didn't work. Edgar was supposed to hold his end of the string and stand still, but he kept following us.

We agreed that 'the Manse' meant the building and the land around it. But how much land? Could she venture into the fields behind the cemetery, or on to Hollow Heath beyond the front garden?

We understood the boundary to be a fixed boundary for all time. Children have a weak perception of change and shifting boundaries, and Sophia and I had almost none. I wanted to award her a greater range in which to roam than she felt entitled to. She would have restricted herself to the garden at the front, the cemetery at the back, and the outbuildings where Father stored his farming tools and jars of nails and rat poison. The fence round the front garden made an obvious boundary, but I saw no harm in her venturing on to the heath so long as she remained in view from the Manse.

Crossing the heath to the railway track clearly had to be forbidden; she would be too far away at the track, and out of sight to anyone looking for her without binoculars. Hollow Wood had to be out of bounds too. It was almost as far away as the railway track. We never went there anyhow. It looked dark and creepy. When the sun fell behind it, it looked like a black wall. Tramps and escaped criminals lived there. They hunted hares for food and slept under tents made from old blankets.

We settled on a fixed object. The lightning-struck tree became her limit. It took a healthy run and skip, from the broken garden gate over weedy clumps, to reach the lightning-struck tree.

Sophia caught a cold, which meant that I caught it as well. Mother confined us to our bedrooms, but allowed me to visit Sophia or her to visit me so long as we kept warm – which meant two crushed together in a single bed. She forbade Edgar access to us in case he got it too. She allowed us to come downstairs for part of each day – the afternoon while Father was at work and the living room was warm – and Edgar enjoyed our company then. We sniffled, sneezed and blew our snouts until they were red and skinned. The cold settled in our chests. Mother was afraid we might take pneumonia and fed us large spoonfuls of foul-tasting medicine that made us sleepy. Father complained about us disturbing his sleep by barking through the night, and promised us the strap unless we barked more quietly. Our nearly pneumonia lasted for ever. Sophia's lasted longer than mine.

Each day, wearing slippers, and a pullover over my pyjama top, wrapped in a blanket, I stared from my bedroom window at the cemetery, and Granny Hazel's grave in particular. Profound thoughts, like the necks of giraffes, twisted towards frightening ones. What if she woke? What if Granny Hazel opened her eyes like Lazarus, and Jesus said Granny Hazel come forth but she couldn't get the lid off? What would happen then? Would Granny Hazel scratch the inside of her box and scream? No one would hear – except Jesus, who would be no use to her unless he had a spade.

I looked at her grave as Sophia barked on the other side of the wall. Granny Hazel's destiny was my destiny too: to be one day still, silent, and buried under earth for ever with no room to move. With no one to hear me if I wept aloud, went mad, and survived a while longer by eating both fists. I would pee myself.

When Sophia started getting better she came to my room at night and we stared out of the window together. 'What are you looking at?' she asked. The sky, a star, the darkness, I lied. 'What are you thinking about?' she asked. I never told her the truth. The realness, the trueness, and the oursness of death seemed to me to be something Sophia needed shielding from. The lumpy mounds of earth around Granny Hazel, the headstones and sculptures of angels, seemed to nod in agreement with my thoughts. Their nods were gloomy, but comforting too. They said, resign yourself to one day dying; get used to the idea; everyone must.

Sophia and I hoped Father might mention the promise, but having brought it up once already he never did. He brooded all day, every day. Mother stayed out of his way while he brooded – but she usually stayed out of his way anyhow.

Granny Hazel's death broke Father like a cup. I watched him slinking up the stairs and down. He never raised his head or looked at me. Sophia said he looked at her in the corridor 'in a funny way'. He said nothing though, just stared, then turned away, into his room. Mother took meals to the bedroom and he ate alone. Normally, he insisted that we ate together at the kitchen table. Ordinarily, Father would say grace. Only when his hands parted and his eyes opened could we raise our knives and forks. When he said we were excused, and only then, could we leave the table.

That way of living became a memory after Granny Hazel died. Gregory, Edgar, Sophia and I were happier at mealtimes because of Father's absence – as well as his mother's. None of us asked Mother about Father for fear that asking might prompt his return.

One day, Sophia stared at, over, beyond or through the graves of Pikes long departed. She stared at the graves often. I stared at them often too, but staring never made them sprout flowers, or enticed their occupants to climb up through the earth and dance a jig.

She held in her hands a posy made of daises from the front garden. I held a similar posy in mine, wondering if I should get the ball of string from the kitchen drawer to tie the stems with. I jumped when a hand rested on my shoulder, and dropped my posy.

Mother smiled at my fright.

Something caught Mother's eye. She started at the grave, troubled by something visible only to adults. I looked where Mother did, but saw only Tennyson's grave – nothing odd about that.

Sophia rose with dirty knees and stood beside us.

'Children,' said Mother in a scolding voice. Then she changed her mind. Bending down to our height, hands between her knees, she said, 'What have you pair been up to this morning?'

'We reburied Tennyson, so he could be with everybody else,' I said. 'I think he was lonely over there.'

'What's left of him. He pongs a bit, Edward.'

Perhaps I should have dug the grave deeper to get all his legs in.

'They're very nice daisies, but don't you think it would be nice to put daisies on the graves of people? Grandparents, for example? Bear in mind, the dog wasn't ours, and blood's thicker than water.'

'Why's blood thicker than water?' asked Sophia, for whom asking for the answer came easier than puzzling it out – such wise economy of thought deserved more credit than she received. I, on the other hand, tended towards puzzling out until my skull hurt.

'It's a long story,' said Mother. 'Your grandparents would appreciate having flowers on their graves.'

Sophia said, 'I'll do it,' and grabbed the daisies from my hand. She would have been off, but Mother spoke her name and fixed her to the spot. 'While you're at it, put the cross back at the head of Granny Hazel's grave. When your father gets home and finds you've given it to a dog he'll hit the roof. He spent hours on that cross.'

Sophia extracted Granny Hazel's cross and tramped across the cemetery to relocate it with its rightful owner.

Mother turned her attention to me. 'And you should know better, Edward Pike. Now, come and wash your mucky paws.' She reached out one of her fine, pale, beautiful long hands for me to take in one of my fine, pale, muddy short ones.

Following Mother, I looked over my shoulder at Sophia on her knees at Granny Hazel's grave, scattering daisies. She had forgotten my existence, and I wanted to call to her, 'Sophia! Sophia! Don't forget about me!' As Mother led me away, I experienced a vast sense of loss, and I swallowed down the lump that rose in my throat.

'Is blood really thicker than water?' I asked. The consequences of blood's being thicker than water must have been important if someone made a saying out of it.

'Is what?'

'Is blood really thicker than water. You said . . .'

'The places your brain goes is nobody's business. It's just a saying, like two wrongs don't make a right. It's called a metaphor . . . I think. Don't worry about it; you'll learn these things at school.'

'Why do two wrongs make a right?'

'They don't; that's the point. You ask the strangest questions.'

In the kitchen, Mother got to work on my hands. She seemed teary and flustered. 'Boys are dirt magnets. I should know. The three of you are the same. Four counting your father.' The notion of Father being the same as Gregory, Edgar and me seemed so mistaken I wondered if Mother and I were thinking of the same father. 'That's to be expected, him on a farm from dark until the cows come home.'

Mother's joke made me smile.

She stopped scrubbing. 'What?'

'We don't have cows.'

'And?'

'So they can't come home.'

She narrowed her eyes, which made me smile again.

Mother resumed her scrubbing. 'I want to ask a favour, Edward. Favour's the wrong word, but will you make me a promise?'

Promises were suddenly popular. I trusted them less than before Sophia made hers to Father, but making a promise to Mother was probably all right. Mother arranged the question in her head while erasing my flesh through scrubbing. 'Here's what it is . . .'

I waited to hear what it was.

'You're both growing up fast, you and Sophia. You'll be young adults in no time. And you're her big brother. Will you promise to be the best big brother in the world and watch out for your sister?'

'Yes,' I said, thinking, naturally, of course, what else?

'Will you promise me you'll be her brave soldier?'

I grinned.

'I needn't ask such a favour; you always do watch out for her and you always will. It's just, now, on our own, now Hazel's dead.'

She choked up.

'Are you sad because Granny Hazel's dead?'

She laughed a cry as if cracked with an insanity-shaped whip. If she washed my hands much longer my upper limbs would start at the wrists.

Mother turned to the sink. With her back to me, she buried her hands in the suds. 'Aye, you've hit the nail on the head, Edward. I'm crying because Granny Hazel is dead. At long last. That's about the size of it.' I rejected the idea that she would ever cry over Granny Hazel. A hundred Granny Hazel's deaths would fail to make Mother sad. They never cared for each other.

'Father is sad,' I said.

Mother removed her hands from the water, dried them with a tea towel, and leaned on the edge of the sink looking at the window.

Mother sniffed. Her hands were red and bloated. After some time, when I thought I might as well sneak off and find Sophia, she began to speak, but quietly, almost to herself. Although she dried her hands less than a minute ago, she put them back under the suds. But the hands were motionless in there, as though trying to drown. I took a soft step closer, but still had to strain to hear. All of the words she spoke joined together like a sadder kind of sigh.

'How is it, I wonder, we get where we end up? I don't know. If there's a god, he's a plan more impossible than I'll ever imagine.'

'Father says God knows everything.'

'What's that?'

'Father says God knows everything.'

'Aye, well, your father doesn't know everything.'

Father doesn't know everything? It was almost blasphemy!

I said, 'He talks like he does.' I meant it to sound more matter-of-fact than it did, and less sarcastic. 'I mean, nobody in the whole world knows everything, so there must be lots and lots of things God knows but people don't. God doesn't tell even Father everything.'

'Holy smoke, Edward, what a mouthful! You're right there. Whatever it was, I'd never thought of it like that and certainly never will.' She looked down at me as if I had fish growing from my ears.

She turned back to the soap suds in the sink and warmed her hands in them. In time, she talked to me quietly again, or to herself.

'There's a connection between sons and their mothers that's stronger than a spider's silk. A mother knows her son for twenty years as a child, but a wife knows her husband as an adult for longer than that. A wife gets to know her husband better than his own mother ever knew him. Hazel never knew him like I do. Mothers only see the good and have a blind spot for the bad. Only his mother could restrain him from wicked excesses without even knowing she was doing it.'

Wicked? Father? Excesses? What were excesses?

'Now Hazel's gone up to Heaven or down to Hell, or to wherever she wound up, there's no restraint. He'll do what he likes.'

Wicked? Father? The two words were hardly fit to inhabit the same sentence. Mother must have meant an adult thing beyond my understanding. Asking her what she meant would have made me comfortable, so I remained silent and a little dizzy with confusion.

'Are excesses like excuses?'

'Well,' she said, turning her brain's dictionary pages. 'Do you know when you have too much of something? That's when you've an excess amount of that thing.' It made sense. Father had too much breakfast, so his breakfasts were excesses. And they were wicked ones because people were starving in China.

'Go now and chase dreams with your other half.'

When Mother smiled the sun shone in my heart. My smile and I went out through the back door to look for Sophia.

Exactly as I had last seen her, Sophia was still arranging daisies on Granny Hazel's grave. Less time had passed than I thought. Although I meant to join her there, I held back and watched. Wrapped in moving daisies around on the palm of her hand. Mouthing the words of some song. Happy. That's what she was experiencing: happiness! If only for this moment, feeling neither too hot nor too cold, lost inside herself, Sophia had found happiness. I belonged to no part of her now. Something of the nature that used to bind us had dissolved for ever.

5

The Horrible Wipple

Wellington boots and dirty hands were permitted in the kitchen, but forbidden elsewhere in the Manse. I kicked off my Wellingtons at the back door and washed my hands at the kitchen sink, then dried them with the tea towel that Mother dried dishes with and said that I mustn't keep using as a hand towel.

The hall sounded normal – like my socks on the floor – and smelled of fresh flowers. The flower smell should have warned me to advance cautiously; the hall normally smelled like wet coats. Innocently, I opened the living-room door, went inside without looking and shut the door behind me – Mother constantly reminded us to close the door and keep the heat in.

Orange and hairy, like an orangutan getting off all fours and on to two! Although I saw the creature for a split second only, that was long enough for it to transmogrify from its demonic into its human form – a head and the correct number of arms and legs. A poker shot up my spine and my hair stood on end. Father said the Devil wears many disguises. I made a noise of fright. Even as I spun on my heels and ran into the shut door, my senses confirmed that I had seen the Devil change himself into a hideously ugly woman who had no right to be there. My hand found the handle, and I escaped into the hall to almost collide with Mother carrying a tray containing a pot of tea, two cups, two saucers, and a plate of shortbread. She spoke my name with considerable alarm while swinging the tray clear of my head.

Nothing spilled, luckily for me.

'There's a, there's a . . .' I trembled, pointing.

'There's a there's a, is there?'

'No,' I whined, tugging her dress, but in no particular direction. I wanted whatever waited for us in the living room to be a figment of my imagination, like the smoke-shaped people I saw in the cemetery from my bedroom window at night. Mother said they were figments of my imagination, which meant I had to ignore them, as if they were unreal. 'You have to look.'

'Let go, Edward. You're behaving like a big baby.'

Mother pushed past me, taking tea and shortbread to the very place where I had seen the ghost – or monster – or disturbed the burglar who had broken out of an asylum – or done whatever I'd done, accidentally. I didn't mean it.

'A dead crow fell on Tennyson's grave from nowhere,' I said, but Mother ignored me the way she expected me to ignore the figments of my imagination. As she entered and rounded the door out of sight, I hung back, half expecting a scream and a clatter as the tray and its contents hit the floor. My feet stayed on the ground, but I jumped when I did indeed hear a dreadful sound.

Not a scream, but a voice. Several seconds passed before I recognized the language it spoke as the same as my own. Its accent was the same too, but different. I had read about accents in the encyclopedia . . . something to do with talking. In the Garden of Eden, the Devil disguised himself as a talking snake. People don't normally expect snakes to talk, so it was a pretty good disguise.

'Oh, shortbread! My absolute favourite! How did you know? What adorable china! You shouldn't have gone to so much trouble for wee old me.' The Devil tempted Jesus in the desert. Don't do it, Mother. Resist. 'I think I made your wee boy jump clean out of his skin. Is he your youngest?'

'That'll be Edward.'

Unfamiliar laughter followed. Horrible laughter. Laughter like the baying of a madwoman. Laughter without sincerity, high-pitched, with each ha distinct and a garden fence between it and its neighbour: ha/ha/ha, ha/ha/ha.

'Edward! Get your sorry backside in here.'

I advanced and peered into the room.

She had a breathtaking ginger head. Without having seen it with my own eyes, I wouldn't have believed that ginger could be so ginger. Her head extended beyond her shoulders and made her seven feet tall.

I entered the room. My sorry backside followed.

The woman had taken a seat and Mother was pouring the tea.

The woman spotted me, and I almost bolted again, but her words – 'Hello, Edward' – accompanied by a smile like the smiles of madmen who die laughing and crying at the same time glued me to the spot, and I could only move when Mother broke the spell by telling me to come in.

This was my first experience of 'a visitor'.

Invited to take a seat, I took one on the battered sofa, as far away as I could get from the scary woman. Mother handed me the plate and I took a slice of shortbread. I sat on the edge of the cushion because if I sat back my feet dangled.

'This is Mrs Wipple, Edward. She's here to cut my hair.'

But Mother cut her own hair! She kept the fringe out of her eyes with scissors and a mirror. The back grew largely unattended, although I did see her once clipping the tail end. If she hadn't clipped the tail end now and then it would have trailed behind her on the ground. She cut Sophia's hair too, and mine. And Father's, Gregory's and Edgar's. When Granny Hazel was alive, Mother cut her hair too. Perhaps Mother and her scissors is why we all looked half baked.

Things became pleasant as we ate the shortbread, Mother and Mrs Wipple chattering and me listening. Mother took the tray and empty cups away, with me hanging on to her tail, and returned with a hard chair from the kitchen – and me still hanging on to her tail. She placed the hard chair in the middle of the floor facing the fire. Mrs Wipple opened her large bag and took out various hair-cutting tools. She pointed a tin of beans at Mother's head and the tin hissed. Not beans but a fine mist came out. She sprayed Mother's hair so much I thought she would empty the can. Mother did have an awful lot of hair. Then Mrs Wipple combed Mother's hair until it looked as if she had been out in the rain without her hat. As a final preparation before the cutting, she fitted a sort of towel with a hole in the middle over Mother's head. Fascinating. I stayed to see the show.

When Mother's hair had been cut, dried and brushed, Mrs Wipple turned her horrendous, toothy grin on me. I panicked as if pressurized to say something in response to a question I hadn't heard. Before I could think of anything, she asked, 'What about you, Edward? Would you like your hair trimmed?' Seeing panic greater than my own on Mother's face, she added, '. . . at no extra cost, of course. After all, I'm here, and you've been kind enough to provide refreshment. Come and have your hair tidied for school, Edward.'

Because Mother simply chopped at my hair when it got too long, I must have resembled a sea anemone removed from its habitat to Mrs Wipple. I sat on the chair. She put the hair-catching thing over my head before tilting it this way and that, frowning at it, and muttering about salvage operations. As she snipped, ruffled and combed she asked me if I thought I would like school.

'Yes,' I said, meaning no.

What did I want to be when I grew up, she asked.

'A spaceman,' I replied, meaning an astronaut but unable to remember the word. The encyclopedia had a spaceman from Russia called Uri something under G. Gargargle: Uri.

'A spaceman!' Mrs Wipple howled. I feared her scissors might put an eye out. I must have said the wrong word. To cover my embarrassment, I said, 'Or a librarian.'

'A librarian!' Rather than laughing, this time she looked impressed. Mother, sheepishly, told her I was a great reader. 'Is he indeed? How wonderful! Why do you want to be a librarian?'

'I don't really know.' I wanted to be a librarian, primarily, because it was less embarrassing than being a spaceman.

'I have no doubt you'll make a first class librarian.'

Just when I thought that Mrs Wipple had shut up, she asked, 'And what school will you attend, Edward?'

Mother answered because she must have seen on my face an unwillingness to cooperate any further in my interrogation. 'He'll board at Whitehead House.'

'Really!' Mrs Wipple's scissors stopped snip-snipping. She came round from behind me, scissors raised in one hand like a weapon, comb in the other. 'Then you'll meet the principal, Mr Mulholland. His wife's a client and very good friend of mine. What a coincidence.'

'It's a small world,' said Mother, trying to be impressed.

I disagreed with her, but kept my disagreement to myself. The world had lots of islands and oceans. In fact, it had more water than land. I'd seen a globe, and an atlas too. An atlas is a flat globe made into pages. You can turn both of them, but in different ways.

'You're in good hands there, Edward,' said Mrs Wipple, who had started clipping, ruffling and combing again. 'I happen to know that Mr Mulholland is the *crème de la crème* when it comes to headmasters.' My ears pricked up, but not too high otherwise she might have pricked one with her scissors. *Crème de la crème* sounded interesting. 'Mr Mulholland is very distinguished in educational circles. Yes. He has friends in high places.' Like, sitting on roofs? Up Everest? 'I'd keep in with your headmaster, Edward. Oh, yes. If anybody can make a librarian out of you, he can. You scratch his back and he'll scratch yours.' I was only five, and still resistant to having my back scratched by a stranger. Nor did I fancy my fingernails working across someone else's fatty, gunky old back. In fact, I would rather have bathed in porridge. Nevertheless, there was something in what Mrs Wipple said that needed thinking about.

'I must tell Edith I've met you,' said Mrs Wipple to Mother. 'You never know, Edward, she might put in a good word, eh?'

What good word? Precocious? Precocious was the best word I knew, although diphthong retained an element of mystery.

'There!' Ten minutes after she started, I had a straight fringe for the first time in my life. She stood behind me, stroking my head, wiping my cheeks, pinging loose hair off my ears. 'Finished! Don't you think he looks just like a little librarian, Mrs Pike?'

'He's a little something all right.'

Mrs Wipple packed her tools. Mother apologized because she didn't have the correct amount of money and had to ask for change. 'Never mind,' smiled Mrs Wipple, counting notes and handing one back. 'Whenever you can, my dear. Whenever you can.'

Mother saw her out the back door.

'Who is she?' I asked, as Mrs Wipple drove off in her red car with the sun roof open and her big red hair sticking out like a bonfire.

'What a nice lady,' said Mother. 'What a very, very nice lady.'

'Who is she?'

'That's Mrs Wipple!' Mother sounded proud to know her.

'I know. But, I mean, who is she?'

'She's a hairdresser. She cuts people's hair for a living, and she owns a salon. When people are old or ill and can't go to her salon, she comes out and cuts their hair in their own homes. Isn't that a fine idea? Now, off you go and show Sophia your new haircut.'

Mother's genuine happiness made me genuinely happy too.

But our happiness was destined to be short-lived.

6
Going to School

An unexpected haircut symbolized abrupt severing from the happiness that went before. Happiness could not return. Time went forward, not back – at least, time as I understood it then did. The time for beginning my formal education drew close like a storm.

Days before I went to school for the first time, Mother said I should be excited. I was terrified. Sophia went off her food. Mother knew what ailed her: missing me before I'd gone.

Then . . .

'It's very kind of you. I'm sorry for putting you to all this trouble,' said Mother, smiling, and grovelling so low she almost scraped her forehead on the kitchen floor. She had her coat on, her boots, a bag over her arm, and wore a headscarf. Farmer Barry beamed red from ear to ear. Mother spat on her fingers and combed them over my fine hair to stick it down.

Although very young, I knew the undesirability of so much gratitude shown to anyone for anything. I couldn't define the undesirability, but I came to think of excessive gratitude as a way of belittling oneself – and in adult life there are folk enough willing, able and ready to belittle you. Schoolteachers are good at it. I wished she would stop behaving like a lackey. I knew what a lackey was because

Mother often told Father she wasn't his. Father usually responded with an 'aye' that disagreed.

Farmer Barry lifted a suitcase in each of his powerful hands. He had fingers as fat as pork sausages, and green teeth that glistened like polished Wellington boots. They were visible when he smiled – and he smiled constantly. He had a round, red, rustic face. A woollen hat sat on top of it like a cherry tomato's hat on a beef tomato's head.

'Not at all, not at all,' he replied, and carried the suitcases out to his lorry. Mother thanked him, and thanked him again as he went.

I'd overheard Father telling Mother that Farmer Barry drank like a fish. That's how he got broken veins in his nose. I drank too, and I had no broken veins in my nose. Maybe I would have them by the time I reached Farmer Barry's age if I started drinking like a fish. Father had some broken veins in his nose. I wondered how, since they had no hands, and fins instead of arms, fish drank. Might Farmer Barry hunker down and drink from a dish like a cat? But fish, unlike cats, have no legs with which to hunker. And if fish are such heavy drinkers, how come the sea isn't empty?

I watched Farmer Barry's boots as they crossed the floor, toes pointing east and west respectively. His boots were the size of small sheds. He must have had terrifying feet. Meanwhile, Edgar puckered his lips and made porridge spew out. Gregory turned away, revolted, and buttoned his coat. Sophia sneezed, and wiped her nose on her hand-knitted cardigan, the one with more holes than wool.

Having to start school meant I had to suffer the agony of separation from my other half. I cried myself to sleep last night – good practice for nights to come. Sophia cried herself to sleep too. Mother had to come to our rooms with a message from Father: 'Tell them pair to stop their gurning.'

Sophia and I would reunite each Christmas and during the summer breaks, but many lonely months were insurmountable obstacles between each of those. I thought they'd let me go home at Halloween, Easter and weekends. But not so.

Being special, Edgar didn't go to school. I wished I were special too. Only Gregory went to school, so I asked him about it. Aware of my bed-wetting anxiety about punishment for starting school a year late, Gregory delighted in exacerbating my fear. School's like a dungeon, he said.

'What's a dungeon?'

'Have you ever seen a smelly, damp cave under a castle on a cliff-edge with iron bars and rats and a torture chamber?'

'No.'

'A dungeon's like that. There's no daylight. You need a torch to see.'

Dungeons were a bit like our cellar, then. I had never seen inside our cellar, but I knew it existed – under the kitchen table – and you needed a torch to see. Mother told Father it had rats, and he said he knew. Mother told him to put poison down, and he might have. So far as I knew, our cellar didn't have a torture chamber, although it might get one when they came to fit the indoor toilet.

Dungeons, my brother enthused, were where torturers chain you to the wall, starve you half to death, and whip you until you're covered in cuts and blood and all your bones stick out.

'What happens when all your bones stick out?'

He got stuck on that one. 'They just . . . stick out. It's horrible.'

'What do they whip you with?' I asked.

'A whip, idiot! Have you never seen a whip?'

I'd seen Mother whipping cream. But she did that with a wooden spoon until she muttered swear words and complained of arm-ache.

In dungeons, Gregory enlightened me, bald, hunchbacked torturers wearing hoods pull off your fingernails with pliers, pour boiling oil on your eyeballs, and stick spikes up your bum.

'Why do they wear hoods?'

'Because they're so ugly you'd die if you saw their faces.'

'How do you know they're bald?'

'Because they are, stupid!'

Puzzled, I pointed out: 'But they've got their hoods up.'

'Shut up!'

He punched my shoulder and it hurt.

I suspected some lies, but it must have been mostly truth, otherwise Gregory would have had nothing to base his lies upon.

According to my eldest brother, the senior boys' half – of the school which would later become my home for the greater part of each year – was bad enough, but the junior boys' half – where I had to board, except for summers and Christmases, until I reached twelve – was ten times worse.

'Every morning the masters strip you naked and hose you down with freezing water, and for breakfast they feed you gruel – if you're lucky.'

'What's gruel?'

'Stuff with the texture of wallpaper paste that tastes the same.'

'Porridge,' I said.

He thumped my arm and that hurt too.

'Gruel! Gruel!' he insisted. 'And the beds have spiders.'

'Same as the Manse, then.'

'The masters beat you with bamboo canes.'

'Pandas eat those.'

'Shut up! These are different. You're so sore they make Father's strap feel like a feather. And if you get your homework wrong they make you clean out the toilets with your bare hands.'

'Is the toilet outdoors, like ours?'

'Yes. And it stinks. You can die from the smell.'

'What's homework?'

Homework, Gregory revealed, was what they made you do in your dormitory, instead of in the classroom, because there were too few hours in the day. I was none the wiser, but homework sounded a lot less painful than having spikes up my bum. Actually, I liked the sound of homework.

Lording over both boys and masters, lording over the whole school like the shadow of a giant storm cloud, hovered the fearful figure of the headmaster. Wanted by the police for crimes against schoolboys too horrible to talk about, they called him Murderous Mulholland.

'Why does he want to murder us?'

According to Gregory, he wanted to murder us because he had a demon inside him. If you disobey one of the rules and a master sends you to the headmaster's office, you're in for it.

'In for what?' I asked.

Stumped, Gregory punched me in the head, but I ducked and he nearly missed.

Murderous Mulholland stood eight feet tall and growled at everybody when his mouth took a break from chewing their bones.

'Bones aren't chewy, they're crunchy.'

'Right, then,' said Farmer Barry, clapping his big hands and rubbing them together. 'Everybody ready for the off?'

Sophia and I held hands. Mother took my other hand and dragged me to the back door. Sophia dragged along too – until Mother disconnected us. We reconnected. Mother disconnected us again, and this time raised a warning finger.

There had been no emotional goodbyes and wishes for good luck from Father, or even a prayer that God would bless us and keep our train from crashing. There had been no unemotional ones either. I had decided to give him the benefit of the doubt; maybe he had prayed for us in private. As usual, he had gone to work on Farmer Barry's farm before we got up, I thought. He might well have met Farmer Barry as he left his farm travelling in the opposite direction. Father would have raised a salute and an aye-aye, and Farmer Barry would have raised his hat.

Sophia, hands behind her back now, and innocent-eyed, rocked her shoulders from side to side as Mother gave instructions. 'Don't go outside, and don't touch anything until I come home. Same for Edgar. Don't let him out unless he needs the toilet.'

Father frightened the wits out of me by passing through the

kitchen and out the back clutching newspaper pages torn into squares. He was in a heck of a hurry.

'Take Edgar to the living room and give him his colouring book when he's finished his breakfast. Don't remove the fireguard, and don't even think about handling anything in here. Stay in the living room. Have you got that?'

Sophia said she had it.

'Bye-bye, Edgar,' I said. 'See you at Christmas.' He waved his spoon and dotted the floor with porridge. 'Bye-bye, Sophia.'

Sophia and I hugged for so long Mother had to separate us like a referee in a boxing match.

Gregory had followed Farmer Barry out to the lorry to avoid having to say goodbye or hug anyone.

'Shut the door behind us, Sophia, and stay warm or you'll catch your death. Sit by the fire and keep your head dry. Don't go out unless you need the toilet. Give Edgar his colouring book . . .'

'I know! I know!'

Mother followed Gregory, pushing me in front of her as I looked back at Sophia with a sort of 'save me' expression on my face.

Sophia, sneezing again, followed Mother and me outside, but Mother sent her back in with an angry bark.

Farmer Barry drove us to Bruagh to catch the train.

The village consisted of two crumbling buildings on either side of the potholed road that ran between them. No other roads turned off or on to this one, just the occasional cattle track, or disused trail leading to a pile of stones that used to be a habitable hovel. Some trails faded away in a field as though having lost interest in a destination. A rusty cow-gate here and there interrupted the wild shrubbery and twisted trees. There were bogs everywhere. There was one on Hollow Heath and we were forbidden to go anywhere near it. It swallowed Father's bicycle once when he took a short cut. The bog would be full of bodies, with no room for mine, if all the tales about it were correct. I didn't know where I heard these tales – maybe from Granny Hazel.

There were farms round about, at the top of winding, bumpy lanes, with dogs that ate you if you came too close. The farms produced enough potatoes, carrots and eggs to sell at a busier roadside, or take to weekly markets in Garagh and other towns far away.

One of the crumbling roadside buildings doubled as a post office cum shop, where handy items such as Wellingtons, dish cloths, damp matches and prehistoric tins of baked beans were available for the desperate. You could get the freshest eggs in the world there, though, and the freshest milk.

I sat on Mother's knee, missing Sophia already, but excited by the prospect of a train ride. Gregory squatted on the floor behind us, between the seats. The lorry had no back window. When I twisted around to see Sophia I saw Gregory, and I had no wish to see him.

I said, 'I thought Father had gone to work.'

Mother explained. 'Sure, isn't he in awful pain this past week. The rebels want out, but the back door's rusted shut.'

Farmer Barry chuckled. 'If he'd eat more cabbage . . .'

'That medicine's doing the job. He never moves that fast.' Mother tittered – she hardly ever tittered.

What they were talking about, a clue I had not. None!

No one spoke for a while. The wipers wiped rain off the window.

'It's a terrible day,' Mother thought aloud, to make sound in the lorry, because Farmer Barry never did anything aloud except smile.

Mother kept reminding Farmer Barry of his terrible kindness, and Farmer Barry kept saying not at all, not at all. God had never created a kinder man, as far as I could tell – except Jesus, obviously. Despite having been stewed in scripture for five years, I still hadn't grasped that Jesus and God were the same person.

The lorry bumped along and made me feel ill. The wipers wiped and would have put me to sleep but for awake nightmares about dungeons, hunchbacks, spikes, my bum and Murderous Mulholland.

We left behind misery – Father wrestling constipation in the toilet, Sophia barking like a hound, and Edgar eating porridge off his trousers – and travelled through misery into more misery.

Nobody said Gregory and I were to travel alone. Nobody said the iron school gates would shut with me inside, in a dormitory, looking out through barred windows with tears in my eyes.

Whimpering like a dog who knows he is going to be put to sleep, but is clueless as to why, I hung on to Mother's coat as the train steamed and rattled to a halt at Bruagh Halt. 'Look after him,' she told Gregory, but it sounded more like a question. She squeezed and squeezed the tears out of me, then tore me from her and pushed me on to the train, both of us contributing to a reservoir on the platform floor. 'I'll see you at Christmas,' she said. 'It isn't far away.'

Christmas was months and months and months away!

The station man helped Gregory hoist our suitcases on board. The station man shoved me in too when I tried to escape. The station man slammed the door shut and blew his whistle, Mother out there weeping and me locked in, bawling. The train jolted to life, and I fell on the seat, but quickly jumped back up. Mother waved to me – to Gregory too – with a handkerchief for her tears. She waved and wept from Farmer Barry's armpit as one of his big arms swallowed her in a hug. I flattened my nose on the window. The train took me away as I tried to press my head sideways through the glass.

I cried myself to sleep on the train. Gregory shook me awake when we arrived at Whitehead House. He did not tease me about my weakness, and I was grateful for that. Once upon a time, he cried himself to sleep too.

The Alf Years

7

Whitehead House and the Monstrous Head

We disembarked at a small but busy railway station and lugged our suitcases to school, a red-bricked cluster of buildings less than one hundred metres from the station, which reminded me of the photograph of a canned soup factory in the encyclopedia. We switched our suitcases from right hand to left and back several times along the way, and Gregory told me to hurry up. Inside the green-painted iron railings bigger boys than me, in various degrees of fear and bemusement, came, went and lingered. Parents, having delivered their darlings, loitered comparing notes with other parents because the rain had stopped and they could. Cloud parted and the sun shone through. Gregory, like the rain, stopped, and I did too, on his heels.

'Ask for the assembly hall,' he said, pointing me at a doorway with pillars that looked like an open mouth with teeth.

I panicked. 'Who will I ask?'

'Have you got your letter?' I panicked harder. I thought Gregory would stay with me until I knew what to do next. Obviously, I was wrong. 'I go that way.' He nodded towards a building in shadow with many black windows that must have been the senior school.

I released my suitcase and fumbled in my pocket hoping I had lost the letter. Without it, they might send me home.

'Here it is,' I said dejectedly.

'New start, young lad?' The speaker, a wrinkly man wearing overalls like Father's, lifted my suitcase and I panicked all over again. 'What's your name when you're at home, then?'

'Edward Pike.'

'Like a fish, eh? You come with me, Edward Pike. Uncle Bob takes care of handsome little buggers like you.'

I turned to Gregory for help, but saw his suitcase and heels retreating towards the dark building. I almost ran after him, but the wrinkly man stole my suitcase and I ran after him instead, calling, 'Excuse me. Excuse me,' and getting no reply.

'Here we are,' he said, setting down my suitcase in a large, busy vestibule with a marble floor. 'Now, anything you need to . . .'

Next thing I knew, I lay flat on my back with a thermometer in my mouth in a quiet room with a high ceiling. A woman wearing a hat watched over me. She looked at the watch on her wrist and took my pulse. A nurse! Seeing my eyes open, she said something too rapidly for me to unscramble the words. Whatever they were, she said them in a kindly way that reassured me. 'You had a funny turn,' she added, 'but nothing to worry about. You're fit as a fiddler's bagpipes.'

Tears formed a lump in my throat that wanted to surge into my eyes. I think the thermometer pinned the lump in place. 'I want to go home,' I told her with the thermometer still in my mouth.

'Everybody wants to go home on their first day. This is your home now. You'll get used to it. While you're here, I might as well do your medical. What's your name?' She took out the thermometer, gave it a wipe and put it in a breast pocket without looking at it.

'Edward Pike.'

'Right, then, Edward Pike.' She drew a curtain on wheels round where I lay. 'Looking forward to school?'

No. 'Yes.'

She grabbed the elasticated waistband of my trousers and began pulling them down. 'Work hard and you'll soon be a brainy little fellow.' My underpants got stuck, so she went back up and pulled them down too. I felt unusually but not unpleasantly exposed. 'Let's make sure you've two of everything.'

I thought she meant arms and legs.

'You poor soul. You must be frozen. Can you feel that?'

'Yes,' I squeaked.

She fiddled around with her nursing duties until content that, in line with expectations, I possessed one of the thing God designed singular and two of everything else.

Declared alive and in full possession of all my bits, I let Nurse help me up with my trousers and off the gurney. She took me by the hand. 'You've missed the induction,' she said. 'But forget about that; it's all been seen to. Come with me and I'll get you sorted.'

Nurse marched me along corridors and up stairs. I ran to keep up as a dark world spun by on a waft of schoolboy smells.

'Here we are. This is your dormitory. It does the job even if it's a bit more rough and ready than you're used to at home.'

I was too distressed by the presence of eight beds to care whether it did the job – or any job. After introducing me to my dormitory, Nurse took me to meet my teacher and classmates.

Miss Walker was tall, broad and deep, and wore spectacles with thick frames. She directed me to a desk at the rear of the class and said it was mine. She left me there. As I watched her expansive posterior walk away, I thought how dreadful it would be if she sat on me.

After calling the register, Miss Walker gave each of us a small carton of milk and a straw. I'd never drunk milk from a carton before. I'd never seen a straw, and only knew what to do with it by watching the others. She said we could talk amongst ourselves and get to know each other. I, however, held my tongue and got to know no one.

I didn't know anything about evolution at the time, but instinctually I knew that the other boys were lesser and more base than me. All but one fellow, that is. I would come to understand that if I stood apart from the others by two steps, Alfred Lord stood apart from me by four steps and from the others by six. At that time, I didn't know him well enough to call him Alf. In fact, I didn't call him anything, because we didn't speak for a year or more. Alf was, somehow, mysteriously, different – although the word different does the degree of his differentness a disservice.

On my first night at Whitehead House, I buried my face in the hard pillow and longed for Sophia. My broken heart bled tears. I imagined Sophia's face. Happy to remember what she looked like, I wished I could magic her there to snuggle beside in bed. I would wish and bleed tears tomorrow too, and the next night, and the next. I tried to weep quietly so no one would hear. But they did hear. And I heard the occasional weep from one or other of them. Weeping intensified until the dormitory vibrated with a symphony of tom cats.

One day, I dared to ask Miss Walker for an envelope so that I could write a letter and send it home to my sister. To my surprise, she said, 'What an excellent idea,' and gave me one. I wrote my letter to Sophia, sealed it in the envelope, addressed the envelope to The Manse, off The Road, near Bruagh, and posted it in the postbox outside the seniors' building. Unfortunately, I forgot to add a stamp.

Before we left Bruagh, Mother told Gregory to look after me. She made him promise. And he did. Some chance! Gregory never had the slightest interest in looking after anyone except number one. If he saw me around school, he must have ducked out of sight before I saw him. I think my existence embarrassed him. Unintentionally, however, he did me a favour when he exaggerated the awfulness of life at school. School was indeed bad, but not as bad as he made out. It was dreadful, but not quite awful, unless dreadful is worse than awful. Perhaps it was just horrible, which has always seemed, to me, less bad than either awful or dreadful . . . It was pretty damn bad, but I lived through it, so it couldn't have been as bad as all that.

Mid-morning we got tea, or milk if we preferred and it wasn't off, and a biscuit – not a custard cream or a jammy dodger, just a plain, edible, more or less crunchy thing, rectangular or circular but always uneventful, which the word 'biscuit' accurately describes. Lunch and dinner were . . . 'dreadful' comes immediately to mind. However, 'necessary to stay alive' comes to mind too. As does 'made me feel ill'. Cook boiled the potatoes and vegetables until they were an unidentifiable sludge. The meat portion looked and tasted something like mid-morning biscuits, and that didn't seem right to me.

My new world of rowdy schoolboys, smelly dormitories and echoing corridors spun and made my head spin with it. I would have fled, but where would I have gone? If I'd walked all the way to the Manse, Father would have taken his strap to my legs, then turned me round and sent me back. Christmas! If only I could survive until Christmas! At Christmas I could go home until the new year.

Thank heavens for Nurse, who gave me treatment in her office daily. After two weeks of school food, my bowels were stationary for four days in a row and my stomach felt wrong. At the Manse, Mother used medicine to get my bowels moving, and I expected Nurse to do the same. Instead, she rubbed ointment on my private parts, and poked her oily finger into my most private part of all. I concluded something amiss, deviant, and possibly illegal about Nurse's prescription, but not until a year or two later, and it was all oil under the bridge by then. Not that I would have complained. I liked Nurse and her over-curious hands. I liked her a lot. Her prescription was odd but not unpleasant, and it got my bowels going again.

Then, like having eaten too much chocolate, she said I no longer needed to see her. Being banished by Nurse came as a disappointment similar in kind to, but infinitely weaker than, my disappointment at parting from Sophia. 'No more ointment?' I asked Nurse. She told me to go behind the screen and drop my trousers, and she would rub some on one more time for good measure.

Although Nurse said I could return to her office any time I wanted seeing to, I knew she was only being nice to a new boy. Undoubtedly she did the same for all new boys. Abandoned, I could do nothing about it. I could do nothing about anything, apparently. School demanded passivity; I must do as instructed. Therefore, I went wherever whichever master pointed whenever he pointed, and performed whatever tasks were asked of me.

In the course of daily bullying, I taught myself the trick of how to hurt without crying. The trick involves teaching yourself to see the world in a special way. You teach yourself how to see it that way by constantly looking at it that way. To hurt without crying, you must constantly look at the world as if everything in it is in it to hurt. The world exists to hurt you. Therefore, hurting is natural. If, one day, the world stops hurting you, then something's wrong. The pay-off is that hurting makes you strong and wise, wiser than those who hurt you.

Another way to stop yourself from crying is by thinking of the funniest thing imaginable – for example, your tormentor naked but for women's bloomers. This short-term solution has no guarantee of success. It worked best for me, for a while, when the bloomers in question were Granny Hazel's.

If no teachers were awake enough to take assembly, Mr Mulholland did the bible reading. Afterwards, he made announcements about forthcoming events, and drew our attention to old problems and new rules designed to overcome them. Mr Mulholland called the playground the quadrangle. A major quadrangle problem involved balls and broken windows.

'You may spend morning break and the greater part of lunch hour outdoors, getting fresh air and exercise in the quadrangle. However, ball games in the quadrangle are no longer permitted. Off the playing field, boys and balls, when combined, are a recipe for disaster. Off the playing field, no boy should be seen in possession of a ball.' I noticed several teachers trying to contain laughter, but did not know why. 'The ball's size is irrelevant. Large balls, medium balls, tiny balls:

they're all banned. Only on the playing field may you play with your balls. I trust I've made myself clear.'

Boys groaned. But not me. I would have been even more pleased if running, shouting and fighting were forbidden also.

While other new boys made friends and formed cliques, I remained alone, doing homework and reading books from the library. I would have welcomed a friend or two, but I did not give out the kind of aura that attracted others to me.

I hoped life at Whitehead House would improve. No such luck! The classroom had a broken window and radiators made of ice. Wind and spits of rain blew through the window. I was used to cold, having lived in the Manse, but other boys were not. I warmed my pyjamas under the pillow and retrieved them at bedtime frosty. My popularity increased slightly, and only for a couple of days, when I introduced the trend of wearing my pullover over my pyjama top in bed. Most nights, I sat in bed shivering with my socks on, the sheets up to my ears and my knees clutched to my chin.

Breakfast was not the wallpaper paste gruel Gregory warned me about; it was wallpaper paste porridge – a totally different thing. Much lumpier. Having survived breakfast, we gathered in the assembly hall to sing a hymn, say a prayer, and have a half-sleeping teacher drone to us from the bible. We sang 'Jesus Loves the Little Children'. But if Jesus really loved the little children – and I qualified as one of those – why did he allow adults to treat us so poorly? And what about the prying, tumbling, rough and tough, loud and foul boys? Many of them – maybe most of them – reserved no space in their brains for thoughts of God and His foibles. Though Godless, they shivered no more or less than I did, and seemed to accumulate more vivacity from and for life in a single day than I had in my lifetime.

The truth soon dawned on me: God was optional.

Father would have been appalled.

*

A senior boy came and spoke to Miss Walker. 'Pike,' she called from the front of the class. Everybody looked at me. 'Mr Mulholland wants to see you . . . Now! Now! Off you go.' Outside the classroom, wondering if I should follow the senior boy, I did. He led me to Murderous Mulholland's office.

I must have been 'in for it' for having fainted on arrival.

Walking the long corridors on weak legs, I wondered how I should knock: two knocks or three, hard knocks or soft, fast or slow.

I didn't have to knock at all; his door lay open.

The senior boy departed.

The headmaster, far from being eight feet tall, topped a few inches over five. Murderous? Based on first impressions, I thought not. His nickname, I discovered later, was Blinky because he blinked a lot. Gregory would end up in Hell. Father said that's where liars went. Blinky Mulholland, standing at the visitor's side of his desk, reading something on it, looked like someone stuck at one down on a crossword puzzle. Noticing me on the threshold from the corner of an eye, he swung round too jovially for a headmaster. Not that I knew much about headmasters, but surely they were supposed to be demonic. Not that I knew much about demons. Father had mentioned them, in the context of constipation, but not in detail.

'Ah, Mr Pike. Come in. Come in.'

I crossed the threshold and reached up to shake the soft, moist and warm hand he offered. 'Have a seat. Do you mind if I call you Edward? Hmm? Good. Good. Well, Edward. My first name is Maurice, but you have to call me Mr Mulholland, I'm afraid. It's school rules, you see. If we all called each other by our first names we would get terribly confused. The place is coming down with Johns, Peters and Patricks.' He consulted the sheet of paper he'd been reading. 'You have an older brother here at Whitehead House, Gregory. I know about him. And, to be frank . . . We had a Frank once, come to think of it. Don't get many, though. We do have a Freddy or two . . . Anyway, to be frank, Edward, I trust you will gain much more from your school career than your brother has gained from his.'

The headmaster smiled at me. It was horrible, but he meant well.

The display of such headmasterly pleasantness made punishment unlikely. I relaxed, but only fractionally. The chair's legs were longer than my own. Most things with length were longer than my legs. Father said that, unless I sprouted, my arse would trail the ground. My feet and the floor had a sizeable gap between. Mr Mulholland retreated to the other side of his desk. I swung my legs nervously and wondered why he had summoned me there.

'Edward. I want you to think of me as someone you can trust. Can you do that?' I squeaked in reply. 'Good. Good. Tell me, how are you finding things? You've been here, what, a week and a bit now?' He waited. I didn't know which things he meant. 'Bed comfortable? Food okay? I know it's not as good as your mother's food, but we all have to make sacrifices. During the war we were on rations. Do you know about the war and rations? No? Well, that's one of the many things you'll learn about. What would you like to know about most? Go on, ask me anything you like and I'll prove to you how splendid an education can be.'

I thought of a question straight away. 'Do dogs go to Heaven?'

'Mmm. Good question.' He opened a drawer, took out a bag of boiled sweets, circumnavigated his desk and offered me one en route. It would have been rude to refuse. 'Butter Balls,' he said. 'My favourites. Take another one and put it in your pocket for later.' I did, while sucking on the first one. 'Do dogs go to Heaven? That's a tough one. Are you a dog lover? Have you lost a dog recently, Edward?'

'No. I found one. It was dead.'

One of his eyebrows hopped – just once. 'In that case, I can tell you, without fear of contradiction, that if there's a Heaven for dogs, and if the dog you found was a good dog, then it has gone to Heaven.'

Since I had no idea whether Tennyson had been a good dog, Mr Mulholland's answer proved nothing concerning the splendidness of an education. Unimpressed, unconvinced, but unwilling to argue with him so early in our relationship, I sucked my Butter Ball.

'I believe you encountered my wife's hairdresser.'

'Yes. She did this.' I pointed at my head.

'Did she indeed? What do you think of it?'

'Father says you can't win them all.'

'Mmm. Very true. Charming woman though, eccentricity with her scissors notwithstanding . . . Wobble. Weeble. Or something.'

'Wivvle.'

Saying Wipple was hard with a boiled sweet in my mouth.

He smacked the desk and pointed his finger at me: 'That's her! I knew it started with W. Good old Mrs Wivvle! She cuts my hair too.' He bent forward and patted his as-good-as-bald crown, which made me snurfle and choke on my Butter Ball.

'Because of our common acquaintance, Mrs Wivvle of hedge-sculpting fame, I shall keenly follow your progress, Edward. Good luck.' Mr Mulholland smiled me back over the threshold.

December came at last. The final days of my first term were upon me. We had two terms each year: the first lasting until Christmas and the second until June. The blessed final day glowed fractionally beyond the tips of my fingers like Sophia's face when she held a torch up to it in the dark – frighteningly exciting in its grotesque otherness. I'd never had a final day of term before.

The entire school spent the run-up to its annual Christmas play preparing for the extravaganza. This year's offering would be a traditional nativity. The student population's good and gifted – predominantly music and drama club members from the senior school – began rehearsing in mid-November. The student population's keen but talentless, those who would fill the stage as trees and potted plants – including me – had been preparing too, painting and cutting out knotty branches and sunflower face masks.

One morning, a senior pupil delivered a note to Miss Walker

while, with blunt scissors, I hacked at cardboard hoping it would evolve into a petal for a kinetic tree – whatever a kinetic tree might be.

Blinky Mulholland had summoned me to his office.

Again? Twice in a single term?

I feared that he had intercepted my letters to Sophia, discovered how much I hated school, and planned to punish me in some unspeakable way.

Counting my steps, I walked many long corridors to get to his office on two very short legs. I walked half of the corridors walking forwards, and the other half walking backwards to see if the backward half got me to my destination in fewer steps and quicker. The forward steps went 12345 . . . and the backward steps went 1 2 3 4 5. I lost count when I backed into Mr Clarke and he told me to watch where I was going, stupid boy. Anyway, I didn't know if walking backwards was quicker because I didn't have a watch.

When I got there, I knocked on his door breathing nervously, but breathing, thankfully, none the less.

'Enter.'

I did.

Blinky's office was bright and dusty, like the man himself. Like the man himself, it smelled of polish and pipe tobacco.

'Edward! How glad I am that you could spare the time to see me. Have a seat. Make yourself at home.' The chair in front of his desk was unusually high. Either it was a different chair from the one I sat on last time or I had shrunk. I managed to mount it with a small leap. 'I know how busy you are, what with the nativity dramatization and so on. That's one of the things I wanted to see you about: the nativity. You're not actually doing anything on stage, are you? I understand that you don't have a role.'

My jaw, I think, hung open for a time. When he said role, I thought of soup. The best reply I could think of was 'Not on me'. But it didn't seem right. In fact, it didn't seem to have anything to do with the nativity – unless they had some kind of Feast of Passover bread in the manger, beside the milk bottle and stack of nappies.

'You haven't been given a part to play?'

Oh! That kind of role!

'Not at first,' I said. 'But I have now.'

'Wonderful! How did that come about?'

'I asked Miss Walker if I could be Jesus, but she said we're having a doll for that because Jesus has no lines to say and He doesn't need to do anything like walk about, because infants don't. She said a rolled-up towel could be Jesus if somebody accidentally stood on the doll and broke it. I said that might be blasphemy, standing on Jesus, but she said not to be stupid. I didn't think it was stupid, but anyway I asked her if I could be Joseph instead, and she said they already had a Joseph. He's got black sticky tape for a moustache and a charcoal beard. She said what about a shepherd or the back end of a donkey, but I said I'd rather be a wise man, and she said she already had more wise men than she could shake a stick at, but I could be a kinetic tree if I want. I said all right even though I don't know what a kinetic tree is. What's a kinetic tree?'

Blinky looked impressed. 'I've never had the pleasure of meeting one. From the Greek, *kinein*, meaning move. We're talking movement here. At a guess, I'd say it's a tree with feet. You have feet, don't you?' I said I did and dangled them at him. 'There you are,' he said. 'You're perfectly qualified for the job.'

'Miss Walker said I could help paint the props.'

'Really? Good. Good. We need a talented prop painter; it's a very important job. And how's it going then, the prop painting?'

'Not bad. It was going better until I ran out of brown paint. There's plenty of green for the leaves, but there's no brown for the trunks. Miss Walker said I could paint the tree trunks blue and nobody would notice because the lights would make them look brown.'

'Excellent.'

'I tried mixing blue with red to see if it made brown, but it didn't.

It just made a bit of a mess. But I cleaned it up, and Miss Walker said I'd have to experiment to find what colours mixed to make brown, but not to worry about it because blue tree trunks would be fine. I need red for the flowers . . .'

'Look here, Edward. Let's set the nativity aside. There's something else I want to talk to you about. How can I put it? It has come to my notice that you are what I can only call a precocious child. Miss Walker is of the opinion that your current study schedule is not challenging enough. Do you agree with her?'

If a teacher says something – anything – that requires a response, the most obvious thing to do is agree. However, intuiting some kind of punishment – such as being restricted to a diet of bread and water until I started finding the work harder, although bread and water might have been an improvement, except on Saturdays when we got chips – I gave him a cautious nod of my head while thinking that a shake of it might have been wiser.

'You're finding the work we're giving you too easy?'

'Well . . . Before I came to school I thought there would be lots of work to do, but it's mostly play things.'

'You're only five, Pike. Theoretical Physics is next year.'

'Is it?' I asked, perking up.

'No, of course it isn't. Don't be silly. Look here: we believe you would benefit if given the opportunity to work harder. Practice, you know. It may not always make perfect, but it improves, it enhances, it opens new doors. Do you follow, Pike?'

Not really. 'Yes, Sir.'

Blinky looked less than convinced.

How could I find easy work hard? I could close one eye, I supposed, but I would see the same thing, and closing one eye wouldn't make half my brain stop working. Then it came to me. When we played spelling in the Manse with Mother, she gave me a handicap of four. First to get ten spellings correct won the game, but I started at minus four. Maybe Blinky intended something similar. It was a good idea, and could be put to use in other areas, such as sports. I could compete with the others on the running track and football field if they were given handicaps such as blindfolds or their legs tied together.

'While chewing over your problem of finding work too easy, Edward, I came up with an idea. What about this. You understand, at this stage I want your honest opinion. What about if, starting from next term – that is, when you return from your Christmas break – what about if Miss Walker gives you more homework to do. And not only more, but work of a more taxing nature. In other words, starting from next term, why not set about stretching that unique brain of yours and seeing how much elasticity it has. What do you think of that?'

I thought of rubber bands. 'If you stretch elastic too far it snaps,' I said, imagining my head in its present shape – not quite round and a bit lumpy – then like a banana on its back, then like a skipping rope, then like the ball of string that we measured the boundary with, and . . . Ping!

Blinky looked as if he had not known that elastic snaps until I told him. 'You're of the opinion that if we make you work harder you'll snap?'

'No,' I reassured him, fully aware that heads are made of bone, and bone isn't stretchy. 'If I got harder work . . .' I said.

'Yes?'

'Doing it would take longer.'

'But the reward, in terms of satisfaction, would be huge.'

'Could I spend more time in the library?'

'Would you like that?'

'I'd like that more than anything,' I said with certainty. More than anything except quitting school and going home, but I kept that to myself.

'Then, Edward, as from next term you shall be found in the library much more than at present, I should imagine. Do we have a deal?' I said we did. Blinky came round to my side of his desk and we shook on it.

'Good. Good. Excellent!' said Blinky.

8

Christmas and the White Lady

The night of the Christmas play arrived. Parents came from near and far to applaud their occasionally stagestruck but mainly inept young. Cameras flashed. Cardboard trees fell over. Tone deaf carol singers sang carols before the final curtain. Stale cakes and stewed tea were served and consumed standing up.

Most parents took their progeny home for the festive holiday. Mother and Father never attended these end-of-term extravaganzas. Gregory had never taken part in a performance. Mother and Father did not attend this year either. I followed in my elder brother's footsteps.

We were allowed to do whatever we wanted – within reason – on the last morning of term. It was a plain-clothes morning, which meant that we did not have to wear our uniforms, not that, as one bright spark thought, we had to play policemen.

After Christmas dinner in the canteen at noon, we were free to leave, be collected by parents, or whatever. Christmas dinner differed from other school dinners by a splash of brown gravy and a cut of meat purporting to be turkey.

The only occurrence before dinner worth noting on that final morning was one that would happen on every final morning, Christmas and summer, during my school career. Miss Walker gave me a sealed brown envelope with 'Mr and Mrs Pike' typed on the front. 'Don't open this,' she instructed. 'It's for your parents.' I would have worried, but everyone else got one too.

Like a small flower out of the earth, I emerged from the junior building. Like a weed, Gregory sprouted from the senior building ten minutes later. We passed through the same gate, but ten minutes apart, and met at the railway station without suitcases, without eye contact, without warmth. Without saying a word, we boarded the train. I had a satchel slung over a shoulder. Gregory carried a cardboard folder with next to nothing in it: his workload. There were a lot of school children like us on board, but neither Gregory nor I spoke to them and they didn't speak to us. I would have enjoyed the ride if Gregory had let me sit at the window.

Some passengers disembarked at stops before ours. Most people lived and worked in the city – I had worked that out. Our stop was Bruagh Halt. Nobody but Gregory and me got off or on. Why would they get off? To sight-see Maud and her shop? Maud and her shop predated the pyramids. The track got smaller and disappeared in the distance. We couldn't see the track from the Manse; we only knew of its existence because the train went by. Just because things are invisible doesn't mean they aren't there. Somebody said that about God. I followed Gregory to Maud's shop unquestioningly.

When he opened the door a bell rang, and Leslie, Maud's peculiar son, came out from an anteroom. Slender and handsome, never smiling, older than Gregory by about ten years – an adult, really – Leslie looked all right to me, but Mother called him peculiar, so he must have been.

'Hello, Les,' said Gregory. Maud came out from the anteroom, nudged Leslie aside, and stood grimly across the counter.

Leslie retreated to the anteroom.

To my amazement, Gregory bought cigarettes: five single ones without a box. Mother would kill him! Father would kill him harder!

After his purchase, Gregory left the shop. I stayed behind. I had a question for Maud.

'Are you really older than the pyramids?'

She called me a cheeky bugger – I didn't know why – and ordered me out of her shop before she called Leslie.

Night had started with teatime an hour off and me, afraid of the dark open space, hungry enough to eat a ghost if one jumped out. Gregory always carried a torch. I wanted one of my own, but Father said I wasn't old enough. How old do you have to be to know how to press your thumb against a button? His actual words were batteries cost money. The tall shrubbery at either side of the road, and who, or what, might leap from it, frightened me. They did that at school: leapt from doorways on to victims returning from a bowel movement after lights out. You could shit yourself twice.

After Gregory finished his cigarette, the rain came on. Gregory walked quickly. I ran in short bursts to keep up.

The first turn on to, or off, the Road in all that distance was the Lane, the potholed, mossy entry that led from the Road to our courtyard, a distance between fields of about half a mile. Father used this lane when going to work. Mother used this lane once a month when she went for the train to get provisions obtainable nowhere other than in a town shop. The workmen would use this lane when they came to build our bathroom.

The rain became harder, faster and wetter, and we ran the last stretch to the back door dodging potholes. I had seldom seen Gregory running. He jumped, tumbled, bounced and skipped a lot, and ran, when he did, only out of necessity. Ahead of me, his lower legs kicked out to the sides like a woman running in high heels. For all I know, I might have looked equally ostrich-like. Panting as if third from last in a marathon, I arrived some seconds after my brother with the longer legs, and found Mother embracing him. Having submitted to the embrace, his arms were limp at his sides.

Sophia entered the kitchen from the inner door at the same time as I entered from the outer. She grinned from ear to ear, and I grinned even wider. Regardless of the fact that I looked like a drowned rat, she launched herself at me as I found an extra lung and launched myself at her. She felt bonier than I remembered. Three months seemed like three years. Mother released Gregory and gave me a bear hug with Sophia clinging on. Edgar came to see what all the fuss was about and leapt on to Mother's back because there was no room for him anywhere else. Gregory, nauseated by the outpouring of affection, slunk off.

Father greeted us with a nod and an aye-aye when he returned from work.

The traditional Christmases celebrated by us Pikes differed from the traditional Christmases celebrated by my peers at school. This discovery threw me into some confusion about the nature of traditions. Gregory, Edgar, Sophia and I never knew the joy of tearing to shreds colourful wrapping paper. Santa, reindeer, mistletoe, stockings, crackers, turkey and the trimmings were irrelevant to Christmas for the Pikes. Father permitted no paganism. The Manse went without adornment. We went without a fir tree. We shunned baubles, stars and fairies. Father said that the gifts from the three wise men, of gold, frankincense and myrrh, were for the newborn King of Kings, and that was no reason for us to reward each other with gifts when we had done nothing to deserve them.

Baby Jesus hadn't done anything to deserve his gifts either. He was a newborn, for Heaven's sake! If one of the wise men had dropped a gold brick on his head and killed him, Jesus would have gone straight to Hell – him not being a born-again Christian. Father said all the newborns that die in China go straight to Hell because they're Communists.

On Christmas Day mornings, Gregory, Edgar, Sophia and I received sensible items we were in need of. Sophia would get 'say' a new pullover. Edgar would get 'say' new shoes, I would get 'say' a new blanket for my bed, and Gregory would get something like a pencil case containing a pen, a pencil, a sharpener, a rubber and plastic shapes you could draw lines against. The gifts were more or less the same each year, with slight variations, such as a coat instead of shoes or trousers instead of a skirt.

The second term of my first year at school, January to mid-June, thanks to the increased workload and greater library access, passed faster than the first. In next to no time my first year had ended. I returned to the Manse for the long summer break.

'There's good news,' said Mother that evening. I thought something good had happened to someone other than me. But not so. 'I hear they're sending you to year three next year.' Sophia looked at me, not knowing whether going into year three was good or bad. 'You needn't look so smug.' I didn't know I looked smug and immediately tried to unsmug my face by frowning. 'I received a letter from your Miss Walker. She says she has reservations about your social development. She says you don't mix with the other pupils.'

Indians lived on reservations. 'I don't like most of them.'

'You'll have to do better on that score in future.'

I nodded my head.

Sophia said, 'Why are they sending him to year three?'

'Apparently because he's good enough at reading and writing. That doesn't surprise me. I wouldn't be surprised if he's a match for anyone in year four or five . . . You're looking smug again.'

'Pride comes before a fall,' said Father without looking up from his bible.

The summer break rained from June to September with occasional sunny breaks like holes in a pullover. Sophia and I amused ourselves, or failed to, indoors most of the time. Edgar showed me his new skill – shoelace tying – sometimes twice daily. Gregory left the Manse in the mornings and didn't come home for days at a time. Father went to work, came home, read his bible, ate and slept. Mother fell asleep each evening in front of the fire, sobbing, because the authorities were sending someone to talk about taking Edgar into care.

One night a dream disturbed my sleep. My heart beat rapidly. A nightmare visited and fled as I woke. A nightmare deposited its seed.

The curtains were open. I could see darkness but no stars. Cloud obliterated the moon. A memory of light came through the window and painted silver abrasions across the glass. The Manse held its breath. In such quietness there are sounds inside your head muttering louder than the occasional tweaks and creaks of masonry and timber outside it. When you listen harder, with one ear pressed into the pillow, the quietness gets louder until you try to stop listening but cannot. I turned from my side on to my back – which partially relieved the suffocating-in-my-own-deafness sensation – and gazed big-eyed into the black.

Something unnatural and external had wakened me. But what? Should I get up and peer into the corridor? Too cowardly and too cold. I lay there for ages, arms under sheets pulled up to my chin.

At last, unable to bear the nothingness any longer, I braced myself to climb from my cold bed into freezing space. Before I moved further, I heard a noise. It came from Sophia's room. I waited for her to knock on the wall – our code: knock-knock meant hello. Knock-knock, knock-knock meant are you happy? Knock-knock, knock meant are you sad? Knock-knock-knock meant yes, I am. Knock meant no. No knocks came. The noise from her room had been something else. Prevaricating, should I or shouldn't I, alertness and curiosity got me out of bed before I had time to question the wisdom of following my instinct.

I moved carefully across the floor to prevent the boards from creaking – not wholly successfully. At the door, I still had doubts about the wisdom of going next door to Sophia's room. Fear of being caught by Mother, or much worse: Father. What would I say? What excuse would I give? And what would I do if I entered Sophia's room and found her fast asleep? Wake her and say I heard a noise but it must have been the timbers? Yes, probably. I wanted to get into bed beside her and snuggle warm. But all Mother's talk of Sophia's needing her own room meant, for some unclear reason, that snuggling and keeping warm, once permitted, had become forbidden. Those days were over.

The cold penetrated my bare feet and into the rest of me. My dressing gown hung on a peg across the room. I could open the door and go into the corridor or go back to bed. Gently, I turned the handle.

. . . but I had no trouble whatsoever resisting an advance into the corridor. Candlelight dimmed dimmer, down and out, and all upstairs looked blind, black as soot. Someone had gone downstairs. In a moment, I put two and two together. The noise in her room; it must have been Sophia who had gone downstairs. Only Sophia carried so little weight on her feet she could descend without making the stairs creak. I considered following, although Heaven knew why if she only intended going to the toilet (we had pots for pee, but plops were outside only). But something told me to wait . . . and listen . . . and watch into the black where the corridor should have been. I heard the back door opening.

The back door had become stiff over the years with damp and needed a tug. If it was Mother, she might have wakened Father, and he might decide to prowl. The corridor would be suicide. I closed my door firmly but quietly and went across the bedroom, less carefully than I had minutes ago, to the window.

A steady light shone outside. Father, or Mother, or Gregory had a lamp . . . a lamp? But the person on the stairs had a candle! Sophia, Edgar and I were forbidden lamps. They were too dangerous and we had to make do with candles, which usually blew out. The strangest thing was that Father, Mother or Gregory – the lamplight – didn't move towards the toilet, but into the cemetery. Then it stopped and

. . . nothing for a long time. Nothing until I shivered, and nothing even then. I needed to get back under the sheets, for dawn might arrive and still nothing, and me standing there, frozen. And somebody frozen solid in the cemetery with a lamp.

But before I got back into bed, the light moved. It moved rapidly, but less rapidly than if it were running away from something. It moved as rapidly as someone would who had completed a task and no longer needed to be there. When the light came out of the cemetery and crossed the courtyard, I saw legs, and maybe an arm. Most clearly, I saw a gait. It was not Father's gait, nor Mother's, Gregory's, Edgar's or Sophia's. And it certainly wasn't mine – not even if I had been down there instead of up here. The only other person I could think of who came anywhere near the Manse was Farmer Barry. But it wasn't his gait either.

The stairs in the Manse were wide with a banister at either side. Sophia and I could walk on the stairs side by side and often did.

Normally, I held the banister on my left going up, and the other banister on my left going down. This time, however, I went up the middle of the stairs without holding on to either banister.

I felt watched.

Aware of the ceiling above me, as I'm occasionally aware of a teacup that might fall off Mother's tray and hit my head, and aware too of the wall above the ceiling that separated my parents' bedroom from Granny Hazel's, I tried to keep the top of my head in line with the wall as if I were balancing a book, or a jug of water like the black woman in the encyclopedia.

'Edward?' I heard Mother's voice as if it came from a world next door to ours. 'Edward?' she repeated. I turned round and shuffled, a little dizzy and in danger of falling, to my left to hold on to the banister. Mother stood at the foot of the stairs, looking up, with a bundle of washing in her arms fresh off the line. 'What are you doing?'

'Nothing.'

'Why are you walking like that?' Because Sophia said that was how the White Lady with the fuzzy face walked up the stairs before Granny Hazel died. Mother didn't know that Sophia had seen her. It seemed to be the kind of thing to hold my tongue about . . . And because of last night too, of course.

'What are you up to?'

'Nothing,' I repeated, as innocently as possible.

'A little white lie, Edward?'

'I just wanted to see if I could go up without holding on.'

'Well, don't. You'll fall, and then where would you be?'

'At the bottom.'

'Don't be facetious. Where's Sophia?'

'In the toilet.' The toilet was the only place we went to without each other – apart from when I went off to school, of course.

Mother, unconvinced of my innocence, asked, 'Where are you going?'

'To my room.'

'Why? What's wrong with waiting for Sophia?'

I shrugged.

'I have to iron these,' said Mother, and went to the kitchen.

Although she'd gone, I still felt watched.

I didn't try walking up the middle of the stairs again because doing so made me dizzy. I held the banister and proceeded, recapturing the thoughtfulness of before. At the top, the landing was a corridor of equal distance left and right. The very old carpet had no colour left, just browny greyness. A word existed that described what I became aware of when at the top of the stairs. I didn't know 'symmetrical' then, but I felt as though if I could fold the Manse like paper all its inner edge would meet.

At the top of the stairs, I looked right and left for the White Lady. But she wasn't there.

⋆

Mother wept again when I left the Manse for my second year at school. I wept again too. Sophia wept too too. Edgar wept because we wept, but mainly he looked baffled. Gregory looked bored. Father, I'm certain – at work on Farmer Barry's farm – didn't care one way or the other who wept, looked baffled or looked bored.

Farmer Barry left Father in charge of his farm – although I doubt that Father's being in charge made any practical difference – while he came for me and Gregory at the Manse in his lorry.

I was too young to appreciate Farmer Barry's kindness, or wonder what, if anything, he got in return. With a wet, purple face, I dug my fingernails into Mother's thighs.

'OW! That hurt! Wee bugger! Let go!'

Smiling, Farmer Barry put his big hands around my chest and would have pulled me free, but I trailed Mother's frock in my talons and between my clenched teeth.

'Let go, Edward!'

Not in her life!

'Do as your mother tells you,' said Farmer Barry.

Frock material ripped. Mother prised my fingers open. She pinched my arm. I opened my mouth, yelped, and her frock came free.

9

Miss Ballard and Satan's Face

I waited alone on the day that classes resumed outside Miss Ballard's classroom door. No one else stood outside, only me, too keen by far. Only Pike, it seemed, wanted to make a good impression. I arrived ten minutes early because I had yet to learn that making a good impression on a teacher is nowhere remotely as important as the avoidance of making a bad impression on other boys.

A rumour circulated that Miss Ballard used to be a beauty queen, and, although forty something, she entered beauty competitions still – scandalous behaviour to boys our age. Exciting too. Standing on toe-tips to see through the pane in the centre of the door, I saw her face when she sensed my presence and looked up. Ducking would have been silly. I knocked on the door and went in. One of Miss Ballard's bare feet perched on the edge of her desk. She was attempting to cut her toenails with the kind of school scissors that I found too blunt to cut cardboard with. Her ferocious big toe, the nail painted purple, looked like a mutant raspberry.

'I'm Edward Pike,' I said, choking on my own saliva. I wondered whether toenail cutting in public was a sin.

Miss Ballard displayed an immodestly bare thigh. I considered backing out of the classroom, but her leg's length held me in thrall. Mother's and Sophia's legs were the only female legs I knew. Miss

Ballard's extravagance in the leg department put theirs to shame.

'Another one.' She surveyed me shoes to hair – no vast distance.

'Miss?'

'Pike. Another Pike. Say Gregry isn't your brother.'

She spoke with a funny voice. Without meaning to be cheeky or precocious or witty or anything else, I said Gregory with two syllables the same way she did: Gregry. 'Gregry isn't my brother.'

'I believe you. You don't look like him.' She narrowed her eyes to see inside my brain and through me. 'Are you sure?'

'I do have a brother called Gregry, but you said to say I didn't. So I said I didn't. Although I do. And one called Edgar. And a mother and father and twin sister called Sophia. We're the same age.'

She looked down at me, past her raised foot, which, when I looked closely – and the foot forced me to look closely – possessed, all beside each other with spaces between making them look like miniature headstones, six toes.

'Gregry Pike's example is not a good one,' she said. 'What's the matter? Haven't you seen a six-toed foot before?'

'No, Miss.'

She removed her foot from the desk. Her thigh vanished. 'The example set by your brother is a bad one. Follow it at your peril.'

'I thought everybody has only five toes. Ten, if you count both feet. But only five if you lost a leg in the war.'

'Wait outside, Pike,' said Miss Ballard.

My effort at making a good first impression having backfired, I waited outside. While waiting outside, I concluded that Miss Ballard, judging by the cracks in her face-paint, had closer to fifty years on her clock than forty. If God sent another flood, and all her make-up washed off, she might be sixty. Could someone that old really lift their foot on to a desk? Maybe old people with six toes could.

I followed up year one's achievement of making no friends by making none in year three either. If I'd gone to year two, I'm sure I would have completed a hat-trick. My peers were too boisterous and competitive for my sensibility.

Miss Ballard gave us official bible lessons daily. We also received bible lessons unofficially during arithmetic, writing and art. Miss Ballard had the sort of piety that would have qualified her to be a world champion nun.

At first, I thought Miss Ballard's odd accent a speech impediment. She came from up north where their words were the same as ours but with fewer syllables. All her sentences, no matter how short or long they were, rose at the end from normal to high-pitched. Everything she said sounded like an attack because it came with a small dog's yap to finish with. The high-pitched ending made statements of fact sound like questions: 'You got tin correct spillings out of tin? I'm awarding you a silver star?'

Miss Ballard also tended to use big words without telling us what they meant. The Lord God is omnipotent and omniscient? He sent His son Jesus to redeem us from our transgressions?'

No more pious woman could exist than Miss Ballard. Alas, she could never be a nun because nuns, like priests, were from a false religion – according to her. They were Cathlics. Cathlics called themselves Christians, but they were not true Christians; they were Aunty Christians and their leader, the Pope, was the Aunty Christ. The crosses of Aunty Christians still had Jesus on them. But Jesus should never be on crosses. He rose from the dead, after all; he wasn't still crucified. Proper Christian crosses were empty. Jesus went to Heaven on a cloud, not a cross.

Miss Ballard frightened religion into those boys who were not infected by it already. As if Christ-bearing crosses were not bad enough, Catholics worshipped the Virgin Mary, Jesus's mother – which I had trouble getting my young head around, although I could not put my finger on why.

According to Miss Ballard with the odd accent and extra toe, worship of the Virgin Mary counted as a posty sea and blast fanny – whatever they were; I dared not ask.

During bible lessons, Miss Ballard encouraged us to ask questions. There were forty of us, but only four or five, including me, spoke. Questions such as 'Is the Dead Sea really dead?' could set her running for fifteen uninterrupted minutes about loaves and fishes or walking on water. Peter McCrew enraged her by asking – perfectly sensibly in my view – if Lazarus was a zombie.

One day, I asked Miss Ballard what Satan looked like. She said no one really knew because he could look like whatever he wanted to? He appeared to Eve in the Garden of Eden as a snake?

During the Christmas break, after I'd been home nearly long enough to go back, I woke, swimming in shards of ice. A dream of sums hurt my head. Miss Ballard, at the blackboard, kept teaching the class that four into seventeen won't go. I kept arguing yes it will! Yes it will! Miss Ballard, pointing her cane at chalk sums, said that four into sixteen goes four times. 'Four fours are sixteen? Everybody?' The class, in one voice, said that four fours were sixteen. Said Miss Ballard, 'But four into seventeen won't go?' I tore handfuls of hair from my head. 'Four into seventeen?' said Miss Ballard. 'Pike! Four into seventeen?'

I replied, although I knew it was the wrong answer, 'Won't go.' 'Wrong!' said Ballard. 'Four into seventeen goes four times, and one over?' Aggghhh! Then, in my dream, I looked from the window of my room and saw Sophia outside. She looked up at me. No matter how tight shut I kept my mouth, I could still breathe. As I looked at Sophia's face, I saw her skull underneath. I saw her skull underneath!

I told Sophia all about Miss Ballard. The woman left an impression on me like a yellow bruise that turned grey but never fully went away.

Sophia was most receptive concerning my ballads of Miss Ballard. She knew no opinion other than Father's in matters of our creator and His enemy, who in turn was ours. Sophia listened with parted lips.

In her pious ranting about the Devil Miss Ballard mentioned spud blights not once! She told us a story of how Satan with the many names had once been God's most beautiful angel. This shocked me, and riveted me to the tale at the time. One day Satan dared to sit on God's throne. As a punishment, God cast him out of Heaven and into Hell. A bit heavy-handed of God, I thought. If Father caught me sitting on his chair he would probably just thumb me off it.

'Hell has mountains made of ice that its fires never melt' . . . that's what Father said.

I never knew whether I would be hot or cold in Hell when I went there, and spent long spells wondering how people in Hell knew whether to take a coat when they went out to get their punishments.

Father described Hell as a place of chaos and eternal suffering – which I had trouble seeing in my mind's eye. I reasoned that it had something to do with the unpredictable weather.

That I would end up in Hell seemed likely. Father said you went to Hell for sinning in all kinds of ways: being cheeky to Mother; bearing false witness – whatever that meant; murder; adultery – which for years I mistook for idolatry; killing yourself . . . that was a strange one.

On the floor, in front of the hearth, almost on fire, I told Sophia more about school. She had asked me to tell her about school every day since I came home. This time, I told her about Miss Ballard, who said that Satan looked like a snake. My parents must have been listening, but they kept quiet until I took the opportunity to get a second opinion on what Satan looked like from Father.

Much later, with Christmas holidays past, Easter gone, and summer on the way, in my hunt for Satan's face I came across a painting of him by William Blake in an encyclopedia in the school library – a muscular, naked young man with wings.

Look behind you! Squint into dark corners! Glance left and right! He may be on the steep, slanted slates and behind the chimney pots, red-brick obelisks that exhaled crematorium clouds. He may lurk in the dark, bare-cold corridors with polished wooden floors. He may be round corners and under creaking beds with lumpy mattresses. You might see him flapping across the playing field at dusk, or rising in flight over the criss-crossed fence that kept two hundred boys from escaping. He might appear, hunched over steaming cauldrons, in the kitchen. I watched warily for him: ugly, not quite human, with wings. I watched for Satan – because God had cast Satan into Hell, and Hell on earth was Whitehead House.

'What does Satan look like?' I asked. And it occurred to me, as I looked up at the grizzled, bearded man on his chair, that I already knew.

Animated by my interest in a subject close to his heart, Father cleared his throat, closed his bible, sat up straight, made a false start and disappeared upstairs for half an hour. When he came down, with a copy of *Pilgrim's Progress*, abridged and reworked for children, I had forgotten that I had asked the question.

'Listen,' he said, with a forefinger. And we did. Father opened the book. Mother's needles stopped clicking. The log on the fire crackled more quietly.

'As I went through the wild waste of this world . . .' He only read four pages of it – thank heavens – and not in sequence. He turned a handful of pages at a time from, say, page one to page seven, then to page fourteen, without losing the narrative thread. Granted, one page had a large illustration, but it still contained more words than the ten or twelve he read. Next turn, he talked more text than could have possibly been on the page.

No doubt Father supplemented the text with bits and bobs of his own invention – which is perfectly legitimate when you consider that 'getting the message across' is more important than adhering to the truth; after all, that is how whoever did it compiled the bible. I doubt that Bunyan presented Christian, at any point on his pilgrimage, knee-deep in the spud fields. I doubt that Bunyan made God, at that very moment in history, blight all the spuds because the population of the land took to strong drink and fornication – which I assumed to be the strongest drink of all: tea stewed for hours and hours that you have to drink black because the milk is sour.

Satan, Father said, confirming Miss Ballard's opinion, could look like whoever or whatever he wanted to look like. He hid his true identity behind many faces, and he wore as many faces as names. Satan, thought I. Devil! 'Lucifer,' said Father. 'Beelzebub! Beast!' Cow, thought I. A cow is a beast.

'That's one good reason why you can't trust him,' said Father. 'He can make himself invisible too, if that suits his purpose, and most of the time it does. He could be here. Right here. In this very room. Waiting to tempt any of us to do evil.'

Father snapped Bunyan shut. I thought of Gregory in the barn with his filterless singles and box of matches. Luckily, there was no hay in the barn or we might have experienced the fires of Hell at first hand.

We went to our separate bedrooms, me and Sophia. Mother tucked us in, closed our doors and went downstairs. We opened our doors, tee-hee-heed in the corridor, and picked our old room, Sophia's room now.

'What's Satan's name when he's invisible?' asked Sophia.

I guessed. 'The Invisible Man.'

Father and Miss Ballard made a good match. They parted, down the middle, black or white without any shades of grey, everything that crossed their minds. There were good things and bad things; nothing sat in the middle and avoided judgement. God received credit for the good, and Satan took the blame for the bad. Obviously, sickness belonged on Satan's side. Miss Ballard taught us to believe that sickness, of whichever shape or size or degree of malignancy, came from the hand of Satan. When I personified sickness – Sickness – I imagined that Sickness looked waxy and blue, like a corpse. She, or possibly he, would have short, flat hair and eyes that failed to focus on anything. Sickness must be unhealthy in mind and body. Whether the blue, waxy Sickness in my mind might have been Satan himself, or one of the demons cast from Heaven with him, I couldn't say. Satan could change his appearance and demons could turn themselves invisible too. Identities and images mingled. The whole thing became messy and merged like butter melting into a pan of boiling water into my nightmares.

10
Junior School Photographs

After fast times with Miss Ballard and Satan in year three, things settled down and time moved much more slowly. At some time, from somewhere, I picked up the phrase 'existential boredom'. I must have chanced upon it in the library while trying to read something too advanced for my years. I, somehow, knew that my existential boredom had, at its heart, waiting. Waiting for something. Anything. Perhaps I'd been bored to death waiting for something, anything, in a past life. Anyhow, that's what I had: existential boredom.

Had I been unaware of what ailed me, I'd probably have done something mad . . . like throwing myself under a parked train, or tying a bed sheet to a light-fitting and hanging myself, or tying a bed sheet to a light-fitting and hanging somebody else, a smaller boy than me – had there been one. There was one, actually: Alf Lord.

I wouldn't have hung Alf from a bed sheet attached to a light-fitting in a million years. He and I had become friends. That is to say, we smiled at each other and said hello. We were friends in so far as, unlike the other boys, we had no need to shout at, strike, kick or bite our peers or charge about the place like demons.

Alf always had a jotter and a pocket full of pencils. He shielded his jotter with one hand and scribbled with the other.

One day, I spoke to Mark Jeffery about Alf, in the sophisticated, extended, abstract and complex way that children speak to each other. The conversation went roughly as follows . . .

Me: Where's Alf?

Mark: Who?

Me: Alf.

Mark: Who's Alf?

Me: Alf! You know.

Mark: No, I don't.

Me: Alf that sits over there.

Mark: There's nobody there.

Me: Is that your soldier?

Mark: Yes.

Me: Can I play with it?

Mark: No.

Often absent from class, Alf, I assumed, had health problems, a swollen brain or something: he was very smart. When present, Alf's presence fuzzed my own brain – like when the dinnertime bell rings and you're nearly sure you ate dinner an hour ago. Quiet and averse to sports like me, small and lightly built like me, Alf sometimes made me jump by looking out of mirrors at me. I noticed him more in year three after Christmas, when, instead of being fuzzy, he came into sharper focus. The other boys were in colour, but Alfred Lord only ever turned up for class in black and white. The other boys had three dimensions, but Alfred Lord, when you looked closely at him – although I don't think anyone ever did – had two.

Nobody except me bothered with Alf.

Each time I left the Manse, I missed Sophia dreadfully. As time passed, I missed her more than anything: more than newly blind men miss sight, more than orphans miss parents, more than Father missed his bible when Sophia hid it under the sink with the washing powder.

. . . which is why I wrote to her and promised that next time I returned to the Manse, I would not return to school. I would live the rest of my life in the Manse and fixed to her side like a loving shadow.

I never questioned whether Sophia still lived, still played, still ate and still got bored in the Manse.

Still she helped Mother with the chores, just like before. Nothing changed at home except my removal from the scene. I never questioned, and yet the absence of her voice, her laughter and the clucking of the hens as she chased them made a gap, a void, where I would have questioned had I been less preoccupied with my own sufferings. I yearned to hear Sophia's voice. Even hearing it without seeing her face would have sufficed.

The senior school had a telephone in the prefects' room, but juniors never went there. Risking my life to use the seniors' telephone would have been fruitless. I knew no number and the Manse lacked a telephone. School encouraged juniors to write letters, even if they were only a few lines long and in crooked block capitals. Sophia and I wrote tomes to each other every week. One of our most commonly occurring words was still, which Sophia spelled with one l. While I still hated school and the food was still rotten, Sophia stil missed me, and Father's nose was stil in his bible. Sophia was stil freezing, and I still missed her too. Possessing her words on paper, and an imagination with which to hear them in my head, was no substitute for having my other half beside me.

In her reply, she wrote that my not returning to school after the next break was wonderful. She left out the d in the middle, but I didn't care. She said Edgar wanted me home too. When she told him about my promise, he was so thrilled he wet himself. Good old Edgar! He never let Mother down when washday came round.

Meanwhile, Mr Hogg, the sports master, had a bigger evil streak than any other teacher. He looked a bit like Satan – which might have been why I never saw him talking to Miss Ballard.

Forced to play sports outdoors regardless of snow, ice-javelin rain, lightning or hurricane, I might have died from pneumonia. Running about a muddy field half naked, trying not to die twice a week convinced me that Mr Hogg wanted me dead or disabled. He favoured sporty boys who made friendships and rivalries, and who cemented their friendships and rivalries through cross-country running and kicking a ball around a football pitch in Noah's Flood weather conditions. I was always the boy third from last in cross-country running, with only the fat boys puffing along behind.

Mr Hogg could always find me, when he felt like a backside to smack with the sole of his running shoe, shivering behind the changing rooms with my hands in my oxters as I endeavoured to stay as far away as possible from everything that looked like a ball or as though you were supposed to run on it. In Mr Hogg's opinion, cold showers first thing in the morning would toughen me up. I failed to see how.

Nevertheless, with my toughening up as his end, he made me get up every morning before everybody else and do exercises, like star jumps and push-ups, naked under the shower while he watched, sitting on the edge of a sink with his arms folded. These sessions lasted about fifteen minutes. The teeming icicles on my body made me quite sick and dizzy by the end. Mr Hogg always said that I did well, and I was a good lad at heart, as he dried me down with a school towel rough as a toilet brush. He paid particular attention to my private parts. Apparently, I could get a nasty rash between my legs without proper drying. The toughening-up programme failed.

Mr Hogg finally gave up on me.

Sometimes, admittedly, I cried and made no attempt to hide my tears. There were few places to hide them. I heard snivelling behind locked cubicle doors, and the echo of that sound in a toilet is truly pathetic. There were no private places. Boys were everywhere. And, when they weren't crying, they were prying, tumbling, rough and tough, loud and foul. But boys were only half of the awfulness. Teachers were the other half. Boring lessons were half of it too, and the food half as well. And we had to go to church on Sundays, which wasn't too bad, just unbelievably dull. When supposed to sing praise Him praise Him we sang braise Him braise Him. That's as good as it got.

When verbally abused by my peers, I shrugged and asked myself, rhetorically, what did I expect? When physically abused, I picked myself up, turned my face from notions of revenge, and knew my tormentors would get what they deserved one day. That's how God works, Father said: there's justice in the end. When the victim of practical jokes, no matter how cruel they were, I pretended to see the funny side. Unexpectedly, my passivity reduced the number of attacks. The bullies grew tired of me.

Life might have seemed tedious then, as I lived it. Of course, looking back, lots of eventful stuff went on: lots and lots and lots.

For example . . .

Mr Ryan taught year fours. I was not in the least looking forward to him teaching me. When Mr Ryan spoke, he sounded like air-conditioning. He always talked as if his listeners didn't care about what he had to say, and, therefore, he didn't care either. Everyone – including his fellow teachers – called Mr Ryan the Old Bore.

Mr Ryan, however – so the rumour went – got himself fired by Blinky for getting his wife pregnant – his own wife, that is, not Blinky's. If Mr Ryan had got Blinky's wife pregnant Blinky would really have fired him – with a flame-thrower, I should imagine.

Peter McCrew, who seemed to know more than most people about such things, said getting someone pregnant involved some kind of shenanigans suggestive of Mr Ryan's being not quite such an old bore after all. Indeed, he stopped being the Old Bore and became the Dirty Old Sod. I knew dirty old sods; Father put them on top of Granny Hazel after he buried her. The connection between a dirty old sod and a pregnant Mrs Mr Ryan escaped me. A deep wisdom stopped me from asking Peter McCrew to explain what he meant. At around this time I discovered that although women can get pregnant, men cannot . . . which I took in my stride. Men and women are different. Sophia didn't have a willy and I did.

I knew pregnant meant the woman in question had a big belly with a baby inside, but remained in the dark about how the mechanics worked or why you would get fired for getting your wife it. Peter McCrew said Mr Ryan couldn't control his trouser snake.

Soon, there were all kinds of rumours about how men got women pregnant. Some of the rumours had pre-existed, but I never paid attention to them before. Other rumours were new – at least, new to me. The stuff about fertilizing eggs sounded like an April fool scam. I knew women didn't lay eggs; hens did that. One rumour – Peter McCrew's invention – was that a man stuck his willy into the woman's bottom and peed.

How on earth? You'd need some kind of shoehorn!

A new teacher, called Miss Fish, arrived to substitute for the Old Bore. Miss Fish came to be known as the Old Cow. She made us take turns reading aloud, and ate sandwiches behind her desk most of the time. I thought we would have Miss Fish all year, but she got pregnant too. It had nothing to do with Mr Ryan: because I asked . . .

Standing in front of the class one day, smiling in a dizzy-headed kind of way and patting her bulge, 'Not long to go now,' she said.

'Did Mr Ryan do that?' I asked.

She had a giggle-fit and never recovered.

I liked Miss Fish after that.

Obviously, her boyfriend couldn't control his trouser snake.

Before the Christmas play, *Pinocchio* – I knew not what Pinocchio had to do with baby Jesus other than that they were both real boys – Miss Fish thanked us for being good children and said that teaching us had been a pleasure. Gosh! We blushed pink, even Alf in black and white. Geppetto morphed into a puppet maker suspiciously like Blinky Mulholland. Miss Fish said she would not be back after Christmas; Mr Ryan would have returned by then.

Blinky must have forgiven him for making his wife pregnant.

I spilled a pot of paint – red for Geppetto's cardboard house – on Peter McCrew's trousers, and he punched me in the head. He would have murdered me if Miss Fish and her bulge hadn't stepped in.

11

Changes

Dear Edward

I hope you have been wel. I have been sick but I am better now. The big news is that Father might put me in Granny Hazel's bedroom. I hope not because I do not want to go. I do not know why he wants to move me about. My legs are making all my dress too short. Mother says we should have a speshal party because we wil reach double figures next birthday.

Yours sincerely, Sophia

Suddenly, time seemed to be running out like the Whitehead House junior eleven from the changing room . . . me in my scarf and gloves, the sports master poking his head back inside: 'You too, Pike.' There was so little time ahead before double figures, and I had been wasting the present, daydreaming through it pretending to be receiving an education. What would be the point of having received an education if time ran out? My education would be of no use to me. When I reached ten, that would be it; no more unique numbers, just the same zero to nine over and over again until all my years ran out. I was afraid. What could I do? Was there a way, like alchemy, to mix the existing single numbers – even though, strictly speaking, zero might not be a number – and create new single numbers?

Extensive experimentation in this field, with a pencil and sketch pad, occupied more of my time than it should have. For several months I mixed fives and threes, twos and nines, ones and fours and eights, every combination imaginable. Uniting a seven and a four produced triangles and made me speculate that creating new single numbers from the already existing ones might be impossible because some numbers from zero to nine have straight lines while others have curved lines; still others have a combination of straight and curved lines. Starting a new single number from scratch might be the only resolution. I made numerous preliminary sketches to that end. Although some were more pleasing to the eye than others, the names I invented for them seemed purely arbitrary, and that did not seem right.

These were days of changes, internal and external.

Internally, school changed me, stripped me from Sophia, my other half, and made me stand alone like a target. My age had two numbers instead of one: 1 and 0 – although the ancient Greeks were unsure about 0 as a number. They asked how nothing could be something. Having thought about this, at length, I concluded that nothing must be something, since if, say, you have something – perhaps an elephant – and someone takes it away from you, you have nothing, which must be something precisely because 'no elephant' is something you have. You can say: I have no elephant. But you cannot say: I have not no elephant, which would mean either that you do indeed have an elephant or that you can't speak right.

Externally, Father set wheels in motion that changed the Manse. In Whitehead House, I missed most of the changes as they happened, but Sophia's letters kept me up to date, and I saw the changes for myself when I went home.

One day, yellow bulldozers appeared on the horizon and out from the edge of Hollow Wood. Lorries came too, stacked with machinery and raw materials and piles of clay-coloured pipes. The rumble was audible if you went far enough across the heath. Father watched from his bedroom window through a telescope retrieved from the loft. Men in orange vests and hard hats turned pristine green into a construction site. They crept along daily, weekly, monthly, like a loud snail leaving a trail of grey in their wake.

Some years earlier, and without telling anyone, the Department of Conveyance decided to construct a motorway – Father called it an abomination – from top to toe of the country and back again. In fact, the abomination ran only half the country's length, connecting north to south (or south to north). It ran parallel to the railway track, but on the far side. If they had constructed it on the near side, the mess would have destroyed a stretch of Hollow Heath.

Instead, destruction threatened the whole of Hollow Heath.

There were rumours of a new town replacing it. They planned to build half of the new town on the far side of the motorway, and half on the near side. The new town would come right up to our door.

Mother brought these rumours home when she went shopping for things we were out of. The notion of a new town replacing Hollow Heath sounded like a notion of Armageddon. Father made enquiries, but I heard no more, and I doubt he did either. They built a halt, and a footbridge over the motorway so new town people could get off the train and walk home.

In time, the new town came, but they only built half of it, and built it well away from us, on the far side of the track and the motorway. Moreover, the planners forgot, or omitted, to build a slip road off the motorway leading to the new town, Bruagh and beyond, thus leaving the new town to starve and die when, as rumoured, through lack of passengers, the train no longer stopped at the halt. Were the rumours true, only an unreliable daily bus would service our sick, small spot of the land.

By the time the motorway was finished, a strip of widely spaced and tall orange lights, as far as the eye could see, from right to left and back again, robbed half my sky of stars. My gloomy sky over Whitehead House seldom entertained stars. But at the Manse, I liked to stand at the broken garden gate and look at them.

Father said, of the planners and executors of progress, as he said of everyone he had no control over or influence upon, 'They don't care about common gardener people like us.' I think he might have meant common or garden, but whatever he meant, for once I agreed with him. He also said, 'All this progress, and all this making us a nation fit for modern times: it's nothing but the Devil's work.'

I had some trouble agreeing with this, despite having a degree of sympathy with the spirit of his argument. I could see that motorized vehicles broke down but horses never did. They died, but that was natural.

Father was a hypocrite, of course. When progress brought hot water into his home, a warm toilet seat, and light to read his bible by at night, Father's condemnation of the Devil's work was absent.

The Manse lost a spare bedroom and gained an indoor toilet. That the simple flush of a loo should put such smiles on faces! Our bathroom boasted a sink too. And a bath! In the old days we put water from the well into the old tin tub and heated it with water from the kettle. Luxury is having a bath with your legs straight and your knees under the water. Father hung the tin tub on a nail in an outhouse, where it rusted – like the whistling kettle and the mangle – for someone, someday, to discover and write into history.

I overheard talk of boilers, timer switches and thermostats. 'Plumbing' entered my vocabulary. I became aware of the connection between these technologies and Science, but it would be more years before I became aware that my scientific tendencies were theoretical, not practical. I couldn't wire a plug to save my life.

The Manse received an upgrade or three. Workmen dug channels and pits. We became proud owners of a new septic tank. Progress consigned the well – although we all had a soft spot for it – to stagnation. Father covered the top with boards and bricks in case someone fell in. He also discovered electricity and came out from the Dark Ages around this time.

And he took a stroke.

I didn't know what a stroke was until he took one.

He had to take time off work, of course.

Where did money come from to see us through? Farmer Barry, apparently – charity, really. Barry could afford it. He owned land as far as the eye could see, which he rented out for grazing and growing.

The doctor from the big hospital far away, where Father had to stay for two weeks, said Father was lucky: his stroke was slight. His speech wasn't affected and his face didn't sag on one side. He had a limp, and needed a walking stick, but apart from that no one would have suspected that he'd had a stroke. I, for one, was heavily disappointed by the prospect that, one day, he might throw away his stick and his recovery might be complete.

But that was not to be.

Mother, Gregory, Sophia and I wanted a television. Father wanted one too, but wouldn't admit it. 'Where's the money coming from to buy it?' he asked. 'And you need to buy a licence and renew it every year. It's a money-eating machine, it is.'

We received a government grant to cover the cost of modernization, but that didn't include a television. I don't know where the money came from, but, in the end, it came.

Two men wearing blue overalls arrived at the Manse in a van that said *TeleIdeal* on the side. We were beside ourselves with excitement. They'd brought us our television. The images on the screen would be in colour. Nothing would ever be the same.

One of the men in blue overalls climbed a ladder and attached an aerial to the chimney. The other man placed the television where Mother said she wanted it, and drilled a hole in the wall beneath the living-room window. When the aerial cable fed through the hole and fixed to the back of the television, and the drill-man switched on our new acquisition, the screen came magically alive. We had visitors in our home, in a box, whenever we wanted them. There were wars, and rumours of wars, that we hadn't known about. Father said it was the Second Coming of Christ.

Our television had three channels with good reception, and two channels that were fuzzy. A blue-overall man said we needed to wiggle the aeriel on the chimney about, but Father said to leave it alone; it was a stupid idea. You can't climb up there in all kinds of weather, wiggle the aeriel about, and watch programmes in the living room at the same time.

In the future, said the other blue-overall man, we would be able to switch channels without getting up from our chairs; we would only have to point and the television would know what we wanted. 'It's satanic,' moaned Father, shaking his head as if powerless and defeated already. In the future, there would be not three but thirty or more channels. The screen would double in size and the images would become sharper. Pictures would come into our living room live from outer space.

The idea of live pictures from outer space thrilled me. The television people must have known things that we did not. Of course they did; they were a branch of the government! What, I wondered, strange, wonderful and other-worldly things went on in outer space that, soon, everyone on terra firma would know about.

Father became increasingly worried. For him, seeing what happened in outer space intruded upon the upper realm of God.

The blue-overall men went away, leaving us watching television. None of us blinked for two hours. Father didn't blink for three. Hours turned into days. Sophia sat too close to the screen and started seeing snow before her eyes wherever she went. Mother took to burning dinner. Burnt meals arrived late on the table. Dishes went unwashed. The noise of clicking knitting needles competed with noise from the television. Soon, the Manse boasted enough woollen scarves to warm the necks of a small army. Pom-pom hats appeared on the floor like mushrooms. At full capacity, the Manse had twelve feet, but a month after our television arrived it had forty-three knitted bed socks, and a forty-fourth on the way.

No one spoke any more in words of more than two syllables – even television became TV. Sentences were short, and ceased being preceded by, or followed by, other sentences . . .

'What's on?'

'This.'

'What else?'

'This is good.'

'What time's dinner?'

'After this.'

'I like him.'

'Hmm?'

'What?'

'I thought you said something.'

'What's for dinner?'

'Shh!'

Sophia discovered that by propping a mirror beside the television she could view programmes without being startled when someone entered the room behind her.

Everything had changed, changed still, and would continue to change. I didn't realize it then, but change is a condition of nature.

Edgar passed out of my life with neither a goodbye nor a departing wave. The authorities persuaded Mother to allow him to be taken into care – for his own good, they said. Apparently, Edgar's long-term care had been an issue for some years. Obviously, things went on between Mother and Father that we children knew nothing about.

Father put his foot down – as far as I understand what happened. He said that Edgar had parents who were fit and able to look after him – by which he meant that Mother was fit and able to look after him.

The authorities sided with Mother, and gave my parents a booklet which explained that, because they had such a low income, the state would pay for all Edgar's needs. The booklet changed Father's mind. He said Edgar's going into care was for the best.

I had daydreamed for years about how wonderful leaving junior school for ever would be. Real freedom at last! I would run like a fast-flowing stream. I would float in the air like a . . . balloon? I would . . . I didn't know what I would do, but whatever I did would feel alive and good. I would feel alive and good! Leaving junior school for ever would be like going directly to Heaven without the unpleasant necessity of dying first.

On the penultimate day, we had an end-of-term party during which I ate too much, and on the ultimate one I felt sick.

I expected to have grown up by the time I left junior school for ever, but I had not – not grown more than a centimetre no matter what variety of instruments of measurement anyone cared to employ. My feet – along with my inches – were disinclined to draw attention to themselves. Their dastardly plan to keep their heads down – and, consequentially, my head too – backfired, and I dreaded returning to Whitehead House, after the summer break, as the smallest ever senior. I would rather have been conspicuous for my ability to see over hedges than for my ability to walk under tables. I would have felt much more grown up if I had spent at least some of my time during the junior years growing up.

In the end, it was an anticlimax. Nobody said goodbye to anybody else. Indeed, everything changes. But nothing changes much or quickly. We would all be back in September as seniors.

I had diarrhoea on the train.

Fortunately, it had an indoor toilet.

Sophia was pleased to see me. Mother was pleased to see me. Gregory couldn't care less. Father . . . God knows. I was pleased to see the toilet indoors.

A little growing up went on during July and August, but not much. Mother promised that I would awake some morning to find that I had grown an extra foot. For a boy who tried to remain as inconspicuous as possible in all situations, an extra foot would have been disastrous, especially if it came attached to an extra leg. There was a little consolation, although not much, in that, with an extra foot, I would have something in common with Miss Ballard with the extra toe. It was a long, dull summer.

12

Senior School Photographs

The shadowy, senior side of Whitehead House awaited. No longer a junior, proudly wearing my longs – which would have covered the knees but not the shins of most boys my age – I walked beside Mother as she carried my suitcase up the Lane to the Road. My strides were the same length as hers now. There had been no rain for a week and the potholes were dry. The clouds were white and fluffy, and the morning sun shone ferocious and cold. Our feet crunched gravel. I heard no other noise. I felt ever so strange.

Sophia hadn't been there this time to wave goodbye from the back door. She missed breakfast. Flu, Mother said. It was catching. I couldn't go to her room, to hug her and say goodbye, for fear of spreading flu to everyone in Whitehead House.

'Why aren't you coming to the train?' I asked Mother.

'You're a big boy now.'

'But why aren't you coming to the train?'

'Don't go on about it, Edward.'

At the top of the Lane, Mother put my suitcase down and we waited for Farmer Barry's lorry. I don't know why he didn't drive down the Lane to the courtyard this time; maybe he was in a hurry. After several minutes, Mother became impatient. 'He's late. I hope he hurries up or you'll miss your train.' She sat on the grass at the side of the road while I kept lookout, jumping up and down to see over the hill – although I would have had to jump ten feet high to see the road on the other side.

We heard the lorry before we saw it. Mother stood up when Farmer Barry came over the hill. 'All right?' he greeted us, stepping down from behind the wheel to get my suitcase. Mother squashed me with a hug, kissed me, flattened my hair with her hand, hugged me again, and sobbed all the words you would expect a mother to sob about being good, keeping out of trouble, brushing my teeth and remembering to write to Sophia – as if I'd forget. Farmer Barry climbed back behind the wheel, closed his door, wound down the window and stuck his elbow out, and restarted the engine because it had cut out while he retrieved my suitcase. Mother gave me a shove to get me going, and in no time I had climbed nearly as high as my neck to get into the lorry. Mother waved, weeping, and I waved back as we drove away. I twisted round to wave through the tiny back window, but Mother wasn't in it.

'We're off, then,' said Farmer Barry, as if I might not have noticed. I had never known Farmer Barry to say much, but he spoke to me in the lorry, maybe to put me at ease, or to try to put himself at ease. We had never been alone before.

'Like school, do you?' he asked awkwardly. 'Good, is it?'

'I like parts of it,' I replied, after consideration.

'Parts, eh? Which parts are best, then?'

That was easy. 'Composition.' Did he know about composition? After all, it had been a long time since Farmer Barry went to school.

'Composition, eh? Anything else?' He was pressurizing me and I began to panic. Now I had to think of something else I liked. I didn't like anything else. 'Sports?' asked Farmer Barry. 'All boys like sports.'

'I hate sports.'

'Not sports, then.'

'Reading,' I said because I thought of Alf Lord who was always writing, but I'd already said composition, so I said reading, which I liked best and should have said before I said composition, in which case I could have done it without thinking of Alf.

'Reading, eh? Reading books never done nobody no harm. Great one for reading his bible is your father. You read the bible?' He was turning up the heat. I thought I should say yes, but that would have been a lie. 'Suppose your reading's a bit more modern than the bible.'

An idea came and rescued me. 'I read stories, mostly. Reading gives me ideas to write stories about in composition.'

'Stories, eh? You like stories, do you? There's nothing like a good story to put you over to sleep at night.' A bend in the road later, he asked, 'What sorts of stories do you like, then?'

I'd never thought of what sort I liked; stories were stories, the way cows were cows. But there were different sorts of cows: fat ones, skinny ones, standing-up ones, lying-down ones, black and white ones, and brown ones. Having no reply, I got out of it by asking him his own question. 'What kinds of stories do *you* like?'

'Oh, now, let me see . . .' I think he panicked. That made two of us. 'Cowboy stories, I think. Or stories about the war . . . Aye, a good cowboy yarn where they have a gunfight in the middle of town.' He took one hand off the wheel and shot me with a finger: 'Boom!' His six-shooter sounded more like a cannon than a gun, but I laughed and said I liked cowboy stories too, which wasn't strictly true because I'd never read any, but I was sure I'd like them when I did.

With a better idea now of what he meant by sorts of stories, I offered, 'I like scary stories too, with ghosts back from the dead.'

When Farmer Barry looked at me sideways as the road rolled under the lorry, I thought we might veer into the roadside ditch. 'Back from the dead, eh?' he said, at last. A corner and a swerve round a badly minced fox later, he added, 'The world's your oyster if you've mastered reading and writing.'

I knew what the world being my oyster meant, and I felt warm inside because Farmer Barry had said it. He said nothing else until Bruagh Halt, where he handed over my suitcase, saw me on to the train, and said goodbye.

This, my first day at senior school, would also be my first day for travelling alone by train. The near certainty that it had something to do with boats, not trains, allayed my fear of being press ganged. Gregory – still in bed when I left the Manse – had finished with school for ever in June gone by. Ostensibly, Blinky Mulholland had let him stay an extra year to resit his leaving exams. More accurately, Blinky let him stay on because he didn't have a job to go to, and the idea of Gregory under the roof of Whitehead House presented a more welcome circumstance to his teachers than the idea of Gregory roaming the countryside bored and terrorizing shopkeepers.

Rocking along the track, it occurred to me that Farmer Barry had done something my own father had never taken the time to do. Farmer Barry had taken an interest in me – only a little interest, but a little interest is miles better than none. Suddenly, senior school excited me. I would have different classes there teaching things like history and geography and science. If I worked hard and did well I could conquer my oyster.

With the handle of a suitcase as big as my torso in my right hand, leaning acutely to my left, I bruised an ankle while staggering from the train to the vestibule where desks were arranged to navigate the confused. An old-timer, I knew the ropes. I knew most of the teachers' faces too, although there were a few new ones. In those days, I thought our teachers, unlike us pupils, liked school. Now I know they hated it more than we did; that's why all their faces looked like their mouths had had spoonfuls of castor oil poured in.

The deputy head greeted me in the vestibule.

'Wipe your feet, boy!'

'On your own this year?' asked a male teacher from the senior side whose name I didn't know. I said I was, because Gregory left in June.

He smiled knowingly and said, in a sleeked way, he would see me around.

The housekeeper loaded me up with sheets, blankets and a pillow. Unable to see over the top, I tottered from the laundry to room seventeen on the senior side sideways. Somebody called, 'You, Pike! 'Zat you under there?' but I don't know who.

The junior school still had a nurse, although not the one who once thought so highly of my private parts. I saw her en route, and thought the other one prettier by far. Senior pupils had a nurse by a different name than Nurse. He was Mr Barmby, the HCA (Health Care Assistant), who I hoped, having genitals of his own, would take no interest in mine.

When I arrived at my room, my suitcase had beaten me to it.

Room seventeen boasted all the living space of a converted broom cupboard. All the other rooms had four or six beds. The secretary, bless her, had put me in a room of my own. Why? Single rooms – each floor had one – were usually assigned to prefects. Whether or not my solitude was due to an administrative error, I wasn't going to complain. In a room of my own, I couldn't have been happier. Long may their error go unnoticed.

A single room was better than a dorm by a mile or six. I grinned broadly and at length to prove it. I was still grinning, and digging paint out of a window-gap with a pen, when the caretaker who brought my suitcase returned with a note from Blinky Mulholland summoning me to his office. The caretaker had gone, and I was just about to obey, when Alf Lord appeared in the doorway. Since he said nothing, but stared, first at me, then around the room, I helped him out. 'Hello, Alf. Do anything good during the summer?' Whether he did anything good or not was of no interest to me, and I'm sure he knew that.

Which was why he said, 'You've your own room.'

He strayed inside as if he'd never seen a single room before. I watched him as he looked around, apparently seeing things worthy of noting that I could not see. Walls, ceiling, floor and a small space between them: that was about it, for me, but I got the impression, there, then, in that room, that where I saw a dust mote Alf saw a whole galaxy.

He made me feel odd inside. I'd never been so physically close to him. It was as though he emitted a kind of electricity that made the fine hairs on my arms stand up. Maybe because I was a touch nervous, I answered my own question as if it had been Alf's question to me.

'We didn't do much. Sophia wouldn't go out, so we just messed around the Manse.' Alf looked at me questioningly. 'It's not really a manse. That's just what it's called.'

'Who's Sophia?' asked Alf. 'And why won't she go out?'

'She's my twin sister. She won't go out because . . . because she just won't. It's a long story. Don't ask.'

He had a quick nibble at a fingernail. 'Long, fine blond hair?'

'Good guess.'

My own hair was blond, fine, and not exactly short.

'Tiny, waifishly thin, fine features?'

'Now you're getting creepy. How do you know?'

Because he knew what I looked like, idiot! Still . . .

'I remember seeing someone like that once . . . Off you go, Edward, or you'll be late for your date with Blinky.'

'You've never seen Sophia. I'm sure lots of girls look like her.'

'And I'm sure you're wrong about that.' He turned to my window, rocked on to his toe-tips and rubbed his hands together.

'You're weird,' I said.

Alf detained me as I left. 'Can I come here sometimes?'

'Where?'

'Here. To your room.'

'Why?'

'Just because.'

I thought he was jealous because it was my room and not his. I thought that, maybe, he saw my room as a refuge from the smelly, untidy dorms and their boisterous madness.

'Of course you can, Alf,' I said.

He turned from the window wearing a huge grin.

I left Alf and his grin, and my case unpacked, and crossed to the junior side where Blinky had his lair.

I no longer feared Blinky. Previous encounters had been benign bordering on amiable. I had what my teachers called 'a good record', which I didn't understand because I couldn't even sing. The summer break had energized the headmaster; he had more bounce.

'You! Edward,' he said. 'Sit.'

My legs no longer dangled numerous inches from the floor. Perhaps Blinky had replaced the old chair for a lower one for short chaps like me.

'You, Edward, are going to be my project.'

'Project, Sir?'

'Yes. Project. As in object of especial engagement. You will be my Trilby and I will be your Svengali.'

I'd heard of Svengali. Wasn't he a violinist? Or was I thinking of Stradivarius? Regardless of whoever Svengali might have been, I couldn't fathom what symbolism might be at play if I were his hat.

'What do you think of that?' asked Blinky.

'It depends,' I said.

'On?'

'Whether my being your project is to my advantage.'

'What a brain! And you're only twelve years old!'

'Eleven, Sir.' Had Blinky been at the sherry?

Being eleven, having lived through two to nine – and zero – my numbers needed recycling. My assumption was that numbers couldn't be recycled *ad infinitum*; with each recycle they would wear thinner, like repeated washings of a pullover. I couldn't imagine being as old as thirty-four. Not ever. Was there a way, like alchemy, to mix the existing single numbers – even though, strictly speaking, zero is not a number – and create new single numbers?

I experienced a long-lasting déjà vu when I was eleven. On some days the sense of recycled time was strong; on other days, I hardly noticed it.

'What's the biggest number possible?' asked Blinky, having done something very like reading my brain.

A billion? A trillion? A squizillion? I didn't know.

'Think about it,' he said. 'No matter what the biggest number may be, you can always add one to it. Thus, there is no biggest number. If you spend all your time inventing a different symbol for each number, you'll need more than one lifetime. In fact, you'll need an infinite number of lifetimes.'

Infinity, I thought . . . and flew through a window, back into myself, the way Sophia and I had done when we were little.

'Have you any idea who in your year gained the highest overall marks in May?' I shook my head. 'You did, Edward. Don't get excited. Stick a pin in it and a balloon will come down faster than it went up. Your task' – he pointed a straight finger at me on the end of a straight arm – 'your solemn task is to keep your balloon in the air. And not only that . . . fly higher! Fly higher, boy. Why? Because you can. Ah! Here we are.' His secretary entered the office with a pot of tea and two cups, one for me.

Since he was staring, beaming like an idiot, I thought I should say something.

'I thought Alf would get higher overall marks than me.'

'Alf?'

'Lord.'

'Bless us and save us! Quite. Now. How's that sister of yours? Cynthia? Last I heard she was late for school by several years.'

I didn't know he knew I had a sister. 'She's . . .' I said – skinny? forgetful? not very clever? worked half to death? sneezing all the time? confined to the Manse because of a stupid promise? 'all right,' I said.

'Does she miss you, her at home and you here?'

'Yes, she does.'

'And you miss her, don't you?'

Wipple, I thought. Blinky wanted me to talk about Sophia and why she had never gone to school. Wipple must have told him. I didn't want to discuss Sophia with Blinky – or anyone else.

'Imagine how proud she will be of you in the not too distant future, Edward. And your mother and father too. You are the great potential in your family. You're the one they have pinned their hopes on. And I know, I just know you're not going to let them down. You're going to work hard in senior school and make them very proud. Aren't you, Edward?'

'I don't want to leave Sophia behind. If I know stuff and she doesn't she feels foolish, and I don't want that.'

He wagged his head slowly. 'That's looking at one side of the coin. But look at the other. If you didn't know stuff who would teach her? How will she know the same stuff as you? Because you do know stuff, and can learn so much more about all manner of things, you can . . . not leave her behind, but raise her up.' He lifted his arms, and that was a very good thing for him to do because it made me understand. He had a point. I could raise Sophia up. I could learn so much stuff I would one day be smart enough to find a way to break the curse.

'Did I hear a penny drop?' asked Blinky. I said I didn't think so. For some reason he chuckled. 'I have something for you.' When he reached into his drawer I feared a Butter Ball. He handed me a cardboard folder. 'This is some information I have put together in simplified form from a variety of universities. You're a big fan of books, aren't you?' I nodded enthusiastically. 'Well, you can study books at university until you have pages of text coming out of your ears. You can study the best literature ever written, from when writing began to the present. What do you think of that?'

It sounded good. I told him so. And, just out of interest, since he brought it up, I asked, 'When did writing begin?'

'When do you think?'

With a shrug, I offered, 'The bible was written a long time ago.'

'Very good. And not too far out. The first writing was called cuneiform, and they used it in Iraq about five and a half thousand years ago. That's the kind of thing you could learn about at university. Not many boys from Whitehead House get to university, Edward. Not any, actually. But I have the highest hopes for you. Off you go, then. For me, for yourself, for your parents and your sister: conquer the world!'

Edward the Conqueror hopped off the chair, said, 'Thank you, Sir,' and, cardboard folder under arm, had some trouble opening the door because the wood was quite heavy.

Some boys in senior school had cameras. Their parents were better off than mine. My camera was imaginary. Here's a photograph of my black, laced shoes – needing polishing – which I took as I lay on my bed with my ankles crossed. My ankles spent a lot of time crossed on the bed, usually when my hands were behind my head and my elbows stuck out like wings. Here's another that looks the same, except my shoes are further from my long trousers. Did I really wear white socks? And here's a photograph of me in the library, in short trousers, bare knees under the desk. Here's another snapped by my brain in the library. I like this one. Standing by a bookshelf, one hand in a pocket, my other hand holding a book by a famous physicist who said the most important thing for people to know is that everything's made of atoms.

Atoms are mostly empty space. Therefore, everything is mostly empty space. Including me. I once told Sophia she consisted of mostly empty space. Gregory, listening in, said, 'Especially her brain,' which I thought cruel.

By the time of this incident, it had become important to me to behave towards other people in the way I wanted them to behave towards me. But in Gregory's case I made an exception. Mother made beef stew for dinner that night, and into Gregory's bowl I crumbled two of Father's max-strength soluble laxatives. Mother caught me doing it. Embarrassed, I apologized, fingers and toes crossed that she wouldn't tell Father. Mother said I shouldn't have done it, because one max-strength laxative would have been plenty, and she'd already crumbled one in. We didn't see much of Gregory that evening, or next morning.

But Feynman and the others came later.

As did Mr Starch, who taught Biology and Environmental Issues – a new subject on the curriculum. Starchy had the unenviable task of enlightening fourteen-year-olds concerning the facts of life. When we heard the facts of life were going to be taught to us, much discussion occurred in dormitories about what they were. Opinion split, almost fifty/fifty, over whether the facts of life involved how women have babies – some boys continued to propose the absurd idea that men stab women in the bottom with their penises – or facts such as that most people get sick at one time or another, and everybody has to die in the end. I came down on the side of the latter. Getting sick in life, and eventually dying, seemed just about as factual as life could get. To my surprise, the boys with the absurd idea were, apart from in the details, correct – we acknowledged this on discovering that the term 'sexual reproduction' related to 'facts of life'.

Starchy was comfortable with pictures of tadpoles in textbooks, but anxious when questioned about the mechanics of sexual reproduction. Much of what we learned about how new humans came into existence came not from understanding the swimming of thousands of doomed tadpoles towards an egg for the purpose of penetration by a last man standing – 'winner takes all', as Mr Starch put it – but from information gleaned from porn – and hard porn if we were lucky – magazines that entered via the caretaker and found their way from dormitory to dormitory. Fights ensued over torn-out glossy pages with their gloss thumbed off. In the dark, at night, beds rattled with rapid hand movement under sheets. My peers introduced me to a new vocabulary, new possibilities . . . new impossibilities, since there were no girls at Whitehead House. Some chaps lusted for Mrs Gordon, the French teacher, while other chaps lusted for other chaps.

I liked Mr Rourke. I found him interesting. He scratched his head and muttered a lot. Chalking on the blackboard, with his back to us, he puzzled everyone by saying things like, 'Twenty into two hundred and seven goes ten times and seven over – that's a nought up there. And twenty into seventy goes three times and ten over – that's a three down there and a ten up there. Add a nought on the end and twenty into a hundred goes five times. Where does the decimal point go? Anybody?' Sometimes he didn't ask any questions, but stuck his chalk behind his ear and left the classroom for no apparent reason. Everybody said he was mad.

I thought of my mind as a camera – a box camera, really, and my memory as a box within the box. The more I thought about it – and my private room afforded me lots of time for thinking about such things – the more the importance of my memory box grew. It grew until it and my mind box were, more or less, indistinguishable. The natural progression of this thought was that 'my' merged with 'memory/mind box' and became 'me'. In short, I was my memory/mind box: a trinity. Three in one.

One mind-box photograph bullied its way to the front of my memory/mind box. This is a photograph of heavy rain on a dormitory window. The window has twelve small panes framed in green-painted wood. The window changes and becomes one pane of glass. Sometimes, when I look, there's no rain. Other times, there's a storm. I'm always in front of the window with my back to the twelve panes and rain, or the one pane and none. I'm in my school pullover and short trousers, or school pullover and long trousers. Sometimes, in the photograph, I've had a haircut. Most times, I need one.

The top of my head is lower than the top of the window frame. The top of my head is higher than the middle panes. I'm comfortable in some versions of the photograph because the radiator under the window works; in other versions, I'm cold because it doesn't.

When I was eight, Mr Brown brought a stuffed alligator to class. When I was nine, I got chicken pox. Nothing so exciting happened in senior school until we had snow one May. Peter McCrew, no wiser as a senior than he had been as a junior, slipped and broke his arm. Word came from our teachers, or from somewhere, that the cold weather was because of a phenomenon called the Greenhouse Effect, or, possibly, Global Warming, which meant the planet was getting hotter. I probably needed my ears syringing.

The senior side of Whitehead House pulsated with acne and angst. It reeked with hormones and stale sweat. I yearned for a spot on my milky face. One or two small ones would have qualified me to join the club, but no spots came. Dark-haired boys shaved with disposable razors while I inspected my chin in the mirror and yearned for fluff. Having been led to believe puberty would put up more of a fight, I thought I might have been suffering from some or other exotic disease: antiadolescencitis.

The puberty war would end with me scarless and pristine. Oh well! I would have made a pathetic veteran anyway. I had lived long enough to be standing at the door to manhood – officially – with a hand on its brass knocker, but I could not enter manhood while I looked like an angel. If only, I speculated, I could lose my virginity. Losing it might corrupt my flesh and make me rough. But did I want to be rough, really? Did I want to be like the others? Did I want to be the kind who gets sweaty and boggle-eyed at the thought of a stiff penis entering a girl's vagina? Would losing self-control please me? To all these: no.

And so I went in the opposite direction (where would I find a girl anyhow?) and became the school monk. The wags called me Brother Pike because I seldom spoke and preferred solitude. Knowing I lived in a place called the Manse, they also thought I was religious. I could have done more to correct their error, but it gave me a vaguely enigmatic identity, and I much preferred to be called the Monk than the Wanker.

In junior school I stayed in one classroom all day, but in senior school I moved to a different classroom every forty minutes to learn a different subject. Each forty-minute teaching session constituted a period, and we had eight periods each day. On a few days each week I got double periods, and eighty minutes spent learning a single subject seemed like eternity – especially Maths. On Friday mornings, I got a double period of Science with Mr Flannigan. Compared to my teachers in junior school, my teachers in senior school were a gruesome lot. I had seen most of them around. Even Father's grim countenance looked healthy and benevolent in comparison to their sickly, cross faces. Mr Flannigan was an exception.

Mr Flannigan had a pinkish red face because of the blood vessels strong drink broke on his nose and cheeks. He was, to his credit, by far the jolliest of my teachers. Flannigan must take credit for my decision, at thirteen years of age, to be a scientist. And not just any old scientist in a white coat, smelling faintly of chemicals; I wanted to be a physicist. And not just any old physicist; I wanted to be a theoretical physicist. I wanted to be a theoretical physicist because I had read about some theoretical physicists speculating that the universe I lived in might be one of many.

I asked Flannigan about this. 'Is our universe the only one, Sir?'

'Good question. Who knows, young Spike. It might be a needle universe in a needle universe haystack. The thing is, this is science, and we need to test our ideas.' He gave a drawn-out shrug like a clown. 'How do we test the needle universe haystack theory?'

How would I know? The science of it interested me less than the mystery.

'If there are other universes, how many are there?'

'Billions!' Flannigan ejaculated, almost literally. 'There might be billions and zillions! But, without a mechanism for testing, how can we know? Are you interested, young Spike? How's your Maths?'

'Slightly better than awful.'

He nodded his head thoughtfully, and said I had to start somewhere. He promised to consult the Maths teacher about extra tuition. I was unsure of how I felt about that, and asked if I could be a theoretical physicist without the Maths.

'Can you eat mince pies through your ears?' he asked.

One day, in my room, I discovered a thin book of poetry that Alf had left behind: *Fifty Great Poems*. As usual, when I looked for Alf I didn't find him. Then I did a bad thing.

I tucked the book away to give to Sophia on my next return to the Manse. Having done so, I did not feel guilty. Something still and deep suggested to me that I had done what Alf intended.

There were only one hundred pages. There were a handful of long poems, but most were short, and I hoped my twin would enjoy them. When I gave her the book, she thanked me, and kissed me, and read poems the way Edgar ate porridge. Poetry wasn't her thing, and after I returned to Whitehead House it never got a mention in any of her letters – which I thought a pity.

13

My Final Year: Blinky's Proposition

I began my final year at Whitehead House in anticipation of an uneventful run through to the exams in May. No such luck. Someone must have had in mind a career for me teaching in junior school – either that or they were short-staffed and I came cheaper than an agency substitute. Whichever: I had no choice. My first assignment was to the classroom of a familiar face.

A decade or so had passed since I, a ragamuffin, first beheld the school siren: Jezebel, otherwise known as Miss Ballard. She had been past her sell-by date then, held together by plaster and paste, bands and straps, and she had in the intervening years passed through her use-by date en route to a date with the great junior school classroom in the sky. She limped along on two walking sticks these days, wore house slippers, and her feet were bandaged up to her shins.

Miss Ballard, still a miss after all these years, had a word in my ear before addressing her class. 'Are you new?'

'No, Miss Ballard. I was in your class many years ago.'

'You'll soon find your way around. We're all friendly here.' She pinched my pullover at the neck and drew us a few inches closer. 'No matter what else you do in life, look after your ankles.'

Then she released me and introduced me to her class.

'Quiet, children . . . Thank you . . . This is Mr . . .'

'Pike,' I said, when she turned to me for help.

'This is Mr Pike. He's from the senior school. Some of you might already know him. Mr Pike is one of our very best students, so listen carefully to what he has to say. And remember, if you work hard, you too might grow up to be as clever as Mr Trout.'

'Pike.'

'Eh?'

'My name's Pike.'

'I know!' She looked at me as if I were stupid. 'Mr Pike is new to Whitehead House, so be nice to him. He's going to read to you from . . . some book or other, while I . . .' She turned from twenty or more bad haircuts behind desks and looked up at me for a clue.

'Assess my reading technique?'

'Reading technique?' Her face crinkled inward like scrunched foil until she looked like a Cyclops. 'You can read, can't you? Why do they want me to assess your technique?'

'I just thought . . .'

'Open your mouth and say out loud what your eyes see on the page; that's technique enough for anybody.' She turned back to her pupils, fidgeting behind desks. Half had sticky mouths after break-time bread and jam. Half had used snotty sleeves of pullovers to wipe their mouths clean. One picked its nose; another sucked its thumb.

'He's going to read while I, like you, relax and enjoy the story. To make it interesting, listen carefully and see if you can tell me, afterwards, who the main character in the story is. Now, before we begin, who can tell me what a character is?'

The nose-picker raised an arm.

'Yes, Gabriel?'

'My daddy says my mummy's a character when she's pissed.'

'Very good, dear. I'll hand you over to Mr Fish now.'

Miss Ballard limped to a chair with arms in the corner, and left me to sweat, eyeballed by wall-to-wall manikins.

I began in the time-honoured way by clearing my throat.

'Good afternoon, everyone. I mean, morning. It's still morning, isn't it?' Oh God! The children of the damned! Stop staring at me!

'Today I'm going to begin reading the first chapter of a very exciting book, and when I've finished I hope you'll continue reading it in your own free time from where I leave off . . . if you can get a copy, that is, from the library . . . which might only have one copy . . . and it might be out. In fact, this might be it. But don't worry, there are lots of other books in the library, and if you can't get a copy of this one, feel free to pick a different book you think you'll like.'

A hand went up.

'Yes?'

'What's a copy?'

'The same book as this, but a different one.'

Another hand went up.

'Yes?'

'If I pick a different book in the library from the story you read will it have the same story in it as the one you read?'

I glanced over a shoulder. Miss Ballard perched on the edge of her seat, staring at me over the bags under her eyes as if her ears had gone the way of her ankles.

'Erm . . . We should move on, I think. The book I'm going to read from is . . .' Miss Ballard had passed it to me when I came into the class, but I hadn't looked at it. I looked now: Samuel Beckett, *More Pricks than Kicks*. 'The book is by a very famous Irish writer who won the Nobel Prize for Literature in . . . quite a few years ago.'

A swarthy-skinned lad raised his hand.

'Yes?'

'I'm called Samuel too.'

'And is your second name Beckett?'

'No. Darisipudi.'

'Okay. Good.' I opened at the beginning and turned the page to start reading. Oh, God! I couldn't even pronounce that! 'It was morning and Bellaquack was stuck in the first of the canti in the moon.'

Oh God . . . 'I'll tell you what,' I said, shutting the book. 'Why don't you tell me your favourite books? Has anybody read *The Lion, the Witch and the Wardrobe*? No? What about *Stig of the Dump*? . . . Has anyone read a book . . . any book?'

My ears rang with silence. I thought the stiff grin on my face might crack it from ear to ear. I glanced at Miss Ballard, but her head had fallen aside, her mouth hung open and her eyes were shut.

'To be honest . . . this is the wrong book, and . . .' And I sweating like a pig. 'I think we should . . .' Should what? Should what? With Ballard asleep, I could walk out. Abandon the sinking ship. Just like that. 'Okay, everyone. Put your arms on the desk and rest your head on your arms. That's right. Now, close your eyes . . .'

The door opened and a boy sauntered in. He might have been in his final year at junior school or first year as a senior, but he was taller and broader than me. I could have reminded him to knock before entering, but he might have taken it badly. 'Mr Pike?' he asked. I acted teacherly by neither replying nor smiling. 'Mr Mulholland wants to see you in his office.'

'Now?'

'I don't know.'

I dismissed the boy with a nod. What power!

'I won't be long,' I told the children – most had raised their heads to see what was going on. 'You can have a sleep or talk if you like, but you must do it quietly. Don't wake Miss Ballard.'

Samuel Darisipudi raised his hand.

'Yes?'

'What if she's dead?'

'You won't be able to wake her if she's dead.'

As I marched along polished corridors to Blinky's office, I thought I should have roused Miss Ballard before leaving the class. I almost turned back; but if she really had died it would be best if someone else discovered her body.

★

Knock-knock

'Who's there?'

I opened the door and looked in. 'Pike, Sir.'

'Pike Sir who?'

'Pike Sir Edward.'

'Come in, Sir Edward. Have a seat. Cigar?'

'Ah, no, Sir. Thanks all the same.'

He sat behind his desk, elbows upon it, smiling, leaning predatorily towards me, hands rubbing together. 'Sherry?'

'No, thanks.'

'You don't mind if I do.' Blinky didn't wait for a reply. The sherry bottle and glass must have been on the floor, because he disappeared under the table for a handful of seconds.

'How's it going?'

'Fine, Sir.'

'Wish I could say the same. They're cutting my budget by fifty per cent. Recession, you know. Hard times.'

'I'm sorry to hear that, Sir.'

'Anyway! My problems aren't yours, are they? The school's problems aren't yours. You'll be on your way soon.'

'Yes, Sir.'

'We've had quite an adventure together you and I, Edward. And now it's almost over. That makes me sad, but all things must end. My work with you, however, is not done yet.'

He drank half his pint glass of sherry in five gulps, expressed his pleasure with an airy exhalation and smiled again.

'What do you mean, Sir?' I asked.

'About what?'

'That your work with me is not done yet.'

'Yes! No! It's not!' He considered more sherry, but decided not yet. 'What is your earliest memory, Edward? If you can't remember your earliest memory, your most potent one will do.'

Umm . . . There were pictures in my mind of me inside Farmer

Barry's lorry . . . Sophia stamping on ice in courtyard potholes . . . Father reading his bible . . . Father giving me the strap . . . church at Christmas. 'I can't think of one, Sir. What's yours?'

'The midwife as soon as I came into the world from my mother's womb. She saw me and screamed. They slap the bottoms of newborns to make them cry, but the midwife slapped my face.'

Having heard that one before, I stared at him. Blinky stared back. I stared at Blinky. Blinky blinked first.

'I've told you mine, now you tell me yours.'

'Days,' I said, having had time to think.

'Days?'

'Days, Sir. No particular day, but a general early memory of a dawning about days. Not nights; you're asleep then.' Blinky had a furrowed forehead. 'Days are of two kinds, that's what dawned on me. There are ordinary days and different days. Different days are ones with names like Christmas Day, birthday, Easter Sunday, and so on. Life is made of days the way sentences are made of words.'

'Are they?'

'There are lots and lots of ordinary days; they're the prepositions, conjunctions and so on. There are fewer proper nouns and verbs; they're the different days. It's the different days that give life its meaning. In the same way, proper nouns and verbs make sentences mean something.'

'Good Lord!'

I fell silent, thinking I'd said too much.

'What makes you think there are more conjunctions and so on than proper nouns and verbs?' While I unknotted a reply, Blinky added, 'Perhaps you mean the same ones are repeated over and over, like the. The cat and the dog went up the hill to fill the pail with the water. That sort of thing. Not more of individually, but individually appearing with greater frequency.' I nodded my head with uncertainty. 'Mmm,' said Blinky. 'Most insightful. Mmm.'

'Burial days are special days,' I said, hoping that saying something, anything, would raise me from my own mess.

'How morbid.'

'My earliest memory is of a burial day. It was before I started school, I think. We buried Granny Hazel. The dog died too, but it wasn't ours. We buried it with the others. We hadn't much space left; the cemetery was overflowing. Not literally. We had reached saturation. There was talk of extending the garden . . .'

'What are you talking about?'

'Our back garden is a cemetery.'

'You mean, there's a cemetery at the back of your house.'

'Yes.'

'What age were you when the cemetery reached saturation?'

'We had to either extend the garden or exhume the bones.'

'Is tending this cemetery part of your father's employment?'

'No. We all do it.'

'Pike?'

'Sir?'

'What age were you when the cemetery reached saturation?'

'Young. That's the thing, you see. At the time, I doubted that anyone could be older than Granny Hazel. I had no idea of myself as unwhole and unstable.'

'Oh, do speak English, Pike!'

'I thought I would always be me, and I would have been horrified that my destiny was to transmogrify into something like Granny Hazel. Ancient. Wrinkled. Smelly. And then I would die and be buried in a hole filled with earth. And things change. Things happen. And that is when I first understood myself as an individual with a separate mind: Granny Hazel's burial day. That's when it began. Sophia and I were wrenched apart. Father tore her from me like a flower from its roots, and the soil that feeds it. That was the day it happened. And it was a dreadful mistake.'

'What, dare I ask, is the precise nature of the dreadful mistake?'

I cleared my throat. 'When my father's mother died, Sophia's grandmother, he asked Sophia to promise that she would never leave home. It was an emotional request in the passion of the moment, meaning never desert the family, or something similar. Being five or six years of age at the time, Sophia thought he meant, quite literally, never leave home. I thought that too, actually . . . And she never did.'

'But someone must have explained to her?'

'But the promise stuck. Sophia deteriorated.' I tapped my head. 'Mother has tried taking her out to Garagh, that kind of thing, but not often. She gets upset and has panic attacks.'

'How ghastly. I had no idea.'

'Somehow she got the idea that she's cursed, and if she breaks her promise to Father she'll, I don't know, die or something.'

'I see,' he said, after rubbing his chin for several seconds.

'Why did you ask, Sir?'

'Why did I ask what?'

'About my most potent memory.'

'Oh! Ah . . . It's . . . I expected the question to lead to quite a different destination from the one it did, to be honest. Mmm. Anyway: you are almost at the end of your Whitehead House journey, Pike. You have travelled a hard but hopefully rewarding road. How have you found it? Are you pleased with what you have achieved?'

'Yes, Sir.'

'Good. We too are pleased. You don't look overly pleased. You look like your goldfish has gone belly-up. Is something wrong?'

'No, Sir.'

'I think you are telling an untruth. Your demeanour lately has not gone unnoticed. Are you worried about your final exams?'

'No, Sir.'

'You don't have much to say for yourself these days.' He awaited a reply. I said nothing. 'I asked you here to enquire what you intend doing when your cosy school days are over. Or do you suppose we'll feed you and provide a roof over your head for the rest of your days?'

'I haven't decided, Sir.'

'I know you've been contemplating spreading your wings. There are arguments for and against pursuing higher education overseas.'

'I mean I haven't decided whether I'm going to go to university.'

'What?' He stood behind his desk and held his hands behind his back. 'Not going to university? Our top pupil? Explain yourself, boy. Don't you want to achieve your potential?'

'I think, Sir, my potential got a hell of a thumping when I happened to be born where I was born with the parents I got.'

He snapped back and made me ashamed. 'Your potential, boy, is what you can achieve regardless of unavoidable disadvantages, not what you can conveniently call upon as an excuse for intellectual lethargy, or the lesser, and in most cases forgivable, crime of failure.'

'I'm needed at home, Sir.'

He was enraged by the notion that anything short of death should stand in the way of a university education. 'Needed? Needed? Fewer constraints and mother's manacles are needs that you imagine, boy. That you use the talent that God has given you; that's an obligation!' His face was red and moist.

'It's Sophia, Sir.'

'Ah!'

'I'm torn between her and . . . My strongest obligation is to her.'

'So that's what's wrong with you!'

'I feel that my moral responsibility . . .'

'Your moral responsibility? One of your moral responsibilities will one day conflict with another of your moral responsibilities. I have a moral responsibility to ensure that my students receive the best education I can provide on a tight budget . . . nay, a laughable one.' He mopped his brow with a handkerchief. 'The question is, Pike: what is to the higher good? What more could you do for your sister than to make her proud of your achievements? How much better could you do than to make something of yourself and by so doing equip yourself to help her in the future? Hmm? Good God, boy, it's either leave your sister now for the space of a few years, or miss the opportunity and spend the rest of your life with one arm up a sheep's bottom, knee-deep in animal clap, married to a farmer's daughter with fat ankles, calloused hands and a wart on her chin.'

I was speechless.

'Is that what you want?'

'No, Sir.' I would have nightmares with my arm up a sheep's bottom. He left me no choice. 'I'll apply for a university place.'

Blinky's eyeballs pierced mine. 'I'm not without contacts in academia, you know, Pike. Would you mind if I put in a good word?'

How unexpectedly decent of him. No one had ever before put a good word in for me. At best they had put in ambivalent words such as precocious. *Illuminati*: that was a good word. There were lots of good words, but nearly all were foreign. University came from Latin, *universitas*: the whole universe.

'A good word would be wonderful. Thank you, Sir.'

'That's settled, then. I'll tell them I've a morbid oddball I'd like off my hands, shall I?'

'I'd be very grateful, Sir.'

Now that the possibility of university was a reality, I had to secure it and make it mine. Blinky put the scaffolding in place. It was my job to climb it. There were exams to pass and pass with the highest grades I could achieve. No one could pack the learning inside my head but me. No one could reinforce it, make it stick, and retrieve it at will on exam day but me. I rolled up my sleeves – often literally – pitched my tent in the library and revised, revised, and revised some more. The librarian said I should take more breaks and get regular exercise. I did. I exercised by turning the pages of textbooks faster.

I studied long hours in my room and in the library. My studies were more than satisfactory as far as my teachers were concerned, but less productive than I, the precocious one, wanted them to be. I lacked study technique. Schools should have a class called 'How to get the best from study'. My study was like pedalling a bicycle in first gear and getting nowhere fast. Having said that, I was a street ahead of anyone else at Whitehead House – except Alf, of course.

One night, I had a strange and unsettling dream. Alf came to my room and kissed me on the lips. We kissed with tongues like giant garden slugs wrestling and evenly matched. The dream was so vivid that, for days, running into weeks, I feared bumping into Alf in case the dream was, in fact, not a dream.

And why was Alf no longer in any of my classes? When I thought about it, he hadn't been for years. Whitehead House had special classes for boys who needed extra help, but Alf would hardly have gone to those. Perhaps Blinky had sent him into a programme of one-to-one tuition for the preposterously gifted. I didn't know of any such programme, but it was all I could think of.

Alf Unleashed

14

Alf and Me in UniversET

A letter from Sophia, in November of my final year at school, warned me that Mother's health was declining. I hardly noticed – self-obsessed, really. Mother had sniffles, I thought – if I thought anything. Concerning the abstract, the theoretical, and matters less immediate than Mother's health, however, I thought a great deal. When Physics became interesting, time became a preoccupation . . . and its heading towards a conclusion.

Time did seem to be concluding . . . and faster than before.

I thought a lot about time. I didn't do it intentionally. I didn't, for example, say to myself in bed at night, or staring from windows at the rain, I'm going to close my eyes and think about time. Instead, thoughts about time happened – like breathing.

My memory is a store for things that happened before the present. The present only exists as a ghost, since it is constantly slipping into the past. Events that will happen later, after the ghostly present – future events – have a space in my memory – a recently vacated one – with their names on. My memory contains countless images different from but like the image of Alf's Adam's apple. I think of these images as photographs because they are still. It seems strange to me that past things – called memories – are almost always still, but future things – called daydreams – are almost always animated. Past things tend to be still because you cannot change the past, and future things tend to be animated because you can create the future. You can create the future by the decisions you make in the fleeting present.

At least, futures have the appearance of being open and arbitrary. But, if you look at the facts, maybe it's all predestined.

'What are you thinking about?' asked Alf, huddled on a corner of my bed, back against the wall, scratching in a notebook while I, hands in pockets, stared through the window.

'Why?' I asked, because it was easier than trying to explain why I was depressed; I could put my finger on twenty reasons and none.

'Your eyebrows: drawn down they are.'

'How do you know? You aren't looking at me.'

'Are you thinking about Sophia, your sister?'

'Yes,' I said, although I hadn't been.

'You're sad for her.'

'I'm perpetually sad for her.'

'Why?'

'Can't you guess? Haven't I told you?' I was sure I'd told him once before. I had a memory of having told him. But it was an animated memory, and so must have been from the future. 'I'm sure I told you.'

'Tell me again.'

'She once made our father a promise that she would never leave the Manse. Our father meant the promise to be that she would never desert our mother and the responsibilities of a daughter. But Sophia took the promise never to leave the Manse literally. And so the promise solidified, hardened in Sophia like cement.'

'She's confined to the Manse.'

'That's what she thinks she promised.'

'What if she breaks her promise?'

I shrugged. 'I think she thinks she'll die.'

He was thoughtful for a while, then replied with a question from a different conversation with a different person in a different time.

'Have you ever been kissed?'

'Beg pardon?' He looked at me, aware that I knew that he knew that I'd heard him correctly. 'Yes. Of course I have been kissed. No. Actually, I haven't . . . Only by Sophia . . . And Mother.'

I was going to ask why he wanted to know, but something stopped me: fear, perhaps. Alf got on with scratching in his notebook. His Adam's apple jumped out from his throat when he swallowed; I'd never seen it doing that before . . . And yet, I had.

That truly happened: the question about a kiss. It was significant enough to ensconce a place in my memory box.

'The boy,' said Alf.

'What?'

Having cast me an annoyed glance, he started over. He was reading from his notebook.

> 'The boy, intensely hands in pockets,
> Glaring t'wards her golden locket
>   Gently on a breast so fair
> Calling him to here from there
>   His sister, far away.'

Obviously, it was about me and Sophia. 'That's nice,' I said.

'It's dreadful,' Alf replied.

'Nonsense. You're a wonderful poet.'

'I'm no poet. I'm only a muse.'

'Amused?'

'Muse. Rhymes with blues.'

'You're a muse.'

'Yes,' he said sadly.

'I see. And who do you muse for? Is that the right way to express what muses do? Or, who's your musee? Musette?'

'Get,' said Alf.

'Get?'

'Get. As in bastard offspring. Not my bastard offspring. It just means human, really. All humans are bastard offsprings.'

'Charming! We humans revere your lot and call you muses, and your lot call us gets. Get a life! Get lost! Who's your get, then?'

He raised his head. I was surprised by his sincerity and anger. Maybe he was just an exceptional actor. 'I can't communicate with him as I should. I can't get through to him.'

Ah! Me? No! Surely . . . Did Alf see himself as my muse? Was I his get? 'Do you mean, you can't get through to me?'

'Not you. God forbid. I'm very fond of my get. Even, dare I admit it, a little bit in love. So it couldn't possibly be you. No. It's my means of transportation. Sometimes the gearstick refuses to go into reverse.'

I laughed. I did! Out loud!

'He has received no communication from me for ages.'

'Oh well,' I said, pathetically and without originality and I wished I'd said nothing. 'No muse is good muse.'

January saw freezing rain, snow, sleet, frosty radiators, frozen pupils and sneezing staff – the ones who weren't off sick. It was wonderful, the best January ever. I'd been back at Whitehead House for one week of my final term at school – which was why it was the best January ever – when Blinky chanced upon me on a corridor.

'Ah! Edward. I've been meaning to have a word. My office.'

He led. I followed.

He asked if I'd like an overnight stay at a university. Blimey! Yes. What for? Orientation, apparently, getting a feel for the place. When? March, prior to getting stuck into exam revision.

I didn't know at the time, but all schools ran these orientation visits for university hopefuls. A master accompanied pupils from each school, but not in my case. Whitehead House couldn't spare a master for just one boy, alone, solo, singular, who already knew how to get on and off a train.

In my excitement I wrote to Sophia and told her about it. I even gave her the university's address and telephone number in case she needed to contact me urgently about anything. When I knew it, I sent another letter with the date of my trip. It was only a one-night stay at a crummy university, but to me it was like exploring the Amazon.

Blinky said I would be an excellent ambassador for Whitehead House. An ambassador. Wow! I hadn't thought of it like that.

March arrived, and the day of my departure for the Northern Island University. I was to go directly there from Whitehead House – no time en route to visit Sophia.

It was six o'clock in the morning, still dark. Unfortunately, everyone was in bed and no one saw me leaving. My ambassadorial overnight bag and I exited the building walking tall – well, tall-er – and swaggered through icy drizzle to the railway station. Plato's *Republic* kept me company on the journey. Feeling sophisticated – although I wasn't – and grown up – although I hadn't – I ate a late breakfast at the railway station in the city across the border before boarding my connection for the university.

Approaching the Northern Island University, my nervousness increased. Plato became an unintelligible blur and I tucked him away in my pocket. The university had its own station, which had so many signposts that getting lost was almost impossible. I arrived in too much of a state to notice anything other than the sky, which was as miserable as the sky down south. I'd to make it to Lindsay Hall by two o'clock, and arrived with two minutes to spare. They had already started – someone's watch was fast or slow. It didn't matter; there were over a hundred boys my age and nobody noticed my entrance.

After the echoing, barely audible introduction by a man with a beard, a girl at a desk ticked my name and assigned me to a room on campus. I walked around some other desks and picked up leaflets advertising clubs and societies because that's what everybody else did. One of these leaflets was the schedule. There wasn't much to it:

16:00–18:00 The library (meet outside main door). I wondered how they would manage a 100-boy tour of the library when, presumably, students would be working in it. *Evening free (dining room closes at 21:00). 9:00–11:00 Lindsay Hall.*

I found my lodgings for the night by following a large group with a few masters to a sort of mini housing estate across car parks and gardens. Actually, it looked less like a mini housing estate than some stacks of mini houses. Each one had an apartment downstairs and another upstairs, and each apartment slept four. My apartment was upstairs, and I was the first to arrive. Except, I wasn't.

'Alf!'

'At your squirrels.' He bowed before me.

'Alf?'

He sang, '. . . a sixpence is better than 'alf a penny,' and did a little dance sideways across the room.

He looked different in jeans and a pullover instead of school uniform. He looked cheerful: most unAlflike.

'What are you doing here?'

'Aren't you pleased to see me, Edward?'

'Yes, but what are you doing here?'

'The same as you.'

'But . . . Have you been drinking? I smell alcohol.'

'There's a bar in the students' union.'

'Blinky didn't tell me you were coming too.'

'I'm here independently, Edward. Whitehead House knows nothing about it. Can you keep my presence a secret?'

'A secret?'

'Can you keep a secret?'

'Yes.'

'Good! You're in, then.'

'In? In what?'

'The secret service. It's a sketch . . . Never mind. I'm glad you're here in one piece and unmolested. Which bed do you want?'

'I . . .'

'I'd prefer this one if it's . . .'

'What do you mean independently? Blinky led me to believe I'd be here alone. I don't . . .'

'You're never alone, dear boy: not with an Alf.'

'What?'

'Look, Edward.' He held my arm and spoke most sincerely. 'I've my own agenda, which may or may not become clear to you one day. For now, our time's our own from six o'clock tonight, and I for one intend to make the most of it. I'm in the mood to let down my hair.'

I looked at his hair, which was much too short to be put up, never mind let down. 'That's not like you.'

'I know,' he said, 'but it's getting near the finale.'

'What is?'

'Everything, really. It's exciting. It's always exciting near the finale. No matter how many times. Exciting, exciting.'

'You've lost me.'

'Don't let lostness trouble your pretty little head. Trust me, I'm an Alf. Moreover, I happen to know there's a seaside town six miles from here and a railway track that goes there. It's called Ruse Bay – not the railway track, the seaside town – and it's where the students go for entertainment and liquid refreshment. Well, their entertainment is liquid refreshment. We can get a train there after the library tour, and a taxi back. What about it?'

'I . . .'

'Good. We should eat first.'

'It's just that I don't have much . . .'

'Money? Don't worry about money. I've plenty of that.'

'How do you know these things, Alf? How did you get here?'

'Where?'

'Here in this room. I didn't see you in Lindsay Hall. You weren't on the train. You just,' I shrugged, 'show up.'

'Let's find the dining room,' said Alf. 'The last thing I want to do is Ruse Bay on an empty stomach.'

What could I do? What could I say? Alf had taken over. To be honest, I was glad to be in the command of someone who seemed to know what he was doing. As for his secretive agenda: Lord knew!

It became clear, during double egg and chips – Alf had moussaka and chips – that my enigmatic friend had in mind an evening of liquid excess. This surprised me greatly because I didn't think him that kind of fellow. He was different, however, away from Whitehead House; an animal let off its leash.

15

The Debacle in Mr Darcy's Arms

Ruse Bay was a pretty fishing port. At least, I think it was pretty. I didn't see much of it because it was night, the rain came down in sheets, and we had to run from pub to pub. Every third door seemed to be the entrance to a pub. By the time we got to Mr Darcy's Arms, we were not wholly sober. We had not been wholly sober for a pub or two. In Mr Darcy's Arms, we decided to remain – in preference to going back outside and drowning, and because a pub quiz would begin at ten o'clock. Alf was ever so excited; he'd never taken part in a pub quiz. Neither had I. Noise more raucous than any I had known previously came from Mr Darcy's Arms that night. Standing room only for new arrivals, a 120-minute happy hour, and much beer on the floor.

Said the quizmaster – more often barman, occasionally DJ, 'Name a palace in Istanbul beginning with the letter T. The official residence of the Ottoman sultans.'

Someone cried, 'The Blue Mosque.'

Someone else: 'The Bosphorus.'

'Not B! T for tits,' corrected the quizmaster. 'Dickheads.'

After much jeering, someone cried, 'Tockpaki Palace.' The quizmaster deemed him either correct or close enough.

'What is the speed of light?'

Alf's voice alone in the silence: 'The speed of light depends on the transmission medium. Light's maximum speed happens in a vacuum.' The quizmaster consulted the sheet of paper with the answer. Alf added, 'One hundred and eighty-six thousand, two hundred and eighty-two point three nine seven miles per second.'

'Give that man a free pint!'

Cheers all round.

'And the next question is for all you footie fans. Who won the final FA Cup of the twentieth century?'

Trick question, thought I; it hadn't yet been played.

Or had it? The pints of beer in Ruse Bay were the kind that made one forget one's decade.

To my left, Alf applied his considerable powers of recall by first holding his forehead in a palm, then knuckling it while repeating, 'Think. Think. Think.' His skull might have thought better without the pummelling. He glanced at me. However, when it came to football, or indeed anything sporty, I was as much use as a keyboard with the vowels missing.

Someone called, 'Blackburn Rovers', which even I thought unlikely. To my knowledge, no team called Blackburn had ever won anything – although I recalled an animated future memory of a radio presenter called Tony Blackburn taking part in a televised game show.

'Wrong,' said the quizmaster. 'Blackburn were the third winners of the premiership title, in the 94/95 season.'

Really? Well done the Rovers! I supped some beer.

Some punters were somewhat drunk, and others were very drunk. A sober competitor would have rifled out Manchester United Liverpool Arsenal Chelsea and stood every chance of being correct. 'Liverpool,' Alf said, desiring that I should affirm it to be so. 'Or Barcelona,' said I, and burped. Meanwhile, other pub quizzers knuckled their heads also. The fellow with the microphone repeated the question, this time in slow motion.

'Liverpool!' called Alf simultaneously with one of our competitors who called, 'Man United.'

'Is the right answer!'

I could tell that Man United won the final FA Cup of the twentieth century by Alf's despair and the delight of our competitors. The quizmaster must have pointed at them.

Unfortunately for us, our competitors took to taunting Alf, who, having purchased a blue and white scarf with a lion sewn on earlier that evening – to keep out the chill as and when, and if, we walked to the station to catch the last train back to campus – had made of himself a Chelsea supporter. We were likely to miss the last train, having consumed more beer than made sense when in training for a pub quiz.

Man U. Man U. Man U. They chanted in unison while jabbing their fingers in our direction. 'Come on you blues,' responded Alf – undoubtedly unwisely – while waving his scarf over his head.

Man U. Man U. Man U.

Alf, blunt-brained: 'Bobby Charlton shags girls!'

I was shocked. Was Alf possessed by a demon? Alf never spoke like a common fellow. Never!

Bobby Charlton went a long way back. I remembered a photograph of him in the encyclopedia. I wondered if Mr Charlton had since died; I wondered what happened to the encyclopedia. Personally, I saw nothing wrong with him shagging girls. I would have been happy to shag girls. There were plenty on campus, but none had spoken to me. My confidence was low. A girl would have to speak to me before I could shag her. Unless she was mute. I'd stand a better chance of a shag if she was blind too. And not particularly fussy.

Man U. Man U. Man U.

'Next question.' The game master tried to restore order.

Man U. Man U. Man U.

Alf, perhaps realizing that he'd inadvertently raised Mr Charlton's street credibility, picked on someone closer to his own age. 'Wayne Rooney fucks chickens.' I knew of a diminutive American actor called Mickey Rooney, but no one called Wayne Rooney. Batman was a Wayne something. The Man U chanters took exception to the suggestion that Mr Rooney fucked chickens. The chorus of Man U chanted still, but quieter.

Cried Alf, 'Imran Troope has only one ball!'

The pointing fingers sagged. Near silence.

'Who?' I asked.

'What year is this?'

'Nineteen . . .'

'Later than that, surely! Sorry. Sorry. I'm getting ahead of myself.' He turned back to the Man U supporters. 'Fergie's gay!'

Alf went too far. I knew all about Fergie: she married Prince Andrew. What she had to do with football, I knew not.

'Language, please,' said the quizmaster, largely unheard.

'Nobby Stiles is a trannie!'

Alf had lost it. I was out of my league. He might happily challenge the entire mob to fisticuffs. If so, although present and his friend, I would have to look away – if not run away. I had my blood to think of. I preferred it on the inside.

'Don't agitate them any more,' I advised.

Collectively: Man U. Man U. Man U.

Alf waved his scarf and sang in classic football supporter rhythm: a spondee followed by an iamb followed by another iamb.

'Geordie Best has shit for brains.'

The chanting and finger-jabbing stopped. One fellow – a skinhead, wearing a Manchester United scarf – stood . . . stood all of six foot five. Another got to his feet. Alf might have been drunk, but he wasn't suicidal. I, keen to avoid death by association, sidled to the exit. 'Arseholes,' I foolishly cried, and hoped the mob, if they heard, misheard it as aerosols.

But, woe! The Red Devils' supporters – four of them now on their feet – heard each syllable of my pre-departure request for calmness and reconciliation. Did the cry really come from my lips? My mouth moved, so it must have: 'Sarah Ferguson has VD!'

Now, upon noticing several Man U supporters looking at each other, I admit to the fear that I had erred. Alf looked at me too.

KILL THEM!

And then we were off!

Oh Lord! The last time I sprinted, years ago, my head and feet began level, but my head soon took the lead and opened a formidable gap before landing on the ground nose first. I rarely trotted unless to get out of the rain. How I kept pace with Alf I'll never know. Fear, perhaps. They were after us: the mob. No need to see it; I heard it. Kill the fuckers and suchlike.

I rebounded off cars. I collided with walls. Where we were going, no one but Alf knew – and even he knew no safe destination. He led. I followed, except when he tripped on broken flagstones and for a second or two I took the lead. Someone behind us threw something, a bottle or a beer glass, that hit the ground ahead of me and smashed. We ran downhill, down Main Street. Our pursuers, as drunk as we were, were no faster. They were locals, unlike us. They worked for a living. They cared not one quark whether everything was made of atoms.

Alf skipped down dangerous steps that led to the seaside. One of our pursuers, the one in front, overtook us on the grass, but thankfully head over heels. He lay there groaning as we overtook him.

The tide was in, and crashed over rocks where sea met sand. The path we ran upon, next to the sea, had no rail, but the drop of several feet could result in a broken ankle or worse. I for one wished to avoid being caught by the mob, bloodied and thrown in. Alas, I realized, grinding to a halt, breathless, it might come to that – for I'd burned all my coal and had run out of steam. Alf too gave up the escape. He turned to face our doom. But they were wearier than us. Three of them remained. They had dropped some distance back, but approached still, panting, wheezing. One of them, near dead with exhaustion, paused to light a cigarette.

Three of them against Alf and me. Three against one!

No more than ten metres separated them from us. None of us had the lungs to curse or engage in last-moment diplomacy. However, a grunt came from Alf as he staggered forward for the fight. The grunt sounded warlike to me, behind him and feeling decidedly unwell. He grunted again, and, with all his might, threw a gallon or two of regurgitated beer at our enemies.

Cheese and onion crisps, a couple of boiled eggs. A cucumber was in there too. Our enemies reeled sideways and back at the stench and power of Alf's fearful ejaculation. Steeled by his example, I followed it, thrusting myself forward until he was behind me. I too let go. I could do nothing else. Beer came up, sewage, my guts. Our enemies, with cries of Oh God and Jesus, toppled backwards, jumping to avoid splashes at their feet. They milled around, as did Alf and I. A lake of undigested chicken skin, diced carrot and beer formed a barrier between us and them. They moaned. They complained. They muttered curses. One of them threw up. A second heaved. Unwilling to cross the steaming reservoir – two of them bent double and unable to attempt it – they retreated to either pick up their fallen comrade or be sick on him. Alf and I gathered ourselves, or what of us remained inside our bodies, and staggered in the opposite direction to . . . somewhere else. A taxi? A sand dune? A hospital?

A taxi, as it happened, thanks to Alf who had some money left. Were it up to me, the dunes would have sufficed. The rain would have come on overnight, and I would have caught pneumonia and died.

By unspoken agreement, and as a consequence of necessity, we missed Lindsay Hall next day.

The first thing that struck me when I woke, apart from sunlight, coldness, shivering and pain, was the image of a cheeseburger. I could almost taste its fattiness, the bland chewiness of its bun and the plasticity of its processed cheese. My tongue and gums were a cocktail of tastes, my molars were mortars awaiting a pestle. Whether

I ate a cheeseburger last night or in my dreams, only Alf might know. I would ask him when he woke – and if.

Deeply and honestly regretting my imbibition, needing to urinate, but lying on in the hope that it would all go away, did nothing to make the suffering stop. I sat on the edge of the bed – and might well have groaned while doing it – and peed into the urinal-shaped Paul Masson wine bottle retained for that purpose. Alf, lying on his stomach with an arm over the edge of his bed, the pillow drooled upon, his face turned towards me across the gap, opened and closed his solitary visible eye.

The drunken sober up with unnatural speed in books. They can do it within a page or two, and sometimes in the space of a paragraph. In real life, however, sobering up can take chapters. My goal was to make sobriety happen as soon as possible. To that end, I placed my head upside down in the sink, my mouth over the tap's opening, turned it on and filled up like a bath. In the meantime, Alf's eye had reopened. He said something that sounded as if he was chewing his pillow at the same time. Returning to the edge of my bed, I asked, 'Did I eat a cheeseburger last night?'

He chewed some more pillow. The initial sounds made no sense, but he concluded with, 'I'm a shit muse.'

The door burst open. A Chinese fellow said, 'Is Edvod Vike he?'

'I'm Edvod Vike.'

Someone at the door wanted me.

I fell downstairs to discover who. And why.

'Hi!' beamed a pretty girl with the whitest teeth I'd ever seen. I'd shag her, given half a chance, when fully recovered and in the mood. 'Are you Edward Pike?' I thought she was a student, but she turned out to be an office worker. The main office had received an urgent phone call from a Mr Barry. He wanted to speak to me.

I knew something was wrong at home, but tried not to speculate – impossible – as the pretty secretary and I walked a quarter mile or more to the building that housed the main office.

'There's a pay phone in your house for making and receiving private calls,' she explained, smiling, chatty, keen to help, and obviously mistaking me for a real student. 'It's a good idea to give the number to your friends, although most people just use their mobiles.' A mobile phone? Me? Mr Lowtec? I made a mental note to buy one. 'You can tell your friends to send mail direct to your accommodation, but who uses snail mail these days?'

Me, I thought, and stopped to vomit at the roadside – there went my chance of a shag.

Farmer Barry probably had a mobile phone. He had left a number that I called from the office. The pretty girl left me to it and went about her business. The phone only rang twice. Farmer Barry answered with a rustic shout that reached up north. 'Hello?'

'This is Edward. Is something wrong?'

He made a noise, as if he wished I'd asked an easier question.

'Here's your mother.'

I listened as Mother took the phone. She breathed into it, dry swallowed, and made a false start. 'What's wrong, Mother?' I asked. I heard Farmer Barry, in the background, telling her to take her time.

'I murdered your father.'

After several seconds, during which my mind scampered around trying to catch a thought, Farmer Barry came back on the line. He had never been a great one with words, but he did exceptionally well this time. 'She didn't murder him, lad. She tried to put him out of his misery, but it didn't work. I advised her against bothering you, but she insisted. There's no need for you to come home, son. You've work to do and I can take care of everything at this end.'

'Did you say she tried to put him out of his misery?'

'That's right. I . . .'

'What do you mean, out of his misery? What misery?'

'That's the thing. You weren't to know. February, it was. He took poorly. We think he had another stroke. It's fairly bad this time. Your mother thought he had picked up something, a virus or the like. A couple of days went by before I knew about it.'

'Was he hospitalized and I didn't even know?'

'No. Your mother didn't want all that fuss. When you have a stroke you need seen to sharpish. It was too late by then.'

'What sort of state's he in?'

'Bad, if the truth be told. It's all but over for him, I'm afraid. But don't worry, your mother will be all right.'

'What happened? I mean, how is he? What did she do?'

'It was an act of mercy. Your mother tried to end his suffering with a pillow. Listen, lad. No one need know. You wouldn't even have known if she hadn't needed to get it off her chest.'

'How did you find out about it?'

'She got it off her chest to me first.'

'What about Sophia?'

'Why would your mother try to murder her?'

'I mean, does she know?'

'Oh, aye. No. I don't know. Yes. Because she supplied the phone number that's this one here we rang. Your father's right as rain. I mean, he isn't dead. He probably thinks he had a bad dream or something. Hard to tell what he thinks.'

'I'll come straight home.'

'No, no, no. No need, and your mother doesn't want you to. You're her pride and joy, learning things at university. You leave everything to me. Why are you at university? I thought you were still at school.'

'I am.'

'Oh. Right.'

Some people are born with good hearts. Farmer Barry was one of those. Expressing my thanks over the phone came more easily than face to face. 'I appreciate everything you've done for us over the years, Mr Barry. I wish I could repay you in some way.'

'You work hard at your studies and make something of yourself, and that'll be repayment aplenty.'

★

Between dry heaving and enduring the hammer in my head, I almost didn't make it back to my room. I was afraid someone in authority would see me, pull up my file on a computer screen, and add to it, at the top, 'Reject application'.

Alf wasn't in our room. I went downstairs and asked the Chinese student if he'd seen Alf.

'Who?'

'Alf? My room-mate?'

'Upstair?' he asked. 'No room-mate. You alone.'

'No,' I said. 'He's so tall. Short hair . . .'

'You dunk last night. Maybe he in pub with bunny labbits and pink elephants. Ha!'

I returned to Whitehead House without Alf. He'd gone. I didn't mention him to Blinky. Nor did I tell him that Father had had another stroke and Mother had tried to kill him. When Blinky asked if North Island University had whetted my appetite, I lied, yes, very much so. In truth, my short university escapade left an unpleasant taste in my mouth: cigarettes, beer and cheeseburger mostly.

16

Mother's Illness

The state of Mother's health only grabbed my attention when a letter from Sophia revealed that she had paid a visit to the doctor. What? Mother never visited the doctor! Something had to be seriously wrong. I asked Sophia what ailed Mother, what the doctor said, and so on. A letter returned the following week: *The doctor wants Mother to go to the hospital for tests.* Sophia didn't say when, where, or anything else that I might have wanted to know, such as what kinds of tests, whether Mother would have to stay overnight in hospital. Nor did she say anything about Father.

I had permission to go home for Christmas and summer holidays only. It was April and I decided to leave Whitehead House and spend Easter week, absent without leave, at home. They could punish me in a manner of their choosing when I returned – assuming someone noticed I was missing. I cared not one jot. On the train, my bravado failed. I decided to spend two nights at the Manse instead of the full week. That way, a much more real possibility existed that no one would notice I'd gone.

As always, Sophia greeted me with hugs. She said Mother was in bed, not long asleep, and I shouldn't disturb her.

I was surprised to find Father on his usual armchair with the bible on his lap. From where I stood, in the doorway, he seemed to be asleep. Turning away, to leave him to it, my foot accidentally hit the door. The impact made a noise much louder than the force of the clash deserved. Father didn't stir. Sophia had approached the room behind me clutching a bunch of daisies. She pulled a face, shook her head, and tapped a finger against her ear. 'Since his latest stroke. He can't go to work.'

'What about money?'

'He's here all day every day,' my twin said mournfully.

'But what about money?'

'The only good thing is he doesn't move or bother me.'

'What are you and Mother doing for money, Sophia?'

'What?'

'If Father isn't working there's no money coming in.'

'Oh, there's still money. Father still gets his pay, only it's called his pension now, Mother says.' Ah. Farmer Barry paid him a pension. 'He prays even louder than ever, but God can't make him out. Neither can I.' She put her daisies in a vase, left it in the hall, and we went to play draughts in the kitchen.

'When are Mother's tests at the hospital?' I asked.

'They said they'll send a letter.' She placed her hands and one counter behind her back. I pointed at her left arm and she revealed her left hand empty. 'Ha-ha. I win first move.'

Now and then, over my years at senior school, I suggested to Sophia that she might venture beyond the boundary at least as far as Bruagh. Not even chocolate from Maud's shop tempted her. 'I'll be here all day tomorrow, Sophia. We should make the most of it. We can take a walk to Bruagh.'

'No we can't. Don't start that again.'

'Why not – if it's dry? You, me and Mother could go together, if she's up to it. She'd like that.'

'Are you nuts? She's too sick.'

'Is she that sick?'

'Any sicker and she'd be dead.'

I took that to be an exaggeration.

'We can go on our own, then.'

'No. Don't keep going on. Mother knows I can't go. She used to coax me all the time. Even to get the train to town. It took ages to get it into her head that I can't.'

'That's news to me.'

Sophia had been here every day for years. Obviously, Mother would at least want to take her shopping occasionally. How self-absorbed I had been to overlook that fact.

'Didn't Mother get fed up and order you to go with her?'

'Huh! She tried.'

'And?'

'I kicked up such a fuss she didn't try for long.'

I stared at the draughts board without making a move, and without seeing a move to make. I should have been here while all this Manse-related drama went on. I should have been here to support Mother and coax Sophia out into the world. The fact that my twin remained in the shadow of her promise was, at least in part, my fault.

'What about the boundary? Did you tell Mother?'

She shrugged. 'What's there to tell?'

'Listen, Sophia: promises, boundaries and curses are child things that adults grow out of. One day, they no longer apply.'

'Mother thought I would grow out of it,' said Sophia, 'but I never did. You can't grow out of a promise, silly.'

'Give me one good reason why not?'

'Because promises are for keeps.' She jumped one of her counters over two of mine – clip-clip on the board – and, landing on the last row, won a crowner – and it wasn't her go.

I placed one of her captured counters on top of the victor.

'I'm going to win again,' she said in sing-song.

'You'll never lose if you keep cheating,' I replied, raising a hand over the board to make my move.

Sophia beat me to it.

Clip-clip on the board. 'I win again! I win again!' cried the little cheat. 'I'm the draughts champion of the universe!' She was indeed. She did a little dance around the kitchen.

It was time to go upstairs and see Mother.

'Where's Gregory?' I asked, standing and stretching my draught-hunched shoulders.

'He was here this morning, but he's taken off. He comes and goes as he pleases. Sometimes he's gone for days.' I knew; she'd already told me about Gregory's comings and goings.

She followed me to the foot of the stairs, but I wanted to be alone with Mother. 'I'd love a cup of tea. Would you make it? I'll come down when it's ready.'

Happily, she trotted off to make tea.

Mother had moved into Granny Hazel's old room to get away from Father.

Half sick in the stomach with the smell of urine, I found Mother half sitting and half lying, half facing me and half facing the window, half sleeping, her upper half hanging off the chair. I had half a mind to turn away and go back downstairs. She supported her head with a spidery hand that hid half her face.

I had never known her to fall asleep on the bedroom chair. A brush, a damp towel, and a bowl of dirty water sat on the dressing table. Sophia had washed and dried her hair that afternoon. I saw the chair-back, and the back of Mother's head hanging askew, in the mirror: thin white strands and pink, liver-spotted scalp. She looked like something spat out of Hell. To my mind's eye came William Blake's engraving depicting Satan's fall.

'Mother?'

She woke slowly. I crouched before her, holding the chair arms at either side of her frail body, unsure whether she recognized me.

'Hello, sleepyhead. I came to visit you.'

She stretched weakly, and as she let out a sigh I smelled the staleness of her breath. Even the most beautiful things are a mirror's reflection away from ugliness. Mother's voice came from her grave.

'Is that you, Edward?'

'Don't tell me you didn't recognize my voice,' I said, taking her spectacles from the table and slipping the stems under her hair and over her ears. 'There. Am I less fuzzy now?' She looked up at me the way cats do, interested but uncomprehending. If I'd dangled a string in front of her face, she might have cocked her head slightly for a second, then tried to clutch it with claws that couldn't fold to make a fist. Her eyes were green. How long had they been green? Maybe it was the light from the window.

'What are you doing home from school? Is it Christmas?'

'I thought I'd pay you all a visit, that's all.'

A panic hit her and, agitated, she struggled so hastily to get up that, involuntarily, I stepped back from the chair. 'Are you okay?' I should have helped her, but feared she might rip my face with her claws. Too weak to get up at the first attempt, she stopped struggling.

'He'll be home soon. I have to make your father's dinner.'

She made a second attempt to get up, but I restrained her.

'It's all right. Father doesn't . . . He's home already and Sophia's seeing to him.' My words were enough to pacify Mother. She relaxed into the chair, breathless after the struggle.

Wondering why Sophia had not cleared away the towel and the bowl of dirty water – she was usually meticulous about that sort of thing – I crossed the room to the dressing table.

'Don't get up yet; I'll be back in a minute.'

'Don't go, Edward. What time is it?'

'About five o'clock.'

Her eyes flickered around the room for something familiar to catch hold of.

'Are the lights from the new motorway bothering you? Sophia said they keep Father awake, tossing, turning and shouting, and that keeps you awake too.' The lights were bright, although they were dots in the distance, and curtains kept them out of the bedroom at night.

'You get used to his shouting,' she said. 'I have to get up. Your father likes his dinner to be ready for the table as soon as he gets home. It isn't easy keeping it hot when he's late. He gets bad-tempered if his dinner isn't ready.' This time, she did not struggle to get up. Her words made no connection with the action they promised. She looked as if she needed to remember something that time had tipped over memory's rim and rendered unreachable.

'And how is Father?' I asked, innocently enough, for something to say. I should have held my tongue.

Mother snapped, 'Your bloody father? Ha!' She said no more.

'I'll take these things away.'

About to kiss her cheek and escape the bedroom, I stayed; her open mouth and held breath froze me.

Mother exhaled. I got the impression that she had given up trying to say whatever it was she wanted to. Instead, she regrouped her hostilities. 'Ask me how your father is? How should I know?' She turned her head aside. Then her head lolled back to me, a sweep that brought her chin down to her chest. Her eyes were lucid on mine.

'I wanted to die and leave you never knowing.'

'Never knowing what?'

'I can't. You should know.'

Did she think me someone else?

'You think you're so clever, don't you? You've always been like that. Always different.' That sounded like me. Then, clearly, she knew Edward stood before her, the twin. 'You think you know it all and that makes you better than everybody else. Well, I'm telling you, you don't know anything. You haven't a clue inside that complicated head of yours.' Pausing to catch her breath and gather her thoughts, she chewed saliva in an off-putting way that I had never seen in her before. Her white eyebrows were down and she looked angry. This woman was pretending to be my mother. I had lost my mother.

'If only you'd been there at the start. I mean the very start: your start. I wasn't always like this, you know, worn down. No man ever looked at me and saw a beauty, I dare say, but whether they were mad or just drunk they saw something they wanted when they looked at me.'

Who, I wondered? She had never known any men. Her life had been here, as much a prisoner as Sophia.

'I remember well the night you were started on your way. I'll never forget it. You could see lightning over the heath, great sheets of it flickering for seconds at a time, flashing globules of lightning through the window and the rain coming down in buckets. It's stamped on my mind. Me looking up at it. I'd been knocked on the floor, you see. That's the memory I have: on the floor looking up. Looking away. On my back. That's how you got started. Pinned to the floor, crying. I screamed, No! No! Stop! Stop? Hah! Expect a man to stop? Your father paying no heed. At least, I think I screamed; I know I wanted to, but at the same time there's Gregory and Edgar upstairs in bed and I didn't want to wake them. How's that for a fool, eh? You're being brutalized and you're afraid to scream in case you wake the babies. Well, maybe I did scream, it's too long ago to remember. And your mother's thinking don't wake the babies at the same time as she's thinking you don't want cuts and scratches or worse; you don't want anything that'll show. So maybe it's best just to take it.'

'What? What are you talking about? Do you mean this is how I . . . how I came to be . . . how I came to be conceived?'

Father raped her? My head spun.

'Your mother's arms flailing like windmills, pummelling his chest without making any difference. Scratching his eyes. What good's that? A woman hasn't the strength. Your father with his dungarees round his ankles and his knees burning on the rug, thrusting and heaving and breathing his rotten breath in my face. Strings of spit hanging from his mouth and me weeping, giving up. Him finishing in me, standing over me, smiling down, pulling up his dungarees, leaving me there on the floor with my knees wide apart and up in the air. And there's you and your sister slithering out of me grey, wet and wrinkled some months later. Jesus Christ, I hated you pair at first. And what does your mother say when her husband wonders why you've a nose, mouth and eyes that are somebody else's, somebody he doesn't know? Yet he's thinking, Maybe this rat-like progeny will grow to look like me, but no one in the family has ears that size.'

'Mother . . .'

'I'm cold.' She tugged at her blanket.

'What have you just told me?'

'I'm cold. Help me get back . . .' She groped and hauled at the chair arms. I helped her get into bed, propped her on a cushion and pulled the bedclothes up to keep her warm. What do I say? I thought. How do I approach this? I had to hurry; she would close her eyes as soon as her head touched the pillow.

'Who is our father?'

'I'm ever so tired.'

'Is Father not our father?'

Her eyes closed.

'Were you raped?'

Nothing.

I left her room and gently closed the door.

What would become of us if Mother died?

I stared at Granny Hazel's weed-covered grave mound. That was dead: put in the ground like a plant, covered but not expected to grow, still, silent, stopped. I didn't know what to make of dead, but thought I should make something of it. I should have had something to say about dead. Dead was like God: mysterious. Why did God give His creatures life only to make them dead? It seemed cruel to me.

17

The Body in the Bog

I kissed Sophia at the broken gate and set off across Hollow Heath to catch the newly scheduled evening train back to school. Without my trusty torch, I would have seen neither my feet nor the track they proceeded along. I helped to make the track with my very own feet. Gregory's and, to a small extent, Sophia's feet helped make it too, and the feet of our parents before we were born. Edgar too, until they took him away. Hard to believe it, but Edgar had become a man: a Superman last I heard, occasionally a Batman, sometimes a Spiderman, and once an Incredible Hulk.

The beam, like a big moon, revealed a lie of the land that looked alien at night. I sometimes sang, but only when alone, and alone I sang now – probably to allay my fear of the dark. Everyone is afraid of the dark, even if just a little. I was a little afraid. 'Moon River, wider than a mile, Father is senile, today.' The rain had stayed away, allowing the mud to freeze. Without Torchy, I would have been wiser to have either left several hours ago or waited until morning.

To keep out the chill I needed to walk quickly. To get off the heath alive I needed to avoid stumbling and knocking myself unconscious. Even if I woke before freezing to death no one would hear my cries for help. The orange-strip boundary partitioned our world from the world outside. Behind me, a solitary small light shone:

Sophia in the kitchen, far away now, boiling milk on a gas ring for her bedtime mug of hot chocolate, and a kettle for her hot water bottle.

Sophia closed the front door after Edward's departure on to Hollow Heath. She stared into the age- and abuse-scarred wood and saw nothing. Her head lowered, like modesty before a superior, like slumbering on her feet, like giving up the struggle. The parents made not a sound. The Manse made not a sound. She sang quietly, slowly, and briefly, to fill some space. 'I fell in to a burning ring of fi-re.'

Sophia raised her head again, but the door had no window for her to see through. She twitched. The dull bronze latch waited there for opening. The wood rested there to thump or kick, or for Sophia to crash her head against. Edward never knew about her thumping her head against the door. If the graze hadn't healed when he returned from school, her hair covered it. Sophia twitched. Why open the door and torture herself with nothing out there, nothing for her. She could run after her twin, catch him and hang on. What kind of madness would he call that? Not one the same as Edgar's. They were sending Edgar home. She'd have three of them to look after then. Edward hadn't a clue. He had a life to get on with . . . beyond the boundary. 'I went down, down, down, and the flames got high-er.'

At last, when she had twitched long enough, twitched and sniffed and hated herself for long enough, Sophia turned round and looked up the stairs. If only Father would hurry up and die! His death would make no difference; living would just, somehow, like a gentle day, be easier. Sophia went up the stairs. She could glide up now, the way Mother used to do.

'And it burned, burned, burned . . .'

Turned the handle softly.

And tiptoed into his room.

*

From the corner of an eye I saw someone else on the heath, off the track, the only track I knew of, and distant to my right, as far from Hollow Wood, perhaps, as from me. I saw a silhouette, which quickly disappeared, leaving me unsure if I had seen a silhouette at all, rather than the movement of long grasses disturbed by a hare, or something caught by a gust of wind, or some trick of shadows. But the wind whispered softly; there had been no gust. And there was nothing to cast a shadow. So why had I seen one?

The silhouette was too far away for Torchy to illuminate. If it had been a person, he or she would have seen my light.

I shone it the other way, to my left, where the heath ended far off at an invisible minor road beyond which were kilometres of fields where cattle grazed in the daytime, weather permitting. That way, the motorway curved away to a point of orange light at the end of the world. Or possibly at the start of it. As a child, I never knew whether the world lay east, west, north or south of the Manse; I only knew that the Manse never seemed to me like part of it.

I returned my attention to where the movement had been. Nothing looked amiss now. Might Edgar have returned sooner than expected? Had he lost his way? Surely he would be escorted home. I cursed Gregory for telling them that Edgar could be safely released into his guardianship.

'Edgar!' I shouted. 'Edgar!'

He might have been playing hide-and-seek.

I noted the approximate location of the movement: close to the right-hand side, as I now turned to approach it, of a crumbling wall – made from the same crumbling stone as the crumbling Manse – that used to be part of a footbridge over a stream that stopped flowing for ever when they built the motorway. The crumbling wall stood two metres high, and radiance from the orange motorway strip made it clearly visible.

I left the track and went to investigate what might have caused whatever I had glimpsed.

Keeping one eye on the wall, and one eye on the ground, and one eye behind me for unwanted surprises, I advanced slowly. I soon realized that I had no idea of how far away from myself and the track the original movement had been. Had it been closer to me than the wall, or further away than the wall? How far should I go? In this direction, I had about a kilometre before the heath ended at the unused access road of a long demolished farmhouse.

I wasn't afraid out there, in the middle of the dark heath with nothing for reassurance but a torch. Granny Hazel and the others meant me no harm. However, after several minutes walking off the track, I began to think myself a victim of the orange light, which had probably played a trick on my senses.

Turning back wasn't an option. Turning back would have left a foolish adventure half complete. If you start something, even if you think it's foolish, you should finish it.

When I had ventured some distance to lumpier ground with wilder undergrowth beyond the wall, I decided that if I had indeed seen something extraordinary, then whatever it was could not have been further from the track than this. Since I'd found nothing extraordinary, I might as well call it a fool's errand and trace my steps back to the track, or take a tangential line to the spot where I customarily exited the heath. Having wasted so much time already – I could have been across the heath by now – I thought I might as well look around my present location.

Feeling like a failed Sherlock Holmes, I trawled the torch's beam across the earth as I moved a dozen or so paces in a direction generally away from the motorway and towards the Manse. As I turned away, something again caught an edge of my vision and I swung the beam back. It had lit a corner of something, and now it illuminated the whole carpet, or large rug, rolled fat, bent in the middle, and dumped here in the heath.

I knew before I touched it. Thrill excited my heart and made it beat dangerously fast. On closer investigation of the roll there could be no doubt to anyone with an imagination, no matter how subdued its vividness, that the floor covering contained, wrapped and trapped within, a body. A human body. One shorn of life. I shone my beam up one end and saw feet in a woman's stiletto shoes. I shone my beam up the other end and saw hair.

Oh, Gregory! What have you done?

Why did I instantly think Gregory was the guilty party? I'd always thought him capable of murder – in a semi-serious-but-not-really kind of way. No one else I'd met in my life was capable of murder . . . with the possible exception of Peter McCrew, and I'd no reason to suspect him. On reflection, I'd no reason to suspect Gregory either. But I did anyway.

Someone had roughly cut the carpet's edges with a knife or scissors. The same knife or scissors that cut the throat or stabbed the heart? Curiosity is a frightful temptress. The carpet had been tied at four places along its length with thick industrial tape. I would need a knife to undo that. Since I didn't have one, and the roll would be easier to manage tied, I left it that way.

Manhandling the bundle seemed like the only option. Digging deep into my shallow reservoir, I did indeed manage it. I got to my knees, wrestled the roll of uncooperative carpet on to a shoulder, struggled to my feet and staggered with it, the torch in my left hand, back towards the track. What am I doing? That was what I asked myself. Why am I getting involved? Moreover, what had I in mind to do with it?

Returning to the Manse in a straight line from where I'd made my discovery, rather than returning to the track, would have been half the distance, but the ground was much more uneven that way and harder to navigate. Having tripped and stumbled my way back to the track, and unable to go further without resting first, I dropped my burden gently – so as not to damage the corpse – and I dropped too, to my knees, gasping great chunks of frozen air into my lungs, my body sticky with sweat, my mind a kaleidoscope. There I recovered for a few minutes before rising to my feet and undoing the recovery.

I discovered that the carpet would not be pushed, which I knew had something to do with Isaac Newton and friction. I had more luck pulling it, but not much more. In the end, I heaved it on to my shoulder again. The track presented no obstacles, and had a slight downward incline towards the Manse. At last, almost in the same physical condition as the corpse in the carpet, I reached my destination. As I had known since finding the carpet and turning back, all the lights were out. Sophia had gone to bed.

I left the carpet on the ground. A little frightened of being caught, a little excited, I felt as a burglar must feel about his crime as I unlocked the back door with my own key. Moving around in the dark, I took a bread knife from a kitchen drawer and returned outside, leaving the back door open because I would have to replace the knife.

Returning to the carpet, I sensed someone watching me from the Manse, an outhouse, or the cemetery. It might be Sophia, or my imagination. Either way, there was nothing to worry about. My watcher might be the White Lady with the fuzzy face, in which case there was still nothing to worry about – but I hoped she didn't show herself anyway. Sophia hadn't mentioned seeing the portentous White Lady with the fuzzy face. She mustn't have seen her. If the White Lady hadn't appeared, it meant that the corpse died somewhere far from the Manse, and was someone unknown to us.

Knife cutting through tape sounded like a car engine revving. The outdoor light on the wall of the Manse cast my own shadow over my work, but I was sawing too feverishly to think about changing my position. The tape parted. I unrolled the carpet. The corpse tumbled out.

There she lay, a woman aged around twenty, well dressed – maybe dressed to go shopping. She had ruffled and knotty blond hair, and looked ghastly by torchlight. There were no violent marks on her that I could see.

The wheelie bin, I thought. No. Put her in an outhouse. Hide her in the coal bunker. The outside toilet – no one ever goes there. No one had been to the outside toilet for years. Taking the corpse by her underarms, I dragged her into the toilet and propped her on the toilet seat.

I returned to Whitehead House and found Alf in my room, cross-legged on my bed, scratching in his notebook. 'What are you doing here?' I asked, surprised to see him because I hadn't seen him for ages, but even more surprised that I was pleased, if not delighted, to see him.

'Sorry,' he said, getting quickly off my bed.

'No. No,' I said, to reassure him that he was welcome. 'Stay where you are. It's just that I didn't expect to see you.'

He stayed in the room, but remained on his feet.

For large chunks of time – whole terms – I didn't see Alf. Did he go home during these spells? Did I simply not notice him? One day, last term or the one before, I went to the dormitory I thought he slept in to find a lost book, which I wondered if he'd borrowed from my room. Alf wasn't there, but neither was a bed assigned to him. When I asked John Morrow, the only boy there at the time, nervously sucking the tail end of a cigarette, if he'd seen Alf, he said, 'Alf who?' and I assumed I'd got the wrong dormitory. I didn't bother searching for him in the others; the book wasn't that important.

I poured Alf a glass of water, and gestured that he take the only chair in the room. We all had a water jug and a tumbler on our bed-side table. Somehow, my room had grown an extra tumbler.

'Where are you from, Alf?' I asked. 'I've always wondered.' Actually, I'd never wondered until that moment.

He tipped his head back, as though consulting the ceiling for an answer, and in that position, with that particular, rainy light coming from the window, seeing that unique angle of fine chin and pale neck, I thought, My God! He looks like me. And Sophia!

He looks like us. Might that be why, so often, I didn't see him?

He was about to speak when the door knocked and a breathless boy opened it before I'd invited him to do so. 'You're in trouble, Pike. Blinky wants you in his office. Now!'

My absence from Whitehead House had not gone unnoticed, of course, but it had been officially noted too late to do anything about it – such as contacting my parents or the constabulary. I like to think that Blinky procrastinated because he trusted me. Whether that is true or not, he opened his mouth and gave me the hair-drier treatment. Was I an idiot? Didn't I know that he was responsible for my welfare?

I told him my reason for going home.

'Mother is very ill. She might die.'

Had I taken leave of my senses? Why didn't I consult him? How was my mother? Did I want more time off?

By the time I got back to my room I'd forgotten about Alf. He'd gone, of course, to wherever Alfs go.

My stature increased in the minds of both pupils and staff. They seemed to have raised me up a notch because of my absence without leave: clearly, word had got around. Blinky made known, to members of staff, the reason for my disappearance, and they, one and all, wished that their children – whether they had any or not – thought highly enough of them to perform such a disobedient but morally admirable action. So far as pupils were concerned, I became some kind of rebel hero.

18

Leaving Whitehead House For Ever

Exam week arrived – Physics, Maths, Chemistry, Psychology, English Language and English Literature. Modern History and Sociology spilled into a second week. After each exam, the teacher of that subject asked how I thought I did. In all of them, I thought I did all right, not great. Language and Literature were probably my strongest, Maths and Chemistry my weakest. As for Physics, my favourite subject – I feared I let myself down. The areas that I revised most did not show on the exam paper. There's an element of luck in passing exams. When I'd finished them I was relieved, of course, but also deflated like a balloon. No one patted my back, no one celebrated; it was anticlimactic – like life itself, I suppose.

A month remained before school officially ended. Boys like me, whose exams were over, loitered unemployed. No reason remained for my presence. I simply packed my suitcase and thought about leaving. I sat on my suitcase and chanted, to the tune of 'Jingle Bells', for the courage to do it: 'Going home, going home, going home today. Oh what fun to ride a train back home down Bruagh way.'

Someone knocked on the door to my room. 'Come in,' I called, and Alf did, armed with a bottle of wine and a corkscrew. I'd forgotten about Alf. Now I felt guilty for intending to leave without saying goodbye to him.

'Hello, Alf. I was just about to look for you to say goodbye. I've decided to clear off early.'

'I thought you might,' he said, uncorking and pouring us a glass each, though it was a bit early in the morning, 'which is why I want to propose a toast.' He handed me my glass and raised his. 'To you, Edward, my best friend. May God bless you and all who sail in you.'

He didn't pour a second glass. Before leaving, he said, 'Can I ask a huge favour, Edward?'

'You can ask.'

'I'd love to visit you at the Manse and meet Sophia. You've talked so much about her.'

I was taken aback. With both parents in poor health, Edgar coming home sometime soon, and Gregory on the prowl, I really didn't want anyone visiting the Manse, not even harmless Alf.

'Of course,' I said, because I could not, realistically, say anything else. 'Sophia never gets to meet new people. I'm sure she'd love to meet you.'

'I'll show up, then, whenever I can.'

'Yes,' I said, still reeling somewhat – as much as reeling is possible while sitting on a suitcase.

'It isn't goodbye, then.' He dashed to the door, left my room, stuck his head back in, said, 'Good! See you later,' and vanished.

A visitor at the Manse: I needed a second glass of wine. I would probably fall asleep on the train, but what the heck!

As I sipped wine, standing at the window, I became agitated by not knowing when Alf would show up. Possibly he didn't know either. A specific date would have been better. If that wasn't possible, a general idea would do, such as before the end of August. I'd be starting university in October, if I passed my exams and got in, and I didn't want Alf to visit in September because . . . because I just didn't. July would be best, early July; that way Alf's visit would be over with quickly and I could stop worrying about it. And did he mean that he wanted to stay for a day or two? I didn't know that either. Suddenly,

I was very unhappy with the arrangements for Alf's visit to the Manse – or lack of them.

I was just about to hurry off in search of him – I didn't even know for sure which dormitory was his, since he hadn't been in any on the few times I'd looked over the years – when I saw him down below from my window, crossing the quadrangle. I sped after him, ran along the corridor and tripped down the stairs. The several boys I passed stood rigid, stunned, unable to believe their eyes. Was that Pike running?

I spun round the quadrangle looking for him. Someone laughed. 'What's wrong, Pike? Is your arse on fire?' Realizing that I was indeed panicking, or seeming to panic, and without good reason, I made an effort to stop spinning. Noticing Alf, however, or what looked like one of his legs following the rest of him into the main junior school building, I set off in pursuit as rapidly as my legs would carry me.

Indoors, I walked swiftly; running wasn't allowed. The leg had definitely belonged to Alf. There he went, turning corners into new corridors some distance ahead of me. I couldn't call him without some teacher coming down on me and telling me to be quiet, and that would only lead to further delay. Now and then, I trotted a little.

Alf went to the junior changing room, where I, so long ago, used to undress for sports, dreading the hour of physical torture to come.

I had Alf now, trapped. What his business might be in the junior changing room, I had no idea.

Inside, the junior changing room echoed with rain, steam and squeaky, hollow voices. There was Alf, his back to me, opening one of the grey steel lockers and . . . and stepping into it? Good grief! He didn't close the door behind him. I stepped up to the locker. Tentatively, I peeked round the door and looked inside.

Nothing. Not clothing. Not sports equipment. Not Alf. Nothing.

There was nothing to see except the inside of a locker, which looked like . . . a locker's inside. I almost went in, as Alf had done.

As Alf could not possibly have done, since he wasn't there.

The hollow, squeaky voices of two dozen junior boys were upon me. Out from the communal shower they'd come, wet and pink, bare-bottomed, bald-pubed, twenty-four little cocks running towel-ward like an army of snails without their shells. And the junior sports master, whom I didn't know – fully clothed, of course.

He viewed me with suspicion. 'Can I help you?'

Quick thinking saved the day.

'Recently finished my final exams, Sir. I'll be leaving soon. Just having a look around the old place. Nostalgia.'

He asked how I'd enjoyed my time at Whitehead House. We chatted for a good ten minutes while the semi-clothed juniors whipped each other with towels. Then he wished me good luck with my exam results and I left the changing rooms, left the junior school – Alfless.

I could have hidden in my cupboard like a mouse until lunchtime, and travelled back to the Manse on a later train. Every lunchtime, except when there were deluges of Noah's Ark proportions, the quadrangle teemed with sweaty, screaming, fighting boys. They were camouflage. I could have crept in the shadows of walls, then dashed through the throng. Feeling at least six inches taller than usual, I did neither. Instead, at twenty past ten, in time for the ten thirty-five train, I strode boldly across the centre of the empty quadrangle, suitcase in hand, as though I owned the place. I passed through the gates of Whitehead House half expecting a hand on my collar to drag me back inside: 'Where do you thing you're going, boy?' 'Home,' I would say, 'and there's diddly-squat you can do about it', or 'so there!' or 'so put that in your pipe and smoke it'.

Crossing the quadrangle, I resisted the temptation to look behind me. No masterly hand fell on my shoulder. I listened, but no masterly voice called my name. Blinky, however, watched my exit from his window. Boys watched from other windows, wishing they were as brave as me. I saw them, and Blinky – his face inscrutable – through the eyes in the back of my head. How eerily strange leaving Whitehead House felt – and leaving without official sanction – knowing I would not be going back, ever.

Outside the gate, my limbs loosened but my confidence decreased. I walked faster. As I approached the railway station, only the awkward suitcase banging against my leg prevented me from jogging. The train had arrived early. It waited for me and my grubby student's ticket. I climbed on board, took a seat and avoided eye contact with anyone on the other side of the window. 'If you're up there, God,' I muttered in prayer, 'make this bloody train move . . . Move. Move.'

But the train did not.

I grew hot and sweaty all over as my heart tried to escape through my ribs. What could I do but sit and wait?

An era had ended. It had lasted for twelve years – a quite lengthy era when measured against a human lifetime. Now, as I sat in the train, waiting for its journey to begin, the era seemed much less long, significantly shorter: from boy to man in the wink of a rusty eye. Would I never again suck one of Blinky's boiled sweets? I almost shed a tear for my cupboard-sized room and the smell of the library. I should at least have shaken Blinky's hand. After all he had done for me, Blinky would think me an ungrateful little escapee.

All on board! A whistle blew. Doors thudded shut. The station guard yelped an instruction to the driver. Steel wheels moved and jolted me back in my seat. The grip of the ghost-hand on my collar slipped, held on by a finger. As the speed increased, the ghost-finger let go. I breathed. And I might not have done that since leaving my room.

I felt sick as I watched the train leave Bruagh Halt, me on the platform, no longer a schoolboy. I went to Maud's shop because I didn't feel like walking home – not yet. At the door, I hesitated. The card in my pocket identified me as a student and qualified me for free rail travel; other than that, and a ballpoint pen, my pockets were empty. I had not even one small coin with which to buy Sophia a celebratory bar of chocolate.

Through the unwashed window, I saw Maud arranging dusty tins on an equally dusty shelf. She looked as old as ever but no older than a decade ago. Maud went on, and on, doing the same tasks daily – like everyone else, really. She existed to be there if somebody needed century-old baked beans or damp matches. If nobody needed anything, she might as well become extinct. I had nothing to buy from her, and nothing to say to her, nothing that would lift her, help her, enlighten or please her. Maud, the post office shopkeeper. Maud in her blue overall: there if needed.

Leslie had disappeared off the radar when I was about seven or eitht.

Did Leslie live with his mother?

Had he returned, the prodigal son, and been forgiven for whatever peculiar thing he did, or continued to do? Had Maud, like Victor Frankenstein, been damned by inescapable love for her creation? *Her* creation? What of a father? Did Leslie have one? Was Maud a virgin and Leslie Jesus returned? Did Leslie Christ drink wine and break bread upstairs with twelve others? Did Maud wash his feet with her hair? Did Alf attend?

As I turned away from the window: 'Hello, Edward.' Farmer Barry, an elbow poking out from the window of his lorry. I returned his hello. 'I thought you were at school.'

'My exams are finished.'

'You came home early, then?'

'There's no point staying.'

'No use hanging around with two arms dangling when there's work to do elsewhere.' He laughed. 'I used to say that to your old man. I'd bark at him and he'd call me a slave-driver behind my back. Deep down it was all in good fun, and he knew that . . . You'll be off to university next, then, according to your mother.'

'If I pass my exams.'

'Oh, you'll pass all right. Jump in and I'll drive you home.'

I did and he did.

'I see that brother of yours has bought himself a motorbike. It's not a big bike, just a wee moped. Fifty cc,' said Farmer Barry as we wound along the Road.

My first thought was: where did Gregory get the money? 'He must have got a job,' I said. 'I can't picture Gregory on a motorbike.'

'Spends his time in Maud's, upstairs.'

Upstairs in Maud's used to be a kind of social club for local husbands and wives. As the years passed, husbands lost wives and wives lost husbands. These days, upstairs in Maud's was a gathering place for drinking poteen and smoking whatever kind of weed they grew.

'I wonder what happened to Maud's son, Leslie,' I said, much more interested in his life than my brother's death by motorbike.

'Strange one, him.'

Farmer Barry did a U-turn at the obelisk, the leaning tower of toilet, before stopping to let me out. 'Here, Edward.' He dipped his hand in a pocket and pulled out a fat wad of notes without so much as an elastic band around them. He separated the wad and forced half on me. 'Buy yourself and Sophia something for a treat. There might be some left over to buy your mother a wee treat too.'

Embarrassed, I thanked him and climbed out of his lorry. I raised a hand: a farewell wave, or a watery Fascist salute. Farmer Barry's lorry, and his elbow protruding from the window, returned the way they came.

I remembered the body in the bog and was amazed that I could have forgotten. I went to our old outdoor toilet to check that nothing had been disturbed. To my horror, an unfastened lock hung from the latch. Indeed, rust made fastening the lock impossible. Had I hung it there? I had no recollection of having done so. I removed the lock, opened the door and looked inside. What a stench! It would have been much worse had our weather been less icy. The body sat exactly where I'd left it. It hadn't decomposed much thanks to the temperature. I closed the door, replaced the lock, and went to greet Sophia while racking my brain to remember having placed the lock through the latch.

Fresh home for ever, I entered the kitchen and was surprised to find Mother washing dishes at the sink, and Sophia at the table ankle deep in spilled flour, both hands a disgrace of lumpy dough – too much water. She beamed when she saw me and ran at me with doughy hands.

Mother looked terrible, like a ghost, as bad as the body in the bog, and she looked at me as though I were a ghost too. 'What are you doing here?' she asked weakly.

Sophia hugged my neck. Now my coat needed a scrub.

'My exams are over, so I came home. I've finished with Whitehead House for ever.'

Sophia gave a cheer, wiped dough off her hands, jumped on my back, smacked me and ordered me to giddy-up.

'I suppose I'd best put on the kettle,' said Mother.

I knew I shouldn't ask Sophia. I shouldn't mention the outdoor toilet. I shouldn't draw her attention to it.

Unable to resist, I asked her anyhow.

'The lock on the old toilet door's rusty. I must take a file to it so it'll shut properly. We never had a lock on the outside latch, did we? Do you know anything about it?'

'I forgot to tell you in one of my letters,' she said. 'The wind blew the door open one day, and when I went to shut it there was a dead body inside.'

'Good heavens!'

'I know.'

'What did you do?'

'Nothing. Well, I didn't know who it belonged to. It wasn't one of ours. So I got the lock. I know it doesn't lock, but at least it holds the door shut . . . We're nearly out of jam. Remind me to add jam to Farmer Barry's shopping list.'

'But what about the body?' I asked.

Sophia shrugged. 'If whoever owns it wants it, they'll have to come and get it.'

'How do you suppose it got there?'

'That's what I wondered.'

'And?'

'Well . . . Tennyson got here . . . What's to stop anybody just walking down the Lane and . . . I don't know.'

'Maybe she came here to ask directions. Before she got to the back door, she needed to go. She saw the toilet, went in, and had a heart attack or something while she was sitting there.'

'Probably something like that,' said Sophia.

My twin entertained me that evening by reciting *The Lady of Shalott* – badly – which she had memorized from Alf's poetry book – partly and imperfectly. Still, it was an accomplishment and I told her I was proud of her. Actually, she looked silly trying to recite a poem in the living room while clip-clopping along on an imaginary horse. Maybe she was supposed to be Sir Lancelot. Maybe clip-clopping along helped her with the poem's rhythm.

> 'There she weaves by night and day
> A magic web with colours gay.
> She has heard a whisper say,
> A curse is on her if she stay
> To look down to Camelot.'

I had neither read the poem nor heard it performed. The word 'curse' made me pay greater attention.

'She knows not what the curse may be
And so she weaveth steadily,
And little other care hath she,
The Lady of Shalott.'

My twin's horse stalled at a jump; she had forgotten what came next. I clapped my hands, said her recital deserved a pot of tea, and escaped to make one.

19

The Cellar

I quickly grew bored at the Manse. Sophia bored me. There! I wrote it! I wrote it because I thought it. Thinking it, I wanted to bite my tongue hard. I hated myself. But, God help us, she bored me. Sophia loved having me at home, and I hid my boredom from her. Hiding it from Mother proved harder. I saw the tiredness in Mother's eyes. 'You'll be off to university soon,' she said – at least once each day – and I couldn't tell whether she said it to reassure me that my boredom would end, or because she felt sorry for herself. Having me hanging around the Manse was preferable to having just Sophia for company; Father was none, and Gregory was seldom there.

A week or ten went by like treacle advancing along a gentle slope. On most days, no matter whether rain or mere cloud ruled the sky, I set out for an afternoon stroll to kill time. Although I didn't like the taste of cigarettes, I smoked one or two along the way because I had nothing better to do. Gregory returned to the Manse once, slept off a poteen hangover acquired at Maud's, and went away again. Father never rose from bed – he couldn't. Mother was heading that way too.

We heard the stairs creaking: Mother coming down in her best coat and shoes, wearing a headscarf despite the sun that day and only a light breeze. I packed counters and board into the draughts box.

Mother had changed since her illness. Her eyes were darker and her face more pinched. Her lips were all but invisible. With crow's feet extending from the sides of her eyes like branches from a branchy tree, and skin the colour of winter, I saw an old woman before me. When she filled the kettle with water, she lifted it with her right hand, but held that wrist with her left hand, adding strength she never needed to add when I was a boy. When she drank tea from a mug, as when buttering toast, her hand shivered ever so slightly.

Yet here she was, getting on with making it to tomorrow, as if nothing had changed. She gave us the usual instructions as if we were still five years old: don't remove the fireguard, don't touch the cooker, and don't go outside without a coat. I said to her, 'Don't pretend to go shopping if you're really sneaking off for a crafty cigarette behind an outhouse,' and she scrunched up her face at me as though I was out of my head.

Sophia bent down a little to hug her goodbye, and I bent down a little lower than Sophia. Some time when we were not paying attention, Sophia's shins stopped growing while the expansion of mine continued. For all I knew they were still at it.

We waved to Mother from the back door. She crossed the courtyard and passed the sealed and secured dry toilet. We watched as her headscarf vanished under greenery bordering the Lane, then reappeared for a while and vanished again. When she was far enough away for us to be sure that she would not return because she had forgotten something – usually her umbrella in case it rained, occasionally her purse – I said, 'Action stations!'

Sophia stood to attention.

'Private Pike, are you ready?'

She saluted. 'Yes, sir.'

'Into the kitchen,' I barked. 'Go! Go!' Soldier-like, she quick-marched round the floor while pointing out, correctly as it happened, that she was already in the kitchen.

'Halt!' She halted to attention. 'Assume position at table.' She did so, standing to attention at a shorter side. 'One end of the table, take in hand! The other end of the table, me in hand take! Table, lift and move aside.'

We moved the table aside.

We removed the mat that covered the trapdoor. Its foam underside tore at the floor underneath. Neither Mother nor Sophia had mopped under there for years. The mat smelled of bacon fat, gravy and other spillages. 'Yuck,' said Sophia with contorted face, and wiped the unidentifiable stickiness from her fingers on to her dress.

The padlock fitted into the centre of the latch – an iron loop, which in turn rested in a groove. That accounted for why the mat had no tell-tale bulge.

I knew where Father kept the key. He kept rusty keys that opened boxes and trunks lost to time, and thus were useless, in an equally rusty biscuit tin in the bottom drawer beside the sink. There were several keys of the type that fitted the padlock; the first of these I tried, and the least rusted, opened it.

'Are you ready?' I asked my excited sister. 'It's heavy. When I lift it, put this in the gap.' I gave her a large paintbrush, the kind used on walls. I'd found it in the bottom drawer with the rusty tin. With hairs stuck as one and solid as wood, it would never paint again. Kneeling above the trapdoor, near the iron loop, I tried to open the door using only one hand but could not raise it high enough. I tried raising it using both hands, standing awkwardly, but that was worse. I went back to using one hand, the other pushing against the floor, but still could not raise the door high enough for Sophia to slip in the handle of the paintbrush. It wasn't just the weight. The hinges were rusted and in need of oil. The door was probably glued to the floor with dead spiders and mealtime spillages. While resting, I decided that I needed a better idea; using the current method of brute force – not that I had ever been brutish – would get me nowhere. I required leverage.

'Now . . . Phase two of operation Raise the Floor requires the deployment of elevating technology, which, although functionality is a prerequisite, need not be mechanically sophisticated.'

'What?'

'We need the right tool for the job.'

Sophia followed me outside to an outhouse. 'What's the right tool for the job? Mother said we're supposed to put on our coats.'

'We need a rope.' The string in the kitchen drawer would be too weak to raise the trapdoor, and would undoubtedly slice into my soft hands like a cheese wire cutting through butter – or cheese, although I seldom ate cheese because it was too expensive for both Whitehead House and my parents. 'This'll do.' The rope was almost black and had been looped on a nail on the wall for years.

'What's that for?' asked Sophia.

'I'm going to tie you to a chair and tickle your feet.' I chased her laughing across the courtyard and into the kitchen.

Sophia watched as I upended the table so it rested on one of its narrower sides a few feet from the trapdoor's latch. Cowboys could have taken cover behind the table and shot round the sides at Indians. I needed something thicker than the paintbrush to slip between the table-top's narrow edge and the floor – to feed the rope through. Mother's rolling pin did the job.

'Now,' I said. 'Here's what you've to do. Stand here.' I placed Sophia behind the table like a cowboy.

'What do I do?'

'I'll tell you in a minute.' I tied one end of the rope to the iron ring and tugged it tight enough. 'I'm going to pass the rope over the table . . . like so . . . down the other side and back under it . . . and go over here.' The rope formed a triangle from the iron ring, over and under the table, and back to the iron ring. I took the rope beyond the trapdoor and stood clear of it.

'I'm going to open the door by pulling this rope. Your job is to put your weight against the table and stop it moving towards me. It'll move a bit, but don't worry; do your best.' I pulled the rope until it became taut, then pulled harder to test how much effort I would need to make . . . a lot. Mostly, I worried that Sophia would be unable to stop the table from sliding towards me.

Seven feet, the height of the table upended, was the rope's highest point, and the greatest leverage I could construct. The rope cut roughly a forty-five degree angle to the iron ring latch.

'Are you ready?' I asked Sophia.

'Ready steady.'

'Lean more weight against the table as you need to.'

At first I thought I had made the trapdoor harder to open rather than easier. As I used muscles previously long-term unemployed, heaving like a tug-of-war champion, the trapdoor began to open. Sophia pushed against the table and prevented it from sliding towards me. The uneven floor tiles helped, immovable obstacles to the table's upended legs. When the door had opened several inches, I asked Sophia to come and hold the rope while I secured the openness by jamming the paintbrush in the gap. Then we rested and admired our achievement.

'It's only opened an inch,' said Sophia. 'We'll never squeeze in there.' I think she was joking.

An inch gap was enough for me to get my fingers in and, with all my modest might, raise the trapdoor fully open, disturbing gunk and rust, then insert a wooden bar that fitted into slots for the purpose of keeping it open.

'It's dark.' She looked in, poised to recoil if something otherworldly flew out. Cobwebby too, I observed. 'There are steps.' Stone ones, but I couldn't see the bottom. We needed a torch. 'We need a torch.' I retrieved Torchy. I felt better about descending now that I could see the bottom of the steps. The cellar looked innocuous enough.

'Watch your step,' I said. 'There's no rail.'

'You go first,' she said.

'How brave of you.'

'I'm not brave. You're a man. I'm only a girl.'

Her self-diminution made me sad.

Standing on the brink, shining the torch into the cellar, I felt a chill run through me, a chill I experienced long ago, although I could not remember when or where. I foresaw tragedy, or disaster, or an extension of my sorrow, and possibly all three; the future 'thing' had no name. Nor did I know where or when in the future it would reveal itself.

'I don't know about this.'

Sophia's voice nudged me forward. One hand holding the torch, one on the wall for balance, I stepped over the brink on to the first step down, then another step down, and another. I could not hear Sophia behind me, but I knew she was there.

The beam of light illuminated damp brickwork, old china spilling out of boxes, sealed crates, a bicycle frame and – the beam stopped – three empty coffins side by side and upright so their future occupants might walk out if they wished. Beside the coffins were three coffin lids stacked against each other.

Glancing over my shoulder, I saw Sophia behind me. She too had seen the coffins. More cautiously, we continued to the bottom of the steps and the cellar floor of dead insects, puddles, moss and concrete. We approached the open coffins as if Egyptian mummies slept inside awaiting reawakening. The soft lining of the first coffin, once pure white, was soiled. There were stains where a head would rest, and others near the centre, which might have been blood, urine, or anything. The other two coffins had similar stains, but lighter.

A loud, echoing noise made my skeleton momentarily flee my flesh – actually, it had been Sophia saying, 'Who'. My skeleton shot back into my body before it collapsed, jellylike. She had almost killed me with a solitary syllable. She completed her question: '. . . are those for?'

'I don't know.' I swallowed hard, put a finger to my lips and asked her to be quieter. The light beam explored elsewhere in the cellar, which was bigger than the kitchen with three supporting pillars. I reassured Sophia, and myself, that we had nothing to be afraid of down here.

'It's where Father stored all the junk after we got the indoor toilet.' It never occurred to me to wonder where all the junk went. I must have assumed it flew out the window and got lost in one of the outhouses.

'But the cellar has always been here. Why not put the junk down here in the first place?' Not for the first time in recent weeks, her train of thought derailed me. Rather than ask her to explain, I moved on.

'Junk ends up everywhere. No one knows how it gets where it does. Corners and dark rooms have a magnetic pull that attracts it.' I remembered Mother telling me I was a dirt magnet.

'Look at that!' The beam had gone by a trunk made more splendid than the rest by its brass studs. Sophia relieved me of the torch and went to investigate.

The trunk was unlocked. The lid needed two hands before it creaked open. I saw white material adorned with lace. Sophia knew what we were looking at straight away. She made no sound, but I heard her inward sigh, or moan, or whatever took her breath away. As I looked at her astonished, open-mouthed face, she passed the torch back to me. I shone it on to the contents of the chest. I touched the material, caressed it between my fingers.

Mother's wedding dress.

Sophia removed it reverently from its container. There were other items of clothing under it, but the wedding dress occupied most of the space. She held it by the shoulders straight-armed in front of her. The dress looked pure white by a trick of the torchlight. The cellar smelled musty and Mother's wedding dress no better, but that mattered not a jot to Sophia. How could she resist putting it on? She and Mother were similar in size.

When she dropped the dress over the trunk, unceremonious with sudden excitement, I took a few steps back but kept the torch beam on her. I had no time to look away, but if I had had time to turn towards the wall I would have rejected the idea and watched Sophia anyway.

Sophia crossed her arms, and grabbing both shoulders of her own drab Cinderella dress she tugged it over her head. I last saw her like that when we were much younger and shared a room. Her ribs stuck out. I do not know why she bothered wearing a bra; she did not need one. Her pants were shapeless because she had no flesh to fill them. Her legs were not much fatter than my upper arms. Did Mother no longer feed her? Had Sophia stopped feeding herself? During those seconds, as she wrestled Mother's wedding dress over her head and wriggled it down over the rest of her, I thought that I might know the tragedy, the disaster, if I focused my mind to reveal it. My penis stirred and I felt like running away and buckling at the knees at the same time. Run away or buckle? I did neither.

Sophia, in Mother's wedding dress, smiled at me.

Beauty warped. Grotesque, hideous, my twin became no longer my twin, but something truly in the nature of a curse. In that moment, I knew that she would never marry, and, worse, if ever she loved, and found her love requited, disaster would come of it. God never made Sophia for happiness.

Did she want me to tell her about her beauty? She would not want to hear what I had to say, for her beauty was a wrong beauty, like a sweet cake that makes you sick, like a beautiful sea that you drown in. I used to be able to read her thoughts. She used to know mine. No longer. Did she want me to say something stupid like 'Who's the lucky groom'?

She sang a song she must have heard Mother singing. 'I'm getting married in the morning. Ding dong the bells are gonna chime.'

'Take it off,' I scolded her.

Sophia's smile collapsed.

I raised my voice. 'Take it off!'

'Why?'

'Take it off!' I shouted. 'Just take it off.'

Sophia's lips began to tremble when I shouted at her to take off Mother's wedding dress. She bunched the skirt in both fists and pulled it inside out, over the bodice and over her head. After a temperamental struggle, her face reappeared red and wet. She flung the dress to the floor, kicked it, grabbed her ordinary clothing and raced up the stairs, out from the cellar, in her underwear.

I raged silently, impotently, in the cellar, more than merely angry with Father for making Sophia promise never to leave the Manse. I raged at Mother for failing to insist that Sophia went to school. I hated the world for its cruelty, and I wanted to die. Most of all, I raged at myself for having raised my voice and shouted at her.

I gathered up the wedding dress and returned it to the chest. As for the coffins, I gave them one last look before I too raced up the stairs. Whichever coffin they intended for me, I hoped it had a pillow.

20

The Seduction

We stayed out of each other's way, and Sophia and I had never done that before. I heard her in the bedroom across the corridor, probably giving Father his afternoon cup of tea and a biscuit. Mother came home and made dinner. She gave Father his first, upstairs, and spent some time up there seeing to his other needs. When she served dinner for the three of us on the kitchen table, Sophia and I could avoid each other no more. No one spoke. If Mother detected tension between us, she held her tongue about it. Maybe she suspected that we had been up to something in her absence, and maybe she no longer had enough energy to care.

After dinner, I went to my room and brooded. As I brooded, in my mind I saw Sophia in her underwear.

I'd had erections. Of course I'd had them – I was in my late teens, for goodness' sake! We had girls from girls' schools in absurdly short gym skirts flapping about on sports days. Sex, however, which I understood to be a sticky and breathless affair, seemed a bit like rugby but without any clothes. Body-contact and balls were involved in both. Not the sort of endeavour that appealed to a chap who hated getting his hands dirty.

I would have thought Sophia the last female on earth, with the exception of Mother, to turn me on. We once urinated in the same bedroom at the same time. In the cellar, when she raised her clothing over her head to try on Mother's wedding dress, my erection came on as suddenly as an electric light. A moment later, I was repulsed and horrified by the sick, lying, mocking hallucination of Sophia in a wedding dress.

Hours later, still I felt dizzy and a little ill.

The anger that erupted inside me when I saw Sophia in Mother's wedding dress melted away. Its departure left me feeling sad – not because anger had gone, but because it should never have been. If I were to be angry with anyone, the object of my anger should have been anyone but Sophia.

Having locked the trapdoor, replaced the mat, and relocated the table so the room looked as it had when Mother left, I went upstairs to apologize to my twin. Her bedroom was empty, and the bathroom door was closed. I almost apologized through it, but I needed to see her eyes. There was nothing wrong with apologizing to her without looking into her eyes, but I had never done it before and it seemed insincere – to me, although probably not to Sophia. I went to my room instead, closed the door and brooded.

Sophia thought I became angry because she put on Mother's wedding dress, but I had become angry because of a sadness so sad that I denied it, and it manifested itself in an angry outburst.

I had seen someone, once my other half, more distinct from me than ever. She stood in a halo of torchlight. Because all around the darkness drifted, Sophia seemed to be an image behind smoked glass. If I went behind her, I would see the back of a picture frame. Maybe not a picture frame, maybe a mirror. The grotesque I had seen in the wedding dress might have been myself. How romantic it would be if Sophia were the name given to my twin sister who died at birth. How beautiful if I had carried her around in me all these years. The truth was sadder than that. I had seen, in the cellar, someone who would never wear a wedding dress of her own. I do not know how I knew, but I knew. No one would ever love Sophia as much as me.

I had seen, somehow, some way, in that wedding dress that did not quite fit or look right on her, Sophia's death shroud. I had seen the coffin that awaited her.

As I watched the darkness moving outside my bedroom window that night, Sophia came to apologize to me. She had apologized immediately after I shouted at her in the cellar. When Mother wandered in with a bag of clothes pegs, Sophia apologized. She apologized at dinner, and again after dinner. I said she didn't need to apologize; I had been at fault, and I should apologize for shouting at her. Never were there two more sorry souls.

'We'll forget it ever happened,' I said, standing with my back to the window, hating the tone of my voice; I sounded like a schoolteacher bestowing mercy on an errant pupil.

Sophia, standing directly in front of me, her arms hanging undefensively by her sides, agreed. We would forget that it ever happened. But although Sophia might, I would never forget. At best, I would try to push it to the back of my mind, a little further each day, like when a loved one dies and the pain hurts a little less with each passing day . . . but not really. It always hurts just as much; you simply get used to the hurt.

I was going to give her a brotherly hug, but what happened next happened so unexpectedly I lost the ability to move.

No one had ever touched my private parts . . . except me, Mother – when she used to wash me – Nurse and a couple of teachers at Whitehead House, a boy once, in the shower . . . maybe two or three boys . . . and the caretaker. Sophia was the first girl to do it except for Nurse and Mother.

She put the palm of her right hand on the front of my trousers, where the zip is, which surprised me more than Nurse did when she applied the ointment for whatever she thought ailed me. 'What are you doing?' stuck in my throat. Silly anyway. Rhetorical question. Sophia rubbed me erect through my trousers, and the feeling was so ridiculously pleasant I allowed her to continue. The poor, open-jawed male twin – or was it twit? – stood there trying to think, but thinking only fireworks.

'Does that feel nice?' she asked. Another bloody silly question.

'Yes,' I replied with vocal cords tight as a catapult ready to shoot.

With big eyes, and staring at her hand working my trouser-front, she said, 'Gosh! That's got really, really hard. It needs to be let out.'

I couldn't have agreed more.

Wanking seemed like such a dunce-headed and juvenile thing to do that I had never tried it. I thought of myself as a cut above. At school, boys wanked in dormitories. They wanked in toilet cubicles. They wanked in the showers. Some of them wanked each other. Senior school crawled with wankers.

When Sophia started to unzip me, I stopped her because of embarrassment. She said, 'Don't you like it?'

'Like hell I bloody like it, but where did you learn about it?'

'From Father,' she replied. 'He likes it.'

She continued to unzip me. I was too stunned to intervene. What she had said, and the pleasure that made my legs weak, were so at odds that they fought to cancel each other out. But the quantity of pleasure was greater than what Sophia said about Father, and it was the pleasure that dominated.

I had an erection you could crack nuts with. But for the wall behind me, I would have fallen. I nearly collapsed anyway. Sophia wanked me slowly, slowly. Faster, faster. Paused, squeezed and teased. Then, she knelt on the floor, and parted her lips, and moved them over my cock, and closed them on it, and wanked me with her whole head, and for the first time in many years, I prayed: 'Oh God! Oh shit!'

Soon, too soon, when I thought I would burst, but did not know if I would burst with the feeling of it or with tears of rage and helplessness, I made her bring her head up and rest it on my chest. The greatest temptation was to push it back down again. I resisted. Nevertheless, my cock jumped and pulsated and made a sticky mess on the front of Sophia's dress. Feeling it happening, she put her hand down and gently fondled my balls, chuckling.

Struggling somewhat to formulate something to say, at last, I managed, 'When did, you know, you and Father?'

'Before he took his first stroke.'

'Bastard! What about now?'

'He never asks.'

'Lie down beside me.' My voice quivered. She lay beside me on the bed, and I positioned her hand back where I wanted it.

I lay a while with my heart in my throat. Sophia sprang up on one arm, as if she had a good idea. 'Do you think I should go to him? Maybe he thinks I don't want to now that he's had another stroke and he's going downhill faster than an Easter egg.'

'No. No,' I told her. 'Never go to him. Never ever.'

The image of Sophia with Father worked to subdue my arousal more effectively than an ice-pack. I tucked my useless penis away and zipped up.

When I rose off the bed, to do I knew not what, Sophia asked, in an apologetic, diminutive tone, 'Will you be angry with me for ever?'

'Does Mother know what Father's done?'

'He told me to keep it a secret.'

'Don't you know that what he's done is wrong?' She cast her eyes downwards without replying. 'Why didn't you tell me? If you'd told me I'd have put a stop to it. I'd have killed him. I still might.'

'Kill Father?'

'Sophia.' She frustrated me so much! 'When fathers do to their children what he did to you, they call that abuse. It's against the law. It's a huge crime. People get locked in prison for doing what he did.'

'But he didn't do much to me. I did most of it to him.'

I raised my hands towards the ceiling in something deeper than frustration and worse than despair.

I walked around like a zombie plotting to kill Father. Every time I tried to look at him, I could not. I could hardly look at Mother either. I hardly knew where I was much of the time.

My incessant browsing through science books in Whitehead House library, books much more advanced than the textbooks I studied for my exams, taught me a number of elegant truths that my official courses of study seemed to think too obvious to bother with. Take, for example, the nature of facts. I learned that certain phenomena are so likely to occur – that the sun will rise each morning, move across the sky and go down at night – we call them facts.

My discomfort with facts began at a very early age, when I was puzzled by the 'fact' that although God didn't create stars until the fourth day, He created light on the first. Today's facts often become tomorrow's mistakes. The earth is flat; that used to be a fact. Besides, if we possessed all facts, every last one possible, and none of them were mistakes, everything would be fixed, and no one could have a new idea. Creativity would have ended. If we had all the facts, we would stagnate. Ignorance is a wonderful thing.

Nevertheless, this world, having relegated religion and mystery, is scientific and factual, and facts must have their due. It's a fact that, given the condition of being alive, no matter where we go in the world, our brains go too. It's also a fact that, given normal biological functioning, we always perceive in four dimensions: height, breadth, depth and time – tomorrow never happens yesterday. It's a fact that when our feet are on the ground, the sky is always above our heads. It is a fact that little girls do what their fathers tell them to do. It is not a fact, it is not known beyond doubt, that the universe, the All, God, or Whatever, punishes evildoers. Punishment of evildoers seemed, to me, to be something human beings had to take into their own hands. And they often did – justifiably. That was a fact.

Next day, when Sophia came to my room to see why I was still in bed, I said I felt ill. When she opened the curtains I turned my back to the light, and to her, and told her to close them. 'You'll feel better after some more sleep,' she said – it's what Mother used to say to us – and left the room. I did feel ill, but not the way Sophia thought.

I didn't blame Sophia, and I had no way of reversing what Father did to her. He did it, and that was a fact. Illegal. Evil. Irreversible. But a fact. All morning, I lay in bed, my back to the closed curtain, thinking. I wanted to die.

Sophia must have known that her admission to me caused a hiatus between us. I truly did not know how she felt. I was unable to read her with any reasonable degree of certainty – a far cry from when we were younger. She might have thought I had fallen out with her. It wasn't true. I'd been hurt, that's all. And I would hurt until, and far beyond, my departure for university.

21

Alf Visits the Manse

One morning, as Sophia flitted about the kitchen sink and I scratched my head and yawned, someone knocked on the back door. Farmer Barry was the only person who ever knocked on the back door, and the knock, which was lighter than his, belonged to someone else.

'Who could it be?' said Sophia, glancing at the door before taking flight to safety in the living room.

I looked through the window in the back door but saw no one there. As I opened the door cautiously, I expected to have to peer left and right. But not so! Alf Lord stood where he had not been a moment ago, a small tartan suitcase hanging from one hand. He looked as if he had broken a window and wanted his ball back.

'Alf!'

'I hope you don't mind my showing up like this. I thought I would find accommodation in Bruagh,' he said apologetically, raising the suitcase slightly, as if it were the accommodation in question. 'Is that how it's pronounced: Brew-rah?'

'Alf!'

'The one and only. Sorry for landing on you unexpectedly. I could get a taxi to somewhere else if it's inconvenient.'

'It's not in the least inconvenient. You're very welcome. It's a pleasure to see you.' It was less a pleasure than a surprise, but a pleasure none the less. I stepped outside and shook him by the hand. I have no idea why I stepped outside to do it, unless it was a subconscious move to protect my sister from the wolf at the door that turned out to be a lamb. 'Did you walk from Bruagh Halt?'

'It's quite a distance.'

'Lucky you walked in the right direction. There's nothing the other way for twice as far. Come in. Come in.' I brought him into the kitchen and relieved him of his tartan suitcase and coat.

'There's not much in Bruagh,' said Alf. 'I thought it would have a guest house where I could stay, if not a hotel.'

'You'd be lucky. The closest accommodation's in Garagh. That's the nearest town, but it's miles away.'

'Your cemetery's amazing. Is it real?'

'Of course it's real. That's where we keep the extended Pike family. How on earth could a cemetery be unreal?'

'I was so impressed I thought it might have been a Gothic extravagance, a kind of folly.'

'Well, it's not. It's the real deal. And, speaking of family . . .'

Sophia's head, halfway up the edge of the door, shook vigorously, and mouthed 'No, no'. As Alf turned in her direction, her head stopped shaking and her no, no mouth turned into a broad smile. She stepped out of hiding.

'Alf, Sophia. Sophia, Alf. Alfred Lord. Or Lord Alfred as I call him, poet extraordinaire.'

'Edward has told me lots about you, Sophia.' Alf extended his right hand. Sophia's right hand gravitated to meet it as though in his hand hers belonged. 'Meeting you is a pleasure. I hope you won't think it improper if I say that you are every bit as pretty as Edward said.'

Sophia grinned. More than grinned, blushed pink while her eyes sprouted leaks – which she tried to hide by lowering her head. No one had ever said that to Sophia before, or anything remotely like it.

'Are you really a poet?' asked my starry-eyed sister.

'Alas, no. I'm just a pretend poet. But I work closely with one of the best. I wish I were as accomplished as he.'

'Any chance of tea for three, Sophia?' I said, offering her an escape route, which she took quickly and without a word. 'I'll give you the grand tour, Alf. Although there isn't much to see.'

I showed him the living room, and told him about how Granny Hazel's bed occupied the centre of the floor before she died. He looked through the window and seemed intrigued by Hollow Heath beyond the garden, although he didn't say anything. I led him to Father's study, and told him the room wasn't used much, not even when Father was able; hence the dust. Upstairs, I indicated the two closed doors, one for each parent within. 'Father's completely immobile,' I explained. 'Mother isn't, but she's going through a bad spell at present. And this is our pride and joy.'

'It's a very fine bathroom,' replied Alf.

'We had none until a few years ago. Calls of nature were answered outside, in an upright coffin with a strip of wood and a bottom-sized hole in it to sit on.'

'How exciting!'

I showed him Sophia's room, and mine, and said he could have my bed tonight; I would sleep on the floor. Alf wouldn't hear of it, and insisted that he slept on the floor.

When we returned downstairs, Sophia had tea ready, fresh bread and blackberry jam – both of which she'd made herself. As we ate at the kitchen table, and Alf and I chatted, Sophia remained quietly timid. While she washed up, I took Alf outside for a closer inspection of the cemetery. There had been an hour of drizzle yesterday, but no rain today, so the ground wasn't too muddy.

He wanted to know who the dead people were, and what were their stories. I only knew who some of them were, and neither Mother nor Father had told me more than a few crumbs of their stories.

'Pity,' said Alf. 'Stories enrich . . . What's this?' He indicated a weedy hollow that looked different, worked on, but only when you looked closely – typical of Alf to notice it.

'I dug a grave and buried a dog on that spot when I was a child. As graves go, it wasn't one of the best. Bits of the dog were exposed to the elements. Mother dug it up and binned it . . . *The Binned Dog*: that's a good title for a story. I don't have the imagination for stories. I used to have it. As I got older my imagination, sort of . . . atrophied.'

'Sadly, sometimes muses desert their gets.'

'Why would they do that?'

'Various reasons. Most often it's because of periods of creative boom when the Department of Muses is short-staffed – especially in winter, when a lot of us are off sick with head colds, flu, Seasonal Affective Disorder and the like.' Alf didn't smile, and I wasn't sure whether I should laugh.

It was getting cold. I should have worn a coat. We wandered back towards the Manse in silence, until Alf said, 'This visit to your home isn't merely casual, Edward.'

I asked him to explain.

'I want to let you into a secret.'

'You came here to let me into a secret?'

'May I?'

'Is it one I have to keep?'

'Not really. It isn't a terribly big secret, and I doubt if anyone would be interested in it anyway.'

'I'm interested. What is it?'

'As you know, I am a muse.'

'You can't be a muse. You're the wrong sex, and you're not even Greek.' Alf smiled. I'd never seen him smiling as he did then, and I thought: Maybe he's the right sex. But he's certainly not Greek.

'I'm working on a poem.'

'No, no, no, Alf; you've got it all wrong. As a muse, your job is to inspire someone else to write a poem. If the poem writers' union finds out you're at it they'll call their members out on strike.' Alf's was an enigmatic smile, not unlike that on the lips of the Mona Lisa. 'All right,' I said, 'you're working on a poem. What's new? You're always working on poems. Every time I see you you're working on poems.'

'This is a special poem. It's the reason why I'm here.'

'To be inspired by the Manse?'

'No, not exactly. It's the reason why I'm here, existent, in this space-time.'

'Okay.'

'I need your help.'

'If you need help writing a bad poem, I'm your man. Turn to me for help and, on completion, you're guaranteed the worst poem ever written. Let's see . . . There was a young man from the Manse . . . who with girls didn't stand a chance . . . the reason for that, was that he was fat . . . umm . . . ahh . . . and hadn't a clue how to dance. Howzat!' Alf's chuckling made me feel warm inside. I chuckled at him chuckling. 'How can I help, then, me a serious non-poet?'

I need your earliest memory, Edward.'

'For the poem?'

'Yes.'

'Granny Hazel. I told you about her, didn't I?' Alf nodded his head. He, or the ambience, or the rightness of the time, roused a feeling in me that felt exactly as it had fourteen years ago, a feeling of fearful doubt, which had been vivid and spanking new to me and Sophia back then.

'Tell me about Granny Hazel,' said Alf.

'All right. I'll tell you what I remember. Not so much about Granny Hazel as how things were after her. Sophia and I had a feeling that Granny Hazel could have been sleeping more peacefully than she really was. Our bones told us that she could have been happier. Granny Hazel was restless. That meant she might become a ghost. We had no idea how we knew such things, but we did. Ghosts were the dead whose spirits leave their bodies and walk about lost. I don't know who told us that, but someone must have. Maybe Gregory. If the White Lady had returned, I would have been less frightened of her than I would of Granny Hazel. The White Lady meant no harm.

Granny Hazel's return would have meant the opposite. It would have been dreadful. She was always so grumpy. Her return from the dead could have been nothing but dreadful.'

I thought I would have been able to recall more, but, when called up, my memory held less than I thought.

I asked Alf, 'Is that any help to you?'

'Oh yes,' he replied keenly. 'I don't know exactly how I can use it, but I shall be able to, I'm certain of that. Yes . . .' He put a couple of fingertips to his lips, but didn't bite the nails. Rubbing my chin helped me to think; with Alf, it was lips and fingertips. 'Who is the White Lady?'

'Our ghost.'

'The Manse has a ghost?'

'At least one. The White Lady puts in an appearance when someone is going to die. She appeared to Sophia before Granny Hazel died. No need to fear her when you're sleeping here tonight. She's harmless. Don't know who she is, though.'

'Fear and doubt, Edward. I wonder if they're why promises are necessary. Do we ask people to promise, and do we promise others, because we doubt their honesty as well as our own? Is that the birth of fear, hand in hand with the loss of innocence: the knowledge that we cannot trust? We can take no one at their word. It's the death of childhood. What age were you?'

'When Granny Hazel died? It was before I started school.'

'Your childhood started dying then, Edward.'

'I know. Sophia's too. Our childhood started dying with a promise, like a kiss of death, she made to Father.'

'She made a promise and, in so doing, cursed herself.'

'That's it, really. Perhaps, since you're here, you can help me to persuade her to leave the Manse.'

'Are you calling upon me in your hour of need?' Strange thing to say, but Alf was a strange person.

'You could put it like that if you like.'

'Good,' said Alf. 'Then we're on the same track. I'll do it. Did you or Sophia talk to your father about the promise?'

I laughed.

'What's funny?'

'He isn't the kind of father you can talk to.'

'Were you afraid of your father?' asked Alf. 'Are you still?'

'Of course not.' My reply lacked conviction. 'Aren't all children in awe of their fathers when they're little?'

Sophia would have been shy with strangers had she encountered any. She was shy with Alf. Doubly shy because she had taken a shine to him. Did Alf reciprocate the shine? With Alf, it was hard to tell. He liked Sophia – he smiled at her a lot and tried hard to nudge her gently into our conversation. However, Alf, I had a notion, was disinclined to take shines to girls.

The sky darkened and the rain came on late in the afternoon. We were trapped indoors, but that didn't matter, because there was plenty of coal. Yesterday I gathered a mountain of fuel from Hollow Wood and carried it home in a sack the size of myself. Approaching an outhouse with the sack over my shoulder, I glanced across the courtyard to the cemetery and saw the White Lady gliding through the headstones as though looking for someone she'd lost.

While Sophia saw to Mother and Father, Alf and I made dinner. A heck of a lot of meat filled the freezer, courtesy of Farmer Barry.

Our misadventure at Ruse Bay having given him a taste for the stuff, Alf brought two bottles of wine to the Manse in his tartan suitcase. That came to two glasses and a dribble each. Fortunately, since Father couldn't object – and thanks to Farmer Barry's generosity – I'd made sure the Manse had a healthy, or perhaps unhealthy, supply of my favourite reds.

During a lengthy, giggly dinner at the big kitchen table – incinerated beef, under-boiled carrots, lumpy mash and lumpier gravy – our conversation took a serious turn. Alf said to Sophia, 'Edward tells me you don't like to leave the Manse.'

'I don't need to,' she replied happily, and drained her wine glass for the fourth time. 'Everything's here that I need.'

'Everything? Surely . . .'

'Farmer Barry brings the things that aren't. He brings the gas and connects it. He pops in at least once or twice a week.'

'No he doesn't,' I said. 'I've only seen him about twice since school ended.' But I'd never had to connect the gas. I assumed Gregory did it – although I'd seen as little of him as I had of Farmer Barry. Connecting the gas was easy; Sophia could do it. But she couldn't leave the Manse to fetch new supplies.

'He comes when you're out on one of your walks, and has gone by the time you return. I love Farmer Barry. He's like a father to me. That,' she pointed at Alf's plate, 'is one of his cows.' It struck me that she said she loved Farmer Barry. Not liked, but loved. She had never said she loved Father. Maybe it was the wine talking.

'Where do you walk to?' asked Alf.

'Round about. Bruagh and back.'

'He goes out to smoke cigarettes. I can smell them off him when he returns. Good job Father doesn't know.'

I pulled a face at my sister.

Alf steered the conversation back to the subject he wanted to talk about. 'The promise was a very long time ago, Sophia. Promises run out after a number of years and you no longer have to keep them.'

'What promise?'

Sophia reached for a near empty bottle and drained it into her glass. Alf looked at me, but my eyes were locked on Sophia for several seconds before I looked at him.

'I wonder how it started,' said Alf to either of us or no one, but looking at me conspiratorially.

'How what started?' I asked deliberately, playing the game, me and him against Sophia with the aim of helping her if we could.

'Sophia's reluctance to leave the Manse.' Alf added, addressing Sophia, 'I wonder why your reluctance to leave the Manse began. Perhaps something happened long ago?'

Sophia shrugged, and sawed into an edge of burnt beef rather awkwardly. 'I don't know. I've just always been like that.'

From behind my wine glass, I watched Sophia chew beef. Had she really forgotten the promise she made to Father, or did she simply not want to tell Alf about it? Sophia and I could no longer read each other's minds. Yet I knew her well enough. She was not hiding the promise from Alf; she had forgotten it.

'What a pity,' said Alf.

'What's a pity?' I asked.

'Oh, you know. It was just a thought . . .' That wasn't Alfspeak; he was pretending to be more casual and tipsy than he really was – for Sophia's benefit, of course.

'What was just a thought? Out with it, Alf.'

'I'd rather hoped that maybe, I mean, if you both wanted to, I could invite both of you to town for lunch some day. We could get a taxi. Who knows, we might even have our meat cooked by a chef who doesn't burn it.'

'Sounds good. I'm up for it. What about you, Sophia?'

My sister must have chewed that particular slice of beef five hundred times. 'No,' she said at last. 'But thank you for asking, Alf.'

'Well, if you change your mind, the offer remains open.'

'If it's Mother and Father you're worried about, they sleep all afternoon,' I said. 'They'll be fine for a few hours. They're alone in their rooms that long while you're feeding the chickens and doing the chores anyway.'

Sophia didn't respond. Then she put her knife and fork on her plate, reclined on the chair and said she was stuffed. She sprang back up, grabbed the plate, and took it to the sink.

I announced that I was calling it a day, and Alf said him too. Sophia said she would stay up a while longer and watch television.

22

Gregory Returns to the Manse

'Where did you go on that day, Alf?' I asked, lying on my side in bed looking down at him lying on the floor looking up at me.

'What day?'

'The last day we saw each other at school. You came to my room. When you left, I followed you to the junior changing room. I wasn't seeing things. I've asked myself all kinds of questions. Did I make a mistake? Did you walk past the locker, not into it? But if you walked past the locker, you walked into a wall. I've even wondered if the locker had a false back that you passed through.' As I spoke, the expression on Alf's face was one of calmness with an almost-smile. 'Come on,' I said. 'Put me out of my misery. Where did you go?'

'Oh, the locker.'

'Yes, the locker.'

'Guess.'

'No, Alf. I can't guess . . . I definitely, unquestionably, absolutely certainly saw you. It was a very, very clever trick.'

After a time, he said, 'It's a secret.'

'No! No, Alf. I'm not letting you get away with that. How did you pull off the locker trick? . . . Stop smiling at me! All right. Answer a different question. Who are you? Where are you from?'

'That's two questions.'

'Where are you from? That's only one. You said you were at the university independently. I never understood that.'

'I'm from here and there, really,' replied Alf unhelpfully.

'What do you mean? Do you mean that your parents travel because of your father's job? What is he, a diplomat or something?'

'A muse is from everywhere and nowhere. I'm from where I'm needed at any particular time – although time is a localized phenomenon; I'm using it now, in this conversation, merely for convenience.'

'You've lost me.'

'You exist within the context of past, present and future, so that's the frame of reference I'm using.'

'Right.'

'My work, and it wasn't in my plan to tell you this but I'm not as sober as a muse should be . . . my work involves travelling all over gathering information on cultures and contributing to their enrichment.'

'What?' I said, after a moment in stunned silence. 'You've only just left school, Alf. You don't work for, or with, anybody. Anyway, I'm talking about what happened before you left school. You couldn't have travelled then because you were at school.'

'My form of travel is unconventional, Edward. Rather than travel from here to there and back in this or that motorized machine, I travel through time – that slippery phenomenon again.'

My penny dropped. I got it. 'You're a time traveller!' Ear to ear travelled my grin. 'Wow!' What an imagination! What acting to pull it off so convincingly! What a storyteller! Why hadn't he revealed this talent at Whitehead House? 'But there's a flaw.' I wagged an accusing finger at him. 'If you travelled back in time and killed your grandfather . . . You know it, don't you: the old time travel paradox? Let's see you get out of that one.'

'It's simple: I can't interfere – much. It's not that natural law forbids interference; it's just that interference is incongruent with stability and nature works to preserve stability . . . Think of stability as your body's health, interference as a harmful virus, and nature as white blood cells produced by your body to fight the virus. On almost every occasion, the white blood cells defeat the virus and preserve the health of your body. But sometimes the virus is too strong, or too sneaky, and stability is compromised.'

'So interference is possible, but it's dangerous.'

'It can make systems sick. Fatally so.'

'Systems?'

'Universes.'

'If time travel's so dangerous, why do it?'

'It isn't dangerous where interference is limited to extracting from an environment non-material phenomena such as ideas. That's what I do. That's what orchard universes are for. I referred a moment ago to cultures. How do you think great civilizations emerge and produce great art? There can't be civilization without art. Art is quintessential to civilization. Design. Architecture. Monuments. Towers. Sculptures. Paintings. Drama. Literature. Technology. Invention. How is it that animals do it?'

'Animals?'

'Humans.'

I stuttered, but came out with, 'Genius. Occasionally, humanity produces a genius and things change.'

'No,' Alf said, in a protracted, condescending way. 'Well, not really. It's because people like me, and you may call us geniuses if you wish, travel, not only in time, but outside space-time too. Don't worry about it. We travel all over in search of . . . in search of what do you think, Edward?'

Oh Lord! What did I think? I thought he was very clever. But I knew that already. He was certainly more imaginative than I'd ever dreamed. What did he and his kind travel in search of? 'You travel in search of . . . solutions. You travel in time to find clues that solve crimes.'

'Ideas,' said Alf. 'We search tirelessly, observing and documenting, developing and eventually inspiring in the production of great art. And sometimes, admittedly, not so great art.'

Art? I felt let down. 'Just art?'

'Yes. Just one, tiny, three-letter word with a single syllable. Art. Art, in its numerous shapes and forms, is the thing, the one and only thing, that makes this animal, human, a significant cut above the rest.'

'Ah!' said I. 'Not so, my time-travelling friend. That would be speech: the power of language.'

Alf nodded his head in agreement, which confused me. 'Like I said, Edward: art. I may have talk; I may have speech. I may say: At a fly beer wine bottom if weasel. Where, then, is speech without art? I may say: And God saw everything that He had made, and behold, it was very good. And there was evening and there was morning, the sixth day. That's art.'

I'd thought I was fairly sober until then. I could have sworn he said something like, at a fly beer wine bottom if weasel. Time to introduce the balm of hurt minds.

'Alf?'

'Yes, Edward?'

'Goodnight.'

Father slept.

'Hello, Father. Hello smelly, shitty fucking Father fucking smelly shitty old fucking fuckface.' He had pushed the blanket down so that it covered only his lower body. He didn't appear to feel the cold these days. The frosty days and freezing nights were too hot for him. Sophia knew why. He'd used all but the last dregs of his life. Close to death and what waited therein, he felt heat from the fires of Hell. Him and his bible! Him and his God! Sophia hated him and his God.

Under a spillage-stained vest, Father's old ribs rose and fell. She watched them rise and fall every night when she'd done with him and he settled. She stood there watching until enough strength returned for her to turn round and leave. Sometimes his ribs rose and fell harder in his sleep. His old lungs expanded to bursting point for ten or more breaths; he inhaled and exhaled as though his whole system needed patching and pumping up just to keep him ticking over. When his ribs settled, when his breathing became less laboured, Sophia imagined herself raising a pillow to press down upon his face. Would she have the physical strength? Could she do it? Could she murder him? Probably. Meeting him in Hell: that's what stopped her.

But if she did it, it wouldn't be murder – at least, not cruel murder. No one could accuse her of that. It would be for the best, like putting a dog out of its misery. What, she wondered, would Edward advise her to do? What would Edward say, if he were in here instead of across the corridor with Alf? She had lost the ability to know his mind. They had grown apart. Everything changes. Everything has its time. Father had had his time. He wasn't going to get better. Better like this than with his dirty fingers up her skirt. Sophia wished she hadn't told Edward and hoped he had forgotten. Of all the things she hated thinking about, she hated thinking about that most. Think about something else. That's the only way to stop it: think about something else.

Best look in on Mother. See if she's asleep. Best leave Father's bedroom. Every time his ribs rise towards her face they seem to say, 'Stop our endless heaving; we can't do it ourselves.'

Sophia raised the pillow. If Father opened his eyes he would see her. Should she set the pillow on his face and gradually exert pressure? Should she push the pillow forcefully on his face, all her pressure at once? She must not startle him awake. She would die if his eyes shot open and he saw her about to kill him.

A clock ticked long seconds. It must have ticked inside her head because there were no clocks in the bedroom or corridor.

Her arms were heavy from holding the pillow. Not now. Tomorrow. With relief, she let the pillow fall to her knees. But she stood on. A voice in her head: 'It's now or never.' And Sophia stood on, convinced that she had no option but to start all over again, here, tonight, talking herself into doing what she didn't want to do and wanted so very desperately to do.

A hand grasped the pillow, but did not pull it away from her. Sophia gasped with shock. Her heart jumped, but not her feet. She quickly realized that Gregory stood beside her and the hand belonged to him. Solemn-faced, he looked briefly into her eyes, then looked at Father. Sophia released the pillow when Gregory eased it from her. The rest was easy. It ended almost as soon as it began. Gregory pressed the pillow to Father's face with one hand. His other hand wrapped around the old man's neck, not choking him, but pinning him to the bed. Father twitched and jolted several times – a token struggle. Gregory held his neck, and the pillow to his face, for much longer than necessary, which seemed none the less like no time at all.

I woke before dawn needing to pee. Had Sophia tapped on my door? I raised myself on to an elbow and switched on the bedside light. Alf gave me a fright; I'd forgotten about him. He sat cross-legged on a pillow on the floor fully clothed, the quilt draped over his shoulders.

'Alf.'

Pale and shivering, he stared at the floor.

'Are you all right?' He looked far from all right. Stupid question. I asked a better one. 'How long have you been awake? You should have gone downstairs and made yourself a pot of tea.'

He raised his head and gave a mad chuckle. 'Tea?' He looked at me with an intensity in which I recognized ingredients of fear: laboured breathing, deep and darkened eyes, a small but perceptible tremble, failure to contain the contents of a bladder. Fear has a distinct and unpleasant smell. Slowly, deeply: 'Have you lost your mind?' Alf asked. I hadn't lost any more of it than I'd been missing yesterday, but Alf looked as if his might have made progress along that road. 'A pot of tea? You're insane, Pike! I wouldn't set foot on those stairs again, down or up, for all the rice in Asda.'

'Again? Do you mean . . . ?'

'I wouldn't step outside this door if . . . if . . .' Alf sobbed.

'Is that where you're from, Asda?'

He shook his head. Watching him broke my heart. But I did nothing other than watch, as he sniffed and regained his ability to speak. 'I woke in the middle of the night. I had to use the bathroom.' He sought the correct words, rejected an approach and decided there were no correct words, just some words that were better than others. 'I'm a grown-up, Edward. You don't know just how grown up I am. It shouldn't have this effect on me. I'm an experienced, mature muse.'

While he sniffed, and wiped his snout on the back of a hand, the idea entered my head that Alf might slip, when necessary, into his muse persona as a tortoise slips back inside its shell when threatened. Being a sensitive soul – certainly a fish out of water – he must have felt threatened all the time at Whitehead House.

'Is this common, Edward? Are you accustomed to this?'

'Accustomed to what?'

'For want of a better word: ghosts.'

'Did you see one of our dead?'

'One? How many have you? I forgot, you've a fledgling city of the dead out there. And, by God, they're in here too.'

'Was it the White Lady?'

His blank stare told me no, not her.

'When daylight's here, I have to leave, Edward. Thank you for your hospitality, but I can't remain another hour in this place. I've seen many things. I know many things. I've had frightening experiences before now. I've even seen what I believed to be spirits disembodied. But last night . . .' He got to his feet and the quilt fell off his shoulders. He sprang at my bed. I thought he was going to grab my neck, but he spoke passionately into my face. 'You must get Sophia away from this place. It's unhealthy and there isn't much time. I'll take her with me, now. You must leave too.'

'Steady on, Alf,' I said, swinging my legs out of bed. 'You're traumatized. This is Sophia's home.'

'It's her prison. She'll die here.'

'No she won't.'

'Won't she? How can you know she won't die here?'

'How can you know that she will?'

'How can I know? The grandfather paradox?'

'Time travel and all sorts. You're a time traveller.'

'Yes. If you travel back to a time before you were born and kill your grandfather, then you'll never be born, and, therefore, you'll never be able to travel back in time and kill your grandfather. I know about Sophia because I've seen your future.'

'I don't believe you. According to the paradox, time travel shouldn't be possible.'

'On the contrary. There are good reasons why it needs to be possible. It's just very difficult, unless you're someone like me.' His eyes were dry now. He had overcome his distress with unusual speed. He cocked his head, amused by my clueless face. 'You can think of such a paradox as a mechanism built into nature's laws to prevent contamination. And . . . I wasn't going to tell you this . . .'

'Tell me what?'

'Unfortunately, I have inadvertently broken the law. I have contaminated.'

'Beg pardon?'

'I have contaminated your environment.'

'Charming. In what way?'

Alf breathed a deep sigh. 'Let me explain something first. Theoretically, according to the Standard Model, contamination through interference shouldn't be possible. However, in practice, things are different. That's why the Standard Model is still only a model and not a unified explanation. Have you read Wineburger's *Principles of Stability and Chaotic Variables*?'

I'd never heard of it. 'Not recently.'

'To cut a long story short, Wineburger says the probability statistics associated with variability dysfunction are unpredictable in relation to the higher degrees of sub-subatomic interaction between matter and conscious thought emanating from a matter-based source.'

'That's what I thought.'

'It follows from Wineburger's formulae that the consequences of contaminating interference can be calamitous.'

'Such as?'

'When I came here . . .'

'To the Manse?'

'No. To this universe.'

'O-kay.'

'I brought a small book of poetry. It contains a poem that was never written in this universe by a poet who never lived in it.'

'That was clever of him, Alf. What's his name?'

'His name is . . . His name isn't important. What's important – indeed, potentially disastrous – is that I've lost the book.'

I dared not tell him that I'd stolen it and given it to Sophia. 'What's so bad about losing a book? You can buy another copy.'

'There is only one copy in this universe. Before I came, there were none. I can't leave without it. If I can't find it, in all probability the universe will have to be shut down as a precautionary measure.'

'Oh, great! And I haven't even had breakfast.'

'We can't have poets from a different universe infecting art in this universe with their work. Where would it end?'

'Personally, I don't see what harm it would do.'

'Oh, don't you? It's happened before, and more than once, with devastating consequences.'

'Like when? Give me an example.'

'Well, for a start, before Galileo Galilei put pen to paper the sun was perfectly happy rotating around the earth.'

Alf played his role so seriously that – if I'd possessed a better imagination – his fantasia might have sucked me in, swallowed, and made me a true believer. I wondered whether speaking his make-believe world aloud to me helped him in its construction.

'You see, Edward, the poem that hasn't been written in this universe, in the book that hasn't been published in this universe, by the poet who never lived in this universe, was written by a famous poet who lived in one of the really real universes. However, it still needs the inspiration to write it because outside the specificality of space-time, and the parameters of matter, it needs to be written. It needs to be written perpetually.'

'The poem needs to be written for ever?'

'Like a mouse on a wheel. You might think the life of a muse sounds like fun, but believe me, it can get mind-numbingly tedious.'

'I see.'

'Do you?'

'No.'

'I think I can still salvage the inspiration for the poem, Edward. The poem's what's important. But I can't salvage the universe.'

'The really, really, really, really real universe?'

'No. This one.'

'This universe isn't real?'

'Don't get me wrong. It's real enough for those, like you, who live in it. But for those who know better, it isn't.'

'That's a spot of bad luck. We're doomed, then . . . Alf, maybe you should speak to someone. A psychiatrist.'

'No need, Edward. I've worked with the best. Who do you think is responsible for the Oedipus Complex?'

Deep down, I admitted that Alf had a point. Deeper down, down in my soul where, until now, until Alf forced me to, I was afraid to look, I knew he was right about getting Sophia out of the Manse. Unless I acted to save her, Sophia would die here – maybe from getting old and worn down long before her time.

'Universes and time travellers apart, Alf, what can I do? Even if I abandon the Manse and take Sophia with me, Edgar's coming home. He'll need looking after, and so will Mother and Father. Gregory can look after himself.'

'You need to look after Sophia, Edgar and your mother. But not your father.' He paused. I awaited an explanation. 'You said your father's immobile? I've news for you, my friend: he isn't immobile any more. Not now that he's dead.'

'What?'

'I met him in the corridor, God help me. One of your dead.'

'Father isn't dead!'

'Believe me: your father is dead. The living don't look like candles in the dark. The living don't float six inches off the floor.'

I started to go directly to Father's room. Alf stopped me by putting his hands on my shoulders.

'You've never seen Father,' I said. 'How do you know it was him?' Alf inclined his head a fraction to one side. I thought he would beseech me, again, to take flight from the Manse.

Instead, he surprised me. 'Edward . . . I'm in love with Sophia.'

My lips parted before I knew what to say in response. Alf thrust his face forward and pressed his mouth to mine. He kissed me and, finding pleasure in it, I kissed him back. Maybe I experienced not genuine pleasure, but real confusion. 'Why?' I breathed, when our lips parted a hair's breadth.

'You are Sophia,' he said. 'She is pure at heart.' We kissed again. Oh God! Had the White Lady appeared, I'd have said, Take me I'm yours. But as soon as Father came to mind I went clean off kissing. I pushed Alf off me and went to Father's room.

. . . where Sophia was already standing over the naked corpse, towels, a sponge and a basin of water on a table at her side.

Alf changed his mind and stayed. The three of us had tea and toast in the kitchen. Mother had awakened and gone back to sleep. Sophia said she wouldn't need seeing to for an hour or two.

Sophia said she would help me to dig a grave for Father, since Gregory wasn't around to help – he'd gone off again after the murder. Alf, restored now to something like his old self, said he would lend a hand too. I, however, didn't want to dig a grave: the ground was saturated. There would be cave-ins, it would take all day, and look at what happened last time I dug a grave; there'd been more Tennyson outside than under.

I suggested, 'Why don't we bury him in the cellar?'

'You have a cellar?' asked Alf.

'The trapdoor's right underneath us.'

'The floor's cement,' said Sophia.

'That doesn't matter,' I said. 'We don't have to dig through it. There are coffins down there. Remember? We can put Father in a coffin in the cellar, and lock the trapdoor. It'll be like a crypt.'

'A foul smell will soon rise upwards,' said Alf, 'no matter how well you seal the trapdoor.'

I had an idea. It came to me all at once. I don't know where it came from. It must have came from somewhere, and it probably came from many places. Suddenly, having bubbled up to my vocal cords, it was there. And I spoke it. 'We'll bury Father in the cellar, take Mother a safe distance from the Manse, douse it with petrol and burn the wretched place to the ground.'

Sophia stared at me, and, staring at me, she appeared to have turned to stone. Then she melted and appeared to be in two minds, perhaps more. I thought I knew what she was thinking, but maybe I gave her too much credit: we couldn't carry my plan through, not least because of uncertainty about the date of Edgar's return; when we fled the burning Manse we would have to take him too.

'This is your prison,' I said to Sophia. 'It's my prison too. To a lesser extent, yes; but it's my prison too.' She remained as stone. 'This is a bad place, Sophia. It took me a long time to see it, but I see it now. It's worthless. The Manse is worth less than nothing. In destroying it we are setting ourselves free.'

'Free,' said my twin as if free were a new word, one she liked the sound of and wanted to surf from her mouth again, and again: free. With two syllables and stress on the second: Fr*eeee*. 'But I live here,' said Sophia.

'Alf saw one of our ghosts last night.'

'Which one?'

Alf said, 'I saw your . . .' but I raised the palm of a hand and stopped him. I didn't want Sophia to know that he saw Father.

Me: 'The ghosts, Sophia.'

Sophia: 'I haven't seen a ghost for ages.'

Me: 'I saw the White Lady the other day.'

Sophia: 'And now Father's dead.'

Me: 'Think of the moans and howls. Think of the Cold. You don't have to live with those.'

Sophia: 'They don't bother me.'

Me: 'The Dark. The Shadows.'

Sophia: 'I'm half-sick of Shadows.'

Alf: 'Yes! Gosh, yes!'

Me: 'What?'

Alf: 'Nothing.'

Me: 'Nothing my left buttock! You had a eureka moment!'

Sophia: 'What's a eureka moment?'

Me: 'What Alf had just now.'

Alf: 'No, I didn't.'

Me: 'Yes, you did.'

Alf: 'I did not.'

Me: 'You did.'

Alf: 'Yes! All right! I did.'

Me: 'What was it?'

Alf: 'A possible line for the poem. A pivotal line.'

Me: 'For the poem that's already been written.'

Alf: 'It's complicated.'

Me: 'What is it?'

Alf: 'If I told you that, I'd have to kill you.'

Sophia gasped and placed a hand on her heart.

'Only joking,' said Alf.

'He can't kill me,' I said. 'He needs me. I'm his muse.'

'Yes,' said Alf. 'I suppose you are, in a way.'

'What's a muse?' asked Sophia.

I told her it was a long story. She said, in that case she didn't think she liked muses much, although she quite enjoyed shorter stories, especially when they were funny.

Mother took the news of Father's death surprisingly well. Her words were, to Sophia, 'That will make things much easier for you.'

I introduced Alf to Mother when she was dressed. She was uninterested. He might have been invisible, or an old brown coat.

It was a bit of a struggle – a huge struggle, actually – but between Alf and me and a bed sheet, we got Father downstairs and into the cellar. He'd lost a lot of weight and there wasn't much of him. Sophia stayed with Mother, dressed in her old Sunday best, in the living room – I didn't want Mother to witness unfortunate spillages. Fortunately, however, there were none.

Alf and I placed Father in a coffin on the floor. I heard a moan and looked towards its source. Mother stood at the open trapdoor, swaying at the top of the steps. Sophia steadied her. They descended, Sophia first, Mother behind her. Her hand rested on Sophia's shoulder. Mother, stiff and slow, took ages to reach the coffin. When she did, she looked down on her husband and stared at him in a way I found difficult to read. She didn't cry. Her face looked pained, but not with grief.

'Should we wait for Gregory?' she asked.

'We don't know when he'll return,' I said.

With a brush of a hand, Mother said, 'Get on with it.'

I hadn't planned any kind of ceremony, but at the last minute I thought there should be at least token formality. 'Would you like me to read from the bible, the way Father used to do?'

'Oh, good God, no,' said Mother. 'If I hear another word from that bloody bible I'll scream.'

I admit to being taken aback.

'Bury it with him,' said Mother.

Sophia hurried up to Father's bedroom and retrieved his bible, and it went into the coffin with him.

I cleared my throat. 'I'll say a few words.' I didn't know which words I would say, but I was sure a few would come to me: We loved him, or We admired him, or We'll miss him. Lies. All lies. More appropriate would be, Good riddance. But I couldn't say that. I cleared my throat and addressed the man in the coffin at my feet. 'Father—'

Mother stamped a foot. 'Oh, shut your mouth, Edward. Just nail on the frigging lid and be done with it.'

Later, when Mother had gone back to bed, Alf spoke with his hands, making solid shapes, less solid shapes, waves and chops. 'Edward already knows about this, Sophia; we've discussed it at length at school.' I couldn't recall having discussed it at school. Certainly not at length. 'Imagine that in a multiverse there's one universe that's really, really real. While there are no other universes that are really, really real, there are multitudinous other universes. They make up fifty point nought, nought one per cent of the rest of each matter-dominated multiverse.'

Sophia went to sleep with her eyes open.

'And the other forty-nine point whatever per cent?' I asked.

'Dark matter, to you. But I don't want to go into that. All the not really real universes in a multiverse are like orchards from which the very best can be picked and added to the really real universe.'

'The very best of what?'

'Correct me if I'm wrong; but didn't I tell you last night?'

'I don't think so, Alf.'

'The very best of just about everything that springs from chance variation, or, as it's usually referred to, independent thought. Poetry, for example, as I explained to you this morning, or possibly yesterday. The poem in the book wasn't created here, and doesn't belong here. That I've lost it here is like having released an alien predator into an ecosystem. Art is the same. Imagine what would happen if you let Rolf Harris loose on the ceiling of the Sistine chapel.'

I cringed.

'My job is in the domain of arts and culture, Sophia. That's where I do my picking. And what I've picked, I take to the really real universe, and I plant. And, by that means, the really real universe gets the best of everything.'

'That's unfair,' said Sophia. 'Poor people should get some too.'

I agreed with my sister. It sounded a tad tyrannical to me, a bit elitist. Alf 's multiverse of not quite really real universes ponged of slavery, exploitation and just plain unfairness. I rubbed my chin, thinking of a way to throw a spanner in the machine of his – admittedly interesting, at a certain level – imaginary construction. I was, however, spannerless. 'Your really real universe is a bit like God's Heaven, then.'

Alf: 'Only if your religion's polytheistic.'

Sophia: 'Eh?'

Me: 'How so?'

Alf: 'The really real universe.'

Me: 'Yes.'

Alf: 'It isn't singular. There are an infinite number of really real universes, each one with its corresponding multiverse of universes that aren't really real.'

Sophia: 'There's infinite not really real multiverses too.'

Me: 'Sophia!'

Alf: 'She's spot on.'

Sophia: 'That's a lot.'

Alf: 'You have to take your socks and gloves off to count them.'

Sophia: 'You'd need to be a cow.'

Me: A what?

Alf: Or an infinite number of armies of millipedes.

Sophia: How many are there in an infinite?

Me: Too many to count.

Sophia: Like the Manse wall to wall and floor to ceiling with Brussels sprouts . . . or frozen peas?

Alf: Oh, infinity is bigger than that.

Sophia: Two Manses full of frozen peas?

Me: About that.

Alf: Plus one.

'Wait a minute, wait a minute,' I said – wait a minute was something I tended to say twice, like a policeman saying two hellos when one would have sufficed. 'What aspect of orchard-cultivated art and culture is it, then, that you've brought here, to this planet, in this universe, to plant? And have you planted it already? Hang on. I think I know the answer to my own question: the poem.'

'Not the poem, no. The inspiration for the writing of the poem is what I've come to get. Alas, I haven't planted anything. Nor shall I. Not here. Again, I must repeat, Edward: you haven't been listening. This, you see, this planet on which you exist, is an orchard planet in an orchard universe.'

'You mean, we're not really real?'

'I've told you that at least once already.'

'That I'm not real.'

'Not really. No. Sorry.'

'Bummer! Tell me if I've got this right: there's only one really real universe in each multiverse . . . and . . . therefore . . . apart from really real universes, nothing else is real.'

'Almost correctish, after a fashion,' said Alf. 'Over and above really real universes there are really, really real universes, or, as you might think of them, extremely real universes. They only exist in extremely real multiverses, and they're a bit out of my league. You'd have to ask an A-plus muse about those.'

'An A-plus muse?'

'I'm only an A.'

Despite the entertainment value of playing imagination games with Alf, the old brain began to hurt before long. The organ in my skull ruminated on my friend's tall tale while I wasn't paying attention, and towards the close of the imagination game I said, 'Wait a minute, wait a minute. It doesn't make sense. You're saying that you've spent years here, child and youth, all for the sake of just one poem! Come on, Alf; it's hardly worth the bother. One poem?'

'One poem,' he affirmed.

'It must be a heck of an important poem.'

'It is indeed an important poem. No canon is without it. But that's not why I have pursued the inspiration for years.'

'Why, then?'

'I could say because that's how long it takes. However, measurements of time are irrelevant. The higher reality exists unfettered by the limitations imposed by time. To keep it simple, you might say that time is where I come to do my day job. Unconstrained, both by time and by finitude, an infinite number of Alfs pursue an infinite number of poems in an infinite number of contexts in an infinite number of universes.'

I added, 'In an infinite number of multiverses.'

'Plus one.'

Sophia screamed and ran out of the room, waving her arms in the air and shouting, 'My head's exploding.'

In the living room, while rain tapped on the window and a log crackled on the fire, Alf recited some of his own poetry to Sophia. My twin was flattered into a state of pink-cheeked awe. I came in from the kitchen and gave Alf two plastic bags and two thick elastic bands. 'They're just what I've always wanted,' he said.

'You'll need them on your feet when you cross the heath.'

'To catch the train? Wouldn't it be easier to return to Bruagh?'

'Bruagh's about the same distance away as the crow flies, but the crow doesn't fly by the Road; it twists and turns for twice as far.'

The Road did twist and turn, but certainly not twice as far. I'd lied, and I think Alf knew it. Why I lied is complex. We had kissed. He loved Sophia. He couldn't bring himself to kiss Sophia because he thought her too pure. My Sofia. To Alf, I represented her. Me: second best. Maybe I read the situation incorrectly, but there you go.

Hollow Heath could be dangerous. Perhaps I wished for Alf the same fate as the body in the bog.

Alf looked out of the window, past the garden, and over Hollow Heath to orange lights far away. 'I'll try the heath.'

We saw Alf to the front door, Sophia and I. The Manse would be quiet after his departure. Sophia would be sorry to see him go. Devastated, probably. I too would be sorry to see him go – although still I half willed him to slither into a sinking swamp in his plastic-clad feet – at least he would die with clean shoes.

'I'm going to destroy our home, Alf,' I told him at the open door, letting the Cold in. 'You don't need to be involved.'

'I do,' he said, looking at Sophia, not me. 'Yes, I do.'

'Can I contact you by telephone, then, when I've had news of Edgar and I'm ready? We don't have a telephone, but Maud has one in her shop in Bruagh. Or Farmer Barry . . . ?'

'I'll contact you,' said Alf.

'But how will you know when . . . ?'

'I'll know when.'

'Oh, yeah, right, I forgot,' I said. 'You'll jump forward and see the future, then jump back and, yes, that's a handy trick.'

'You don't believe me,' he said with a smile.

'Believe you? Of course I believe you! You're the most honest fellow I've ever met, and I doubt not a single word. Indeed, not a single syllable. Do I believe you? Absolutely!'

Said Sophia, reassuringly, 'I believe you too.'

'Bring back a nice painting to decorate a wall,' I joked, 'if you bump into Michelangelo. Or a ceiling; that would be good.'

He took my hand in what was, for him, an unusually strong grip. Oh, God, don't kiss me again! Yes, please do! He didn't. 'Goodbye for now, Edward. This has been an incredibly profitable experience.'

'Is that what it was? Was that what it is?'

He released my hand and took Sophia's – much more gently.

He raised her hand to his lips and kissed it.

After Alf's departure from the Manse, Mother's memory deteriorated. She only remembered that Edgar was coming home when I reminded her – as I did almost daily. A letter from the institution, containing the date of Edgar's release, might have been lost in transit. We had no plan for what to do, where to put him, or how to treat him. They say you can plan to succeed but you can't succeed without a plan. I had a plan. It started and ended with attending Northern Island University. I had a sub-plan: to lose my virginity while there. While waiting for my plan to start, I walked to Maud's shop each morning to see if the post van had left my exam results. If out of cigarettes, I bought a box and smoked one on the way home. Then, one day, my results arrived. Standing outside Maud's in light drizzle, heart beating like a frantic woodpecker's beak, I tore open the envelope.

I passed my exams, but my science grades were too weak for the science faculty. I no longer had to worry about mathematics turning my cerebral cortex to pulp. Someone else would have to come up with a unified theory of the physical universe. It was Humanities for me.

University drew near. I itched to get started. Preparatory books in a box, courtesy of Blinky Mulholland, arrived at Maud's shop.

Then, disaster . . .

23

Oops!

'I'll save you!' cried Edgar, and jumped off the bridge.

24

The Ballad of Edgar and Mrs Wipple

Mrs Wipple continued dressing hair for five years after her visit to my part of the world – the time she prepared my head for starting school. She gave up the mobile arm of her empire and bought a salon in a city – if one is to make a fortune hairdressing, one's salon must be in a city because that's where most people's heads are. Soon she'd made enough money to retire and spend the rest of her days on luxury liners cruising the oceans and visiting exotic locations. On the day of Edgar's return to the Manse, two bulging suitcases occupied Mrs Wipple's boot as she drove south to an airport, where she would board a plane and fly to a cruise ship somewhere sunny and hot.

No one knows why Edgar did it. I suspect he did it because he relapsed into one of his boyhood personae, probably Superman, because of his proximity to home after such a long time far from it.

It's reasonable to assume that he expected to soar, and my older brother must have been disappointed, to say the least, when he plummeted like the proverbial lead balloon. His fall, from leap to thud, lasted only a second. During that second, although he fell at speed, the world outside his eyeballs became infinite. Infinity penetrated the heartbeat and a half and Edgar's fall lasted for ever.

In all his years of cloudy skies, he had never noticed anything about them other than that they were skies and they were cloudy. However, he noticed now, he 'took note of' how louring and splendid a cloudy sky could be. A cloudy sky was a universe of possibilities.

'Oh,' he uttered, as if, until then, he'd missed the point.

Although upside down, head closer to the macadam than his feet, Edgar's brain interpreted everything as though it were the right way up. Everything would indeed have been the right way up had Edgar been the right way up too.

All this in the space of an oh.

At the same time as Edgar saw her face the right way up although her head was upside down, he saw big hair. He saw the awful, open-mouthed face of the motorist behind the wheel, the horrified eyes in her head. Behind Edgar's oh, as behind a cloud, he had a thought: I know her from somewhere.

Midway through infinity – if infinity has a midway: epiphany!

It happened between the o and the h of the oh. Edgar realized that his error was momentous and irreversible. Meeting God should occur at a time of God's choosing. They taught him that at the institution, subsequent to attempted suicide by overdosing on custard creams.

Endeavouring to fly like Superman had been, at best, a bad idea.

Acrobatically, and maybe in defiance of one of Newton's laws of motion, he twisted one hundred and eighty degrees in mid-air. Perhaps he hoped to scramble back on to the bridge.

Unfortunately, in equal measure for both parties, the car approaching the bridge as Edgar jumped did not have time to scramble one hundred and eighty degrees also. Neither could it manoeuvre up or down, left or right. Edgar faced the car the right way up, legs off the ground like the rest of him. The car, the hair, horrified eyes, mouth wide open for a bloody kiss: all were on course to impact crunchingly.

Yes! He knew that face!

The eyes behind the wheel latched on to Edgar's. Four eyes met.

Two thought bubbles in unison: *Shit!*

Had the motorway been less busy at that hour, had no vehicle been so near to the bridge, Edgar might have hit macadam and broken a leg or legs, mangled an arm, punctured an internal organ with a displaced rib, and perhaps suffered spinal and cranial injuries, although that is something no one can know for sure. Fortunately, however, the vehicle approached at just the right time and fast enough for its bonnet to fill the gap between Edgar and the macadam. It broke his fall. The vehicle that broke his fall was a large four-by-four with huge wheels. Its underside was thus some distance off the road.

Now, Edgar's body was some distance off the road too.

Having bounced off the bonnet, Edgar flew like Superman . . .well, perhaps not quite like Superman, but he did fly.

The squealing of birds sounded like footbrake, rubber and macadam all in a spin. Superman ran out of propulsion fuel. He dropped like seagull poop and, for a second time, hit metal like an over-ripe tomato thrown at a wall. He lay there motionless – but, oddly enough, spinning. Edgar lay there wetly and awkwardly, face – what remained of it – looking at his right shoulder, all four limbs bent at their joints and splayed, mostly on the four-by-four's bonnet – as it spun for the million and umpteenth time – although his head and shoulders were on the windscreen, which miraculously remained intact, but cracked and in need of replacement.

You can cover a crack on a windscreen with brown tape to stop it spreading, but they won't let you drive it in that state. The rest of the four-by-four, which was metallic blue and bloody in the proximity of Edgar's landing, was relatively undamaged – quite a large dent up front, though, visible when they got round to peeling off Edgar.

The four-by-four spun on to the hard shoulder, and now, motionless like Edgar, it faced the direction it had been coming from.

Mrs Wipple's hair needed dressing now. On impact – Edgar with the bonnet of her four-by-four – her hair took a turn for the worse.

She needed a vodka top-up. In fact, she'd had a couple or three before commencing her journey. Thus, drink-driving was on her mind as she passed out, a fine, losing her licence. And murder.

Mrs Wipple regained consciousness.

The entire incident came back to her in a trice. Indeed, her mind could scarcely have been better jogged than by Edgar's head so near and upon the cracked glass. The door was a little stiff, as was Mrs Wipple, but a weighty shoulder and a desperate kick shifted it. Before she could say 'I'm lucky to be alive but that poor sod isn't' she was outside, dazed and bruised. Scratched and sore. But intact.

Having limped around her four-by-four, hands in the pockets of her fur coat, and taken a good look at Edgar from several angles, Mrs Wipple sighed and concluded that there wasn't much she could do. Nothing, in fact – she being knowledgeable in the ways of haircuts but knowing nothing at all of bones, and those other kinds of cuts.

She stood akimbo, looking some hundred metres along the motorway at the pile-up of several cars framed by the bridge. The pile-up was fresh, new, still steaming. When did that happen? Funny, she hadn't heard a single crash!

That's going straight back to the manufacturer, thought Mrs Wipple. What use are air bags if they don't work?

Under normal circumstances, she loved being at the centre of attention. This circumstance, however, was decidedly abnormal. The centre of attention would involve ambulances and police cars. She had no option but to flee, to get out of there before someone saw her. Her hair was a mess. Doubtless, someone had already seen her.

Mrs Wipple ran away. Staggered. Walked. Tottered.

She tottered along the hard shoulder for ever such a long time.

Someone had best contact the police. Mrs Wipple had a mobile phone, but it was in her bag, and her bag was in the car. They would breathalyse her if she went back. They would find the vodka bottle in the glove compartment. She found a relatively dry patch of hard shoulder. There, she sat down on her gnarled, expansive bottom. 'Thinking cap on,' she said. 'First things first. Don't panic.'

The distant siren, soon to be followed by flashing lights, got her moving. She flung herself – in so far as a woman her age in a fur coat can fling – over a grassy rise and tumbled into a shallow stream on the other side. She lost a shoe and stood ankle deep in icy water. There, Mrs Wipple hid until the police car sped past.

Mrs Wipple retrieved her shoe and climbed out of the stream on the opposite side from the motorway – on the side of dense woodland and escape. Tears cut lines through her make-up and her face looked like the surface of Mars. It was no consolation whatsoever that dusk changing to night meant that no one could see. Who could see her anyhow, in this jungle where the thickness of overhanging branches made the darkness darker? She stumbled on, near blind, whimpering, carried forward by the logical belief that if she walked in a straight line – or as straight a line as possible given all these woody obstacles – she must emerge from the other side sometime. But, then what?

The fingers she touched against her head came away bloody. I'm concussed, thought she, I need a sticking plaster.

Night would be harder to survive than day. It gets colder at night and you can't see. By daylight, you can gather berries and leaves. There might be apple trees. Wood! She could build a raft using vines like Tarzan to bind the timbers. Mrs Wipple had never before hunted rabbits or deer. Learning to throw a spear would be easy; setting traps and gutting fish – that would be a challenge.

'Survival.' That's what came first: food and shelter. Regardless of whatever else she had to do, she had to survive until the rescue team found her. They were bound to send one when someone noticed her missing. There was plenty of kindling. It was a bit damp, but if she rubbed two sticks together hard enough . . .

In the better weather, when the season changed and sunshine dried everything flammable, a passing ship might see the smoke from her fire. Survival packs of juice and nutritional chocolate bars might drop from the sky when she ran low on berries and rabbits. Protection from the elements. The Swiss Family Robinson. 'Cover,' said Mrs Wipple. 'I shall build a tree house.' Building a tree house required a saw and a hammer, and she had neither. Nor did she have a large sheet of industrial plastic for the roof.

Night fell. Mrs Wipple got to her feet – although she couldn't remember having sat down – and looked around her. If she moved off now, to find a better spot, she might only find a worse one. She gathered fallen branches, woody lattices and moss clumps. With these, she built two walls – of sorts – at either side of her spot against a tree. They were quite low walls, as walls go, and more like two piles of knee-high woodland, really, but they served to demarcate her private and secure spot from the badlands beyond it. 'Tonight I must sleep,' thought Mrs Wipple while staggering about, 'and restore my strength. Tomorrow, I must build a raft.'

Until noon the next day she stirred not once. When she woke, beside a puddle of vomit, she had a pneumatic drill in her head.

Remembering, as soon as her eyes opened, that she ran over someone in her car – a day ago, a week ago or whenever – Mrs Wipple burst into tears. The victim was dead. Mrs Wipple didn't know how she knew. Nevertheless, she knew. No number of buckets of tears, no amount of guilty sorrow, no heart and brain and soul-felt apologies could undo, or even reduce, the fact that she had killed him.

And her such a kind and tender thing, girl and woman, all her life. Yes, thought Mrs Wipple, as she lay there, sobbing in dewy dampness, I'm loud, I'm clumsy, I'm big, I'm annoying, but my heart has always been in the right place. I'm not a murderer. Yet I have murdered. As her sobbing turned again to wailing, 'I deserve to die,' she told the living trees, dead leaves, and fullness of nature's woodland of living and dead things. Sucking her thumb and whimpering, she had a thought: I could eat a horse. On that thought's tail came another: I could hang myself from a tree.

But she didn't have a rope. Or a horse.

After more hours of fruitless wandering, sweating inside her fur and drunk on despair, Mrs Wipple suddenly stopped dead and sobered when it hit her. A moment of lucidity struck like lightning. She looked all round at so much woodland that looked like so much woodland at night, and thought, calmly, In my distress and disorientation I've been travelling in a circle. Oh dear me.

A beast in a tree shook its branches. Monkeys, thought Mrs Wipple and fled at speed, throwing off her fur as she went, ripping off her cashmere cardigan, silk blouse and pearl necklace. She ran, in a bra like two tents drawn tight over footballs, like Xena the Warrior Princess, expecting a monkey to land on her shoulders.

And one did – sort of.

Mrs Wipple stopped dead and screamed like a car trying to start with a flat battery: ah-ah-ah. Her hair would have defied gravity and stood on end if finer and less plentiful.

'Sweet Jesus,' said Alf.

Mrs Wipple's arms made crossbones across her breasts. Paralysed, she didn't run away.

'Hello,' he said. 'Sorry to have startled you.'

Mrs Wipple's cavernous mouth hung open to fill, empty and refill overworked lungs. Her two amazingly plump breasts heaved up and down, in and out, and side to side as one. They juggled turn about as two, headed off east and west and reunited in the middle.

'I'm Alf,' he said.

'I had an accident.'

'I know,' he replied, with a kindly smile.

'What are you going to do to me? I've no money. And I'm old.'

'I'm not going to do anything to you.'

'Then what do you want? Can you help me?'

He shrugged apologetically. 'Sorry. I can't intervene. I can't undo what's been done. It's against the laws.'

'There's money in my bag. In the car.'

'I don't want money.'

'What, then? You can't have sex it won't be nice I haven't washed in days and I have my period.'

'I'm not obliged to tell you this, but I want to. No one should die with a bad conscience. I want your conscience to be clear. For that, you must know that no one blames you. No one will ever blame you. You are innocent.' His smile, this time, was a flash. 'It is an unqualified good to die with a clean conscience.'

'Die?' Mrs Wipple, having calmed a degree, started up again.

'All of us die some day. You have nothing to fear from me.'

'I don't want to die!'

'And you have nothing to fear from death.'

'Don't hurt me! I can't stand needles! I . . . I must be on my way,' said Mrs Wipple.

'Not yet.' Alf walked to where the fur coat had fallen, picked it up and gave it to her. Mrs Wipple accepted the coat with one arm, the other trying to hide both breasts and failing spectacularly.

'Goodbye,' said Alf. 'Watch your footing . . . in the dark.'

Mrs Wipple escaped. Her head spun. Everything else spun in the opposite direction.

'Stop!' called Alf. Mrs Wipple did, but she didn't turn round. She listened. 'That's the wrong way. The track to your right.' Mrs Wipple thought about taking it. Then she did.

When she believed herself far enough away from the would-be rapist, she knelt with an ear to the ground – John Wayne did it once in a movie. The rapist had lost her scent.

Her feet were so numb, soon she'd be walking on her shins. Mrs Wipple's mind turned to those television documentaries she'd watched about how to survive in extreme conditions. But she didn't have a penknife with which to skin a snake for food, nor a string with a bent paperclip tied to one end to dangle in a crack in the ice in hope of a passing, short-sighted fish.

*

Dusk would arrive in an hour. I closed the curtains, wished I had Alf for company, and strayed to the kitchen to see what Sophia was up to. Water boiled in the stock pot. I watched as my sister brushed vegetables off the chopping board into it with the back of a hand. She added a crushed stock cube, gave the brew a stir, and put on the lid.

'Have you seen Gregory?' I asked, wondering what my chances were of borrowing his wheels. Probably zero.

'Last I saw him he was mucking about outside.'

I hoped for a pot of tea, but Sophia dusted vegetable residue off her hands and retrieved flour and eggs from the pantry.

'What are you making?' I asked.

'A pie,' she replied, cheerfully enough.

'What kind of pie?'

'I don't know yet. A pie pie.'

'My favourite.'

I put on my coat, scarf and gloves and lied to Sophia that I had a date with Alf in Garagh and she shouldn't wait up; I'd be home late. I'd be home exceedingly late – some time tomorrow – if I tried to walk it. Besides, Alf was almost certainly somewhere else. But I didn't know where else to look for him. While in Garagh, I might have a few beers and brood on regrets about our evening in Ruse Bay.

I intended to hitch a ride part of the way, or all of the way if possible, on a passing tractor. The chances of encountering a passing tractor were slim, but if I did it would surely stop, local tractor drivers being what they were. Meeting a hitchhiker is a major event. In reality, I knew I would probably only make it on foot to Bruagh. Maybe I would buy cigarettes in Maud's shop, with a little of the money Farmer Barry had given me, and cough my guts up in the rain while walking back to the Manse – that counted as entertainment around Bruagh.

I kissed Sophia on the forehead, avoiding her floury hands, and left by the back door. I saw a light on in an outhouse and went to investigate. Gregory, mottled black with oil, tightened the bolts on his baby's rear wheel as it lay on its side. 'What are you doing?' I asked.

'Having sex with a prostitute. What's it look like?'

'It looks like you're screwing your nuts.'

Gregory, like Father, had no sense of humour. It was so obvious I'd never noticed it before. 'What do you want?' He looked up at me. 'Going somewhere?'

'Would you lend me your bike for the evening?'

'No! Piss off!'

'Would you rent me your bike, then?'

'I said, no.'

'I'll pay you as soon as I get some money.'

'I won't live that long.'

I removed one of Farmer Barry's notes – a generous denomination – from my pocket and tempted him with it. Wiping his hands on a rag, he took an interest. 'It'll take more than that. Nobody rides the Wasp but me.'

'The Wasp?'

'Yes. The Wasp.'

'Wasps are fast.'

'Your point being?'

'It's all I have,' I lied.

He thought about it. My brother wanted to say no, not at any price, but temptation got the better of him. He snatched the note. 'Bring it back exactly as you see it. One scratch, one tiny scratch, and you're dead meat.'

'Yeah, yeah.'

'I mean it. Scratch it and you're next for the cemetery.'

'Yeah, yeah.' Actually, I feared I might indeed be next for the cemetery. But not at Gregory's hands. I'd never ridden a moped before. I picked it up and sat on it.

'It'll need petrol,' Gregory warned.

'Do I need a key or something?'

'It's already in it.'

'Oh. Right. Where's the steering wheel?'

He showed me how to change gear and threatened to kill me again. I turned the key and an earthquake of noise almost brought down the outhouse.

I started out with extreme caution. Whereas some fool advised: live fast and die young, Edward Pike advised: live slowly and don't die.

'Watch the potholes!' called Gregory as I shot across the courtyard a little faster than walking speed. I soon realized that going faster made balancing the machine between my legs easier. Vroom-vroom! Up to the speed of a battery-powered wheelchair.

Borrowing his moped had been a lot easier than I expected. He knew that I knew he'd murdered Father, although nothing had been said. Maybe he was afraid that I'd go to the police. I was aware that he might try to eradicate that threat with a second murder. Mine.

I saw what Gregory meant about the potholes. The headlight blinked out once or twice. Getting to Garagh took twenty minutes, and I encountered no other vehicles on the way. The closer I got to town, the more certain I grew that Alf was there.

The town was neither large nor exciting. It shut at five o'clock. One hotel graced the main street, McGibbon's, a bar-restaurant really, with guest rooms upstairs. There were a couple of bed and breakfasts, but I didn't see Alf as a bed and breakfast kind of guy.

I parked Gregory's bike in the small car park and hoped there were no moped thieves around, since I'd no way of immobilizing it. There wasn't much happening inside, no one at the reception desk and a few locals supping beer in the bar. I rang the bell, and a flushed-looking woman came from an anteroom fixing her hair and blouse.

'I'm looking for Mr Lord; I believe he's staying here.'

'Oh, he's in room five,' she said without hesitation. He might have been the only guest. 'He arrived this afternoon. Friend of his?'

'University colleagues,' I said, and wished I hadn't. Lying had never been my strong point. I nodded at the stairs, 'May I?'

'By all means, dear. You go right ahead.'

When I had one foot on the bottom step, she said, 'My name's Laura, by the way.' What does one do in such a situation? I lacked experience. Do hotel receptionists introduce themselves? Do barmaids? I thought, not usually. 'It used to be Leslie. But I changed it to Laura.'

I said um, ah, or possibly er, and followed it with, 'I'm Edward. Pleased to meet you, Laura.'

'Lola!'

'Sorry?'

'Hasn't he mentioned me? I'm Lola.'

'Sorry. I thought you said Laura.'

'I did, but my friends call me Lola. C.O.L.A. cola.'

'Right.'

'Friends,' she emphasized. 'My friends call me Lola.' Lola sang, 'See my friends, sailing down the river,' and then spoke, 'You can be my friend if you want. Any friend of Mr Lord's is a friend of mine.'

'Right. No problem.' I fired a forefinger-arrow at her. Got it! And hurried up the stairs, clueless as to what to think. I only made it halfway. Lola, at the bottom, fists on hips, called after me, 'He didn't mention a university colleague.' What could I say?

'How well do you know him?' I asked. My amusement with Lola was beginning to turn to frustration.

'It's a long story, dear. I could tell it to you over drinkies if you've got the time. There's more comfortable spots than halfway up the stairs.'

As I reached the top . . . Leslie! Maud's weird son, Leslie!

Lola was Leslie!

Leslie simply vanished off the planet. An ancient memory stirred. Someone – probably Mother – said Maud's boy's head went and they took him away, though I might have been muddling my memory of Leslie with them taking Edgar away. Whatever state my memories were in, Leslie would be in his early thirties now. Lola was about that age. I knew a transvestite. Good grief! Had he had a sex-change – his parts removed and what remained tampered with? I briefly thought of Nurse in junior school with the fiddling, prodding fingers. Were sex-change people still called transvestites? I didn't know. The stair carpet smelled of stale beer. So did the walls and ceiling. The door handle looked sticky. So did the door, but I knocked it none the less – with an erection in my underpants that I half hoped Alf wouldn't notice.

While the other half of me hoped that he would.

The door opened.

'Surprise, supplies!'

Alf should have been surprised to see me, but looked anything but. 'What's the matter?' He stood aside and I entered a typical pub guest room: mattress three and a half feet off the floor and furniture from the French Revolution.

I sat on the mattress and sank, springs going off all around. Alf was wearing his coat and boots. 'Are you going out?'

'I've just returned,' he said.

'By broomstick, no doubt.'

'You shouldn't be here – although I knew you would be.'

'Well, I'm overjoyed that you're so pleased to see me.'

'I'm always pleased to see you, Edward; it's not that.'

'What is it, then?'

'It's not yet time.'

'Time for what?'

'I can't tell you that. But I can tell you that you must return to the Manse. You have a destiny to fulfil.'

'Wow! A destiny! Is this one of your time travel stories? Are you in some kind of role-playing syndicate?'

'Yes, yes, something like that,' he snapped, making me angry and hurt that he seemed to take me for an idiot, a pawn in his game.

I brushed off his insult. 'Look, Alf, why don't you come back to the Manse and get to know Sophia better? You can stay there for free instead of paying for here . . . Is there something going on between you and the receptionist? She's a man, you know. At least Sophia's a real woman. You've only met her once and I know you like her. She likes you too.'

'There must be mystique,' he replied. 'I want to be, and I am, her knight in shining armour. Sophia can know me, but only from a distance. It's magic. If you see the trick close up, you spoil it.'

'I know what you're saying. But you have to get close to her some time, or let her get close to you. Is that what you're hoping: that because you're here, in town, she'll be tempted to break a promise she seems to have forgotten and come to you?'

Alf said, 'Let the poem play out and reveal the ending.'

Let the poem play out and reveal the ending. I liked that.

And I found myself falling in a kind of love with Alf, who had kissed me, and who had fallen for my sister. I wished he was a woman, and felt perfectly content with my wishing.

'Let's go down to the bar and talk about poetry,' I said.

'Return to the Manse. You're needed.'

'I'm not. Honest. Do you know who the receptionist is? Come down to the bar and I'll tell you.'

'Go home, Edward. Now.'

Through the trees, she saw a light. Salvation. The star of Bethlehem. An angel. And that angel, so long as it didn't move off, provided Mrs Wipple with the straight line she should have been walking all along. The trees became less densely packed.

'I'm saved!' cried Mrs Wipple. Having climbed over bracken that tore her legs, and waded through a stream that stung her fissures, she found herself on some kind of farm track. The light that saved her was maybe a mile away. It was no angel, but an electric light in a room with a window. She had no option but to head for the light. And in a straight line too, for Heaven knew where this farm lane led to or from – not the light, so far as she could tell.

Mrs Wipple yelped as rusty barbed wire tore into her inner thigh as she straddled it. From here to the light was like walking on air in comparison to her struggle through the wood. Occasionally, the moon peeped out. The star of Bethlehem came from an upper window in a large rectangular house. 'Hang about,' said Mrs Wipple. 'This is . . .' the place she came to years ago . . . 'the woman with the hair . . . and the little boy who looked like an angel.'

A second before Mrs Wipple reached for the big, black knocker on the door, she thought to take a look through the nearest window. One never knows what one is letting oneself in for, does one? Although the curtains were closed, they had a wide gap at the side closest to the door, which Mrs Wipple peered through.

What she saw came as a shock, and instantly made her change her mind about knocking on the door. There was a healthy open fire dancing on the far wall and, silhouetted before it, what looked like, unless she was very much mistaken, a thin man standing rather bent at the knees masturbating, or . . . Mrs Wipple couldn't see; the curtains were in the way. Was there someone else in the room, and were they . . . ? She was a woman of the world. She'd given birth and become familiar with body fluids. Mr Wipple had been a sailor!

Well . . . whatever people do in the privacy of their own homes is entirely up to them, but while they're doing it you don't knock on the door and ask to use the telephone. If you interrupt a man mid-sexual excitement there's no telling what the impulses that drive men might drive him to do. When Mr Wipple got that way it hardly mattered if one was in the cornflake aisle at the supermarket. Through the window, he, or they, were taking an awfully long time over it. Was that normal? Mr Wipple was in and out before one got one's knees settled . . . Suddenly, Mrs Wipple needed badly to urinate, and she wrenched her gaze from the window.

Rather than return to the wilderness for relief, where someone might see her from an upstairs window – and a lady peeing in the open is so unladylike – she looked for a suitable wall or something similar to drop her ruined tights and crouch beside. Feeling most definitely unlike a lady, she saw, noticeably askew, a rectangular erection standing on end, which she knew to be an outdoor convenience. What else? Some of these old places still had them. She was old enough to have used one herself as a child, at her grandmother's house in the country, a plank with a hole in it, and her feet dangling.

Even if they've taken out the pot, this will do, she thought as she hobbled towards the inconveniently located convenience, removed the rusty lock,touched the handle, turned it and opened the door.

'Sorry! So sorry,' said Mrs Wipple, smiling stupidly despite the stench, and shut the toilet door. What had that woman eaten? The occupant was a woman, wasn't it? God, what horrid, hard lives these rural people lived. She turned round, and shrieked. The wanker!

The Dark and the Cold were there. And me. And a moped in an outhouse where I'd left it beside a cigarette butt.

Brave of me: I'd seen a shape – not Gregory's, an intruder's shape. I'd stamped out my cigarette, taken the ice-cracking pole that Mother broke years ago and gone to investigate.

And Mrs Wipple was there too, whom I recognized, and whose name I had never forgotten. And the leaning tower of toilet had always been there, with the rotting corpse inside.

'I, a, that is, there's. I needed to, you see. It's engaged,' said Mrs Wipple. Although she remained conscious throughout the seconds that followed, her legs gave way and she crumpled in a heap.

I helped her to stand.

Mrs Wipple said many words and bits of words, but not one sentence, and made hardly any sense. She defended herself – against possible rape? – swiping a fist at my head from too far out to hit.

'I hope you came, you beast!' she cried.

'Steady on,' I replied. 'I don't want to hurt you.'

'Just try it! Just you try it! If I'm trespassing, that's all very well, but you shouldn't . . . I've a black belt in Jakarta. My husband's a sailor. I'm a policeman. Woman. Goodbye.'

She took off across the field.

'Where are you going? Don't go that way. There's nothing that way for miles.'

'I have a bus to cat—' Mrs Wipple stepped in the Hole and went under with a splash.

Oh Lord! My instinct was to save her. But she was big and heavy. And under water. And had seen the body in the bog. I might have been able to save her. At least, I might have tried. But I didn't. What a mess. What does one do with a mess? One cleans it up, of course. With the broken pole, I prodded into the freezing, muddy water, detected the Wipple-bulk, and ensured it stayed under.

Having dispatched the woman, I realized that I felt, and had felt for some time – maybe an hour – much as I had felt here and there during my adolescence, serendipitously tipsier than intended, comfortably out of myself and prone to weighty, convoluted sentences. My mind transcended the limitations that flesh and bones imposed upon my being. I had achieved, without trying, enlightenment – of a sort.

I knew that what had been had to be and what would be would be. Blissful powerlessness.

Gregory came out from the kitchen – presumably for a smoke because Sophia complained when he smoked inside – as I approached the back door. Startled at seeing me, he said, 'I thought you'd be out all night.'

'I didn't say I'd be out all night.'

'I know, but . . .'

'Is something wrong?' He looked like he'd seen a new ghost.

'No,' he said. To my surprise he offered me a cigarette.

We smoked cigarettes at the back door.

'I'm going to burn down the Manse,' I said.

Like, it's for the best, he said, 'Yeah.'

⋆

I had either murdered Mrs Wipple or been responsible for her death. Manslaughter involves, I think, killing without malice aforethought. Therefore, I might have been guilty of manslaughter – or, in Mrs Wipple's case, woman-slaughter – for I never had malice in mind: not in aforethought, not in contemporaneous thought, and not in afterthought. I have always been, and remain, malice free; a touch unsympathetic perhaps, but completely without enmity.

If I had not caused the Wipple woman to take flight from me she might not have fallen; indeed, she might have taken flight from the Manse in a different direction. I did, it's true, hold her under the water, but she was probably dead already and my action served only to conceal that which I'm sure no one could have the slightest wish to look at – there are concealed bodies enough rotting around the Manse without one rotting fully exposed.

Although I did not want to do what I did to Mrs Wipple, we found ourselves there, and I did it without premeditation.

In time, I am sure, I will come to believe that our lives are predetermined. We think we have choices, and act as if we do. But of the options we think we have all but one are ghosts, and that one is the one we must take. I did what I did because, in the infinity of options, I could do nothing else.

I have always tried to be good, but appear to have failed as often as I appear to have succeeded. 'Appear' is the significant word. When I have been good, I have been so by accident. When I have been bad, I have been so through no wicked impulse of my own. Whether good or bad, then, I am nothing. I have made no decisions. I have made no impression on the world. I am a footprint on Hollow Heath on a snowy day. More snow has fallen and covered me. I did not ask the snow to fall and I cannot make it stop. Sophia cannot understand. I have no one to tell about the way I feel. I feel as though I am the message in a bottle that no one will ever read. Everything started to rot years ago, and rots still. Maybe there is nothing but rot.

I suffered deeper depression than I had previously known following the dispatch of Wipple. But what can one do? One cannot undo the past. I toughed out the depression caused by the bad thing, unaware that a worse thing was imminent.

25

Edgar Comes Home

With a cup of tea on my lap and one leg dangling over a chair arm, I settled to Alf's book of poetry. I turned to the scruffy-edged poem: *The Lady of Shalott*, by Tennyson. That's the one that Sophia recited, and, in so doing, made me yawn mightily.

Sophia appeared in the doorway and said someone was at the Manse's back door. 'Who?' I asked. She didn't know. I went to resolve the mystery and found a rotund police constable with his cap under an arm. There was a police car behind him and an officer inside it.

Wipple! It must be Wipple. She survived the Hole and went to the police. No. She couldn't possibly have survived the Hole. Not Wipple, then. The body in the bog! The police couldn't touch me for the body in the bog; I hadn't killed her.

'Yes?' came from my mouth as it dropped open.

'I was hoping to speak to Mr Pike senior.'

'He's indisposed.' My mouth was very dry. 'What is it?'

'Is he at home?'

'He can't speak to you; he's too ill.'

'Your mother?'

'They're both too ill. How can I help you?'

'I'm afraid I have some bad news . . .'

I saw a moped, a ditch, a body face down, and felt mightily

relieved. I'd happily bury Gregory in the shallow grave where Tennyson used to be before Mother binned him. The officer mistook my sagging shoulders for a near faint.

'Would you like to sit down, sir?'

I didn't want him in the kitchen. 'I'm all right.'

'There's been a road accident . . .'

'Yes?'

'It's just . . .' He choked. Swallowed. Policing was probably a bad career choice. I thought he was going to cry. 'I've never done this kind of thing before. I don't know how to say it.'

Just my luck to get a wimp.

'Would you like me to guess?' I asked.

He shook his head: a negative.

'I'll guess. You can nod yes or no.'

The officer whimpered, biting his lips, nodding his head with a single teardrop in the corner of one eye.

'There's been an accident involving my brother.' Whimper – him, not me. Nod. Nod. 'My brother Gregory.' Shake. Shake. Whimper. 'Not involving Gregory, but my brother none the less.' Nod. Nod. Sniff. 'Edgar. It's my brother Edgar.' Nod. Nod.

'There's been an accident involving my brother Edgar.'

The officer pulled himself together. 'I'm sorry to have to tell you that Mr Edgar Pike . . . lost his life. He's dead, that is.'

The officer continued to speak. I heard what he said, but his voice came from far away. Edgar's body had been taken to a hospital. The medics there did exactly the same as the ambulance medics had done on the motorway: they acknowledged that Edgar was dead.

'What happened?' I asked.

He'd just told me what happened, but I was in shock.

'It looks like a hit and run,' said the officer. 'I mean, we have the vehicle belonging to whoever hit him. But the driver ran.'

'Edgar died, but the driver suffered no injury,' said a voice that came out of me, angry at the injustice of it.

'Yes. Er . . . How do you mean?' asked the officer, presumably because of my angry, or possibly just puzzled, tone of voice.

'You can't run away if you're injured.' I looked over my shoulder to see if Sophia was listening, but she must have gone upstairs. How would I break the news of Edgar's death to her? How would I break it to Mother? 'Where is he now?' I asked.

'Like I said, he ran away.'

'I mean Edgar, my brother.'

'Oh, we've got him all right; he's at the mortuary. We need someone to identify the body. You, sir, if that's all right. If you could pull on a coat and come with us now.'

'Mmm,' I said, but my mind was elsewhere, everywhere and nowhere all at the same time. 'What's the car like?'

'That's it,' he said, turning to the police car.

'I mean the car that hit Edgar.'

'It's drivable.' The officer juggled a scenario briefly. 'I mean, it's drivable now the smashed window's been removed. That'll be why the driver didn't escape in the car: couldn't see out. Your brother's head landed on the windscreen: splat! I mean, not his head by itself, the rest of him was there too. But don't you worry, sir. We'll trace the vehicle's owner, and you'll have your man in no time. Or woman.' He cleared his throat. 'Unless the vehicle was stolen, in which case it might take a bit longer.'

'I'll get my coat.'

Sophia was upstairs with Mother. I entered Mother's bedroom and Sophia looked at me without speaking.

'I've got to go out for a while, but I won't be long.'

'What is it?' asked Sophia.

'It's nothing to worry about. Nothing any of us can do anything about. I'll tell you when I come back.'

'How long will you be?'

'Not long,' I said, although I had no idea how long I would be.

Sophia stayed with Mother. Gregory was farting around the

countryside on his vacuum cleaner. The drive in the police car to the hospital lasted two hours. The hospital was somewhere I had never heard of and had never been before.

Identifying Edgar in the mortuary lasted a couple of minutes. Half of his face was cut and grazed. The other half was missing. He'd put on some weight since last time I saw him. Other than that, he looked just like himself but bluer. They'd traced him to the institution, apparently because of documents on his person – probably his release certificate. The institution directed them to the Manse.

The drive back to the Manse – I felt less like I was under arrest driving back – lasted the same amout of time as the drive from it, but passed more quickly.

The night was very dark when I returned. I asked the officers to drop me at the top of the Lane; I wanted to be alone with my thoughts. They nodded their heads, pretending to empathize with my grief. The truth was that I dreaded the thought that the hump of Mrs Wipple's corpse would appear, floating in the Hole, silver under moonlight.

'I came out without my cigarettes,' I said, before getting out of the police car. 'You couldn't spare one, could you . . . and a light?' The driver was a smoker. Discovering only three left in his box, and feeling sorry for me, he gave me the box, and a book of matches.

Gregory had returned to the Manse while I was identifying Edgar. The three of us, him, me and Sophia, didn't go to bed until well after midnight. Neither Gregory nor I fancied digging a grave for Edgar. We decided that when his body came home we would put it in the cellar with Father, temporarily, until we had a better idea. My plan, to burn down the Manse, was set to one side. I didn't mind burning down the Manse with Father still inside. But not Edgar.

'Well then, slimeball,' said Gregory to Slimeball – presumably me, since he looked at me as he said it, 'that's the end of Edgar. I can't say I'll miss the poor blockhead; I hadn't seen him for years.'

'The police will be here again,' I said.

'Why should they be?'

'They told me they had to ask some questions. It's their investigation of the accident.'

'I'll take myself off for a week or so, then. As from tonight. No use—'

'No you bloody won't, Gregory.' He was shocked, and perhaps a touch impressed by my ferocity. 'They'll be here tomorrow, and Farmer Barry's bringing Edgar home tomorrow; I phoned him from the mortuary. You're older than me and Sophia and you've a duty to play the role Father would have played. Mother isn't able.'

'Stiff types in uniforms make me uneasy.'

'Tough luck,' I said. 'It's your job to speak to them.'

'Frankly, slimeball, I'd rather not.'

'You want me to do the talking.'

He grinned.

I would make a better job of talking to the police. I agreed to do it. 'You'd probably say something stupid and cock it up.' Gregory didn't deny it. 'I'll talk to the police tomorrow and you can break the news to Mother. Don't be your usual dickhead self; break it gently.'

Gregory, Sophia and I entered Mother's bedroom. She had been dozing, but turned her head when the door creaked.

Gregory couldn't find his tongue. Awkwardly, I said, 'Hello, Mother. I suppose you're wondering why we're all here together. Gregory has something to tell you . . . haven't you, Gregory?'

Sophia and I held hands.

'Guess what,' said Gregory, a little too cheerfully for my liking. 'Edgar got run over by a car. He's dead.'

On the following day, we were on our best behaviour. And sad. We were sadder than we had ever been before. Although at the centre of the scene, I felt detached from it, set to automatic, as though wound up like a clock and left to run in the constantly shifting present. No past and no future. Only now, and now and now.

It was the day Edgar returned to the Manse.

*

We four are standing outside with the Cold at the back door, dressed in our tattered best, watching the Lane across the courtyard: me, Sophia, Mother and Gregory in a line. We are in black, except for Mother, who is in white like a brittle stone angel. Her energy, this morning, might be one final power surge to enable her to say goodbye to the idiot child that – I believe – she loves the most.

Farmer Barry drives Edgar's body down the Lane. We watch the top of his lorry over the hedge. We can't see the trailer behind it or the coffin within, bumping over potholes. A police car tails the lorry. Farmer Barry has brought all kinds of things down the Lane over the years: gas canisters, bread and vegetables, sausages, and now a dead brother. Edgar is returning to his home. To his second home, really; his first home is the institution that spat him out without so much as an escort to see him safely back to the Manse. I've been angry with the institution, but I'm too sad to be angry now. Edgar is no more, and there's nothing I can do about it.

This morning, Gregory senses an edginess, and is wary of me. Our relationship has flipped over. He'll do whatever I tell him to do today. Tomorrow? Who knows?

Farmer Barry and the police car pass the dry toilet, which leans to one side more than it used to. He stops his lorry in the courtyard, and the police car stops behind it. There are two policemen inside it. They're not the ones who brought the news of Edgar's death; this is a different pair. Farmer Barry drops from his cab to the ground, goes to the back of his lorry to unload Edgar, but looks at the policemen through their windscreen instead. Something's wrong.

The policemen look back at him. The passenger policeman speaks to the driver. The driver restarts his engine and backs up to give Farmer Barry space to unload Edgar's coffin.

He's a smaller man than he used to be, Farmer Barry, shrunk with age, but still strong and capable. He has a trolley that rises up like a melodeon when he cranks the handle. It makes getting the coffin off easier. While Farmer Barry is about his business, the policemen get out of their car and saunter towards us with peaked hats under their arms. The passenger, who is smaller than the driver by a head, hesitates and elbows his colleague, who looks where the passenger is looking and hesitates too. But they keep advancing until the small one meets a pothole and, with a painful yelp, twists an ankle. They reach us outside the back door, one walking and the other hobbling.

'I'm very sorry for your loss.' The tall one addresses Mother mainly, but his eyes flicker on the rest of us.

The small one is still looking at the cemetery.

The tall one nudges him.

'What? Oh aye! I'm sorry for your loss too . . . like him.'

They're not sorry. Why would they be sorry? They never met Edgar. Mother says thank you and bows her head.

I think the policemen are a pair of pricks.

Farmer Barry's trolley, let down to its normal height, with Edgar on it in his coffin, rattles over the courtyard avoiding the larger potholes. It's all a bit unreal. Dead grandmothers is one thing, dead strangers another, but a dead brother is disconcerting – especially when he's heading straight at you in a box on a trolley. I can't help thinking that Farmer Barry is bumping Edgar's head, and, on the tail of that thought, I think that the coffin's interior is probably cushioned and uniquely comfortable.

Farmer Barry mumbles an excuse me.

We part as he steers the coffin towards the back door. Mother raises a gossamer hand to his arm and he pauses. 'It's very kind of you,' she says. And he replies 'Not at all' before encountering the doorstep. The tall policeman helps him to get the trolley over it without losing Edgar over the side. The small policeman just stands there looking like someone with a broken ankle and I feel a strong urge to punch him in the head.

The tall policeman helps Farmer Barry lift the coffin on to the kitchen table. Farmer Barry takes a screwdriver from a pocket and begins to unscrew the lid. We have followed Edgar, Farmer Barry and the tall policeman inside. When Mother whimpers, I raise a hand to Farmer Barry and shake my head. He nods and retightens the screw. If we change our minds and want to look in, we can manage to come up with a screwdriver of our own, I am sure.

Farmer Barry puts the screwdriver back in his pocket and stands a while in front of Mother not knowing what to say. Then he does a very strange thing: he falls on her, and, to my surprise, she falls on him. Mother's little arms spring up round his broad rustic shoulders. After what seems like an hour or two, they part. Mother says it's very kind of him and he says not at all. Then he leaves.

The tall policeman says to Mother, 'I realize it's an inconvenient time, but would you mind if we have a chat?'

She dithers because she didn't expect to have a chat and doesn't want to chat. And I don't blame her. My anger returns, and I'm about to say something, although I don't know what, when the tall one asks, 'Is there a Mr Pike?'

'I'm Mr Pike,' says Gregory, and looks at me. 'So is he.'

'Our father is ill and confined to bed,' I say. Lying is probably a mistake, but I want to avoid the possibility of the policemen's asking how Father died. 'He's too ill to see anyone. Anything you want to say, you can say to us. What would you like to chat about?'

It must have been my tone; the tall one is taken aback.

'Let's go through to the living room,' I say.

'You'll have to excuse me, officers,' Mother says in the hall. 'My sons are capable of telling you whatever you want to know.' She holds on to the banister as if she's about to faint. Sophia takes her other arm and helps her up the stairs.

The fire smoulders, an orange glow behind the guard. Sunlight enters the front window and cuts an acute line across the room. Gregory slumps in an armchair with its stuffing escaping – which annoys me. I say, 'Can my brother pour you a glass of wine?'

The small one grins a yes please, but the tall one says not on duty, adding, 'You have a graveyard in your back garden.'

'Cemetery,' says Gregory.

I add, 'Graveyards are in the grounds of churches and chapels.'

'Is that where . . . ?'

'Yes. We do all our own.'

The tall officer eyes round the room as if looking for clues. The small one looks out of his depth.

'Is there anything specific you want to chat about?' I ask.

The tall one: 'Your brother, Edgar. Is he your older brother?'

'Gregory is first born. Edgar next.'

'You're younger than him, then,' concludes the brain cell, while his tall colleague strays to the window and looks over the heath.

'That's the motorway.' He turns to me with his hands behind his back. 'He jumped off the bridge.' When I make no reply – since his statement doesn't call for a reply – he adds, 'On his way home from a psychiatric hospital, I believe.'

'That's right.'

'Which one?' As the tall one asks, the small one takes out a notebook and pencil.

'You'll find the name of the institution and other relevant details on file,' I lie. 'Your colleagues have already interviewed my mother. She found the experience stressful in the extreme.'

'How long had your brother worked there?'

'He didn't work there.'

'He was a patient,' says Gregory.

I add, 'As information already provided will verify. Our brother had been in care for many years. Mother couldn't manage him at home. Over the past few years, his minder accompanied him home, here, to the Manse, for occasional short stays.'

'What was wrong with him exactly?'

'There was nothing wrong with him; we loved our brother.'

'There must have been something wrong with him. I'm no expert. Schizophrenia or something?'

'I'm sure you'll find that in the file too.'

The tall officer's face looks as if, out of initiative, it has decided to await instructions. The small one scribbles something out, then keeps writing. When he stops, he looks at me for more.

'On his way home,' I say, 'in fact, having all but arrived at the door, inexplicable and unlikely as it seems, Edgar jumped.'

'You've got it badly wrong, then,' says the small one.

'What do you mean?'

'There must have been something wrong with him.' I grind my teeth and try to hold my tongue. Were my gums able to do anything, they would be involved too. 'People don't jump off bridges when there's nothing wrong with them.'

My voice becomes louder all by itself. 'Edgar was essentially the same as anyone else. Are you the same man while on duty as you are while on holiday in the sun? Are you the same man arresting a criminal as you are when making love to your wife?'

'Yes.'

'No you aren't, you fool. You're a different man depending on the place and the occasion and how they affect you.'

The fellow with the pencil looks to his taller colleague for help. The taller one says, 'I think what he means is that freedom for Edgar, after so many years of living in an institution, did something to his brother's delicate brain.'

'Not just freedom,' I say. 'The sight of this place. Have you seen it from the motorway? You can, just about. The Manse must have looked like more of a prison than the institution he came from.'

The tall one: 'If that's true, Edgar couldn't have been well enough to come home. That's how it looks.'

'His care was state-funded. Sending Edgar home had more to do with cost-cutting than his welfare.' I don't want to continue talking to them. I want them to leave the Manse. 'If you need our help with anything else, please call again. I'm sure you can appreciate that we would like some time alone, as a family.' I sidle towards the door.

'Just the five of you here, are there?' says the tall one.

'Six. Including Edgar.'

The tall one asks Gregory, 'Do you have an occupation, sir, if you don't mind my asking?' Gregory's the only one of us who looks old enough to have an occupation.

'I am an actor,' my brother lies grandly. 'And he's off to university soon. He's the smart one.'

I add, 'And our sister, Sophia, works harder than either of us looking after the Manse and our parents.'

'Would you mind if we have a look around, sir?'

'It would be a treat; we don't get many visitors. Let me give you the guided tour.' I make for the staircase as Sophia comes down it. 'You'll have to excuse the untidiness. Give me a minute to—'

'I meant outside, sir.'

'Of course.' I know he meant outside, but I don't want him snooping. I lead them to the back door, past the coffin. Gregory and Sophia come too. 'Perhaps I should have shown you the view from the front first, but we hardly ever use that door. Where to start? Over there: they're the outhouses where Father used to potter when he was able. The barn's no longer in use; hasn't been for decades. The cemetery you've already met. Feel free to walk amongst our ancestors. There's a septic tank over there. And that's the outside toilet. Of course we no longer use it since we had a proper toilet installed. Still pongs a bit in summer. I mean, even worse than it pongs now. Can you smell it from here? I can't, but I'm probably used to it. I think the tank's leaking. It gets bunged up. I have a padlock on the chemical toilet to lock in the stench, but it escapes through the cracks in the wood.'

The tall one reaches a decision. 'Some other time. I'll leave you and your family alone with your grief for now.'

'Thank you,' I say, mightily relieved, and walk with them to the police car. Gregory and Sophia watch from the back door.

★

After the police left, Gregory lit a cigarette and paced the courtyard while Sophia and I went indoors. I sat at the table beside Edgar's coffin. She leaned against the sink. We didn't look at each other and we had nothing to say. We felt the same way: empty. Funny, how we missed Edgar. We hadn't seen him for years. He was a part of us, none the less.

'What's Mother up to?' said Sophia, and headed for the stairs.

In the absence of something better to do, I followed.

Mother had undressed and got into bed. She stared at the ceiling. 'Have those people gone?' Her voice was quiet and weak. Sophia said they had. 'Your father doesn't like strangers.' I thought it peculiar that she referred to two police officers as 'those people'. I also noticed that she referred to Father in the present tense.

'Hungry?' asked Sophia. Mother, still staring at the ceiling, didn't answer. 'I'll make soup. It'll be ready in about an hour and you'll feel more like it by then.'

She went downstairs to chop vegetables.

In want of something meaningful to say to Mother, I strayed to the window and looked out. Evening had arrived in late afternoon again, and the motorway lights were on. Like a string of electrified fence posts illuminated orange, holding us imprisoned. I hated those lights. I strayed to Mother's bedside. She didn't look at me.

'We're going to put Edgar in the cellar for the meantime.'

'Why? What's he done?'

If she'd asked why, and left it at that, I would have said something about grave-digging, rain and mud. However, asking what he'd done resonated with referring to Father in the present tense.

'He can keep Father company down there,' I said, nonsensically, in a panic, my brain having registered Mother's confusion and scrambled itself – temporarily, I hoped.

'What's your father doing in the cellar? He hasn't been down there for years.' Mother turned her head, and her eyes, towards me for a moment. Then she turned back to the ceiling, and her eyes closed.

While trying to think of an answer, I heard Mother lightly snoring. Relieved that she required no reply, I left the room.

I had to get away from the Manse. It was all too much. The mess had been accumulating for ages. It had been too much for years! Now, Edgar dead, a corpse in the outside toilet, Mrs Wipple in the Hole, the Manse a conflagration waiting to happen, the roof collapsed in on me. I had whatever medical people call it when your roof collapses. All that weight had been piling up since, since, since . . . since Granny Hazel died and Sophia promised Father she would never leave the Manse.

'Where are you going?' said Sophia as I stormed past her.

'Out.'

'Out where?'

Out to steal a moped or walk to Garagh, whichever came first. If I found Gregory sitting on his moped, I'd punch him off it. If walking to Garagh made my legs fall off, so be it. I needed Alf. If he wasn't in Garagh . . . He was in Garagh. I knew he was in Garagh, waiting for me, the way I knew North Island University was no place for the likes of me and I'd never get there, never mind get a degree there.

I was wrong about Alf being in Garagh.

'Haven't seen him,' said Leslie.

I didn't believe her at first. 'Are you sure?'

'I should know.' I ran up the stairs to Alf's room anyhow. 'Oi! It's guests only up there!' I entered the room without knocking. It was empty. On the way back down, I passed Leslie coming up the stairs after me. 'You need a lesson in manners, young man.'

Alf had deserted me. That's what I thought. My mind was, and had been for some time, all over the place. I'd forgotten to check how much petrol remained in the moped's tank, and it choked, spat and died before I reached Bruagh.

I pushed it the rest of the way back to the Manse.

26

The Final Stanza

Dusk. I looked out on Hollow Heath from upstairs. The motorway lights were an amber necklace far in the distance. Hollow Heath seemed smaller than it did when I was a child. Funny how things change but nothing really changes. This bedroom used to belong to Granny Hazel. It was Gregory's now, although Mother had moved in.

What's a bedroom anyhow? A space between walls. It would no longer exist when I burned down the building – and if. Me, Sophia and Gregory would be all right, but Mother needed a sanctuary. The only sanctuary I could think of was Farmer Barry. He'd helped Mother in the past. He would help her now. Why should the future be different?

Something caught my eye out on Hollow Heath. Something moved – or I thought that something moved. It might have been a gust of wind blowing something into a ray of moonlight. It might have been a bird. It might have been a floater in my eye or a ghost in my imagination. I looked long and hard into the heath, but didn't see it again.

Granny Hazel breathed on my neck. Or Edgar breathed on it. Or, God help me, Father. Or Mrs Wipple or the other body in the bog breathed on it.

Nobody breathed on my neck, really, but the perceived movement on the heath had me spooked. The bedroom was colder than a moment ago. I left it, and closed the door to contain whatever was inside.

Sophia's voice: 'Edward.'

The door to her bedroom lay open and she was inside. She was standing at her window. I joined her. Together, we watched the White Lady in the cemetery until she faded and vanished.

'One of us is going to die,' said Sophia. She turned away, 'I've dishes to wash,' and went downstairs.

I followed shortly afterwards.

At the foot of the stairs, I paused to look through the open door at Sophia in the kitchen. She had changed her mind about washing dishes. Framed in the rectangle of electric light, she looked like Cinderella. Alf, a dreamer, was as good a Prince Charming as any. My sister picked eyes out of potatoes and didn't see me. Nor did she see me as I passed behind her and looked through the window in the door. Gregory, black and shining with oil, entertained his beloved in an outhouse. When I left the kitchen, closing the door was like tucking Sophia in bed, cosy and warm at night.

I wanted to switch on the light in the living room to read, and went to the window there to close the curtains. To my horror, there was indeed someone on Hollow Heath; someone still some distance from the garden gate, but – unless I was mistaken – moving towards it.

I hurried to the door and opened it – fool that I was! What was I thinking? I should have run in the opposite direction. If I'd had time to think, I would have armed myself, then run in the opposite direction. There might be time, later, to analyse why I opened the door. There again, there might not be.

That unusual gait! She was running. He was running. Leslie, Laura, Lola, in jeans and a denim jacket, blond hair molested and wild. She'd been searching for something on Hollow Heath – or someone – and

I thought I knew whom. But why would Alf be on Hollow Heath? It didn't make sense.

Leslie hurtled through the gateway, into the garden, up the weedy path, and – breathing heavily – ground to an untidy halt before me. No need to bang on the door, Lola. I'm here, and I have confronted scarier entities than you.

She was big and I was small, but when I extended my neck and stood on my toes, and when she hunched over, we were almost the same size. Her face was a rage. It met mine, almost nose to nose. She snarled. Her eyebrows lowered and met in the middle. I tried to do the same with mine, but I don't think I pulled it off. Lola contorted her upper lip like a bad Elvis impersonator. I did likewise.

Breath like maggot-infested beef, she roared so hard my cheeks flapped, 'WHERE'S MY BODY?'

I roared less ferociously, 'Under your head.'

She was on a roll, still hot from steaming across the heath.

'WHAT HAVE YOU DONE WITH MY BODY?'

'I didn't touch your body!'

'LIAR!'

'I wouldn't touch your body with a barge pole!'

'YOU STOLE IT! ADMIT IT!'

Hang on a bit . . . A body that I stole?

She was clearly nuttier than a fruitcake. 'Calm down. Take it easy. This body of yours; it obviously means a lot to you. I might be able to help. Would you like that?'

'YES,' she roared with an oral pong.

'Then I'll see what I can do.'

'THANK YOU!'

'Who was she . . . your body?'

'WOULDN'T YOU LIKE TO KNOW!'

'Why did you kill her?'

'I DIDN'T KILL HER. HOW DARE YOU!'

'Then . . .'

'SHE WAS . . . my best friend.' Tears burst from Leslie's eyes. She howled. 'I loved her, and she died on me. I loved her so much.'

'This body . . . this friend of yours; did you, by any chance, roll her up inside a carpet and leave it on the heath?' I could tell, from the width of her grin, that I had accomplished some nail-on-the-head-hitting.

'But why did you dump her body on the heath?'

'I don't know. Whaahhh!'

'It's all right. Shush. I know where she is.'

Lost for words, her big mouth flapped twice as she gasped air into her lungs. Then . . . she had me. She had me by the head. Her big hands were a vice and my head was in it. She planted her mouth on mine. Teeth clashed. She sucked my tongue into her mouth. I flapped. I threshed. I stumbled backwards, but she held me erect and dangled me by the head, my kisser stuck to hers, tongues like umbilical cords uncut. For a moment, I found myself embracing her, but thought of Father, my real father, raping Mother, and I struggled again: punched, slapped, kicked, all to no effect. She had a massive mouth; half my head was in it.

Thunk!

My head shuddered.

. . . but my head was free of the vice-like hands and vacuum-cleaner mouth. I looked up – for I had fallen on my back – and when my vision came right I saw Gregory standing over me with a shovel.

Wetness touched my right hand: Lola's blood.

Gregory spoke down to me. I thought he asked if I was all right. That was my expectation, and I replied, 'Do I look all right to you?'

'I said, is she a friend of yours?'

I perched myself on an elbow and rubbed my head. Rubbing my head did no good, but the rubbing of one's head is the done thing on such occasions. The image in my mind of Lola hospitalized became an image of a police car coming down the Lane. I would tell the officers that Gregory whacked her with the spade, not me. Why did he whack her with the spade? Because she attacked me. Did she attack me with a weapon? Yes. What was the weapon? Her mouth. Why did she attack you? I don't know. Did you know her? Not very well.

The police would get to the bottom of it in the end; they always did. It would come down to this: she would not have crossed Hollow Heath to attack me without a reason. You might as well spit it out, the officer would say. Refusing to tell us why she attacked you is tantamount to withholding information, and doing that will only make it worse for yourself. I'll ask you again: why did she attack you? I don't know. Did she speak to you prior to the attack? Yes. What did she say? She said, what have you done with my body? And, what did you do with her body? I put it in the toilet.

No! No! No!

Gregory remained standing over me and Lola.

'She doesn't look good,' he said.

'It's not a she. It's a he.'

'What sort of people do you hang out with?'

We took a closer look at Lola. Neither he nor I was a doctor, but we agreed that she was as dead as she was ever likely to be.

'Now you've done it,' said Gregory.

'Me? You're the one that hit her with the spade.'

'And I saw everything.'

'Sophia!' said Gregory and I simultaneously.

'I couldn't very well not see, with all the noise you lot were making.'

'When they swab her mouth it's your DNA they'll find,' said Gregory. 'You were all over her. It's your DNA they'll find on her coat.'

'Not if they can't find her coat.' On the tail of that thought came another. If I could dispose of the coat, I could dispose of its owner – admittedly, with less ease, but I was hardly a beginner when it came to disposing of – or, at least, concealing – bodies.

'We can't afford to let the police get involved,' I told my only surviving brother, and impressed upon him a convincing reason why. 'You know what they're like. They'll pry. They'll want to know how Father died and why no one informed the authorities.'

'You can lie to them.'

'Sophia was there when you dispatched him. She's not much good at lying.'

'That's true,' said our sister.

Gregory had the solution. 'The cellar!'

'I'm not putting this hermaphrodite with Father and Edgar. I'd put it with Father, but not Edgar.'

'What's a hermaphrodite?' asked Gregory.

Sophia didn't know either. 'Is it like a hermit or a termite?'

'Never mind that now. Gregory and me have to bury her. Not a word to anyone, Sophia. Could you be a star and mop up the blood?'

'Why bury her?' asked my clever twin. 'Why not just put her in the toilet with the other one?'

'The other one?' asked Gregory.

'Come on. Take her legs.'

We lifted Lola with great difficulty – unfortunately, we both pushed, Gregory towards the front door and me towards the back.

'Out the back,' I said. 'She'll drip all over the flag stones if you go out the front.'

'She'll drip all over the floor if you go out the back.'

'The floor's easier to clean,' I told him. It didn't matter which way we went; Lola would drip all over the courtyard anyhow.

We carried her through the kitchen to the back door where, unable to carry her any further, I hurried to an outhouse and brought back a wheelbarrow with a flat wheel. Gregory waited, spade in hand. I told him we wouldn't need it. Together, we broke our backs again hoisting Lola into her ride. Pushing her weight with a flat wheel was as arduous as carrying her.

'Where are we going?' asked Gregory as he pushed one arm of the wheelbarrow and I pushed the other. Sophia had already answered that question. We reached the toilet breathless and sweaty.

I removed the latch and opened the door.

'Give us a hand, Gregory,' I said to a face that had looked Medusa in the eyes, a face I had to lightly slap. 'What's up? Have you never seen a body in a bog before?'

Later that evening, in an outhouse, in his heavy coat, woollen hat and gloves because it was cold enough for snow, Gregory polished the rust on his moped. I smelled petrol and saw a canister with the lid off.

'I need that,' I said. He stepped away from his pride, such was my insistence, complaining that I hadn't paid him for the last time – which was a lie. I threw a leg over the seat. 'Give me the key.'

'Piss off. Get off my bike!'

'Give me the key or I swear to God I'll kick your head until you're toothless.'

'It's in it.'

'Oh.'

I made the machine roar and took off across the courtyard and up the Lane like a . . . like a child on a two-wheeler with stabilizers.

Damn those potholes.

'Come in,' said Alf. 'We don't have long.'

'Before what?'

He closed the door behind me. 'The finale.'

'And about what dost thou speak, pray tell?'

'Did you come by taxi?'

'Gregory's moped.'

'And Lola?'

'What about her?' I asked, all innocence, but deep down suspecting that Alf, somehow, knew.

He winked at me knowingly. 'You must return to the Manse, but not directly.' He looked at his watch, rather a fancy watch with lots of knobs. He looked at it for longer than he needed to tell the time. 'An hour should do it. Don't arrive back at the Manse until one hour has passed.'

'Might one ask why?'

'You'll find out. Trust me. You've time for a slow pint of beer in the bar. Leave in good time to get back to the Manse in one hour from now. How many hours from now?'

'Six.'

'One hour. Off you go.' He opened the door and shooed me out.

'What about you?' I asked. 'Are you joining me?'

'I've things to do. You won't see me again. Not here, anyway. One hour.' He shut the door in my face.

Fine! 'Time travellers will be time travellers,' I muttered, descending to the bar. Maybe he'd arranged some kind of surprise party. Or something. I didn't know!

True to my word, with help from the clock on the bar wall and a pint of stout in my belly, I arrived at the Lane at exactly, give or take ten minutes, one hour after Alf ejected me from his room. Halfway down the Lane, navigating potholes, I decided it would be easier to get off the moped and push it the rest of the way. I paused at Mrs Wipple's hole and looked in. No sign of her under the thin ice. I paused at the outside toilet. And . . .

Frizzle.

I turned my face towards Hollow Heath.

I couldn't believe my eyes. Something was on the heath, near the Manse, something that had never been there before. It looked like a haystack as broad as it was tall. Walking on, wary of potholes, I kept my eyes on it. In daylight, I would have been able to identify the shape. It seemed to be moving, and the only way I could know was to stand still. So that's what I did. The shape must have turned side on to me, because now I made out the shape of – unless the beer in town was stronger than I thought – a man – a person, anyway – on a horse.

Alf sat not far from the garden gate. On a horse. Not much of a horse. On the small side. Lumpy, as if stuffed with old clothing. A horse in need of a haircut, that had seen better days. On its saddle, the rider wore a washboard for armour on his chest. His lance, a mop the wrong way round – working end where the point should have been – looked unlikely to pierce anything. Despite the tin bucket on his head, the sort you catch rain in, masking a third of it, Alf, magnificently and unmistakably: it was he!

I smelled danger.

Sophia!

Farmer Barry's lorry in the courtyard. Why?

To the Manse! I didn't run, but walked swiftly like a fleet-footed zombie. In the Manse, happenings had happened and were happening still. Happenings that would, when complete, tie the string round the bag that contained the tale within. Soon after the string tied it shut, the universe of the tale in the bag, a universe not unlike a numberless number of other universes, could fizzle out of existence, contaminated, yes, but with its job done.

I experienced a further change.

Whether physical, in the environment, or psychological in my mind, or whether the change came in some part from both, I couldn't say. But change came. It came like rapidly working medicine, a powerful drug. And after it had happened?

. . . after change happened there existed inside me a progression, a rolling – slowly at first, like the flow of thick lava. Gradually, the lava rolled to a stop. As it thinned and cooled. I experienced this change as though my thinking, as though thought itself, began to decrease, dry up, run out and harden like lava. And instead of thought, action began to take over. The thinning of substance.

Fleeing from the living room in tears – I had my own agenda and did not wonder why – grotesque-faced, Sophia almost collided with me in the kitchen. Failing to recognize me, or seeing something different in me, she skidded to a halt, then backed off.

'Get Mother,' I said, 'and get out of the Manse.'

She ran for the stairs and Mother.

As I approached the living room-door, which lay wide open, I saw feet – large, horrible feet, the toes pointing Heavenward – and halted on the spot. No one who lived here had feet so awesome as the pair I saw through the doorway – not since Granny Hazel. These feet were attached to legs that ceased at the door frame. Toes with high, yellow nails behind which grew potatoes in Guinness-coloured soil. Who possessed such feet?

I stepped forward and dared to look inside.

Gregory's face rose like that of a rabid tiger with a thorn lodged firmly in its dick. The living room, the fire ablaze in the hearth: Gregory hadn't heard me entering by the back door. He'd been deaf to my instruction to Sophia, as he was blind to me now. My brother, about his mission, needed no assistance from me.

Having returned to the Manse half drunk from Maud's shop, where poteen flowed freely in a smoky upstairs room, my only remaining brother had stumbled upon a fat male arse thrusting with all the inflexibility that arthritic hips are capable of. Appalled – for although he never showed it, Gregory loved his sister – Gregory hated the fat male arse with an intoxicated and murderous hatred.

Who owned the fat arse, he hadn't a clue. Nor did he care. He grabbed the first weapon that came to hand. However, deeming Father's bible insufficient for the purpose, he discarded it – hesitating only for a quarter of a second when a voice inside his head said, 'Didn't we put that in the coffin with Father?' – and grabbed the second: Sophia's knitting needles. With all his might, he plunged the needles into the fat neck some feet above the fat arse. Not only did they fail to go all the way through, they invaded the neck by only an inch. But an inch proved enough to startle and confuse Farmer Barry and put an end to his feeble thrusting.

With a moan of stupefaction, Farmer Barry toppled sideways as Sophia's skirt fell down to cover her naked bottom and she scrambled over the sofa's back on her knees and cowered for a while in a corner before taking flight and bumping into me.

As Gregory had pummelled Farmer Barry with his fists, then with a vase, choked him with his bare hands, and had another go at his fat neck with the knitting needles, I had sent Sophia to get Mother. It all happened so mindlessly that time had no involvement. And now, out of ideas concerning new ways of punishing Farmer Barry, Gregory looked up and saw me in the doorway.

That's what happened!

'Is he dead?' I asked.

'I don't know,' said Gregory.

Farmer Barry was certainly unconscious.

'Torch it,' I said, pushing the palms of my hands upwards, meaning, as Gregory well understood, the fat arse, the whole bloody Manse and everything within.

He looked over his shoulder at the blazing fire. Realizing that he straddled Farmer Barry's exposed organ, he quickly jumped off and took to repeatedly kicking my real father's head. I didn't mind. I tore a handful of pages from Father's bible, miraculously risen, set them alight and placed them under the curtains, which were thin and worn so that the flames caught easily. Seeing what I was doing, Gregory booted Farmer Barry's head one last time and fled the Manse.

'Sophia?' I shouted upstairs, then ran up to see if she and Mother were still there. They were not. Having scampered through all the rooms like a madman in search of I knew not what, I hurried downstairs as Gregory returned from an outhouse with a canister of what I took to be some kind of flammable liquid. As the curtains burned, he splashed it around the carpet, chairs and sofa. Not forgetting Farmer Barry's organ. The Manse's walls were stone, but the ceilings and roof would go up like a bonfire. Good riddance!

In the courtyard, Sophia wept, sniffed, paced, approached the back door and retreated. Her trauma kept the Cold at bay, but not for long. She hugged herself and shivered, but couldn't bring herself to return indoors.

Then, she caught sight of it . . . and him. Her knight in shining armour appeared from the side of the Manse – mounted. His helmeted head turned towards her, Alf raised his mop in salute and the horse sauntered off towards the Lane.

'Go on,' I called to her as I emerged from the back door. 'Get after him! Follow him while you have a chance.' Judging by the speed of the horse, Sophia could easily catch up if she ran – even if she ran out of puff after a hundred metres.

Sophia panted and delayed, looked at me then at the horse's waggling bottom. 'Gregory's burning down the Manse,' I said, shouting probably because of the cacophony inside my head. 'Where's Mother?' Sophia turned to Farmer Barry's lorry. Mother sat inside, hugging herself small and frightened, looking out. 'Get after him, Sophia. You're leaving the Manse. You have to leave it. It's now or never. There won't be a Manse tomorrow.'

We both looked. Alf and his trusty steed were further along the Lane. Soon, they would be too far along it to see.

Then: light. Frizzle. Gone.

My heart sank like a knitting needle into Farmer Barry's neck.

'It's too late,' cried Sophia.

Yes, I thought, but what could I say? 'No, it's not. It's not. Take the . . .' Farmer Barry's lorry. She didn't know how to drive it. Neither did I. 'Gregory's bike! Take Gregory's bike!' Sophia dithered. She hesitated. She started out and stopped short. 'Go! Go! Go!' She threw a leg over the bike, looked at me, saw Gregory emerging from the back door and froze. 'Go! Go! Go!' I commanded, jumping up and down, jabbing a finger towards the vanished horse's waggling posterior. Sophia turned the key and revved the handle bar. My last advice: 'Watch out for potholes.'

And off she went. Moped like a space rocket. The rear wheel skidded to the right. Her left leg stuck out to the left. They swapped positions a couple of times, hurling up gravel and mud, before at last Sophia got her balance. 'Turn on the light!' I yelled in her wake.

'Come on, you,' I called to Gregory as I marched to Farmer Barry's lorry, with Mother safe within but looking . . . actually, looking the spitting image of the White Lady.

The resemblance broke my stride.

'Where to?' said Gregory.

'I don't know.' But I did know: after Sophia.

We would never catch up with Sophia on foot. I climbed into the lorry behind the steering wheel. Gregory climbed into the passenger's seat, which meant sharing it with Mother. We had enough room because Mother had little meat on her bones. The lorry faced the wrong way. I asked my brother, who knew more about such things than I did, 'How do you make it go?'

He waggled the gear stick thing. 'Turn the key.'

'What key?'

He leaned across to my side, causing Mother to cry out as he squashed her, looked for a key, then jumped out of the lorry and ran back into the Manse – presumably to retrieve the key from Farmer Barry. Which was very brave of him because, although no flames licked through the roof yet, and there were no signs of smoke or flame, the living room must have been an inferno. I considered going in after him to help, but Mother looked so imploring, and I had always been and remained so cowardly, that I didn't.

Gregory ran back out of the Manse in less than a minute, lightly smoked but not overdone. He entered the lorry on top of me and I climbed over to Mother's side. Gregory turned the key in the ignition, the engine started, and we were off; the first time we had been in Farmer Barry's lorry not going to or coming from school.

The headlights showed what I already knew: the Lane was almost narrower than the lorry, and had more pothole than lane. There were potholes like moon craters on the Road too, but far fewer of them. At the top of the Lane, Gregory turned on to the Road. A single eye, the headlight of Gregory's moped, came towards us. Gregory stopped the lorry. The eye advanced more slowly. I opened my door and stood on the lip as Sophia pulled up before me.

'What are you doing?' I shouted, aghast.

'Coming back. He's gone.'

'He isn't gone. He can't be.'

'He is.'

'What happened?'

'He was there, ahead of me on his horse. Moonlight made his bucket shine in the dark. Then, the horse sort of disintegrated.'

'And Alf? What . . . ?'

'He was on it.'

'You can't come back. We're leaving. You have to find him.' I was by no means certain that she could. Sophia might have been correct: it was too late. Nevertheless, I didn't know what else to say. We could stop and reassess the situation at Bruagh. Or in town. Or somewhere. 'We'll follow you,' I called to her. I think she wanted to find Alf even more than I wanted her to find him, because without argument she walked the moped one hundred and eighty degrees and took off the way she had come. Gregory put the lorry in gear and followed.

Soon, perhaps six hundred metres and nearly as many bends along the Road, on a strip of straight, two yellow eyes opened in the dark ahead of us, and ahead of Sophia. My sister, I'm sure, had been watching for potholes. Gregory didn't have to: the lorry bounced over them . . . but not the moped. The yellow eyes must have taken her by surprise – they certainly surprised me – for she took her eyes off the road for a second or two and . . .

She left the moped and took to the air. *After all these years, Sophia has remembered how to fly!* She flew in one direction moonward. Unable to trick gravity, like my twin, the moped fell in the other direction. Sophia's flight, doomed to be short, ended. She dropped like an Edgar and hit the Road. I can't say which part of her hit it first. Her body rolled off the Road and into a Roadside ditch.

Gregory brought the lorry to an abrupt halt.

Mother's eyes were huge and round. A hand covered her mouth. Gregory and I leapt out of the lorry and hurried to where our sister had fallen. Unable to locate her at first, my thoughts only returned to the yellow eyes when they began to move towards us. Caught between looking for Sophia and looking at the eyes, the eyes had it. The eyes had it for Gregory too. We watched, captivated.

I don't know what Gregory thought or remembered, but I remembered a dream I must have had once, a long time ago. The vehicle in my dream said MORRIS MINOR on the front, and the man inside it had a beard not unlike Father's. He was my friend.

Morris Minor, if the driver owned the name his vehicle bore, couldn't steer it past the lorry on the narrow Road. He didn't even look out of the window at us – which I thought discourteous – but turned the vehicle round in five tortuously slow forward and reverse movements before heading for Bruagh . . . or wherever.

The darkness was fresh and icy and the air thinner than normal; it stole colour from everything. Gregory looked almost like a life-sized cardboard cut-out. 'Wait,' I heard someone say, quietly. Me.

'There she is!' shouted Gregory, and leapt into the ditch.

'Wait!' I bawled after Morris Minor. 'Wait for me!'

The lights stopped receding. They came back towards me.

Morris Minor stopped beside me. Aware of Gregory's reappearance from the ditch, I ignored him. I ignored Mother – screaming now like a far-off banshee.

A window came down and I looked inside, across an empty seat to the bearded driver. 'Can I go with you?' I asked. And, even as I did, my voice faltered. I knew him from somewhere.

And the door came ajar all by itself even as I heard, in the background, Gregory calling my name and asking if I'd lost my fucking brain. I entered the vehicle because, instinctively, I knew I had no option but to do it if I were to continue. If I were to continue when the tale ended. As the window went back up, I heard Gregory for the final time. His words were clear, inside my head, and I knew I would never forget them. He said, 'I don't know if she's alive or dead.' Then the vehicle thrust forward, me in it. That's the last I saw of Gregory. And Mother . . . And my beautiful twin.

I don't know if they were even there to see Morris Minor's back lights shrink. Frizzle. Vanish. Nothing. Dead silence.

ABOUT THE AUTHOR

Born in Belfast in 1960, **David Logan** underwent neurosurgery in childhood and lost most of his hearing as a result. He left school at sixteen and worked briefly in various unskilled jobs before returning to full-time education. He has a BSc in Sociology and an MA in Ethics and the Philosophy of Religion from the University of Ulster, and also a BA in English Literature and Language from the Open University. He has written fiction for the SF, Horror and Fantasy small presses and has edited and published his own magazine. David and his wife live in Carrickfergus but escape to sunnier lands at every opportunity. When in Carrickfergus, David can be found loitering in coffee bars, staring out of windows, dreaming up ever more fantastical excuses for not going to the gym – again.